Cloud to Cloud

J.J.M. Czep

&

Bob Frank

Metrix Source — Publisher

Phoenix, Arizona, USA

Cloud to Cloud

ISBN-13 eBook: 978-0-9838416-8-5

ISBN-13 Paperback: 978-0-9838416-9-2

First eBook Edition: Dec 2019

First Paperback Edition: January 2020

1- Fiction 2 - Adventure 3 - Spiritualism 4 - Science Fiction

Metrix Source - Publisher; Phoenix, Arizona, USA

Mailto: publisher@cloud2cloud.com

Novel and author websites: www.cloud2cloud.website

Acknowledgements:

Cover design by Michael W. Leone

Cyber Cloud Vector by Freepik

Editing by Avily Jerome

Preface

While this novel is a work of fiction, much of the information concerning NDE's (near death experiences), past life phenomena, precognition, and advances in technology is based on published research in science, quantum physics, and metaphysics. Readers rooted in metaphysical connections, are more likely to relate to the deep nature of the story. More physically grounded readers will enjoy the adventurous sci-fi concepts contained in the story. We invite all readers to research the subjects to discover more.

The cuneiform language symbol on chapter headings derives from the ancient Sumerian civilization (4000 BCE) and the Assyrian civilization (2000BCE) of Mesopotamia (modern day Iraq). The character represents the ***Interface between the divine and earthly realms***, a principal theme of interconnecting the two clouds in this novel.

The dilemmas and challenges for the characters in this story are as ancient as the oldest of humankinds.

"The distinction between the past, present and future is only a stubbornly persistent illusion."

Albert Einstein

Theoretical physicist

Chapter One

"Come on, Evan! Get on frequency!" the confined space of the military communications van filled with Linc's voice, as his partner heard the demands through military-issue headphones.

"Hold your horses, cowboy! I don't have them yet!" Evan adjusted his position on the thinly cushioned metal seat.

He reached to turn one of the multitudes of dials on the board occupying the wall in front of him, causing the static in the headphones to merge with the squeal of the metal stool.

Evan winced at the noise. "Billions of dollars on state of the art modern tech, and they can't get us a comfortable chair that won't squeak."

Sleek monitors mounted above eye level flickered to life, before reverting once again to static. The snap of an image caught Linc's eye before it was lost in a haze of pixels and scrambled data.

"That was it!" Linc straightened his lanky form in his seat. The energy of the moment coursed through his tattooed arms. "We're almost there!"

Another flicker of images, and both men sucked in a breath. Anticipation and adrenaline coursed through Evan's rigid form.

Linc wiped his palms over the camouflaged pants of his uniform.

"Hands on the wheel, man." Evan grabbed at the dials.

Linc gave the comment a brief grin. His hands struck the keyboard stationed in front of him, fingers flying.

Code and commands screamed across the faces of the monitors below the flickering screens. Evan's eyes flitted between each of the four main viewing channels. The images and data streams were joined by a garbled audio feed.

"Yes!" Evan locked in the dials within his reach. "Okay, okay, I'm in! I got it! I got the link!"

Linc's smooth shaven face ripped into a broad smile. "Yes, you do! Right next to you, brother!"

Evan's gaze tore from the screens long enough to roll his eyes at the comment.

"Whatever, man. There! Decryption set!" The screen directly in front of Evan blossomed with encoded text. "Let's get this!"

Linc wiped his face on the sleeve of his uniform. "Enemy tank battalion closing forward line. Grid six, tango-five-two. Is the drone in position?"

Evan's hands surfed across the board below the monitors. "It is now. Ready to jam when you say."

Evan glanced to his side at a small Army Cyber Command motivational poster taped to the front of a door panel. He smiled as he recalled its words:

> ***Einstein never guessed the weapons of World War III would be information, data, and control of the Infostrada.***

Evan keyed in another myriad of code.

"Okay... Now! Block 'em out." A flicker of dots scattered across the screen as Linc whistled.

"Done! Look at those dots bounce the battlefield. They have virtually no electronics. They're blind! Total confusion!" Laughter echoed off the walls of the communications van.

"Shit. They're all over the place." Evan smirked.

Linc shushed Evan with a wave as he sent a verbal all-clear through the headset. "Red Rover Four, this is Snoopy Three. The battlefield is yours."

Another voice filled both Evan's and Linc's headsets. "Roger. We can probably hold jamming for twenty. We'll tell you when they finally knock down our bird. Clean 'em up while you can. Out."

Linc's eyes flashed as he accepted the go-ahead for the real prize. "Let's get back to the data. I see the signals. You are dead on frequency now."

Evan's eyes locked on the screen in front of him. "Crypto key cracking routine... set! Let's grab these data streams. They're in a panic out there and trying anything! Their guard is down. Transmissions are sloppy."

"I've got your data sample! The routine is cracking on the keys on four, three, two, one, busted! Got their crypto keys," Linc called out over the headset.

"Good." A smile plastered Evan's face. "I've got the first data streams downloading. Shoot me the keys."

A long pause sucked the air from the small cabin. "Okay." Linc's voice was barely a whisper. "Decrypting... decrypting... Yes! Clear text. I can't read their characters, but it's clear text. Let's send it all home!"

Chinese characters flashed across the screen.

"The decrypted keys are on the way to Intel at G-2." Linc slammed the return key at the corner of his board.

"Packaging enemy data streams. Ready. Link established and three, two, one, data streaming is on-line." Evan tagged the keys of his board and relayed the command through Linc's screen.

"Full download complete!" Evan whirled his stool to another monitor and keyboard station to his left. "Now, we have to send it home!"

The new monitor sprang to life with the same streams of code and text sync echoing in the other screens. Evan glanced at another memo above his station:

> ***Ours is a war of devastation equal in mass to a nuclear bomb, yet with minimal toll on human life. A war of minds and data; a game of codes and keys.***

The two young men, sweating in full military uniforms, slumped their shoulders only a moment before spinning their stools to face one another.

"Heroes again." Linc sighed as he stretched in his seat. "Coffee break."

"I wish they hadn't fried all the satellites months ago or we wouldn't have to be so damn close to the front line," Evan lamented as he returned to watch the dots bustle on the screen.

Linc laughed. "Oh, but this makes it more interesting. We're not rear echelon monkeys sitting in an office in Nebraska."

"True enough." The slap of their hands meeting in a double high-five echoed through the small space. There was barely enough room for the pair of communications soldiers within the tangle of wires between screens, keyboards, and various LED spotted electronics. Linc pointed at the small poster above his station and jabs his finger in the air:

> ***We are Spartans of the mind, elite warriors with a keyboard and screen.***

"Yeah! That's right! Never a problem when you've got the Linc on your side!" Linc wove his fingers together and stretched his arms over his head.

A series of audible pops followed as his tired back realigned.

Evan twisted on his stool with the same result. "Damn straight! Communication is key to modern war!"

Evan took in the steady stream of data flowing from one screen to the next. Linc's gaze rose to the images on the monitors. A team of soldiers slammed a battering ram into a door. The camera angle, poor image quality, and lack of color obscured their faces. He felt another rush of adrenaline, different than the thrill of the hunt.

Linc turned a haunted gaze on his partner. "Evan, man, you have been on your ass in here longer than me. Why don't you go take a break? Don't you need to take a piss or something?"

Evan shrugged. "Meh, there's still a glitch or two in this stream to work out."

Linc lowered his eyes to the monitor over Evan's shoulder. "Let me give it a go."

Evan smiled at the suggestion. "Serious? I thought cleaning and gutting the beast was the boring part for you?"

Linc waved off Evan's jest. "I gotta learn. Someday, I might not have you by my side to do the tedious stuff.

Linc kicked the base of Evan's stool, rolling both man and seat aside. Evan caught himself on the far wall.

"Well, okay. The ship is in your capable hands, sailor."

Linc waved Evan off, totally focused on his work.

Evan glanced up as he passed through the narrow hallway of cables and shelves to a small metal hatch:

> ***The spoils of war are simultaneously infinite and infinitesimal. The secrets of nations, the wealth of empires, all controlled by invisible streams of data coursing through wireless echoes and oceans. He who controls access, controls the world, even from an ivory tower.***

He stole a moment to look back and smirked at his friend's hunched form furiously striking at keys before he turned the latch and pushed through the door.

He squinted and shielded his eyes with a salute to the high sun. As his pupils adjusted, he took in the clear, pale blue sky. His combat boots crunched the gravely beige earth as he dropped from the metal steps of the communications van. Desert brush did little to camouflage the dirt-colored vehicle.

Evan gazed out over the surrounding hills as he stretched his aching limbs. The heat of midday brought a glisten of sweat to his brow, even as he breathed a sigh of thanks for the weak but present breeze. The van's air conditioning was to protect the equipment, not the soldiers. Vents were mandatory, windows were optional.

He walked up the rise of the hill that sheltered the van from sight. It only took a few steps before Evan crested the ridge far enough that he no longer had a direct view of the van.

***

A strange aura swept the sky. A flash emitted from above and a violet bolt of electricity struck the tallest of the steel array of antennae protruding from the roof of the communication van. Electrical striations of colorful magnetic threads pulsed in all directions surrounding the van and its antennae.

Within the confines of the van, Linc rubbed his eyes to clear away the strain pressing at his lids. The screens suddenly flickered between light and darkness in a rapid, random succession of energy. His headphones hummed an unbearable droning pitch. Linc groaned and gripped the device connecting him to the network of cables and electronics.

Before he had a breath of a chance to remove the head gear, the screens crackled. Wires deep within the walls popped against thin metal shielding. The whole of the cabin came to life in a sudden surge unharnessed electromagnetic energy. As equipment voltage meters rattled, needles violently pegged the warning zones. The smell of heat and electricity burned into Linc's nostrils. The inside of the van burst into a vibrant fireworks display.

***

Evan clutched his temples, clamped his eyes closed as he stumbled over the plateau toward the van. He fell to his knees, doubled over and grasped the back of his head. The ringing in his ears, the throbbing inside his head became so intense that he folded over in the fetal position. As calmness returned, the ringing remained in his head. He slowly rose and wiped a thin line of blood from beneath his nose. He stared for a moment at the red smear maring his hand. In a daze, Evan meandered toward the van.

The violent rings of magnetic vibration left the earth surrounding the van rippled, small rocks and debris scattered away from the tires. The entirety of the episode hardly lasted more than a heartbeat.

Evan's gaze caught the glint of light on metal as the door to the van squealed open below. Evan stumbled toward the vehicle, still uncertain what transpired, yet knowing full well he needed to get out of the open field.

***

Shafts of light splintered the darkness within the van as Evan swung the door wide. The smell of hot wiring assaulted him as he lingered in the entry hall.

"Yo. Linc." Evan's shadow cast the space into darkness. "I felt the weirdest pulse out there."

Evan picked his way into the van, covering his face with his sleeve, stifling the acrid smell filling the confines of the space.

"Linc? What the hell, man? Why is it so dark in here?"

Evan fumbled for the touch lights adhered to the ceiling of the vehicle. He tapped a dome once, twice, a third time. He pressed as hard as he could. A wire popped, snapping a flicker of electricity near enough to his arm to singe a few hairs.

As he passed into the primary work space of the van, he squinted into the shadows. "Linc?"

Evan struck another plastic dome with his fist. A pale glow illuminated the wall of monitors. Liquid crystal screens burbled melted images. In the half-lit glow of mangled tech, a blue-grey glow illuminated the cabin.

The air was thick with the odor of electricity, fire, and something else, something Evan feared to recognize. The smell for a moment reminded him of home and weekends and summer barbecues, but the sick scent mingled, turning Evan's stomach to darker thoughts.

Unprompted, Evan's gaze fell to the empty stools set before the decimated workstation. Evan fought to will his eyes to travel no lower, but his body refused to obey. His gaze settled on the smoldering mass crumpled on the floor. Charred fabric, still red-trimmed with dying embers. Flesh blackened at contact points - the fingertips. Molten remains of headphones and charred flesh around what were ears formed a seamless mold.

Words refused to form on Evan's gaping lips. In their place, a breath caught in his throat before the scream of anguish and confusion released into the van and escaped the twist of sparking wires out across the barren wastes of the desert.

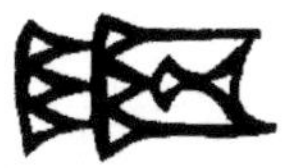

Chapter Two

Evan straightened as he adjusted the lines of his dress uniform. The memory of the attack which stole Linc away two months ago haunted his eyes as he scanned the screens mounted along the wood-paneled walls. He had not looked at a screen since the incident. Even the sight of the mobile devices carried by the medical staff in the infirmary drew a sickening lump of dread in his core.

Evan had ignored the therapist's suspicions until several weeks into the sessions. Technology of any sort caused his mind to go blank and his heart rate to skyrocket. The first time was in the recovery room days after the attack. A nurse clicked on the wall mounted television. His vision went dark. He vaguely remembered jumping from the bed, grabbing a chair and launching it at the screen.

The therapists insisted it was PTSD. They suspected he'd wanted the shards of plastic in order to harm himself. Several sessions later they connected the incident to the television itself and diagnosed him with severe technophobia.

The doctors made it clear Evan needed more specialized care. It was also clear it would be some time before he could return to the field. If he ever could.

The men, most in decorated military dress, and a pair in the white coats and suits Evan had grown accustomed to seeing, seated themselves along the far side of the large, U-shaped table. Evan noted the table served as a fine barrier between himself and the board. His thoughts, however, flipped instantly to the touch screens as each man set his black, handheld device into a dock on the table.

Evan found himself counting breaths as generals and doctors settled into their seats. He hoped he had not been speaking the numbers out loud.

As he took in the expressions of the men, reality settled on him. At this point it did not matter if he was talking to himself or not.

"It has been a long time since we have had any casualties in a war." A general with grey hair and more medals on his breast than the others, slid a weathered hand across his screen before raising his eyes to Evan.

Evan winced as a familiar pain fired through his skull.

"Well, that's a fine thing to make the history books for?" Linc's voice groaned in caustic annoyance. "First to cook their carcass in the all new, all tech battlefield."

"Yes, sir." Evan nodded, ignoring the din inside his head.

His lips felt drier than they had in the heat of the desert sun that day. He swiped his tongue over them.

"This blame is not on your shoulders, soldier." Another man, this one with fewer medals and far less hair on his head, offered a soft expression, though his words were level. "This was an oversight."

The commanding officer cut the man off with a flit of his fingers. "It was outside of our standard strategic plans. This new information is being reviewed for future missions."

"Translation, they will slide this whole shitstorm under a plush government carpet. Class act all the way." Linc's words hissed in Evan's head.

"Of course, sir." Evan maintained a stoicism, allowing him to step this far out of his hospital room.

"The EM—electro-magnetic—assault on our communications vehicle was not something our intelligence had made us aware of." The commanding officer glanced back at his tablet against the glossy black of the table.

"It is not a new technology," the officer to the right, his shoulder bearing the ropes of a communications squadron, inserted. "But it was something we thought exclusively in use by our allies."

"The world is still changing as we continue to colonize the Infostrada." The commanding officer nodded.

"Colonize the Infostrada, geez!" Evan's head began to ache from the strain of containing Linc's words. "You would think we were sticking a flag in the damned cyberspace or some shit."

"What was once considered high technology is now commonplace, and while the methods of fighting a war have allowed both sides to see far less bloodshed, when an otherwise backward group of extremists gets their hands on a new weapon, it is hard to say where they will make first use of it."

Linc's voice persisted against Evan's skull. "Bull shit. They knew all about the crazy faction and all their new toys helping them track our asses. They're lying, man."

"I understand, sir." Sweating palms were a sign Evan had become familiar.

He knew the tremors would start soon. If there were some way to hurry this along, he would have given anything to make it so.

"Sirs, if I may." Evan breathed through his nostrils, forcing calm over his raw nerves. "Is there anything further required for our report?"

The commanding officer's eyes narrowed. A look passed between the men at his side. Looking down at the tablet before him, he waved his hand over the screen.

"You are free to go, soldier." The commanding officer nodded, his eyes still locked on the tablet screen.

Evan saluted as he rose to his feet. He hoped the momentary waver in his posture was not enough for the men to take notice.

"Medical will need to see you again, Lieutenant Gabriel. You will report there as soon as you are able." The voice was so flat Evan was unable to discern which of the men spoke the words.

Evan took the moment to face the panel of men once more. He offered another curt salute. He wavered yet again before continuing on his way.

Most soldiers only saw Medical for standard appointments anymore, even those could be performed remotely if the right equipment was available on base. Of course, it had been quite a length of time since any soldier had seen a battlefront not locked in the frame of a computer monitor. Drones and field robotic soldiers did the dirty work. Death on the field more often than not was due to suicide, or rare accidents.

Those deaths went all but unnoticed, or unreported. It was all part of the job. No one had seen what destruction war could do in more than a decade. Evan was a new case in the modern battlefield. A study.

Sterile, white walls, the scent of antiseptic alcohol on cold metal, and the raw taste of the wood tongue depressor did nothing to ease Evan's nerves.

"When did the shaking start?" The examiner rolled her wheeled stool across the white linoleum floor.

She stopped short of the paper-covered bench where Evan perched. Her deep, grey-green eyes flitted over the information on her tablet screen.

Under normal conditions, Evan would not have hesitated to ply the blond nurse for personal information or convince her to join him for dinner or a night on the town.

These were not normal circumstances.

"Oooh. She is a pretty one. No rings on her finger either." Linc's voice snickered in Evan's ear.

"Shouldn't I be telling the doctor?" Evan avoided the woman's pale eyes as he leaned away from the digital thermometer she aimed at his mouth.

"You will, but I'm supposed to ask, too. For the record." She rose from her stool and made certain Evan understood she was in charge at the moment.

"Right." Evan mumbled around the plastic stick jutting from his mouth.

The nurse removed the digital thermometer and recorded the digital readings into her tablet.

Evan caught a glimpse of the chart. Below his name, a series of notes and numbers filled the screen. One set of letters stood out.

"PTSD." Linc's voice tutted the diagnosis. "They are pegging my death with making you nutty."

"I'm not emotionally unstable," Evan assured the pretty young nurse.

"I'm sure the doctor will take it into consideration." She jotted a few more notes with the stylus and set the tablet on the counter. "Have a nice day, Lieutenant Gabriel."

"Did you see? She didn't even bat an eyelash at you. You're losing your touch, man." The scorn in Linc's voice was tempered by a convivial sarcasm.

"Yeah," was all Evan could muster in response to either party.

The silence surrounded Evan once the examination room door closed behind the nurse, leaving a vacuum of thoughts and rising anxiety. Evan dropped his feet to the floor and crossed to the tablet resting beside the small sink.

"Do you want to see the whole shopping list of medical mumbo jumbo?" Linc's voice fluttered at the back of Evan's neck.

Evan reached out, hands shaking, not wholly from the implications of his impending diagnosis.

He tapped the tablet and brought up the information screen. He read.

"Possible physiological side effects of electromagnetic exposure. Possible PTSD. Possible neurological dysfunction."

"Possible. It's not positively bad." Linc's voice attempted a reassuring tone.

Evan slammed his fist into the cabinet above his head.

He was so engaged in his conversation with Linc, he did not hear another person enter the room.

"Hey, now, that's government property." The doctor's voice shocked Evan out of his anger. "And so are the cabinets. We just had those fitted."

"Busted," Linc's disembodied snicker taunted.

"Sorry, sir." Evan handed the tablet to the doctor and returned to his seat on the padded bench.

The doctor offered a gentle smile. The loose cut of the man's greying hair and his relaxed demeanor betrayed his civilian credentials.

"Evan." His name fell like a sigh as the doctor lowered himself to perch on the wheeled stool.

The man's years were clearly lined across his brow as he looked over the records displayed on the tablet screen.

"Tell him to get to the point already." Linc's voice interrupted the silence of the moment.

"Tell me what the burst did to me." Evan wiped his palms on the dressing gown. "Then please let me get back out in the field."

"You wouldn't go back out there without your partner, would you?" Protest filled Linc's voice.

"You aren't going back out there, son." The doctor's demeanor shifted to a more stern tone.

"What?" Evan's brow creased.

"Evan, Lieutenant Gabriel, look." The doctor raised his attention from the screen to the young soldier seated in front of him. "The official record of your condition will be post-traumatic stress."

Evan shook his head. "Fine. So? No one has had a case since the early forties. So what?"

"But this is more than PTSD. Something happened to you outside that van. We will be investigating the effects of electromagnetic pulse on the human body. But, until we know more..." The doctor sighed once again and set the tablet aside on the table.

One more sigh and I'm going to get annoyed. Evan was uncertain if the protest was Linc's or his own.

"Evan, look, I know you military guys are stoic, and you are your work." The man removed his glasses and rubbed at the bridge of his long narrow nose. "If I had the authority, I would begin testing on you right away." He paused. "If you were open to it, of course."

Evan put his hands out. "Of course! I'm up for anything. MRIs, CAT scans, whatever it takes. Don't send me out of this office saying I'm crazy or shell-shocked when I know that's not the case at all."

"Guinea pig." Linc's voice was accented with a snort.

"I have to." The doctor replaced his glasses and rose from the stool.

He walked to the door of the examination room and set his hand on the lever of the door. "I truly am sorry, Evan, but this is not my call."

Evan's breath caught his protest before he could speak it. The doctor opened the door to leave.

"Get dressed, Mr. Gabriel. You are relieved of duty. Welcome back to civilian life." The doctor's closing left no question on how final the decision was. "I'm prescribing some medications, sleeping pills, and something for your anxiety. The Veteran's Directorate will continue to monitor your physiology in addition to your stress issues."

"Wow. And he doesn't even know about the voices."

Evan did not register the doctor's exit until the click of the door cracked the silence.

"Well. Shit." Again, Evan was uncertain where the words derived , or if they broke the silence of the room.

Evan stared down the closed door, willing it to open again. Willing the doctor to return with a sudden change of heart. He stared, then he slammed his fist into the padded examination bench.

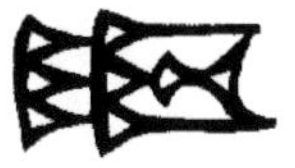

Chapter Three

The incoming call alert rattled the mobile device resting precariously on the bedside table. In the year since his medical discharge from the Army, he had grown lax about jumping out of bed in response.

From beneath a tangled pile of bed covers, Evan groaned. His hand jutted from the folds to silence the device.

With one eye open, still bleary from sleep, he read the caller ID blaring across the smooth screen. "Mother".

Evan groaned again and swiped his thumb across the screen to meet with the red phone icon. The thought passed his weary mind as to why they still chose to use the icon at all. No one alive had ever used a handset phone.

The alert silenced. Evan tossed the mobile device onto the bed stand once again. He rolled over and buried his face in the pale yellow locks of the woman sleeping on the far side of the California king bed.

A secondary alarm chimed menacingly, notifying Evan of a waiting voicemail message. The chirp lit his last nerve. Evan flipped over in the bed, sending tremors over the full surface of the mattress and causing his bedmate to grumble. He dropped his feet to the cool wood floor of the bedroom and rubbed his palms over his face. Snatching up the mobile device he finally noted the digital readout on the lock screen, ten a.m.

The woman beneath the covers lolled her head to face him. Her delicate features had seduced more than Evan's interest. The young model was well recognized as the newest face of GlobeNet's Wired Women campaign.

Her eyelids fluttered open to lazily reveal a pair of stunning blue eyes. Evan's thoughts had wandered far from the woman, yet her waking princess routine was such a part of her programming she failed to notice his lack of attention. A silent yawn parted pale pink lips. And a pair of slender, perfectly tanned arms extended from beneath the blankets. It was only as her palms fell on the empty space beside her she realized Evan's absence.

"Where do you think you're going?" She propped her head on her crooked arm, momentarily forgetting herself.

"Work beckons." Evan picked his way across clothing scattered over the floor.

Recovering from her annoyance the woman fluttered her lashes as Evan turned to her. "So early?"

The words could have been recorded, so eloquent was their execution.

"It is past ten." Evan offered.

He fastened the button on his dark slacks.

He wouldn't make it into the office until well after noon by this point, yet he should make the effort of an appearance at the downtown office anyway. It also made a good excuse to escape the apartment of his latest conquest.

"Shit." The woman kicked herself free from the plush comforter to reveal a pair of equally slender and tanned legs. "I'm always late when I spend time with you."

Evan disappeared into the adjoined master bathroom, leaving the door open.

"Ugh." The woman flopped onto her back letting her hair pillow beneath her head. "Must you leave the door open while you pee? At least put the seat back down."

Evan thunked the lid down, and returned to the bedroom following his basic morning rituals.

"Did you use my toothbrush again?" The woman loosely knotted the belt of her pastel satin robe. The garment barely served to cover her breasts, and the bottom hem stopped long enough to be revealing.

"I think we've shared enough fluids for it to not be an issue." Evan scoffed at the question. "But, no, rest assured I used my travel one this time."

"Happened to have it with you when we bumped into one another at the bar last night." The woman crossed the studio apartment toward the kitchen, and though Evan could not see her face around the dividing wall, he sensed the sarcasm in her voice.

"Boy Scouts taught me to always be prepared," Evan called out.

"You could leave a few things here, you know." The woman sidled up behind Evan as he drew his grey button-down shirt onto his shoulders.

"That's not necessary." Evan sidestepped, as he fastened the last button on the shirt and tugged the cuffs of the sleeves.

He turned his attention to the scattering of clothing on the floor and spied more of his garments intermingled with a black slip dress, sheer stockings, and black lace that belonged to his current annoyance.

"You could call in sick." The woman tugged playfully at the waistband of Evan's slacks.

"Nope." Evan drew her hands to his lips and kissed her knuckles before stepping out of her reach again.

He looped the ends of his deep blue silk tie around his neck like a scarf. Taking a quick backtrack toward the bed, Evan snatched his mobile device from the bedside table. In a smooth, practiced motion he dropped the device into his shirt pocket and hooked his finger through the collar of the jacket slung over the nearby chair.

"I started coffee." The woman cut into his path of egress.

Throwing the jacket over his shoulder he danced around the pretty obstacle.

"Evan?" He paused at the door but did not turn to face the woman. "When are we going to discuss this relationship?"

He smiled to himself at the idea of discussing anything of substance with this woman. "Later."

Evan was out the door and in the hallway of the apartment building without so much as a second glance over his shoulder, his "date" left standing in the midst of her disheveled apartment, arms crossed. It was a pose for an audience no longer tuned in.

The metal doors of the elevator slid open as sensors observed Evan's approach. They closed once he fully entered the carriage.

"Lobby." Evan ordered the machine in a tone casually accepting yet firm.

Slipping his device from his pocket as the elevator lowered, he checked the time. As the doors opened, Evan strode through the opulent entryway of the building. A quiet ambiance of music filled the otherwise quiet lobby.

The doors to the street opened and closed as they sensed movement.

Evan was buffeted by the sudden din of the world. The street bustled with late morning traffic. He adjusted the jacket on his arm before weaving through crowds of similar business attire. Sighing through the chaos, he shook the need to pop one of the pills stuffed in pocket.

His late model Tesla sport coupe waited at the corner. The vehicle had been a hand-me-down from his uncle. To hear the man talk of the thing, one would think it a high quality machine. Evan was almost ashamed to claim it.

Parking the night before had been fair. At this hour, though, the large engine and out of date tech was certain to set off a global positioning system or parking alert as soon Evan offered the start command. He released the charging dock from the vehicle.

Evan popped his mobile device from his pocket and slid his fingers over the screen. A series of codes, applications, and effects streamed beneath his nimble digits. The headlights on the Tesla blinked to life. The horn sounded two short bursts. He winced at the audible click of electronic locks as the driver's side door released.

Evan gripped the slim door handle and manually opened the door the rest of the way. He sank into the plush comfort of grey leather seats.

Uncle Fred had taken great care of the vehicle even though it was technically worthless.

Evan lobbed his jacket into the empty passenger seat. He glanced a moment at the space and sighed. Another typical night--the string of clubs, bars, and restaurants the past week afforded as entertainment.

"GPS activated. Location, GlobeNet office, downtown Phoenix." Evan uttered the command in controlled monotone. The car's equipment was nowhere near as nuanced as the elevator doors.

Evan repeated the command once more before screens on the centermost portion of the dash illuminated.

A scroll of recent searches flickered past as Evan touched the start button beside the steering column. The list of women's names with attached addresses, five star rated clubs, restaurants, concert halls, and event locations streamed in full color. The data finally paused on the requested location and set directions into the mapping program.

"GlobeNet Offices, 103 North Central avenue, Phoenix, Arizona. Distance to destination, twelve miles. Estimated drive time in current traffic, thirty seven minutes." The sensual preset voice emanated from the surround-sound speakers within the cockpit of the vehicle.

"Search alternate routes." Evan dropped the car into gear.

"You are currently on the fastest route to your destination. Estimated drive time, forty-two minutes." Evan thought the tone of the robotic female as irritating as any human woman.

"Fantastic." Evan whipped the wheels of the sport coupe toward the street and dropped his foot on the gas.

The nose narrowly missed connecting a passing car as he burst into the flow of traffic. Horns blared, tires screeched. Evan cursed the out-of-date safety and alert system on the aging vehicle. The incident did nothing to slow his maneuver as his focus remained on the road ahead. A mile later he blessed the failing tech as it allowed him to hit the gas and sneak under a traffic signal as the light flipped red.

"Satellite radio. Station 17785." Evan relaxed into the seat. Music blared from the speakers.

The global positioning navigation application chattered turn by turn directions, interrupting the beat of the music whenever the soulless computer deemed it necessary. Evan followed the system's orders, never considering the turns for himself, nor committing the information to memory.

Streets and pedestrians blurred past, as Evan focused solely on the traffic as it affected him, the next direction his only concern.

The music cut out again, this time an alert sounded in place of the navigation.

Evan glanced at the monitor nested in the center console of the vehicle. An image of his mother appeared, a picture from some family picnic Evan had long forgotten the purpose or date of. He made mental note to update the image in his contact records.

"Call recognized, send to voicemail." Evan commanded.

"Rerouting navigation. Make a U-turn at the next intersection." The voice of the navigator almost sounded perturbed at having to reassess its task.

Evan grumbled. He did as ordered, whipping his vehicle around the median at the next intersection.

With the system content again, the next direction followed.

Evan pulled into the parking garage of GlobeNet's campus. He cruised into the level-one space open despite the line of cars moving through the narrow path within the garage.

In the dim confines of the parking garage headlights illuminated the metal placard mounted to the wall. The reflective lettering read: Evan Gabriel, Technical Consultant and Special Security Projects Manager, Level Seven Clearance.

Evan tapped the starter switch on the dash of the vehicle. The engine cut out, followed by the radio.

His mobile device activated before Evan stepped out of the parking garage. Tracking activated the auto update on messages and calendar data exclusive to his security clearance. Algorithms, mostly ones created by Evan and his team, also checked recent histories for anything potentially suspicious.

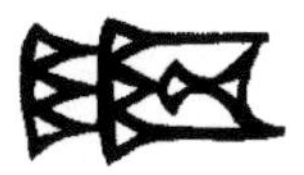

Chapter Four

Safety and security of millions of users depended on Evan. It was little different from his military service. Evan entered the building. His mobile device emitted an alert as each door recognized Evan's security level, confirming identity with an imperceptible flicker over his retina. Scans had greatly improved over the past four years, allowing more expedient ingress and egress during emergency situations.

"Evan." The receptionist seated in the security offices lobby leaned over her desk. "Are we still on for lunch this afternoon? I booked a booth at that new cafe off Central."

Evan responded with a quick tilt of his head and little more than a brief pause to his step. The receptionist rolled her eyes and returned her attention to the infrared keyboard illuminating the stark surface of the desk.

Evan wove within the lab-like maze of cubicles lining the security floor of ITower's GlobeNet offices. He passed busy cube workers chattering via headset to customers across the United States and the world. Physical boundary lines meant little in the age of ITower's Infostrada empire.

He caught snips of complaints and client requests, ignoring names and unimportant personal data. He could gauge his day by clips of half-heard conversation.

In terms of global control of big data and the Cloud in the Infostrada war ITower had won, but in so many ways, Evan and others like him were still fighting. The industrial revolution drove humanity into an era of mass construction, movement, and expansion in the physical reaches of the globe. The digital age had created a new space to explore and control, a new era more akin to the golden age of exploration and colonization.

ITower controlled all cloud access and the data stored therein, yet a constant battle of code, passwords, biometrics, and grid maintenance was required to retain a seat of power.

Few employees raised their heads from the business of consulting GlobeNet clients to notice to Evan, and fewer still enjoyed making eye contact with the young man.

Evan remained a soldier, albeit a far more well-paid one in the private sector. Hired gun might be a more suitable title.

Evan's reputation for being less than friendly to cube rats was far reaching. Dealing in office politics was not in his job description since moving down the hall, and into deeper levels of Infostrada security.

A light above the keyless entry handle framed the door to Evan's office in a faint glow. It blinked green as Evan approached, activating the inner circuitry of magnetic locking mechanisms. Passing the couch against the wall, Evan allowed the door to close and latch behind him. He strode into the sparsely decorated space and glanced through the glass door to ensure the light had returned to it's previous red glow.

He tossed his jacket onto the dark leather couch. The windowed wall across the room overlooked the sprawl of the desert city. Adjacent, a nearly wall sized LCD screen rotated a multitude of certificates, awards, video clips of presentation ceremonies, and event photos, a constant reminder of how far Evan had come since military dismissal.

It meant nothing.

Propping his mobile device into the docking station at the corner of his desk, and his body into the plush seat of his chair, Evan sighed at the enveloping silence of the office.

"Video screen, image night lights." Evan ordered.

The rotation of honors flickered to a cityscape at night, complete with lights and passage of time demonstrated by subtle changes.

"Smart glass, transparency zero. Color grey." As the words left Evan's lips the large window became opaque and the glass shifted to match the walls of the office.

Had anyone entered without prior knowledge of the layout of the room, or time of day, one might think Evan was working late into the night.

The lighting within the office adjusted to appropriate brightness ideal for working. Evan sighed into his chair and tapped the keyboard in front of him. He still enjoyed the haptic response of an analog keypad. The large screens mounted to the desk blinked to life. Data streamed over one to the right while a series of tabs revealed e-mail messages, open websites, a digital calendar, and a feed of the latest news.

Within the square of open programs, the left screen centered a small frame to reveal a man's face, blocking Evan's view of sites and applications behind it.

"Mr. Gabriel." The audio on the computer popped to life. "Building data says you arrived only fifteen minutes ago. I hope you are late for a decent reason this time."

Evan smiled cordially at the man on the screen. "My mother called, sir."

The man's image nodded. "Right then. Not a problem, Evan. But what have I told you about calling me sir?"

"This is not the military." Evan nearly saluted the man who was, for all intents and purposes, his superior officer.

"Calling me sir makes me feel like an old man, and I don't need any further notes on that file." The man laughed.

Evan held a vacant professional smile on his face as he waited for his boss to continue.

"Ahem." The man in the chat composed himself. "Have you been updated on the current state of the outages?"

Evan allowed his smile to fade, grateful to shift the topic to business rather than foolish small talk. "I was about to check stats and media reports on the issues when you called, s—Mr. Marshal."

"Good. I will leave you to it." Mr. Marshal coughed. "Contact me as soon as you have a grasp on the extent of the damage; technically speaking as well as on the public relations machine."

"Will do." Evan dismissed the man with a salute-turned-curt wave.

Mr. Marshal returned the gesture before the chat window dropped from view.

Evan confirmed audio as well as video link had been severed before sighing at the stress of the interaction. He replaced the cardboard squares over the cameras. Some of the old tricks Uncle Fred taught him still had uses. The authority of the man wasn't offensive to Evan—no matter what Mr. Rod Marshal thought his rank was within the company, Evan held the real power. He and his team did the groundwork. It was a solid gig no matter what the big guys in the boardroom tossed around.

Evan tapped the keyboard and brought up the news feed. A wave of tempered concern flowed through him as he scanned the morning list of files and links including outage reports, security leaks, and assumptions of terrorist activity. Marshal had been correct, the media misinformation machine was in full cog-buckling mode, freaking out the ill-educated masses.

It had been the same for the entire era of GlobeNet's take over. Once all information and networking shifted into a global array, people with less understanding of how their old cellular phones worked began spewing conspiracy. No one understood the power and freedom of complete connection to all networks.

Stronger signals, increased bandwidth, the potential decrease in overall cost, including security, networking, and service from the bottom up.

It wasn't about monopoly--financial or political. The Global Network was a tool for the world to harness together.

Evan's anxiety piqued, however, as he clicked a site focused on the inner workings of tech industry. A site Evan himself subscribed to, primarily because it wasn't known for hype and circumspection rallied by weak sources.

He scanned the text, absorbing the first few lines of information. He expanded the link with a click to the full article.

Outages linked to breakdown of cellular signal and process. Are the rules of cellular communication changing? Numerous public health concerns due to extensive exposure to cellular frequencies may require a shift to safer communication transfer. As the reliability of safety also comes under fire with the latest attacks by the group calling themselves Wave7, many seek a new answer.

Evan chewed the cuticle of his thumb. This site's discussion of system breakdown might actually signal a threat to job security.

Worse, another war between ITower, world governments, and hacker gangs like this Wave7, over the rights to data and connections.

Evan minimized the articles and info sheets and tapped a new video chat command connection.

When the window opened, Evan was surprised to see Mr. Marshal was not alone.

"Mr. Gabriel." Mr. Marshal's tone was nowhere near as jovial as the earlier meeting. "I trust you read through most of the information sent to you this morning."

"I have." Evan swallowed the lump growing in his throat.

The profiled faces filling the board room were cut off by the edges of the screen, yet Evan could tell none appeared to be particularly pleased.

"The issue with cellular frequency." Evan almost hesitated to ask, though it weighed the back of his mind. "Has any of this information been substantiated by our more reputable sources?"

"The last article by the journal was not reputable enough for you, Mr. Gabriel?" Mr. Marshal's tone took on a special tenor in the presence of the GlobeNet board of directors.

"Of course. I'm not certain what it means to my position." Evan dared to allow his voice to match his superior's. "A frequency glitch is not something security is set up to handle. Ultimately, the level of fallout is the responsibility of networking and signal representatives at ITower main station."

"Mr. Gabriel, if you are suggesting the issue is not something your team can handle, the board is in a position to question the reach of your security team. As well as your position in it."

Evan sensed a rapid decline into a serious case of scapegoating with him as the goat.

"Not at all, sir." Evan didn't bother to correct the title. "I am simply saying as we work on the problem on this side, it may be advisable to take a step across the way to consider where our partners in the Ivory Tower are standing."

Evan hadn't realized he had dropped the pet name of the superior company until a new face replaced Mr. Marshal's on the screen.

"Mr. Gabriel." An older gentleman--and gentleman would be the best descriptor for the well-coiffed, white-haired man. "If you have some idea of what those of us in our Ivory Tower might do, we are open to suggestions, but save sarcasm and petty remarks for those at Mr. Marshal's clearance level. Are we clear?"

"Yes, sir." Evan knew a military man by the tone. There was no doubt this weathered face was more than a line-man in his day.

A man in his position today would not have been a fool before the GlobeNet era. His demeanor was nimble-minded tech buff, with more than a dash of sharp-edged soldier.

"We will be sending a higher level clearance packet shortly. Despite your youthful missteps, the ITower board feels you might have potential to save GlobeNet from complete collapse. Mind you, failure is not an option. In case you were unclear."

"Yes, sir. Of course, sir." Evan's breath caught with every word as he struggled to push through the remainder of his final military mission.

The video chat cut without so much as a flicker back to Mr. Marshal. Evan didn't bother to check the audio feed. He rose from his chair and paced. His arms arced over his head in an attempt to open his breathing and squelch the waves of anxiety gripping every heartbeat.

"Damned Ivory Tower thugs." Evan coughed. "I'd rather be back on the front lines."

Evan knew the lie in his words, it wasn't the point. He dropped onto the couch and drew his jacket toward him. He rifled the pockets for the blister pack of yellow pills.

He sneered at the small round pill before firing it into his mouth and swallowing. Pride went down with it. Authority figures never bothered him before. Even in the military, he never balked at a barking drill sergeant.

The communication van incident changed everything.

It was not merely the loss of Linc that shifted his emotions and reactions. People, being around them, felt different. Evan shook off thoughts of Linc and the past. He needed to focus on the issue at hand. This new war was sparking. He would need to tap into his old self to get through it.

Evan summoned the receptionist from the front desk through the video chat. Her bright eyes and bubbly smile appeared on the screen.

"Hey there." Evan plastered a smile across his face as he greeted the young brunette. Her name escaped his memory.

"Hey there, yourself," she bubbled. "Did you decide on lunch? Or, I mean, is there anything I can assist you with Mr. Gabriel?"

"That's sort of what I am calling about." Evan feigned a frown. "I am going to have to rain check on our lunch. Casualty of this mess we're in up here in security."

The woman's pout was genuine enough to cause Evan to stir. "Oh poo. Well, I guess if it's for the security of the company and nonsense. We both need to keep our jobs, after all." She paused in her thoughts. "If I see you waltz out of here at noon with some other woman on your arm, your rain check is so cancelled. I remember what you did to me last time, Evan Gabriel."

"No lies this time. They got me working to the bone on this one. In fact, I would love a special delivery around the hour of lunch, if you feel so inclined to make a quick drop off."

"Whatever, Evan. Text me your order." Her tone was terse, but Evan knew she would come through on delivery of a quick snack if nothing else.

"Damn it." Evan rubbed his eyes for the hundredth time in the last hour.

There was little accomplished through the streaming data on the screen. Though the untouched lunch bag and stacks of error messages popping across the windows should have meant otherwise.

Tapping screens to shut down systems wasn't the therapeutic action Evan needed after this day. He wanted nothing more than to punch the streams of data and code.

"Begin close of day save protocol." Evan commanded the computer. "Dim lights. Initiate."

Technology and communicating with people online or through a phone or through social media - it's a false sense of intimacy and connection.

Carly Chaikin

American Actress

Chapter Five

As Evan entered his apartment, lights followed him from entryway into main living area. Cued by his mere presence, the screens hung on the walls blinked to life with images and videos of weather, current time, and news bulletins. As he moved from room to room, information followed, never skipping a beat as it streamed along Evan's side.

His life flickered over slimline monitors. Awards and ceremonies intermingled with family photos, vacation clips, and calendar entries.

He paused in front of a screen before entering the bedroom. Above the bed, weather reports and a flicker of local news illuminated the room.

An alert on his mobile device instantly transferred to the nearest screen, in the kitchen.

A pop-up window filled the center of cabinet-mounted screen. Bright blue text read: MOM.

Evan sighed at the alert but conceded there would be no further avoidance.

"Answer," he commanded into the empty space of the room.

His mother's image appeared in the expanded box on the screen. Her pale blonde hair lay neatly coiffed in a short pixie style framing her wrinkled but joyful face. Her bright blue eyes lit up, though they searched the room with mild concern.

"Evan, dear!" His mother's shrill voice cut through the silence of the apartment as the audio surround system picked up the signal.

"Hey Mom." Evan continued through the kitchen, opening the refrigerator and ducking his head into the lighted space.

"Evan, are you okay? I've been trying to get a hold of you all day!" The glint of joy shifted to one of worry.

"I'm fine, Mom. Busy day is all." Evan emerged from the refrigerator with a block of cheese and a container of cold meat slices.

"Busy?" The shifting expression on his mother's face transformed once more to one of mild annoyance. "Too busy to check in about arrangements with your dear mother."

Evan winced as he recalled the date. He set the meat and cheese on the granite countertop and returned to the refrigerator for a jar of mayonnaise and one of sliced pickles.

"Right. Well, all is well." Evan shrugged as he retrieved a loaf of bread from the pantry. "I did not forget our plans for Thanksgiving."

"Well, I certainly hope not." His mother's tone was still ripe with annoyance, though she seemed to be simmering down. "Evan, I wish you would at least look at a screen when I'm talking to you, dear."

Evan turned to shoot a smile at the screen across from the countertop as he prepared his sandwich. He continued to smile as he chewed around the slice of cheese protruding from his mouth.

"Evan." The knot between his mother's eyebrows brought a broader smile to his lips before he closed them around the remaining tail of the cheese. "At least chew with your mouth closed," the woman reprimanded.

"Yes, Mom." Evan mumbled around a mouthful. "I haven't eaten all day. You wouldn't want your poor only son to starve to death."

"Dear Evan." His mother rolled her eyes. Her sigh filled the surround sound system.

Evan completed the construction of his sandwich and returned the materials to their places. Sandwich in hand, he stepped through the archway from kitchen to main sitting room of the apartment.

His mother's face appeared in a new screen, this one over sixty inches, and in high definition, mounted across from the couch.

"Whoa." Evan mumbled around a bite of sandwich. "Now you have me questioning this latest purchase."

"Evan, can you please tell me if you received the electronic passes for the train to Las Vegas?" His mother's image panned back enough to display her upper torso. Her arms crossed in annoyance.

Evan admitted defeat. He meant no real harm in irritating his mother. He simply enjoyed getting the woman's ire up a bit now and again.

"I received the e-passes this afternoon, Mom. Don't worry so much. I will make it out there by tomorrow evening," Evan consoled her before taking another bite of his sandwich.

"Good, dear. You know I still have a hard time trusting GlobeNet's newest transit integration system. It doesn't seem to notify me when the tickets are cleared." Evan could see his mother's eyes wandering over the screens on her side of the transmission.

"Be sure to call the main line if you're worried, Mom. They are good people and they will help you out. Promise. It's not magic." Evan drew his mobile device from his pocket and keyed in a set of commands on the touch screen.

"You know, I'm not even sure I would want to bother your friends over something so silly though, Evan dear." She reset a stray lock of blonde hair back in place with her neatly manicured nails.

Evan thought he could make out autumn leaves on her thumb nail.

"I have been calling the hotlines nearly every day this week as it is." She shook her head and the stray lock freed itself once again.

Evan frowned. "Why all the calls to tech support?"

"Well, the outages of course." His mother waved her hands at the screen dismissing the inquiring as if her son were pulling her chain again. "You know."

The frown on Evan's face deepened. "Mom, how long have you been having outages?"

"Well, it's been over a week now, at least, dear. I mean it's been a real disturbance. Before the few flickers and the strange error codes."

Evan grumbled under his breath. This outage issue was more than a localized glitch as he had been hoping all day.

"You know this is stressing your poor uncle Fred out too." His mother's words drew Evan to raise his attention back to his mother's image on the screen.

"Fred?" Evan scoffed at the mention of his mother's older brother. "What does he have to worry about? This is a networking issue. It has nothing to do with the old Big Data systems."

"Big Data? Oh, dear, don't go into the lingo and techno speak with me. You know it's all the same systems to me." His mother waved her hand again at the mention of making a distinct difference between networking, signals, security, and data systems.

"Seriously, Mom, I tell you about all of this all the time. You know Fred has nothing to worry about with a few spotting outages in cellular signals." Evan tried to keep his tone less than condescending.

"Oh, I don't know, Evan darling, but I do know he was quite a bit frantic when I connected with him a few weeks ago. He mentioned some new hackers. Wave7 I think it was." His mother sighed in concern for her brother. "The two of you are so alike."

Evan shifted from annoyance at his mother's lack of technological knowledge to one of sincere concerns as he listened. "Wait. Mom, are you saying, uncle Fred was genuinely stressing over the drops in connectivity?"

"That's what I said, Evan dear." A condescending tone from his mother was not something Evan was wholly accustomed to, especially during a technology based conversation.

"And you know such things aren't something Fred should be going on about in his condition. Getting his blood pressure up is only increasing the poor man's risk of a stroke, or worse yet a heart attack. Oh, I shudder to even think of it." Evan's mother waved a hand in front of her eyes.

A red rim rose around the pale blue.

"Right. Well, a little bit of on-the-job stress comes with the territory. You should see what the board of directors over at GlobeNet dropped on my lap today. I think I'm in more jeopardy of having a mental break down."

"Oh, but Evan honey, you handle these things so much better, and you don't go off and drown your stress in alcohol or eat your way out of troubling thoughts."

"Right, Mom." Evan nudged the coffee table, home to more than a few beer bottles, out of camera view.

"When you do meet up with your uncle Fred on the train tomorrow morning, please at least try to get him to order one of the more health-conscious meals for lunch. I tried to block in the order but I think he messed around in there and had it switched." Evan's mother contrived to control her brother nearly as much as her only son.

"Yes, Mom." Evan paused. "Wait. What do you mean when I meet him on the train?"

"I got such a great deal on the electronic passes when I set an order for the same routing stations, I saw no reason not to book the pair of you together on the same train." Evan's mother shrugged her shoulders and twitched her nose, as she often did when she thought herself more clever than typical.

"Why did you do that?" Evan groaned.

"Oh, Evan dear, don't be like that. You and your uncle Fred have quite a lot in common. I wish the pair of you would talk more often." Her arms crossed again in the manner Evan knew better than to disagree with, at least vocally.

As much as it was best not to argue networking and security with Evan, it was equally unwise to make motions on familial and relationship with his mother.

"I'm sure we do. Maybe we'll find out how much on our journey." Evan offered a feigned smile to appease the woman.

"Wonderful!" His mother's perfectly painted lips broke into a wide smile, revealing equally perfect teeth. "And remember to pick up some nice flowers when you get to the Las Vegas station."

As if the journey and subsequent visit to his mother's home for the holiday dinner could be any more straining. His mother was forever going on about some new fad religion, political agenda, or protest of some manner. Evan didn't dare ask what the drama flavor of the month would be this time. The day had been too long as it was to go into more with his Millennial mother and her activism.

"Of course. I will remember. Tiger lilies like last year?" Evan offered the same faux smile.

"Perfect dear." His mother smiled back with genuine pride at her son's memory.

"Right, then. I'll see you tomorrow, Mom. Love you." Evan offered a half wave to his mother's image.

"I love you too sweetie! Take care. Travel safe." She blew kisses at the screen before Evan tapped the end call button on his mobile device.

Evan sighed into the back of the plush couch and tore a bite from his now dry sandwich.

There is no aspect of reality beyond the reach of the human mind.

Stephen Hawking

Theoretical physicist, cosmologist, and author

Chapter Six

The train station buzzed with holiday travelers as Evan shuffled along. He squeezed between throngs of clustered families and outbound urbanites packing off from downtown to suburban family gatherings likely equally enjoyable as the one Evan would be subjected.

He caught the eye of one bleary-eyed mother, hair disheveled, four small children in tow. The youngest, still stroller bound, tapped at the screen of a tablet, and a colorful story book of images flickered across the screen. The eldest, not more than ten, scrolled through lists of songs on a mobile device. Wireless audio earbuds jutted from a pair of pastel pink bedazzled cat ears set atop the young girl's dark hair. The middle two children tapped at mobile devices, causing images of mini explosions to alternate in the space between the pair. The mother's attention flitted from her brood to the GlobeNet connected tablet resting on the awning bonnet of the stroller. Evan made out the numbers of the same gate he was bound for. He flagged the woman down and gestured her to follow.

"Thank you so much, sir." The woman smiled. Sweetness and gratitude alighted genuinely on the woman's face. "It's such a trouble to travel during holiday rush don't you think?"

Evan grunted in response to the woman's attempt at thanks and small talk. "Right."

"And with kids in tow." The woman shifted her attention to make a head count over her offspring. "Do you have any kids?"

Evan didn't intend to openly sneer at the woman, but he knew by her facial reaction his disgust at the thought had been made quite apparent.

"I guess not." The woman smirked before shifting her pace and direction of the stroller slightly. "Well, thanks for your help."

Evan shrugged and saluted loosely at the woman and her gaggle of children as they hurried into the crowd ahead. Evan refocused on his destination. Small talk and big crowds, two of Evan's least favorite things. Nothing would please Evan more than to turn the entire crowd off via remote to avoid conversation. This was not the scene he was accustomed.

Evan reached the platform for his departing train without further occasion to talk to or rescue another human. His mobile device alerted the train of his permission for passage via his electronic tickets. Evan passed through automatic doors into the cylindrical carriage of the train.

He double-checked carriage and seat number against the screen, glancing now and again to confirm he was heading in the right direction as he wove through tightly packed aisles. His eyes remained loosely trained on his mobile device as he awaited signal he had neared his designated seat. The chime sounded as he paused in front of the section. Evan frowned at the only empty seat directly between an overweight older gentleman and a young woman with a snoozing infant in her arms. This leg of the journey was certain to include overt snoring, and probable squalling. Typically both would start around the same point Evan was getting comfortable.

Evan positioned himself between the two annoyances and shoved a set of earbuds into his ears. He slipped into a zone of music from his cloud playlist and opened his tablet to the connection to his office desktop.

Through the window Evan watched as Fred's eyes never left the screen of his mobile device. He ambled his slightly overweight form through throngs of travelers swarmed along the train station platform. Following the blinking green dot on his screen, Fred navigated the station to the waiting train carriage. The doors slid open allowing Fred to enter, still following the direction of his mobile device.

The mapping system on the screen shifted to an image outlining the seating of the interior of the train. Noting each doorway he needed to pass through, the navigation system displayed red flashing squares indicating the seat reserved according to the electronic pass. Fred's blinking blue icon closed on the doors of the next car and he paused, eyes ever on the screen, to wait for the doors to part.

Evan glanced from his business on the tablet long enough to catch a glimpse of the slightly large, balding man waddling through the car toward him.

Fred passed Evan's seat and frowned at the screen of his mobile device.

Evan coughed.

Fred waved the device in a slow circuit, as if searching for a signal. He watched the blinking dot hover short of the red seat square. It was clear the navigation system had locked up.

Fred wandered past Evan a few more steps. Evan sighed as he watched.

He considered a moment before calling out. "Uncle. Fred. Hey."

Fred turned toward Evan, head still down, eyes on the screen of the mobile device.

"Your seat is right here, old man." Evan rolled his eyes.

"I know, but it doesn't seem to be registering on the navigation program." Fred paused directly in front of Evan, uncertain whether or not it was safe to sit. "Do you think it's a local system glitch, a service error, or a mistake in program coding?"

Evan snatched the device from his uncle and dropped it onto the small table set between the two seats.

He returned to his work on his tablet as Fred dropped into the seat across from him. Fred retrieved his device and closed the train station navigation app. He slipped the device into his shirt pocket and fumbled with the satchel hanging across his chest. The strap flipped off his shoulder onto a dozing passenger beside him, earning Fred an unnoticed scowl from his nephew. He drew a tablet, similar to Evan's, from the valise and propped it on the attached kickstand.

Both men stared at their respective screens as the cityscape dissolved into sparse desert. Most passengers settled into similar positions.

Fred broke the silence to inquire about dinner. "Have you seen this menu? Damned near thirty bucks for a basic bacon burger with cheese, fries and a milkshake."

Evan glanced from his tablet to raise an eyebrow at his uncle. He sized up the man at about two hundred and sixty pounds, possibly closer to the three hundred mark.

"Do you think you need all that anyway?" Evan returned to scrolling the menu application on his own tablet. "I mean we're going to be eating a pretty big meal tonight. You know how mom loves to stress herself out over the perfect Thanksgiving feast."

"Hmmm." Fred grumbled at Evan's comments. "You know, typically I wouldn't pass up a good burger, shake, and fries combo, but you may have a point there, Evan, my boy."

Evan released a sigh and allowed his eyes to roll back to the screen. "Well, it's good you think so, Uncle."

"What are you getting?" Fred bowed the small plastic table with his weight as he leaned to spy at the screen of Evan's tablet. "What on earth are you looking at? A menu from Mars?"

Evan let the tablet slip to the surface of the table and rested his hands at the sides of the device. "What are you talking about?"

"What is this tripe?" Fred flipped his fingers over the tablet and set the images reeling.

"It's the sushi and sashimi list. Tripe is not on this one. That's English not Japanese." Evan tapped the screen and the mad scroll jolted to a halt.

"If you want to eat the bait, remind me never to take you out fishing." Fred snickered.

"Right. As if I am going to take dietary advice from a man who is on more pills than food." Evan snatched the tablet and leaned away from the table.

Fred scowled. "Well, aren't you your mother's kid." Fred pressed the image of the send button to confirm his order of burger, fries, and large chocolate shake. "And you shouldn't be talking about who's on drugs for what. I've seen your charts."

"What?" Evan glared up from the tablet. "What the hell, you old hacker."

The minor outburst earned Evan a glance from the sleepy passenger beside Fred, as well as a quirked eyebrow from the young woman with the baby.

Fred shrugged his broad slumped shoulders. "Old dogs don't need new tricks, kid."

"Whatever. Privacy hasn't existed in twenty years anyway." Evan returned to his tablet. "Besides, it's post-traumatic stress. Not the same thing as killing myself with food."

Fred sniffed. "Post-traumatic stress. 'Whatever' is right. Come on, kid."

Evan let the tablet settle to the table. "Seriously. We're going to get into this again. Now. You know how pissed my mom will be if we show up and we're not speaking to one another. You know this is a real thing."

"Oh I know it's real." Fred leveled with Evan. "I had my wars too. I watched my buddies get shot down. More than once. With bullets. This tech stuff makes war too easy."

"Look. There was more to that incident than Linc's death." Evan sensed adrenaline coursing through his chest. "I cannot do this with you right now, Fred. I'm going to get a drink. Service here sucks."

Evan shoved himself out of the seat, jostling the overweight passenger to his left and irking once more the young woman on his right. He grunted an apology to both before making for the service and dining car.

Fred sighed into his seat and crossed his arms. "Shit."

"You are so right, friend," another passenger murmured over Fred's shoulder.

Fred turned to see a man somewhere between Evan and himself in age, alone in the next set of seats.

"I heard what you and the young punk were chattering about." The passenger peered between the seatbacks at Fred.

The man moved to rise from his seat. He turned and rested his knee in the seat of the chair and quirked a nod at the empty seat Evan had occupied.

Fred shrugged.

"This is a screwed up era of war we live in, my friend." The stranger leaned his arms on the back of the chair between himself and Fred.

"In many ways it is, but there are new dangers as we remove the old." Fred searched for Evan through the doorway to the next car.

Evan stood at the bar, a shot glass set in front of him. Fred shook his head. "That punk kid has seen things that could mess with the mind. I spout off sometimes."

"The mind." The stranger's harsh tone snapped Fred back to the conversation at hand. "The mind has ways of repairing itself, as long as we are not continuing to poison it with this techno garbage."

"What are you talking about?" Fred quirked his brow at the strange man.

Fred took a good look at the man for the first time since he had begun talking. He wore a threadbare military jacket. The display grids for rank and insignias had been disabled and deep gouges marred the blank black squares. Fred thought the scratches had a pattern but the reflection of light on the plastic surface made it hard to make out. A symbol on the man's tee shirt caught Fred's eyes as well. It was partially visible under the open jacket.

"Poisoning our minds?" Fred shook his head. "With what?"

"All of this, of course." The man tapped hard on the surface of Fred's tablet to make his point. "It's as you said. War lost the personal hand-to-hand combat. We are nothing but children playing a video game. Only bodies which hit the floor are real. Technology has stolen our humanity."

Fred glanced again around his seat to the dining car.

"Linus." The man's hand jutted into Fred's view.

"Come on. Plenty of space in this row. I sense we could do with a face-to-face conversation to break the ennui of the journey."

Without pause to await Fred's answer, Linus dropped into his seat.

Fred slid his tablet into its bag and coaxed his rotund hips from the seat. He wedged his valise into the chair and shuffled around to the next row.

Linus met him with a smile as Fred dropped into the seat across from him.

"You work for the Tower." Linus nodded.

Fred's brow furrowed. "Yes, but how-"

Linus waved off the question. "The young man was right about one thing. No privacy in this world."

"You seem to be working on keeping yours." Fred gestured to the damaged uniform.

Linus brushed a hand over the insignia. "Yes. Well. Every little bit helps."

"My studies require I maintain a somewhat more discreet persona." Linus offered a sly smirk. "As do yours."

Fred frowned.

"You have been prodding at a pet project." Linus continued. "A means to expand the storage capacity of ITower's Cloud."

"How do you know about that?" Fred lowered his voice to little more than a whisper. "Only half the company board knows."

"I know because my organization knows." Linus leaned in. "They have been studying the answer for almost two hundred years."

Fred released a short laugh.

Linus scowled.

"Oh. Damn, man. You had me." Fred glanced around the car. "Who put you up to this?"

The look on the man's face stole Fred's mirth.

"This is where it begins, Fred." Linus leaned back into his chair. "You don't have to believe."

From the dining car Evan glanced through the window to catch a glimpse of his uncle Fred talking with a man in a military uniform. The short cropped hair and olive green jacket gave away the man's enlistment, but little else.

***

From the bar, Evan's attention was caught up by a male voice chattering loudly behind him.

"I understand what you're saying Hannah, but seriously. You cannot expect the average person to grasp the depth of what you are intending to offer them."

"How would we know if we don't offer them at least the chance?" A young woman's voice drew Evan further into the conversation.

He turned to see a young woman scowling defiantly at the man seated across from her. An array of necklaces and charms covered what the woman's low cut blouse failed to. The man's cascade of heavy dreadlocks blocked Evan's view of his face.

"We are so connected today. Everyone has a cellular mobile device. We no longer call locations hoping to connect with the person we seek, we call people knowing they are within reach via a small device constantly on their person. How far of a stretch is it to do away with the device and contact the person over these same invisible waves?" Hannah continued her speech, her flowing sleeves punctuating her movements.

"We do it all the time and don't even realize it. Everyone, even normal people, as you call them. I have seen so many people do it. They look at their devices a moment before an alert signals an incoming communication. They know. Their minds are connected to the waves and the messages. We are amplifying our psychic levels and we don't even know it."

Hannah smiled, her serene expression surprised Evan. The woman appeared to be delighted though her stubborn tone displayed otherwise.

"Some even have expressed knowing who is going to call, or they at least have some emotional idea. I have seen it in their faces. They experience an emotional shift before they even look at the screen to confirm who the message is from."

Hannah paused, eyes intent on her partner. Eyes Evan wished would flit his way, if only for a moment.

"Yes, but Hannah, my dear, it is exactly as you say. These people have no idea what they are dabbling in. They are monkeys with a rock. It happens to spark fire against another stone. There is no real understanding of the connection they are making. Why give them more? They are happy as they are. And probably so much safer." Evan stifled a snicker as he considered how right the dreadlock man was in referring to himself.

"But they are ready," Hannah pressed. "And you know as well as I do people today are not truly happy. And what about us, those who do understand? We could be accepted for what we do. We could be the generation that heralds a new era of communication."

Evan watched as the woman leaned forward in her seat and the tangle of crystals and charms shifted.

The mention of communication advances could draw his attention no matter the situation or the speaker. In this case the view was as alluring as the commentary.

"Imagine it all the more—we may not be the first civilization to have even gotten this far." Hannah drew her mobile device from her pocket and shook it in the space between herself and her counterpart. "This, this brick of silicon. What is it without the connection to the cloud? Nothing. Why do we deny more ancient civilizations the power of electricity, mass communication, technology? We have so little understanding of the languages they made use of. We have even fewer clues to the meaning behind such works as the great pyramids of Giza. Or what about Stonehenge? Have you thought about the stones at Carnac?"

"What on earth do all of those have to do with cellular communication? They were holy sites. They were places for the soul to connect to some God, for goodness sake, my dear woman, they were not a place to plug in your wi-fi." The man sitting across from Hannah shook his head and waved at the mobile device in the dejected woman's hand.

Evan rolled his eyes. He had heard more than enough of the nonsense in this overheard conversation. He returned his focus to the bartender and requested a drink to take back to his seat.

As Evan worked his way down the length of the train car, his focus suddenly shifted to a buzz of activity surrounding where he and his uncle had been seated.

A throng of passengers had cleared the way to allow medical personnel to kneel over a fallen passenger. The glass slipped from Evan's grasp to shatter against the floor of the train car. Glass and ice mingled in the spreading pool of liquid as a wave of some unknown feeling wafted over Evan.

He strode through the doorway into the travel car. Time and space slowed around him, allowing him to experience a teleportation through to the scene of the activity.

Evan spotted the man he had seen chatting with his uncle Fred. Time slowed all the more as Evan's focus tuned into the man. He was a little older than Evan, though not quite the same age as Fred. He was uninteresting in all senses of the word, yet he arrested Evan's attention.

The man's close-cropped hair and clean-shaven face in partnership with military uniform left Evan to believe this strange man a fellow soldier. The insignias bothered Evan more than they should. From afar, the panels had looked obscured, but in the closing distance Evan could see that the panels themselves were completely blank. Black and scarred with some sort of etched symbol, the military rank and branch missing as if eradicated with more than violent intent.

"What happened? Where's my Uncle?" Evan fired the question at the man, but only maintained eye contact a moment more.

"Connecting." Linus offered.

The spell shattered as Evan scanned the floor where the emergency medical technicians huddled.

Dark brown and grey striped tennis shoes stole all of Evan's thoughts. Sticking out from the cluster of medical workers and their equipment, the shoes remained on equally familiar mismatched socks.

The man in the deformed military uniform put a hand on Evan's shoulder.

Evan spun. He glared into the strange man's pale eyes. The man was so cold and matter-of-fact it froze Evan to his soul. Military training could make a man colder in emergency situations, yet this seemed inhumane, dark, almost smug.

"What happened to my uncle? What did you do to him?" Some part of Evan feared to raise his tone. The uncertainty of his military rank, the bizarre sensation of connection, the ice in the man's eyes. Evan grappled with a pained cocktail of respect for a brother in arms, a desire to act against an enemy soldier, and fear. This man weighed Evan's nerves. Beneath it all, an energy about the man made Evan feel more than a little nauseated.

"What happened?" Evan ripped his attention from the strange man to drop to the level of the EMTs.

The curse cast upon him by the man broken, Evan's mind absorbed the full scene sprawled out on the train floor.

Fred's eyelids lay closed, as if the walkway of a train would be as good a place as any to take a quick snooze, but the steady rise and fall of breath was absent.

Medical workers tore open Fred's cardigan. The drab, olive sweater lay splayed, buttons peppered the floor, stripped free from their place along his grey and green plaid shirt. The sight of the scattered buttons shook Evan once again.

"What is going on?" He shouted over the volley of commands conveyed between the pair of medical technicians.

"Sir, please step back!" The young man's firm tone preceded his taking up a pair of paddles, each attached by a thick wire to a box set at Fred's side.

"Step back!" The other technician barked in echo, his voice carrying to the crowd of anxious spectators, including the man in the military uniform.

Evan turned his attention once more on the man in the uniform. "What the hell did you do to my uncle!"

The cynical, curt response fired back, "Maybe he choked on his hamburger… maybe he got milkshake brain-freeze."

Evan's hand moved as if on its own volition, powered by a force seemingly beyond his own, curling into a tight cannonball of anger driven by fear and concern. His arm swung out arching his fist into the face of the strange man in the military uniform.

The man's body flung into the seat. The force of impact rattled Evan's tablet on the table. Evan took in the crowd surrounding him. None seemed to have noticed the violent outburst, so entranced were they by the distress of his uncle.

Evan dropped to his knees beside the emergency worker. The man glared at Evan again for overstepping the boundary of his work space.

"Please." Evan pleaded with the young man. "He's my uncle."

The emergency worker glanced at his partner. With a nod, the pair argued no further with Evan and returned to the business of saving a man's life.

***

One car away, Hannah's conversation held in the abrupt halt. The young woman's eyes sparked with an inner light. Her face held rigid as she stared vacantly at the man across from her in the small booth.

Within the dining car Hannah jolted from her seat startling her companions. "Access the code."

"Hannah?" The ire brought by the heated conversation instantly melted to the warmth of sincere concern. "Hannah are you there? Are you having a vision?"

Eyes from the bar and surrounding booths shifted to the woman. Hannah's expression remained stoic, her breathing slowed. Physically, Hannah sat motionless in her seat, yet deep in her spirit, images scanned through her mind, stealing her into another level of reality.

It is a mistake to look too far ahead. Only one link of the chain of destiny can be handled at a time.

Winston Churchill

United Kingdom Statesman

Chapter Seven

Fred's lungs opened to allow air into his body, but the sensation was unlike anything he had experienced before. He could no longer feel the rush of air filling his lungs—rather, he felt as though he had become one with the air itself. He opened his eyes, yet he felt it was as if his eyes had not been closed. Sensations, more than visions, filled the space he occupied, shifting as he moved within the energy. He felt lighter than usual as well. As he worked to wrap his mind around the experience, he could only relate it to floating in the waters of the Great Salt Lake, or the feeling of open air in the middle of a skydive. Even those experiences had other sensations that could be heard as well as felt against the skin. No. This was none of those things, yet it felt more familiar than any act he had recalled in his life.

Fred floated, for lack of a better term, seemingly in the direction of a bright light. His only sense of movement, though, was the endless streams of information coursing around him. These were not images he saw, and Fred couldn't make out tangible numbers, letters, or symbols from the bright greenish glow rippling and encircling him.

Fred allowed his body to be drawn through streaming data and fields of imagery that had become his entire world.

As he moved through space it moved through him. Fred sought means to locate any part of his body. He willed and envisioned his hands moving in front of his eyes, but he neither saw through his eyes nor experienced the sensation of moving his hands or any other part of his body.

He was nearly to the point of maddening confusion when he finally felt a solid shape filter around him again. The glory of the great bright white light he had been tumbling, or flying toward, opened around him, swallowing the entirety of his being in the powerful warmth of its glow.

"Fred." He turned at the sound.

It was not so much the sound of his name drawing him, but the action of sound at all. Light had been the only experience until this point. Fred opened his senses to the settling vision that shifted around him like a curtain settling in the breeze.

Streams of neon blue-green data continued to ribbon through the air around him, as if the air itself was information. As he took in strange, pressureless breaths, Fred felt the data ribbons fill him. As he breathed out, the ribbons created twists and ripples in cords of his exhalations. Fred coughed, yet it caused no pain.

"Fred." The voice became a beacon of sound rippling the data like a rock tossed into a pool.

Fred rotated in space and gradually made out a vision of pillars; pale white, as if made of cream, and near as liquid in the way they wavered within the ripples of the data streams. He took in the settlement of new sights--arches, tables, all as alabaster as the columns. All as solid as a soap bubble.

Then new movement was born into view.

Silhouettes of entities shifted and floated through Fred's field of vision. One, then two, then as if stepping from a fog, dozens filled the space, then hundreds, and then Fred's mind twisted at the idea of keeping a count. More shadows than stars, and many nearly as bright. A shifting menagerie of ghostly figures both hollow and luminous.

As thoughts surfaced in Fred's mind, realization began to dawn on him. Ghostly figures indeed, and he among them. This revelation could mean only one thing.

"Fred." He spun this time to greet the voice so close it could have come from within his skull.

He felt as if the tone had suddenly become mocking in its insistence. "What?"

The word escaped into space, though he had not felt the pull of it passing his lips. The purse and pull of his lips was equally absent as the draw of breath and shift of tongue.

"Fred, you are not supposed to be here now." Fred's field of vision suddenly filled with the crystal clear face of a man.

His white hair and beard shimmered in the same way as the creamy pillars. It framed the soft, tea-stained glow of his face. His eyes glinted, bright as a child's.

"Fred. What are you doing here?" The melody of the man's voice summoned a feeling of joy within Fred he could not recall experiencing in his life. Still, a familiarity to the meeting of this man resonated in the depths of Fred's memory.

"Do I know you?" The sound of his own voice startled Fred.

It was not the harsh tone indicative of years of poor diet, lack of exercise, and the more than occasional cigarette in his youth. The lilt to his voice should have belonged to the child Fred once was rather than the embittered older oaf he had become.

"Where am I?" Fred did not wait for the man to answer his first inquiry before barreling into the next question and rolling his vision to either side of the man to see the milky surroundings again.

"Fred. You do not know me in this form, but you and I have met many times before, and over many lifetimes." The melodic voice drew Fred back to the pale, glinting eyes.

"What?" Confusion filled his senses even as the understanding of the man's words dawned on Fred's mind. "Many lifetimes?"

"You will understand in due time, but for now you need to return to your life as Fred Newman. Continue the task assigned to this current life experience." The eyes of the ethereal figure softened as he spoke, but a firmness permeated the words. Fred sensed little room to argue.

"I don't even know how I got here." Fred's mind whirled to wrap around the moments before the streams of data.

"Return to the train, Fred. Before you are missed." The being's voice and eyes enveloped the entirety of Fred's universe.

"Yes." Fred allowed streams of data to embrace him in their tendrils.

"I will see you after the meeting, Fred. Until then, we have much work to do. The activation has begun." Fred felt the urge to wave farewell to the fading figure.

The pillars melted into the mists of shadowed figures and the man along with them. The data stream took full hold and Fred plunged into darkness once again.

All this technology for connection and what we really only know more about is how anonymous we are in the grand scheme of things.

Heather Donahue

American writer and actress

Chapter Eight

Fred's momentary dip in the data stream had passed as weeks in the physical realm.

"Reports are scattered at best as news of major losses to the cellular network signals are expanding from localized centers in outlying areas to more densely populated cities and business districts. This could be a slow week in the business world as we cope with lack of communication and steady decline of connectivity. It is difficult to say where the issues have stemmed from, but there are many who see this as a global problem and hold out for government and higher powers to create a safety network for transportation, banking, and important emergency services. Is this an attack by Wave7 or similar organization, or evidence we are overstepping the current capacity of our technology? "

Evan flipped the channels on the television mounted in the corner of Fred's hospital room.

According to the doctors there were many more signs, but there had been little change since the incident on the train.

He thumped his head into the high back of the reclining chair. His eyes watered as he squinted sleep away from his mind.

It was not too late. He wagered from the fading light through the hospital room window, it was barely near seven in the evening. He had not eaten since lunch, before that he was served the announcement his job was nowhere near as secure as the now faltering networks he had worked so hard to protect.

"Well, it's all down now, so there you have it," Evan mumbled at the muted television. "Fat lot of good that did, firing me. I'm not so great a scapegoat after all."

Evan stretched his legs out on the lift of the recliner. He rolled his head to face the hospital bed opposite the chair.

Machines flickered, wires and tubes creating a sort of network all their own. An IV bag offered the steady drip to mark the passing of time. Within it all Fred lay on his back, thin hospital blankets covering his nearly motionless body. The steady rise and fall of Fred's chest was the only sure sign of life.

Evan clenched and released his right hand. His fist ached at the joints, though the bruising had gone down considerably since his overreaction on the train.. He remained grateful the emergency medical technicians on the train had been so willing to comply when Evan claimed the stranger threw the first punch.

Having a relatively intact military service history versus the apparently spotted record of the stranger in the damaged uniform likely helped Evan's case quite a lot.

Many of the other passengers who had witnessed the confrontation between Fred and the strange man in the uniform jacket also backed Evan's cause. Evidently the man had been menacing others on the train prior to his argument with Fred. Evan felt bad for the guy for all of a minute as police escorted him off the train directly behind the gurney carrying Fred.

It felt to Evan as though the moment marked the beginning of the spiraling doom his life had become in a matter of a few days. A busted hand. Communication brownouts. A security lockdown. A furlough of indeterminate timeline looked more like a firing of most of the security team at ITower.

Evan was left to wonder how long it would last and how far down this spiral would plummet as he continued to ponder the wires maintaining life support systems to his uncle Fred. He fixed his gaze back on the television. He watched as the flickering stream of data could blink out again at any moment delivered news and weather.

Rising from the chair, Evan stretched his legs in a slow pace around the room. He plucked his tablet from a wheeled table set in the corner of the sparsely furnished room.

There were no messages on the queue of either text or voice. He wondered if this was how his life would be now he found himself jobless. It was a furlough. Things could pick up, if the issue was due to a larger problem—hackers, tech terrorism. This was certainly even more than a security breach. Once ITower realized this, they would need him more than before, and his paycheck would certainly reflect it.

Evan tapped the screen to reveal a popup window containing a listing of current articles. The stream seemed to be feeding in, though there was little telling how long it would last, or if he would have to wait until he could get to his car radio.

It was interesting to experience how quickly radio shifted into a power play as the only media still clinging to a scattering of the former primary broadcasting system. Radio signals had begun to fill the airwaves almost immediately after the first dip in cellular communication. None of the same could be said of any other medium. Evan smiled to himself at the thought maybe the whole crash was something contrived by grumpy HAM radio hacks.

He flopped back into the chair across from uncle Fred. He sighed as he read the latest posting about the outages in communication. It was not looking good for GlobeNet services companies as a whole. ITower had, as yet, dodged the blame bullets as the chain of blame was inverse to the chain of command.

Cellular network companies at the bottom of the communication food chain felt the crunch first. One by one they lost service and felt the tidal waves of customer service complaints. It was likely nothing anyone of this generation of service agents and cube slaves had ever encountered. The sheer volume of calls alone might have been cause for some of the outages. Not that anyone had considered this when they were attempting to gain access to their contact lists, dropped calls, lost text messages, and email dumps.

Once more, Evan rolled his eyes as he imagined the riot squads of media-based socialites. The shriek of discovery that all record of their narcissism was lost to the ether.

It was, in the dark truth, likely smaller, portable businesses felt the initial punch to the gut of communication. So many current businesses survived entirely on the cellular networks. Not only calls and messages, the entire currency exchange system was built into the capabilities of tablets, mobile devices, and fingerprint guarded bank accounts.

Evan skimmed through off-mainstream news blogs. Sure enough, conspiracy theorists were running as rampant as ever, only now Evan felt almost inclined to be sympathetic to their thinking. The crash would indeed be a grand way for larger companies to decimate competition in one sweeping stroke.

Yet, when the big boxes began to release complaints of crippled commerce, the world began to shudder a little bit in their designer and knock off boots.

While grocery and supply markets were not the first to feel the pinch of the cellular brownouts, they were the first to beg for government assistance.

Food and transport of essential products were valuable and should be protected at all cost. That big move piqued the conspiracy theorists' ire.

It wasn't mistaken markets, not at all, it was something the bored and crazy could latch on to. Nevermind the only reason they were not starving or cities were not slowly degrading into hives of cannibals or raiding parties was because of forethought. No, let us blame it on commercial big guns.

Evan continued his flip through articles on his tablet as he allowed his mind to wander. There would be bigger issues if all of GlobeNet went down. People, average people, had little understanding of the big picture.

It was not that other means of communication no longer existed, but the base of much of the infrastructure was in something more than disrepair. It would take more than blowing a bit of dust off some old server rooms.

True it may be for more than forty years the cellular network had been the sole means of communication, the switch brought the ideas and scientific magic of Tesla to life. The world had done away with landline phones an age ago, and though Evan recalled his grandfather talking about how he had walled up the phone jacks in the house even though his grandmother had sworn it would be a bad idea, no one ever thought that anyone would ever need those squirreled away rotary dial phones, or touch tone with a cord to the handset. Evan had always laughed at the story when his grandfather told it, but now, Grandmother's lunacy seemed too close to reality.

Evan allowed his eyes to scan the walls of the hospital room. His mind wandered as he questioned if there were even cables in these walls? The building was old enough to be sure, but did the wiring still remain? How many updates had the structure experienced? At what point did the construction crews and city regulations teams agree all the wiring would be more hazzard and hindrance than back-up plan?

While in communications meetings, Evan had heard underground wire systems still existed. They had been used to transition to fiber optic lines connected the original cellular towers. Those lines had long since been put out of service.

All these systems, well beyond the need for cables of any sort, were suddenly failing. As long as satellites captured and transferred frequencies, the world had taken for granted it was all around them, in the air. Including the Cloud.

The data, the memory of an entire generation, the Cloud was ITower's greatest achievement following the infrastructure overhaul to an entire communications network. GlobeNet was the greatest monopoly in recent history, left to stand because of the smaller networking agencies and their commitment to bickering over the price of communication plans.

The Cloud made it all seem like a foolish game in comparison, and yet, there it was.

Evan rose from the recliner and waved a silent farewell to Uncle Fred as he left the room. He had waited out the rush hour traffic, but there was little point to staying late into the night. It was not as though Fred would be bored without Evan there by his bedside. Guilt, thus far, had not overridden a desire for the comfort of his own bed.

Evan returned to his car. A moment of anxiety overcame him as he awaited the action of the automatic lock to click open. The vehicle's reliance on cloud-based software made it possible his car would be rendered unable to be driven, or at least accessed. Evan allowed a snicker to escape his lips. He was not sure how bad this would get, but his loss of gainful employment was starting to look like a small problem in a much more grand and global concern.

Coming off of his PTSD medications was beginning to allow darker thoughts to seep into Evan's mind. The idea to ration the pills was meant to keep him sane longer, instead it appeared to be making the path to a breakdown a smooth slide.

Evan continued to consider the cloud as he maneuvered through steady downtown traffic. He listened for the next direction from his mobile global navigation system fed directly from the car's tracking systems. If the cloud went down, would he even know how to do something as simple as get home? Evan watched the signs pass by his view. It was not as though he had never taken this route, he simply never looked directly at the signs. Evan realized there was little more than numbers to guide him. Naming new streets was a banal novelty meaning little when most everyone knew the pseudonym of their global positioning system coordinates.

Evan found himself strangely grateful his uncle Fred's home was built when streets still had names and homes had clear numbers on the outside.

Within the confines of the dim, quiet house, Evan allowed his body and mind to relax as much as the rising panic attack would allow.

Welcome home, man. Linc's voice sliced through the silence.

Evan gripped the edge of the nearest wall. His heart lurched in his chest.

"Screw this." Evan made a beeline for the medicine cabinet.

Man. Those pills were some powerful stuff. Took long enough for them to wear off. The familiar voice rattled Evan's mind.

He stumbled for the couch.

Take a load off, partner. I've got a little something to show you." As Linc's words ripped through Evan's skull, he collapsed onto the floor shy of the sofa, his consciousness slipping away.

A vision of a desert filled Evan's mind as the sensation of sand dusted a fluttering scarf covering his face.

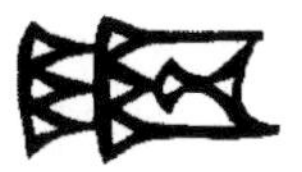

Chapter Nine

Orange goggles reflected a steadily rising sun. As if by instinct, Evan checked the compass dangling from a pocket chain.

He would be at the gates of the city at the base of the dunes before the noon sun threatened to bake the leather of his jacket to the point of cracking. He shrugged his pack into position between the growing blisters on his shoulders and trudged on.

Desert cities never struck Evan as pretty, but this one called to him like an oasis. It was against his usual code to enter inhospitable gates--no Northern cities in winter, no Southern ones in summer.

People were mean most times, but even meager hospitality died with the crops.

Care for a closer look? Linc's voice filled Evan's head and the world tipped for a moment.

Evan found himself peering through the window of a dingy bar. He slowly pushed open a creaking wooden door, well-worn from years of parched summers. Evan scanned the room as he dropped his bag beside a bar stool. He perched on the narrow seat and monosyllabically ordered a drink.

His hair plumed into a spiked and disheveled mass as he slid the scarf off his head and pulled it loose around his neck. Pushing the goggles up over his forehead didn't serve to tame the style, but it cleared his vision. Evan made note of the patterns in the chapped wood counter, avoiding the expressionless patrons.

"How you paying?" A familiar looking bartender held the beer out of Evan's reach.

Evan sighed. He dug in the multitude of pockets to find a large flat circle of silver inside his coat. He pun it lazily on a knot in the wood. The bartender stopped it mid-spin and swapped it for the bottle.

Bone dry hospitality, not even a 'hello, mate'. Linc tutted in Evan's ear. *At least summer booze isn't watered down.*

The bottom of the bottle may as well have been parallel with the ceiling before Evan could claim the first swallow.

"Staying long or passing through?"

Evan turned his gaze enough to glimpse the man in the seat beside his.

"Why? Are you the man in charge of room fare?" Evan took another swig of his drink.

The man flashed a look behind the bar. "Might be that I am."

"I'm not looking for a room, sorry." Evan looked the man in the eyes this time.

"Passing through, then. Fine, fine."

Evan could tell when he was not wanted.

"But, I say there. I couldn't help but notice the glint of tags at your neck there."

Evan looked down. Unsmiling since the conversation began, now he smirked as curiosity and bemusement washed over him. The tags the man had indicated had fallen free of Evan's jacket when he fished for the coin.

"What of 'em?" Evan clapped a hand over the bits of metal.

"They don't look like military rank and file, but things change fast outside remotes like this place," the man noted. "We are not kind to run-outs who might bring trouble our way."

Evan raised a brow and shook his head slowly. "So are you kind to those who won't bring trouble around your way?"

Linc's laughter tickled in Evan's skull. *Well done.*

The man beside Evan stifled a snicker and mumbled, "'S got a point, Coach," before taking a shot from the row in front of him.

The bartender glared and picked up a glass. The man in the stool guarded his face. But the move had served its purpose. The bartender snatched a towel and wiped the glass as if that had been his intended purpose all along.

He turned his gaze back on Evan. Evan knew an answer was more than recommended.

"I'm not military. Not anymore." Evan could tell by the silent exchange he hadn't upset them in the statement.

No surprise.

Big as some cities were, the further from the main seat of politics, the less they gave a damn.

"A man who leaves home for long stretches has to carry reminders, and a man never going back carries all he can."

Evan fingered the pair of embossed tags dangling side by side on the chain. He thumbed a slider hiding a plug on one, the other had a split in the center with a cap.

This city, like so many others, lacked the technology to read the files, but Evan knew what they were. That was all he needed.

"Boy, you make not a bit of sense." The man beside him finished off two more shots.

"Maybe not in this town." Evan grinned. "But where I came from, memories don't come more organized." He clutched the USB drive tags a moment, then hid them safely inside his shirt.

Linc's voice filled his thoughts. *The important things can be taken anywhere; the photos, letters, drawings, papers, who we are, were, and loved. May be they are only copies, digitized moments frozen in points of data, but it is enough. A hundred years ago, no one cared you could not feel the warmth on the face of a photo in a locket.*

To confine our attention to terrestrial matters would be to limit the human spirit.

Stephen Hawking

Theoretical physicist, cosmologist, and author

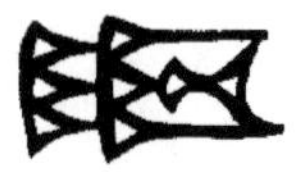

Chapter Ten

Evan awoke to a bright sliver of sunlight burning into his eyelids and the ringing in his ears being replaced by the call alert on his phone.

He knew his lack of steady employment had begun to wear his nerves. That, combined with lack of schedule, created a disastrous mix of late nights and later mornings.

The lack of his usual medication had done nothing to help his anxiety about the instability of his financial situation, Fred's failing health, and the Cloud crashes. The cocktail of dramas was enough for Evan to write off the feelings left by the bizarre, vivid dream, as well as the return of Linc's voice.

Evan rolled to his feet to check the time on the mobile device propped on the coffee table.

The screen was dark.

Evan tapped the side of the device, searching for the unlock key along the edge of the frame. Locating the fingerprint recognition surface, the screen blinked to life.

The home screen, however, was not what Evan had set. A bright blue background with an error message in bright white text assaulted Evan's eyes.

He rolled to his side and drew the device to him, holding it between his palms. Evan examined the handheld computer. His brow furrowed as he considered the meaning of this error message.

He tapped screen.

Nothing. The image remained the same. He swiped the surface, the panel shifted. The same error message met him no matter which direction he slid his fingers. This was not a typical failure in connection. There should at least be applications and icons on the home screen.

Evan strode across the living room of his uncle Fred's home. He wandered into the master bathroom and set the device on the edge of the sink counter.

The blue screen disappeared as the preset sleep mode activated, returning the screen to black. At least *that* still worked. He washed his face before taking up the device again.

He crossed into the kitchen to start coffee, eyes all the while on the device. The ritual of making coffee was never something Evan bothered with when the networks were fully functioning--he would leave that up to settings on the communication between the internet of things. With the networks behaving as they were, it was not worth the stress wondering if settings and alarms would remain functional.

Evan flopped into the closest chair. He let the mobile device clatter to the table and drew his tablet to him. It was possible the tablet could still get a signal when the mobile was down. Evan tapped the screen to wake the tablet from sleep mode.

The same blaring blue screen met his eyes.

"Oh, come on." Evan prodded the screen.

Here. Let me help you out with that. Linc's voice buzzed in Evan's ears.

A moment later, the mobile device began to vibrate and sing the message alert Evan set for the hospital.

Evan lunged for the device that suddenly chose to function.

"Hello." Evan panted the word out past the startled jump of his heart rate.

"Is this Evan Gabriel?" A woman's voice on the other end of the connection offered vague concern.

Noting the woman's tone, Evan and prepared for the worst. "This is Evan. Is this the hospital my uncle Fred is at?"

"Oh, good! Evan, we have been trying to reach you all morning."

All morning? Evan rose and peered through the shade covering the kitchen window. Another blast of light accosted his adjusting pupils. It was brighter, and later, than he first thought.

"Is my uncle okay?"

Evan glared out the window at the high morning sun, and swallowed his emotions for the moment.

"He's asking to see you," the woman replied.

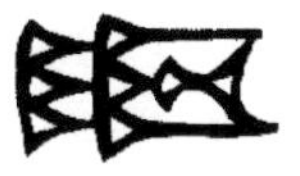

Chapter Eleven

Fred shuffled along the walkway within the courtyard of the hospital. Sunlight warmed his shoulders and the top of his head. It was a welcome shift from the cold lighting and air conditioning in his room.

It felt good to soak up natural light. He had never enjoyed the outdoors much, but an extended stay caged within hospital walls made him long for fresh air. His eyes wandered as he pushed the metal walker steadily along the open-air path. The strange realization weighed on him, he could be dead right now instead of meandering the little manicured garden. The silence of the space left Fred moderately uneasy. Nothing stood out to alert him to the day or the time. Neither of these things seemed to matter much at the moment, either.

The slight breeze sent a chill over his arms, but not so cold as to want to adjust the hospital robe resting on his shoulders. The scrub pants and shirt were the most clothing he had access to since being freed from a hospital gown. He did wish he had some shoes in place of the rubber gripped socks.

Convincing the nursing staff to remove the varied devices that had kept him alive for nearly a month had been a chore that had taken much of the night.

Anyone in technical support knew, the overnight support was rarely as in-command of things as day shift. The medical field was no different.

The staff insisted on the walker. Fred was grateful after trying to stand. That was the first moment he realized he must again be among the living. Death or a dream would not have been so tiring.

“Uncle Fred!” Evan’s voice broke the silence of the garden and any lingering thoughts Fred had that this was not reality.

Fred pivoted in the frame of the walker to see his nephew. The young man did not look as vibrant and cocky as Fred recalled from their last encounter on the train.

"Who dragged you in?" Fred laughed.

Evan sighed, but gratitude exuded in his demeanor.

"You can't go wandering off." Evan strode toward Fred.

He stopped short after a few steps. "Are you okay?"

Fred released a cool smile. "Eh, it's nothing a burger and fries won't fix."

"Good luck with that request." Evan rounded the chair and took hold of the handles. "You'd best get used to rabbit food.

"Nonsense." Fred shrugged. "I feel better than ever. I was starting to think this might be heaven."

"Sure." Evan smirked. "And what tipped you off it wasn't?"

"Your sorry ass," Fred quipped.

"Well, best get used to me, too. We're gonna be roomies for a while." Something in Evan's tone told Fred this was not only due to his health. In silence, Evan walked Fred back to his room.

"I can pack my own bags." Fred protested as Evan puttered about the hospital room.

"You are supposed to be resting. The doctors are impressed with your seemingly spontaneous healing, but you still need to take it easy."

From his perch on the edge of the bed Fred watched his nephew.

"Am I going to have to put up with you mothering me for long?" He complained.

Evan shoved a stack of get well cards into the side pocket of the small satchel.

"I certainly hope not." Evan scanned the room for any stray items.

He lifted a tablet from the bedside table and turned it in his hands as if it might bite him before adding it to the clutter of other small items and articles of clothing.

The nurse entered as Evan zipped the closure on the bag.

"I apologize gentlemen." She struggled with a folder of papers.

"The systems are down here too?" Evan scowled.

The nurse nodded. "In some wings yes, others no. It's sort of skipping around."

"What systems?" Fred's interest drew him from the bed to Evan's side.

"The Cloud has been … a bit glitchy." Evan took the papers from the nurse. "Which is why we are going hard copy I assume?"

"Yeah." The woman patted at her uniform. "Shit."

"Not used to needing a pen?" Fred snickered.

"I'll be right back again." The apology was implied in her tone as she scurried away.

"I wonder where they found enough spare paper kicking around?" Fred pulled the folder from Evan's hands and flipped through the pages.

"So, what did you break while I was gone?" Fred tapped at the embedded touchscreen in the Tesla. "Tablets down. GPS spotty." Fred paused to turn a serious gaze upon his nephew. "Will I be able to watch my shows while I'm stuck on recovery?"

Evan batted Fred's hand away from the frozen GPS screen.

"They're still trying to figure it out. And until then, my security clearance is revoked. I'm on indefinite furlough."

Evan glanced at the smear of notes etched on the palm of his hand.

Fred raised a brow at his nephew. "You know, that cool stuff called paper. I hear the ancients used it to write directions on."

Evan shot a scowl at Fred.

"Where are we going, anyway?" Fred turned Evan's palm.

"Your place." Evan pulled his hand away.

A short laugh escaped Fred. "Take the next left. Then north to thirty-sixth street."

"Right." Evan put his hands on the wheel.

"No, left." Fred laughed. "Don't you know how to get to my place? You've been there often enough."

"Why would I commit that to memory?" Evan scoffed.

"In case of apocalypse?" Fred winked as he tapped again at the non-functioning dashboard screen.

A physician without a knowledge of Astrology has no right to call himself a physician.

Hippocrates

Greek physician- "Father of Medicine"

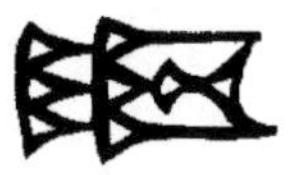

Chapter Twelve

The reason to commit more than directions to memory became abundantly clear by the end of the week.

In a matter of days the minor hiccups in connectivity had grown to full blown blackouts. The furlough of ITower employees had become an exodus. Blame was passed from the highest ranks to the lowest, and back up again.

The security teams led by Evan and others in his position were dragged in for questioning on corporate and criminal levels. It was no one's fault, and everyone was to blame in the same stroke.

It was the next wave that shocked Evan most however.

"We will be opening a limited line of connectivity in our ongoing efforts to discover the root of the issues, and continue to serve our most valuable customers."

"Hotspots." Evan growled at the radio.

"It does make sense." Fred moved a pawn to block the path of Evan's bishop. "Your move."

"How can you be so calm about this?" Evan paced the living room. "We are listening to radio broadcasts. In a week the tech company heads are going to start hopping out of windows. In a month it will be much worse."

Fred leaned away from the chessboard. "The backup systems will be online by then. Bo patient. Your move."

Evan halted mid pace to stalk over to the board. His eyes flit across the pieces a moment before he snatched Fred's rook from the corner of the board.

"Check." Evan returned to his circuit of the room.

Fred frowned at the pieces. "Maybe we should take a break. You seem stressed."

Fred rose to stretch his legs. Out of habit he reached for his tablet to check the time.

The screen was dark.

"Look at it this way, hospitals are running again since the ethernet hardline bypass. Libraries, police and fire stations have the same safety net. We will be fine."

"How can you be so calm about all of this?" Evan followed his uncle through to the kitchen.

"Mankind has come a long way, and most of the journey happened without nearly the technology we have today." Fred opened the pantry and spied a bag of pork rinds."

"Yours is in the back." Evan reached past Fred and snagged a bag of air fried banana chips.

Fred offered an ungrateful scowl as he claimed the bag from his nephew. "Right."

"At least the stores kept their backup inventory files on the hard drives in the clerk handhelds." Evan joined Fred at the table.

"They are only daily lists but it allowed them to retain most of the data required for supply updates."

"I'm calm because a lack of data connectivity isn't the worst thing in a world where I am denied pork rinds and hot dogs."

Evan smirked as he popped a rind into his mouth. "And long walks as soon as you get the all clear."

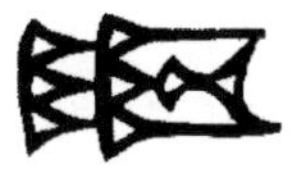

Chapter Thirteen

Fred let the tip of the cane press into the hard concrete of the sidewalk. He breathed in the afternoon air and straightened to take another step.

"Day three. Walking." Fred stated to the empty sidewalk. "Let the day's journey begin."

The prescribed therapy for a man who had gone through a major heart attack and bypass surgery. It was not the walk that bothered Fred, though--it was lack of purpose. With two weeks of work leave--a mandatory vacation, as the human resources department referred to it--following nearly a month on his back in la la land, the banality of his days was becoming too much for Fred's typically busy mind.

It wasn't as if he could do much at work anyway. Connections were so sketchy, he had given up watching streaming video or listening to digital radio. Walks were, in sad truth, the most interesting part of his day. It had only taken Fred one trip around his neighborhood for boredom to push his adventures further.

Fred absorbed the mundane wonder of finely manicured lawns, drab walking paths, and the blasé similarity of quaint front porches. He offered vacant good mornings to disturbingly adorable gnomes and rigid figures of forest animals whose living counterparts would likely never venture this deep into human habitation.

Potted plants and geometrically imperfect stone paths meant to emulate dried rivers dotted the waterless neighborhoods. Fred counted the number of green yards against gravel patches, and pondered how to properly categorize a xeriscape yard.

It was as boring as he always knew it to be.

He could be fighting with streaming data systems. He and Evan might even have been able to fit the remains of land lines to the house, if they tried, but that boy was making him crazy.

Evan had cared for Fred and visited him every day in the hospital since the incident on the train. Fred was grateful, though he had no idea at first why Evan was helping him. Now he realized there was little else for the kid to do, with GlobeNet systems laying people off left and right. Fred sighed as he took in yet another perfect gravel yard complete with river rock ribboning through it, off of center.

He continued down the street, further than he had ventured before. His strength and stamina had been improving enough Fred no longer felt he would have to call Evan for a ride home if he wandered further than his body could take him back.

Manicured front yards gave way to open lots and office parks. Fred eyed the commercial gardens and parking lots, before averting his attention in the opposite direction.

Opposite the business district, the street was dotted with a row of two-story homes. These lawns were unlike those in the neighborhood.

Fred glanced back the way he had walked. He was easily two miles from the entrance of his neighborhood. Three miles was a decent walk. He sighed, considering the three more it would take to return. They would not be easy miles.

"I can always ask Evan for a ride. That boy needs to get out of the house. It will give him an excuse to take a shower."

As Fred pondered Evan's employment situation, he continued down the street into undiscovered territory.

The quality of the houses were lower here. They were not necessarily dilapidated, but the perfectionism of lawns and overall appearance dwindled comparatively.

Gravel patches were scattered with weeds and leaves. Paths needed more sweeping. The figurines and porch decor leaned more toward tacky, second hand, or handmade.

Fred wandered on, a renewed energy from the unique discoveries fueling him, drawn by some deeper energy. Halfway down the street, Fred's eyes fell upon a sign jutting from the front lawn of a two-story structure might have been a home at one point, and now doubled as commercial property.

Fred adjusted his glasses and squinted at the twist and swirl of the ornate letters. A sudden rush of understanding struck him. He shot a glance up and down the street. He had indeed wandered into the back streets of historic homes and business district of the chichi downtown.

He considered how proud his doctor would be when she took the readout from today's walk. A full six miles. Fred averted his attention to the sky. The sun was high, and the growing afternoon was warm. He'd walked the morning away.

Whether from the sudden realization of the time, distance, or heat of his adventures, a wave of dizzying fatigue overwhelmed him. He leaned on the sign post.

"Maybe a moment inside to cool off." Fred meandered the short walk to the porch of the business-slash-residence.

He offered a bemused smile to dangling porch chimes tinkling in the gentle breeze. His eyes protested in a flurry of blinks and squints as a string of crystals trapped the afternoon light and glinted it back in an array of prisms. A pair of brightly colored pinwheels with petals like flowers spun at either side of the porch stairs.

Yet another wave of vertigo bucked through him as he gripped the rails. He caught the step with the foot of his cane and allowed a moment to lean on the hook. His eyes rolled and focused on the bright yellow door at the top of the short flight of steps.

Inside the window, a small paper sign was taped to the glass. Fred's brow knit at the sight of a printed page and realized that the lawn sign had been on a printed board as well, rather than a digital advertising screen.

Fred read the words on the paper.

"Have you recently had a Near Death Experience? Do you want to discover more about past lives? Do you see, hear, or otherwise experience unexplainable or unusual phenomena?"

Fred's mind suddenly returned to the strange images and visions he experienced before waking in the hospital bed.

He looked through the window beside the door. A woman within the building wandered into Fred's view. She was young, possibly the same age as Evan, yet there was a way in her walk that caused her to seem much more mature than Fred's playboy nephew.

The woman paused mid-task and moved out of sight. A moment later the door of the little shop opened. She leaned on the open screen door. "Come on in, you're a little early, but that's good for your first time."

Fred's confusion was consumed by the calm of the woman's energy. His vertigo evaporating, Fred didn't hesitate to enter the little store.

Chapter Fourteen

Evan continued to prod the rainbow array of wires protruding from the walls of his uncle Fred's aging house. Cobwebs and dust tickled at his face, threatening to unleash yet another wave of nasal convulsions. He toed along the beams as he stretched to reach wires merging in a cluster against the rafters within the ceiling.

"This is ridiculous." Evan snorted as he swiped the webs and shook the grit from his face. "Guh."

Evan backed toward the ladder and tossed a handful of coiled wire into a tool chest on the floor.

"This is so not worth the trouble." Evan glared at the wires before descending the stairs from the crawlspace.

It would be as easy to hit a library converted into an information center since the crash. Evan might even have gotten over the volume of people in line for connected devices. Watching women search for recipes annoyed him more than it should, while tweens checking messages and chatting in drama clusters was even more tiring. Evan sighed as he shook off the thought. All he wanted was to surf job postings. A man with his caliber of technological savvy belonged behind a screen, not digging in a dusty crawlspace rooting for old wires.

Evan made his way through to the living room and glared at the tablet collecting dust beside the couch. Forget the furlough due to potential security breaches, with all of GlobeNet down there were no security issues at all. It was a something Evan had wished for on an almost daily basis, especially when things were exceptionally tough and his social life suffered with the swell of overtime hours due to some petulant breach. Instead, this calm and lack of network did equal damage to his social life.

What he would give for one big security project to sink his claws into right now. And, the huge paycheck that would come with it.

Evan glanced at the screen hanging in the kitchen to check the time. A habitual action now produced no result. He flashed his attention to the watch strapped to his wrist. It had been his great-great-grandfather's. No one in the family had ever taken it out of the box after he passed away. Evan received the device as a graduation gift after finishing his master's program in technical security systems. To wear the thing pained him, not for the risk of causing damage to such an antique, but for having to wear anything at all to check something as simple as the time.

"Hey. Hey, Uncle Fred!" Evan called into the empty kitchen as he crossed the floor to peer into the rear guest room.

"Fred?" Evan called again.

Fred had been taking longer walks since hospitalization, but usually returned before the sun began to set.

Evan slumped his shoulders and looked at the rumpled shirt he was still wearing from yesterday. He made sure his mobile device was docked into the temporary landline station and trudged for the guest bathroom to take a late afternoon shower.

It would be nice if Fred considered letting Evan know when he decided today would be a day to get a ride. It wasn't like before the crash, where anyone could call from anywhere, at any time. Information centers and communication hubs were few and far between, and catching someone near a phone was even more of a hassle.

Evan knew the station only worked if the mobile device remained docked. He would have to take a quick shower and hurry out to listen in case of a call. Messaging systems no longer worked unless both parties were on tablets and logged in to ITower's GlobeNet backup. It was like living in the dark ages of technology.

Evan soaped and rinsed as quickly as he could, his ear ever attentive to possible sounds of ringing from the communication device.

"Communication device. What a misnomer." Evan grumbled as he stepped from shower to plush bath mat.

As Evan rounded the doorway into the kitchen, still wrapped in a towel, he heard a car pull into the driveway. A moment later he caught the sound of his uncle Fred's voice.

Evan scowled in confusion before hurrying to get some clothing on. He disappeared into the guest bedroom and listened for the door. He pulled a pair of jeans from the pile, threw a shirt over his head, and tossed the towel into the nearby hamper.

"Thank you again for the ride, Hannah!" Evan heard his uncle Fred call out from the front door.

"You old dog."

Evan smirked from the doorway between the kitchen and front room. The smile on the younger man's lips was one of curiosity as much as mocking.

"I know the doctors told you to get that heart rate up, but don't you think it's a little soon for anything too strenuous?" Evan snickered.

Evan grinned as the double meaning of his words dawned on his uncle. "Oh good gods, Evan, my boy! What do you take me for? That woman is nearly the same age as you are and I couldn't keep up with someone like her even before the time bomb in my chest went off."

Evan shrugged. "Sure. Whatever you say, old man. So who's this chick that gave you a ride, then?"

"If you must know, Hannah is the owner of a new shop I discovered today in my travels." Fred closed the door and swung his cane out of the way.

He began his steady march toward the kitchen, passing Evan.

"Sure. So what did you buy? Besides a ride, home of course." Evan opened the refrigerator door and drew out a beer.

"She doesn't sell too many things, more so she offers support." Fred waved for Evan to hand over a bottle.

Evan returned to the refrigerator and tossed a container of carbonated water to his uncle.

Fred frowned as he caught the bottle. He moved to the kitchen chair. "That's beside the point. She was also kind enough to take me to the public information center up the road to check my messages."

Evan set his beer on the table. He eyed Fred a moment before turning back to the refrigerator.

Fred continued to relay the adventures of his day as Evan fished out a handful of vegetables and a packet of hot dogs.

"None for you, and you know it," Evan caught his uncle's grin at the sight of the hot dogs. "I'm not enabling another heart attack here. What did you find out from the information center?"

"Yes. There's news from the ITower front lines, sir." Fred mused in military tones. "It looks like I'm going back into the fray."

Evan dropped the pan he held and let it land heavily on the stovetop. He breathed before turning to acknowledge his uncle's statement.

"That's great," Evan lied.

"My mandatory leave is over, and while I've enjoyed this little vacation with you, nephew, one of us has to have some sort of income."

Fred gestured at the hot dogs with his cane. "I mean, if we want to keep up this extravagant lifestyle."

"Of course." Evan sighed.

He stared at the sizzling dogs in the pan.

Chapter Fifteen

Fred awoke to an empty house. Evan had been leaving earlier every morning, it seemed. Though Fred had begun to be concerned his nephew was not sleeping at all. He knew the signs of anxiety and stress. He had once been far too intimate with them as well.

Since the incident on the train, the near death experience, or NDE, as Hannah and the others in the support group had called it, however, Fred seemed to have lost the ability to be anxious. It was a symptom, a sort of side effect of touching the other side. At least that's how Fred understood it.

He rolled out of bed and made his way to the kitchen. Tea, in place of coffee, had become his new drink of choice. When he mentioned this to Hannah she had given him a sample bag of hibiscus flowers.

Fred pulled the bag from the cabinet and turned back the small tabs holding the mouth of the bag closed. The aroma of the flowers filled his senses.

"Smells as purple as it looks." Fred mused as he fished a tea cup from the cabinet.

Following the hand written instructions on the back of the little bag, Fred spooned a few dried petals into the tea strainer. He set the strainer in the tea cup and the kettle on to boil as he wandered to the front of the house.

A few scoops of dried petals were not the only gift Hannah had offered Fred on their meeting.

He took a canvas tote from the hook by the door. He grunted as he remembered the weight of the contents. He peered into the bag.

"Homework time." He mumbled.

The whistle of the tea kettle drew him back to the kitchen.

He laid the bag on the kitchen table while he completed the task of brewing tea. Hannah had also mentioned the ritual of making the perfect cup of tea. Using a tea ball was more than enough ritual for now.

"Smells nice enough." He admitted as he sniffed at the curls of steam rising from the cup.

He settled in at the table and drew the books from the tote bag.

He scanned the titles spread before him. "Evidence of Life after Life, Tomorrow's Return, Dying to Become Me." He turned one of the books in his hand.

Many of the men and women in the support group had mentioned the titles as guides that allowed them to understand their experience, yet as Fred flipped the pages he found little fully explained the man he had spoken to in the vision, or the scenes whirling in his mind.

Fred moved to try the tea. "Shit! Hot!"

A spattering of pinkish liquid speckled the table and the pages of the book as Fred thumped the cup onto the table and fanned at his open mouth.

"Great." He muttered as he rose to snatch a towel from the counter to mop up the mess.

As he patted at the pages of the book something caught his attention.

He put the towel aside. "The Akashic records are a compendium of all of existence. They are considered by some to be a sort of library of data stored in the greater consciousness of reality. Contained in this library are the past, present, and potential of all existence."

Fred laid the book on the table. "A library of data." He repeated the words aloud.

Glancing again over the books before him he wished he had more than a table of contents to guide him to more information on this Akashic library. Undeterred, he flipped through the next book in search of keywords.

"Hey! Fred! You here?" Evan's voice sliced through the fog of Fred's thoughts.

He lifted his gaze from the stacks of books and notes spread across the table as his nephew appeared in the doorway.

"How goes the day, old man? Any adventures with lady friends today?" Evan mused as he opened the refrigerator in search of food.

Evan turned to his uncle when Fred didn't reply. "Have you been sitting here all day?"

Fred blinked at the analogue clock across the room. He lifted the now cold tea cup.

"I need to get online."

The purpose of human life is to serve, and to show compassion and the will to help others.

Albert Schweitzer

Nobel Peace Prize: writer, humanitarian, philosopher, and physician

Chapter Sixteen

"It's good to see you back in the saddle, Fred."

Fred rotated in his office chair to see a young woman with a mailroom cart blocking the entrance to his cubicle.

"Thank you." Fred frowned at the disheveled stack of envelopes and file folders. "What's all this?"

"Afternoon message run, and packet distribution." The woman flipped through the stacks. "Better known as my midmorning tour of the campus."

Fred's attention turned from the young woman as he flipped through the envelopes.

"You are looking pretty good." She winked as she handed over yet another stack of folders and letters. "That little vacation did wonders."

"It was mandatory." Fred frowned. "I would've been back sooner had they allowed me to be."

"Oh." The woman shrugged. "Well, you may need a real vacation soon. It's like a war around here. Everyone has their boxers in a twist."

"I'm a new man, ready to bail you young slackers out of this little mess." Fred nodded.

The woman waved off his statement and continued through the cubicle maze.

Fred turned his attention to the dusty early 2000's desktop computer in his office space. The chair wheel hung up on a wire as Fred rolled closer to the desk.

"Crap." Fred shifted and lifted the chair.

He tracked carefully toward the desk. "Maybe this is a little different than before the crash. A bit more like the old days than I would like to admit."

Fred adjusted the cascade of wires across his desk. He checked connections between tower and screen, wiggled the tail protruding from the keyboard, and adjusted the wired mouse on the pad. Use of the Cloud had not been limited to data transfer. Everything wireless was forced to rely on hard line connection to avoid strain on the already unstable bandwidth of the data stream.

Fred scowled as he ran his fingers through his hair. The building had maintained a backup infrastructure. There were enough wired devices in storage, it appeared. Somewhere, he was certain, there was a warehouse of rotary phones.

Fred depressed the switch on the face of the tower and waited for the machine to boot up. He sighed as he heard the shriek of the connection. Things were indeed different, but at least he was linked in. There was comfort to the familiar hum of electronics and the bright white of a Cloud-connected screen.

"Takes me back to college." Fred muttered as the screens connected to the computer tower blinked to life.

He settled in as loading screens abated and a familiar desktop image appeared. He set his fingers flying across the keyboard. It was strange to feel the haptic feedback of solid keys beneath his fingers.

Windows of code filled the screen. Fred's eyes flitted across the alphanumeric strings as he deciphered incoming errors and messages. ITower was a mess.

Wired connections seemed to be functioning, yet wireless cellular connectivity was a mystery. It appeared to be a hardware issue. Yet, that made sense only if the disease of the data stream infected only certain devices.

Fred removed his glasses a moment. He rubbed his weary eyes. Returning his glasses on the bridge of his nose, he stared at the cluttered screen. His eyes wandered to the icon tray. He slid the mouse and the cursor hovered over the browser icon.

He clicked.

The window appeared to be a typical information center start page. The difference, information center connections contained locks and nanny-bot programs. It was like working in a small, cramped cage with the whole of the data stores on the outside.

Combined with the time limits, navigation was nearly impossible.

Fred typed his search terms into the text box. He was greeted with more than a million returns, a reaction much more akin to what he was used to.

Fred slapped the desk in his excitement, and instantly hoped no one in the surrounding cubicles had heard the report.

He considered the tidbits of information offered by the owner of the whimsical little shop. He wandered into her world a few days ago, yet since then, Fred's mind filled with new ideas and questions. Attending the support groups offered at the store were not nearly enough to quench Fred's knowledge-starved mind. His hunger for more data was never satisfied with a mere morsel. Fred sought the buffet of understanding.

He opened several tabs as he read the headlines of links listed on the screen.

Near Death Experiences: Signs and Related Consequences; Astral Travel and the Near Death Experience; International Association for Near Death Studies; Reliable sources of Near Death and the Afterlife; Share Near Death Experiences with Others. The list was more than Fred could have hoped.

Fred opened the last link. After a moment of allowing data to load, he realized it was a chat system. There appeared to be several members. A key along the left side of the page displayed a live list of members currently signed on.

Fred hastily created an account.

He awaited the registration message and was shocked at the speed of the response. Even ITower interoffice messages were slower on the vintage wired systems.

It took longer for Fred to choose a catchy handle than for the confirmation to go through. The site must have been on a well-connected server or had minimal data.

Fred, using the handle Cloud Master, opened a thread on near death experiences. Many in-depth answers had been entered by a user under the name Coach333.

Fred noted the little green dot hovering beside the name, indicating the user was currently available. Fred clicked Coach333's highlighted link. He was surprised when a live chat opened. This site offered a lot compared to others. Since the crash, most had given up live chat due to the burden placed on data connections. Even basic text transfer lagged pages, leaving communicating parties frustrated and confused by buffered dialogue exchanges. Audio and video were a lost cause.

Fred typed a short greeting and introduced himself as one who had recently experienced near-death.

CLOUD MASTER: *I have a few questions.*

His user title Cloud Master appeared beside the block of text:

CLOUD MASTER: *You seem knowledgeable about this near-death experience stuff. I was wondering if you had a minute to answer a few questions.*

Fred awaited a response, wondering if he might need to reload the site page in order to actually see the reply. To his excitement, the chat box alert sounded and a new block of text filled the space beneath Fred's initial query.

COACH333: *For you, of course!*

Fred considered the response strangely personal, yet he was learning from the Connections support groups that there were extremely friendly people in Near Death and metaphysical communities. Fred adjusted and began to type his response.

CLOUD MASTER: *Thank you! I'm not sure where to start. I guess I should ask if it's typical to see streaming data during an NDE. I've asked others, but they don't seem to be as techie as I am.*

COACH333: *What an individual sees can depend much on the life they are released from. Programming and lessons experienced thus far can shape near-death experiences in many ways. Your job is likely the reason you saw data streams. It could also be connected to your task, your purpose.*

Fred's brow furrowed at the mention of his job. How had this stranger known he worked in data? Fred tabbed to his site profile. Did he post the information? He had been hasty with the entries, it was possible he ticked a box inadvertently. He found nothing to reveal his employment.

CLOUD MASTER: *How do you know I work with data?*

Fred typed with care. He read the words to be certain he had not given further information away before clicking the send key.

COACH333: *You told me it would be your interest in this life. You were quite excited at how far technology has advanced and you would be able to dabble in data as you had lifetimes ago.*

Fred read the text multiple times. There was quite a bit to unpack in the statements. He leaned on the easiest and most pressing.

CLOUD MASTER: *Have we met?*

COACH333: *Several times, but you might not remember. It has been a while.*

Fred returned to his profile. His name wasn't listed publicly as far as he could tell. He tried to review Coach333's profile.

CLOUD MASTER: *You must be mistaking me for someone with a similar handle. I guess code monkeys aren't unique thinkers when it comes to usernames.*

COACH333: *Perhaps. I'm still happy to answer your questions, friend.*

Fred smiled at the Coach333's openness. Awkward as the conversation had become, he couldn't deny a connection with this character, even through basic text chat. A sense of connection overcame Fred.

CLOUD MASTER: *Well, you're right. I'm in Big Data, currently tasked with this issue of connectivity.*

COACH333: *We're all working on that issue. And have been for quite a long time.*

Fred was once again confused. He pushed his chair away from the desk. He rose to peer over the walls of his cubicle. Could this Coach333 be someone on the floor toying with him? He scanned the tops of the spaces, searching. Fred dipped back to his seat. It occurred to him this person could be a higher level employee, someone spying to access the Cloud for personal use.

"Shit." Fred practiced the breathing technique Hannah had showed him as he fought to regain control of his heart rate.

His eyes flicked to the screen.

COACH333: *There is plenty of information in the Library. What do you want to know?*

CLOUD MASTER: *Which library are you referring to?*

Fred hoped this would reveal if Coach333 was a ITower employee. The upper floor of the main ITower building housed a traditional library of archival technical manuals, company histories, and pieces from personal collections. No one ever read the books though. All the information had been scanned into files and uploaded ages ago for ease of access. It was no more than a museum.

COACH333: *The Akashic.*

True knowledge exists in knowing that you know nothing.

Socrates

Ancient Greek philosopher – "Founder of Western Philosophy"

Chapter Seventeen

Fred's heart all but stopped as he recalled the attendees of the support group mentioning the Akashic.

CLOUD MASTER *What do you know about that?*

Fred was too caught up in the twist the conversation had taken to be concerned with spies or pranksters.

COACH333: *This is something you have been tasked to work on. Connection. To the Akashic. As you said.*

Fred swallowed a growing lump in his throat. This unknown chat room user, with no accessible profile, had touched a topic on Fred's mind since he stepped into Hannah's Connections shop. A topic he had mentioned to no one.

Fine, he thought. *This character wants to mess around. Let's see where this leads.*

If this was a prank, Fred was about to nip it right in the bud. Fred's fingers flew over the keys. He clicked the mouse with more haste and force than intended.

CLOUD MASTER: *I might be working on the possibility technology can access the Akashic Records. Is it not one big Big Data cloud? Should be easy, right?*

"Damn it all." Fred grumbled and took to the keys again before his Coach333 had chance to respond.

CLOUD MASTER: *I'm not sure if you noticed the connection to the data cloud and wireless cell nets have been more than a little out of whack. I'm supposed to be working on that mess.*

COACH333: *Same thing.*

He stared at the screen, wondering if this guy was tech savvy as Fred thought.

COACH333: *Your theory is not a joke. It is what you have been tasked to do.*

Fred peered over the cubicle. Someone was playing a prank, or worse, testing his sanity and threatening his job.

CLOUD MASTER: *No, they're completely different. There is reality and there is mythology. Where did you say you were from again?*

COACH333: *Are you not paying attention during support group at Conscious Connections? You should listen to what Hannah is trying to tell you.*

Fred froze at the specificity of the statements. He snapped a glance over his shoulder to be certain no one was watching. He scanned the components on the desk and waved a hand over the top frame of the screen. Was the camera recording?

His gaze fell to the screen. He read the words in the message box once again.

Fred's fingers twitched as they hovered the keys. He could end the chat now, tap the little red X in the top corner of the window, and be done with it. He adjusted in his seat.

CLOUD MASTER: *How do you know about Hannah? Are you an NDE group member too?*

It was the most logical answer, Fred reasoned with the tingling at the back of his neck. It was possible another ITower employee could have had a similar experience and attended the NDE group. Fred peered over the top edge of his cubicle wall. This time searching for a kindred soul.

Before Fred could read the response from Coach333, the message chime drew his attention to a secondary window blocking the chat.

"Fred." The Cloud systems repair project lead appeared on the screen.

"We need to see you in the east boardroom. Now." The audio hiccupped through the audio relay as the image jerked like a flipbook of stills.

The image disappeared as soon as the audio ended. Fred shifted back to the chat window. The interruption had disconnected Coach333. Fred slumped into his chair. He would have to wait until after the meeting to continue with Coach333.

Chapter Eighteen

Fred entered a space already filled with more men in suits than he was accustomed to. He straightened the gig line and collar on his button-down shirt. He was grateful he had not rolled and wrinkled the sleeves earlier in the day, though not so grateful he had failed to wear at least a sports jacket. It was awkward enough he had not checked to see if there were visible sweat stains on his shirt.

At the far end of the large oval table, the head of ITower Cloud Services' Big Data branch sat with hands folded in front of him. The man's perfectly coiffed head of grey hair and tailored black suit were enough to make Fred nervous even without the rest of the suits in the room.

In the military, a rank on a sleeve higher than his own had been enough to make Fred cringe. It didn't take so much as a word from someone in power to make Fred sweat bullets.

Then the high ranking corporate officer spoke.

"Fred. I'm glad to see you're on the mend and ready to get back to work here for ITower. We are well aware the world of communications has gone through some serious changes since you had your leave of absence. It is our sincere hope you are not too overwhelmed by these shifts." The tone in the man's voice was almost apologetic.

Fred would not allow himself to be lulled into a relaxed state. He knew better than to fall for such basic corporate mind games. Fred simply sought an empty seat as close to the door as possible.

"Please, we also ask that you be sincere about your opinion of the current wired systems. We are trying hard to maintain some semblance of normalcy at least within the confines of ITower offices."

This time, Fred was certain the man meant to be apologetic, if not ashamed, at the disastrous state of communications systems. Systems that had been the highest and most reliable technology for over forty years.

"I think ITower is honestly doing the best they can." Fred lowered himself into an empty chair between a pair of suited businessmen and took stock of their expressions. "I have worked for this company for more than half my life. I wanted to work in Big Data and Cloud Services since I was a boy messing around on a home device." Fred's brief but deep speech seemed to suffice for the moment to relax the suits in their high-backed office thrones. "I want to help ITower and the people we serve."

"That is wonderful to hear, Fred. We trust you are fully recovered?" This from his direct boss once again. "This is a stressful time and we are in dire need of your expertise, but we also want to keep an asset such as yourself in good health."

Fred smirked at the earnest concern on the man's face. The truth was out--the only real concern here was the health of the company, but by proxy, Fred was getting star treatment. There was a small voice inside Fred's mind telling him there might be some incredible benefits to this new position if he played his cards right.

The man at the head of the table cleared his throat and began his explanation of the information at his disposal at the moment. "The Cloud Services technicians who have been working closely with the crashed systems believe this is a terrorist problem. The issues with the organization calling themselves Wave7 and their apparent bone to pick with GlobeNet may well have expanded into Cloud Services."

Fred folded his arms as he listened with a furrowed brow. The concern of connectivity was not the only issue at stake here. He knew this from the moment the Data Cloud was taken from the easy grasp of public and private control.

The boss continued. With no wireless tablets available, every eye in the boardroom was on the man. It was obvious by the way he worked to avert his eyes he was greatly unaccustomed to having anyone actually look at him while he spoke. "Our fear here at Cloud Services division of ITower is we could have a sort of global amnesia if this Wave7 gang of terrorists is able to compromise the integrity of the Data Cloud. That could hurt us."

Fred held back a sudden urge to speak up for the real issue. The fall of a corporate empire aside, a form of global amnesia was not a matter to take with a light heart. And it was completely plausible.

For the last fifty years, all information had been shifted to digital. In that time, all formatted material had also been moved from even the most advanced solid state storage devices to the Data Cloud. It was an entire generation. The retro uploads would be more devastating if lost. It started with video and image files from the middle to late nineteen hundreds. All information was converted and uploaded. Sure there were some VHS tapes and CD or DVD discs in storage somewhere--the nostalgic or hyper-cautious certainly kept something. The further issue was access to devices required to read these formats of information storage.

During Fred's waxing consideration of these issues, the boss cut from the presentation. "We are talking about every piece of data in the world. Everything is stored in the Data Cloud. When was the last time anybody printed anything?"

Fred mused about empty library shelves, and how the purpose of a librarian had become more research assistant, data communications trainer, or archivist continually uploading information of the past on to storage system of the future.

Fred leaned forward. Leveling with his supervisor he felt the weight of this mission upon him. "You have more than adequately captured my attention. What do you need me to do?"

The offer seemed to enliven the room.

His immediate superior spoke first. "We need to find out if they, Wave7, hacked ITower data or if their sole concern was to knock out communications branches through GlobeNet. We need to know how Wave7 works--their systems, where they're striking. We need to know what ITower Cloud branch needs to lock down to maintain security."

Fred's mind reeled from this insurmountable task, but something else bubbled in his brain as his superior spoke. "Half of what you're asking is networking and access security. I feed data clouds, others specialize in protecting it. I'll need assistance, possibly a team."

"Of course." The way his superior spoke the words gave Fred the sense it would be no trouble at all to ask for the moon or sun to power the mad system he might build.

Fred continued. "I happen to know a guy. Ex-military, so you can be assured he'll follow orders. A hacker and communications man on the field. More recently a contractor for GlobeNet branch in Silicon Valley. He's a bit of a hot shot. A challenge this large wouldn't frighten him in the least."

It wasn't the moon, but it was nepotism. Fred was encouraged by the softening of the boss's features. "Perfect. You get whatever or whoever you need. Promise me progress, and fast. Get on it."

Chapter Nineteen

The door to the narrow utility closet slammed open. Evan glanced up from where he yet again fiddled with the wiring in the walls to see Fred grinning down at him.

"Do you want a new island to dig for buried treasure?" Fred grinned.

Evan turned from his crouched position within the wall to survey his uncle Fred's face.

"What is that damned grin for?" Evan grumbled.

He pulled himself from within the wall.

"Feeling smug now you are gainfully employed? It's not like I'm not trying to enjoy this garbage work, you know."

"Oh, I know you're trying, but you should still be nice to me, since technically I *am* your boss." Fred's grin continued to spread wrinkles of joy across his face.

Evan scowled. "Being the big breadwinner does not make you the boss, old man."

Fred waved his free hand as he balanced on his cane. "No, no, no. I wish I could say you're my personal assistant and maid service, but that's not what I meant."

Evan's eyes narrowed. "Get to it, then. I'm getting more annoyed than usual."

"I got you a new job." Fred lowered to a conspiratorial tone. "At ITower. Cloud Services Branch." Fred clapped a hand on Evan's shoulder.

"Front of the lines. Security work, and networking, for the whole sector."

Evan's breath caught as he realized what his uncle was offering.

"Same pay as before the crash?" He pressed the most pertinent issue.

Fred waved off the question. "Bah! This is bigger than a paycheck, my boy! This is history in the making. We are tasked with catching bad guys, getting the world back on line, saving the day."

The older man offered a smart nod and marched for the hallway.

"It does pay, though. I mean come on Fred, be serious a moment." Evan followed, brushing dust from his hands.

Evan stopped short as the older man pivoted on his cane to halt, toe-to-toe with his nephew.

"Of course it pays." A wily grin emerged on the man's face. "Double what you did with that corner office gig!"

Evan swallowed. "Double."

Fred's brows wriggled. "Double. Speaking of which, I think we should celebrate. Drinks are on me."

A broad smile split Evan's face, then he frowned. "You know you're not supposed to drink anymore."

Fred's shoulders slumped. "Killjoy. Fine, you can have mine. I'll order a Shirley Temple."

Evan clapped a hand on Fred's back.

It was good to see the man in good spirits. "And you can tell me all about saving the world."

* * *

Evan made his way through the maze of open office spaces filling the floor. Many of his military buddies laughed when Evan first told them about working security for corporate communications, yet something about the energy thrilled him. An office was safer than a van in the middle of a nowhere battlefield, but the adrenaline rush was there. He wasn't as excited with the step down to working in a cubicle, even if it was on the top floor. But he was certain it wouldn't take long before both he and his uncle moved to more elite accommodations.

Evan rounded a corner and smiled with his former confidence at a pair of women chatting over the cubicle walls. The women shrugged him off, but they did smile. He was grateful he'd chosen to shave the two-month overgrowth on his face. A clean look suited his features best.

Evan took a peek into the cube he would call home for more than eight hours a day. He assessed the situation with deflated enthusiasm.

Woven among the standard monitor, keyboard, and mouse setup, and a master tower, sat a leaning stack of file boxes. Wires and cables as dusty as the gaps in the walls teetered against the sides of the cubicle.

This was as desperate a situation as the buildings and server rooms. At least here, wires were easy to access. Evan considered the situation. He had never had to plug anything in when setting up a new office.

"Shit. This is going to take forever." Evan sighed at the futility.

He wasn't certain why he initially thought he would come in to a fully operational wireless system.

Evan dug into the nearest box to reveal a trove of dust-covered, yellowed papers, notebooks, and faded covers of hard copy manuals; books.

"What the hell is this?" The protest was louder than intended.

The outburst drew Fred from the next cubicle over.

Evan slammed a particularly large book onto the center of the desk as Fred peered in through the opening at the rear of the cubicle.

A box of wires to shifted. The towering filing boxes gave way. A cascade of wires unraveled across the floor as they pooled around Evan's ankles.

"Damn it all to… Seriously!" Evan tugged at his hair.

"I have a few extra high blood pressure pills in my desk." Fred's snide remark whirled Evan around.

"That is not even funny." Evan growled.

Fred shrugged. "Who says I was totally joking?"

Evan muttered a few more choice curses. He snatched up another book and a fistful of cords.

"Seriously though. What the hell am I supposed to do with this waste?"

"You're supposed to get to work." Fred folded his arms and leaned against the edge of the cubicle. "And I don't want to hear grumbling or complaints over the wall." Fred's brow quirked. "You're good at what you do, but it took more than pulling wires to get the big guys to ignore your dismissal from GlobeNet."

Evan turned his gaze from Fred as he fought to connect monitor to tower on the desktop.

"That wasn't my fault. GlobeNet was looking for a fall guy to sacrifice to the ITower gods. I happened to be the goat they decided to scape with. Not to mention I was probably the highest paid employee on the security floor."

Fred nodded. "I know you're probably right about that, kid. Still, they look at the writing on the screen, not the soul of the employee. You're a punk sometimes, but you're good, and you have got passion. Especially if you can prove you can do it better than anyone else."

Evan hadn't so much as raised his eyes to Fred through the pep talk. His hands fumbled with connections as his feet danced between the loops of wires.

Evan could feel Fred's eyes on him as he struggled with the cords and connections. It was completely outside the younger man's realm of understanding. Firing up strategic mobile unit communication stations was much more demanding than plugging in a corporate cubicle on fifty-year-old technology, but Fred opted not to mention this to Evan.

"Better than rooting in dusty walls all day. You're doing what you love, even if you don't recognize it yet." Fred pushed away from the cubicle wall and straightened. "At least the money's good."

Evan flopped into the rolling office chair as he plugged in another wire. He finally turned to look at Fred.

He sighed. "Yeah. Thanks. That much is true. I haven't made a real paycheck since before the crash." Evan scanned the disaster surrounding him.

"Good. Now you can start paying rent." Fred winked.

A relieved smirk grew on Evan's face. "This isn't so bad, I guess. Crawling around in the dust and crawl spaces of your house isn't payment enough? Even before I got into the business of being a wire rat, your house needed work. You should have been paying me for having to sleep on your curbside-catch of a couch. My back and my social life certainly paid this past couple months."

Fred laughed. "Don't go blaming our living arrangement for your social fall out." Fred tapped at his temple. "Maybe if you had a real address book instead of trusting everything to the Cloud, you could contact all those lady friends you used to have. Bet their beds would have been much more comfortable than my old couch." Female snickers could be heard coming from surrounding cubicles.

Evan feigned hurling a thick volume on computer networking. He dropped the tome into an empty cardboard box instead.

"Whatever you say, old man." Evan wheeled his chair around the small space. "You're like the godfather of this whole Cloud deal. Big data, instant transfers. You've never owned a print copy of anything. You can't possibly tell me you don't put your trust in that masterpiece of data storage."

Fred smiled and allowed his eyebrows to raise. "That, young man, is precisely the reason why I don't trust it."

Fred's laughter was cut short by the sound of an alert hailing him to his cubicle.

"Well then, speaking of keeping in touch with lovely ladies." Fred offered a curt salute before bowing and disappearing around the cubicle wall. "You will have to excuse me. I have an important date."

Evan rolled his eyes. He slumped in the chair and scanned the cubicle made all the more cramped by oodles of wire yet to connect everything to every other thing.

Nature is the source of all true knowledge. She has her own logic, her own laws, she has no effect without cause nor invention without necessity.

Leonardo da Vinci

Italian Polymath - 1400's

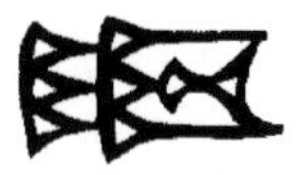

Chapter Twenty

Fred returned to his cubicle and eyed the computer. A smile spread across his face as he realized the picture on the screen was not a still chat room avatar.

"Well. If it's not one miracle it's another." Fred sighed as he slid into the chair to face the monitor.

Hannah's image smiled back from a small pop-up window.

She, too, grinned as Fred entered the cubicle and shifted into view.

"Fred!" Hannah's voice exploded from the speakers.

Fred had not expected the sudden, incredibly audible outburst. He dove for the volume dial and cranked to the lowest possible setting. He twisted in his chair to throw a nervous glance at the cubicle opening to check if anyone, especially Evan, had overheard.

Fred fished within his own boxes of connections and devices. From beneath a tangle of wires he drew a dusty headset. Turning back to his work station, Fred fumbled with the audio jack and the openings along the monitor frame. At last the pin found a home and an audible click announced the audio shifting to the headphones.

"Hannah?" Fred eyed the video of the owner of Conscious Connections.

Hannah's lips moved in the video, yet there was no audio. Fred leaned to the speaker dial again. He rotated the dial, to no avail.

Hannah gestured calmly.

"Ahh!" Fred drew his hands to the wire connecting headset to monitor.

His fingers fumbled along the cable to pause on a small switch and rotated a miniscule dial until Hannah's voice could at last be heard at a reasonable level.

"Fred. I can see you!" Hannah's excitement seemed more subdued with the low volume. "Can you see me too? Can you hear me okay? Say something so I can hear you. This is exceptional! You're the first one I have been able to video conference with since all these glitches." Hannah rambled joy into Fred's ears.

Fred stared at the woman. It wasn't the first video conference he had experienced, yet it felt like a new discovery. Systems between them appeared to be behaving as before the crash.

"Hannah. I can see you. And I can definitely hear you, but how are you getting through?" Fred adjusted the headset as he whispered to the woman on the screen. "Even internal networks here at ITower aren't getting a feed solid enough for streaming."

Fred could tell his words fell on ears with little knowledge of networking system function.

It wasn't that Hannah lacked the savvy for business and social applications. To the contrary, Hannah took pride in how much she learned on her own. Self-taught, yet aware only of what she needed to keep her business running.

The inner workings didn't mean much.

Fred had little desire to waste time guiding Hannah to a greater understanding of technology. Yet, he wished she understood enough to be able to explain how she had rigged a streaming chat session.

For the moment, however, it was far more important to share his concerns with the last online chat he had experienced with the stranger, Coach333.

"Never mind the connection stuff for right now." Fred shook his head. "I can explain it to you later. As exciting as this is, I have a more pressing concern. I'm glad we can talk about it instead of trying to make sense of it in text."

Fred shifted in his seat, concern knitting his brows. He could only imagine how the encounter he experienced would be perceived in an email.

Hannah fumbled with the volume controls on her end. It was clear she finally realized Fred was whispering and would likely not be raising his voice.

"I'm concerned." Fred's voice rasped over the speakers. "I have reason to believe the security and integrity of your Conscious Connections shop and the NDE support group have been compromised. A spy perhaps, from ITower, trying to catch me at something the company might see as troublesome."

Hannah's image shook her head. "Well, that's a fine way to shift a conversation."

Hannah's smile sparkled as Fred worked to keep the woman focused on the immediate concern.

"Are you okay, Fred? Do we need to talk more privately? Maybe you can come by the shop later today? No meeting, just to chat."

Fred shook his head. "No, no, no. I think this is okay for now on my end. This might even draw out the spy. And you should be fine where you are, no one pays any mind at information centers."

He glanced over his shoulder once again, to be certain no one wandered by. He adjusted the headset, uncovering an ear to monitor the sounds around him as he continued his exchange with Hannah.

"I have to tell you what happened yesterday. I was on this chat. A supposedly anonymous metaphysical chat board. New login and username. I was posing questions to a user with the handle Coach333. I asked what he thought about ITower using current technology to connect to global consciousness, you know, the Akashic records thing you talked about in group."

Hannah's face lit up. As if that was possible, as bright as the young woman's smile always seemed to be. "Fred! You are paying attention when I go off on my little tangents about the way technology could be used to move humanity forward in truly communicating with one another and multiple dimensions!"

Fred's anxiety plowed through the woman's excitement. Hannah's face fell slightly, as the man's concern dawned on her.

Fred continued his retelling of the incident in the metaphysical chat. "This Coach333 guy got even more strange. Along with weird responses, he started talking about me, and you, and attending the group. He mentioned you by name, Hannah."

Hannah's image froze a moment as she composed herself. She waved a hand between herself and the camera.

"Fred. Relax. Are you centered? Take a few deep breaths. Are you grounded, do you have some means of grounding?" Hannah clasped her hands. "When you mentioned Coach333 there was a shift. It's curious. I'm getting some strange energy."

Fred sighed at the maternal tone in Hannah's voice. "Yeah, yeah. Grounding. Yes. And took my pills. Drank lots of water." He snagged a half empty bottle of water from the desk and shook it within view of the camera.

Fred took a few deep breaths and blew each one out at the screen. "I'm fine, Hannah. And I'm not kidding about that guy. He was an odd duck. He also said something about laws of the physical realm. He made it sound as if he wasn't on the planet."

Hannah's lips pressed together at the mention of other worlds. She narrowed her eyes and Fred noticed her shoulders seemed suddenly burdened.

"Hmm?" Hannah looked into the distance. She rose from her chair in front of the camera. "Wait a second Fred. Let me get a quick read on this."

As Hannah moved out of the camera frame revealing the room behind her. Fred stared at the familiar string of fairy lights and glass shelves heavy with crystals, shells, and small statues. The display cases behind the register at Conscious Connections.

Fred frowned into the camera as he leaned to see more clearly.

"Hey. Wait, Hannah. Are you at your shop?" Fred called out, forgetting for a moment to whisper.

As Fred continued to try to make out the background image, Hannah returned to the frame.

She waved a deck of tarot cards in front of the camera. "This will be fun. I haven't done an online reading in at least a month. So many more face-to-face, and phone readings lately."

Hannah glanced at her cards as she laid them out off-screen.

"Hannah." Fred's surprised tone drew the woman's attention.

She looked from her cards. "Oh, I'm sorry. Did you say something when I walked off?

Fred waved at the screen. "How is it possible you're in your store and connected?"

Hannah thumbed over her shoulder, confirming she was indeed perched at the counter in the retail portion of Conscious Connections.

Hannah jabbed a finger toward the second floor of the shop. "I am always connected, Fred. It must be great, I have customers coming in so often complaining about service outages plaguing GlobeNet, and I've never lost access to my files. It's difficult to contact others via messaging systems, though."

Fred shook his head. "No, no, Hannah, I'm serious. I mean your computer, our connection. How can your computer be connected to the network outside of a wired network center?"

Hannah's confusion rose as her face fell to the cards laid on the counter top. "Um. Well."

Turning from the camera Hannah turned a card from the top of the deck. When her gaze rose to meet Fred her eyes were wide. She displayed the card to the camera.

Three figures in long robes held a trio of goblets above their heads.

Hannah lowered the card to show her face once more. "I think you know the answer concerning the chat room, and maybe our current connection as well."

The tinkling of the doorbell at the store jostled both Fred and Hannah from deciphering the potential meanings of the card. Hannah turned her head to call out a welcome to the entering customer.

Turning her attention back to Fred, Hannah offered a short wave. "I gotta go, Fred. I'll ask a bit about the Akashic and chat rooms. We'll talk later, okay? I'm super curious about this!"

The chat box closed on Fred's screen before he could utter a response.

Confusion and a renewed sense of need to reconnect with Coach333 overwhelmed Fred.

Who controls the past controls the future. Who controls the present controls the past.

George Orwell

English novelist, essayist and journalist

Chapter Twenty One

Fred slumped into his chair to stare at the pale walls of his cubicle. He considered Hannah's words and the card as he pulled the headset from his ears. The card meant little—more important to Fred was deciphering how Hannah was still connected.

Fred murmured. "She never lost connection to Cloud Services storage systems."

Fred hadn't thought Hannah a foolish or stupid woman when he walked into her store. A little flighty and harboring more than a few strange beliefs, still she was grounded, business savvy, and personable. She certainly wasn't what Fred considered technical-minded, though. Hannah used technology to maintain her business, make connections, but she lacked the understanding of systems function to bypass blackouts.

Fred pushed free of his chair and stepped from his cubicle. He popped his head in to check on Evan.

His nephew was still on hands and knees in a nest of wires. Desperation curved his back as he fought to read manuals and connect devices.

"There's no easy way to search for anything in paper volumes!" Evan cursed as he caught a glimpse of Fred leaning into the cubicle.

"Did you try the index?" Fred offered.

"Yes." Evan glared. "That only works if you actually know what you're looking for. Basic troubleshooting to probe a help menu with reasonable questions, not so much."

Evan tossed the manual at a box near the edge of the desk. The weight of the book tipped box and contents onto Evan's lap.

"Damn it to hell." Evan cursed. "Fred, this is insane. No one should have to work like this."

Fred stifled a snicker at his nephew's plight. "Well, I may be working on a way to limit the number of wires required. I'm going to be focused in my cubicle for a while though. I wanted to check on your progress, see if you needed anything, before I dive in."

Evan sighed. "How about a solid connection. Bluetooth? Something akin to a miracle."

Fred held his hands up. "Above my paygrade at the moment. I'll be in my office. The do not disturb sign will be up."

Fred backed out of Evan's cube. Evan kicked at the closest pile of cords and snatched the manual again. "I need a disturbed sign," he grumbled.

Fred returned to his chair. As he sat a moment with fingers hovering the keyboard, he took a few more deep breaths. He typed the first few letters of his last query, allowing the automatic search to return a list of possible sites Fred had recently visited. He spied the metaphysical chat site. He clicked the link.

Fred reclined to wait for the connection to load the page. His breathing steadied as he contemplated what to ask this time. He wanted to ignore the growing feeling he had connected to some alternate plane.

The chat box with Coach333's name in the title bar popped up before Fred could scrutinize further. Shocked by the speed of the connection and the instant redirect to the chat he had been looking for, Fred moved the cursor to the input box. He typed a brief greeting as he pondered his first question. His username appeared beside the text as soon as Fred clicked on the send icon.

CLOUD MASTER: *Good afternoon. Or morning, depending where you are connecting from.*

A breath passed before the chat filled with the username and response from Coach.

COACH333: *I'm at the library. Morning, afternoon, either one works.*

The vagueness of the reply caused Fred to sigh. He tilted back in his chair before requesting further information.

CLOUD MASTER: *What library?*

COACH333: *THE Library.*

Fred pressed his palms to his brow. He grimaced as he entered a more specific request.

CLOUD MASTER: *What is the library's GlobeNet protocol and address?*

COACH333: *We're on our own protocol. The Library doesn't need an address.*

Fred froze and whispered aloud. "This has to be a gag."

At least he knew it wasn't his own nephew pulling his chain. And access was so limited even in the building, most people could barely get daily work completed, much less have time to troll someone.

Keying into the script screen of the site, Fred tapped into the data to search for current user addresses. As the codes populated Fred located his current IP within the building. All other addresses however returned in a confused combination of numerics and script.

Fred's hands hovered the keyboard and mumbled. "What sort of prankster would be capable of accessing networks without a traceable address?"

Fred was so busy mulling his thoughts he failed to notice the newest reply at first.

COACH333: *You don't need an access address either.*

Before Fred could type his response, windows popped in rapid succession on all monitors within the cubicle, including one perched sidelong in a box.

"Shit." Fred hissed. "Hacked. I should've known better. Fuck. Rookie mistake."

Fred's fingers flew across the keys as he fought to block the data shift flooding his computer. Screens fluttered with images depicting scenes from the past as well as present.

COACH333: *Watch.*

The words filled the central screen tearing Fred's attention from his futile battle against the data. He glimpsed a date far in the future on one window. Entities with alien features as well as those more human in shape flickered in and out of Fred's view. Maps of star systems, planets, the rise and fall of empires blossomed and blinked across the screens. Fred recognized blurbs of scientific data, mathematical equations. It was a data dump of epic proportions.

Fred allowed his hands to fall into his lap. On the primary screen, Coach333 continued his chat.

COACH333: *You have always been connected. Consider this merely an update.*

Fred's heart raced, he dared not blink. It was all over in a matter of a few short breaths. His heart fluttered, the speed of the connection seemingly transferred to his heartbeat. As the screens settled to a single scene of serene waves meeting the shore, Fred's trembling fingers found the keyboard.

CLOUD MASTER: How did you access my computer?

COACH333: *I didn't. I accessed you. You transferred it to the devices.*

An avatar image appeared in the corner of the chat window. Immediately, Fred felt the full weight of recognition. It was the bearded man he had seen during his near-death experience on the train.

CLOUD MASTER: I know you!

COACH333: For quite a long time.

Fred's voice rose with his excitement and confusion. "I have to tell Hannah."

COACH333: She knows.

The words on the screen brought an amused grin to Fred's lips. "Of course she does."

COACH333: *Glad to see you smile, but you have work to do. You have the data, but this time around, the technology is different.*

As Fred read the screen, he realized the scope of the connection. "I have to reverse engineer the connections. We can get back online!"

Fred clapped his hands over his mouth. He tossed a glance over his shoulder at the opening of his cubicle, hoping no one heard his outburst. The chat window had taken over the center of the screen again when Fred turned back to his desk.

COACH333: *Have fun. Keep in touch.*

In another blink and flicker, the chat window closed.

Fred was left to consider the task laid out before him by a contact he knew, and yet in so many ways did not know. The wonder of the offerings blinded Fred to the question of whether Coach333 was friend or foe.

"Well. He's not a hacker in the typical sense." Fred let a short laugh escape his lips.

A quick rap on the metal frame of the cubicle, startled Fred from his thoughts. Evan popped his head into the cube.

"Hey, I'm heading to get a late lunch." Evan's words fell on ears cluttered with the fog of research.

Fred offered a slow nod and muffled murmur.

"Right." Evan paused. "Well, I think I can finally get to tracking Wave7. It only took half a day to get this rig hooked in."

At the mention of the hacker group Fred spun his chair, eyes wide. "Great!"

"It's not that exciting." Evan frowned. "I have no idea where to start."

"You'll come up with something. We're going to need some progress to feed management." Fred shooed Evan away.

"Wait. Don't you have anything on your end?" Evan's brows tucked to the center of his forehead.

Fred tipped a gaze over his shoulder at the cluttered screens. "Of course. But this is a completely different angle I'm working. I'm not sure how to present it yet."

"Right." Fred's unconvincing tone drew a deeper frown to Evan's face.

"We've been in worse situations." Fred swept a hand between them and rotated back to his keyboard. "You've been on the front line of bigger battles than this. Be careful where you tread."

"Right." Irked by Fred's dismissiveness, Evan stepped into the walkway.

"Looks like your uncle is back in the game." Fred pretended to ignore the conversation from a passing coworker who met Evan in the pathway.

"Yeah." Evan peered into the cubicle.

"I wouldn't be able to begin to understand what you tech heads are doing. As long as I can check my messages without shuffling this rig all day, I'll be happy." The man continued down the corridor of cubicles pushing a squeaky mail basket.

Lingering a moment more in the entrance to Fred's cube, Evan shook his head and walked away.

Fred knew the boy wouldn't fully understand what he was doing. He would have time to explain once he had a better grasp himself.

As the days passed, Evan set up shop at the house as well as two separate ITower offices. Once he figured out the wiring it wasn't as bad as he had made it out to be.

If he was actually tracking an operation as large as Wave7 was reported to be, he needed to be up his game.

Running a set-up powerful enough to handle constant searches, IP tracking, and data mining would have been no problem a month or so ago. Now, the lag even one machine caused was enough to bog down the system for hours.

Evan spent his days mostly in a state of waiting. Waiting for data to load. Waiting for downloads and uploads. Waiting.

The three locations and constant checking in to see if data had moved at all caused he and Fred to keep opposing schedules. On the up side it allowed the two to alternate driving and public transportation. As one worked security concerns and the other connection updates their paths rarely seemed to cross.

Evan's least favorite part of it all, moving data via transfer sticks. USB wasn't Evan's idea of a good time, "At least it can't be traced or compromised." He mused as he fumbled with the narrow plastic device.

The crossed schedules also meant Evan remained primarily in the dark about Fred's work. Something about their last conversation left him with feelings of uncertainty about what the old man might be up to.

Evan flicked the lights in the kitchen as he abandoned his bed to construct a midnight snack. Another issue had wandered into his dreams and pulled him from the comfort of sleep. Passing Fred's room, Evan noticed the bed still made. He wondered when his uncle had last slept, or been in the house.

"Feels like I'm living alone either way." Evan shrugged off his uncle's absence.

He continued back to the flickering screens arranged in the center of the living room. The couch had become Evan's sleeping quarters to be nearer the chaos of intel he fought to tame.

As much as he had wanted to set up shop in his own room, as his uncle had managed to do. The signals seemed more effective at the center of the house.

He took another bite from his sandwich as he watched the location dots flit across the screen. The pattern seemed to take shape as Evan focused on a set of clusters. It was the one in Silicon Valley that provoked his curiosity.

"That site's been down for years." He mumbled around a mouthful of ham and cheese.

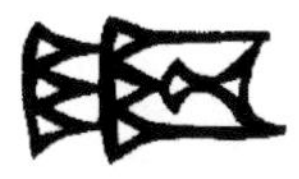

Chapter Twenty Two

"Professor." A scattered young man in polo and jeans entered the auditorium.

The man at the front of the room turned his attention from the white board to the cluster of students seated around the room. "Forgive me a moment."

A dower expression creased the professor's brow as the intruder approached.

"Sir. I apologize." The young man cleared his throat. His eyes darted to the other students in the auditorium. "I was told it was urgent."

"Well, get on with it then." The professor's scowl deepened.

The man offered an envelope with trembling hands.

The professor's breath caught as he spied the seal. He snatched the paper from the student. "Thank you. Go."

"Yes, Professor Atticus." The young man offered a curt nod and scurried out the way he had come.

Atticus took a moment to stare at the envelope before a cough from the seats returned his mind to the waiting students.

"Class is dismissed for today." He passed a dismissive glance over the small crowd.

"You are free to go." He barked at the confused expressions staring down at him. "Review the chapters on connections between Giza, Cahokia, and Ji'an."

Without further explanation he pivoted from his audience and slipped out the door.

As Atticus strode down the hallway, his hands creased the edges of the envelope. His fingers itched to crack the seal. He flipped his keys from his pocket as he reached the door.

"Linus!" A fellow professor called down the hall.

Atticus ignored him as he closed himself into the confines of his office.

Linus stared at the envelope as he leaned against the door. "This is it."

He sighed as his heart raced. The wax seal crumbled away as he tugged at the folded paper. A disk tumbled free of the envelope as Linus drew the letter out.

Linus bent to retrieve the device.

"A replica of Phaistos?" The words shattered the silence of the room.

Linus paced toward the large oak desk that dominated the small, cluttered room. Sliding aside a stack of folders, he lowered into the high backed leather chair. He set the plastic replica of the ancient clay disk at the center of the desk as he read the handwritten letter.

Professor Linus Atticus,

It has come to our attention that the systems you maintain have been recently experiencing increased activity. We feel it is in your best interest to move closer to your operations in order to ensure increased probability of success.

You will find a replica of the Phaistos disk to be used to access your grid site. We have also made arrangements to host further excavation and restoration to your secondary site in Pueblo del Sol.

The message closed with a set of stylized waves in place of s signature.

Linus pressed the letter onto the desk. He stared at the replica disk.

"He did it." A smile spread across the professor's lips.

He pushed free from his chair and navigated his way to the door, he grabbed his camouflage jacket from the hook on the wall and dropped the replica disk in the front pocket below the scarred insignia panel.

***

As he waited for the train, Linus struggled to keep his emotions in check. He counted back the three decades he had made his life's focus on the grid restoration project. He sighed as he thought of the years his mentor before him had spent. How the man had died only three years ago.

"You would've been so pleased." Linus muttered.

The train slowed and announced the stop. Linus rose from his seat. His excitement urged his steps as he made the short walk to the glass doors of the GlobeNet building.

A neon orange sticker covered the GlobeNet name on the glass.

Glancing along the street Linus stepped into the alcove of the entryway and pressed his palm to the panel on the door. The green light activated at his touch and he entered the darkened lobby.

Painter's cloths hid the furnishings in the lobby, giving the space lumpy natural landscape in place of sleek lines. Caution tape barred three of the four elevators. Linus waved his hand over the infrared scanner and waited for the metal doors to slide open.

As he watched the numbers on the screen within the elevator carriage Linus rubbed at his cheek and thought about the men from the train.

"The messages from those crazy psychics had been right all along." A smirk spread across his face. "Trust the ancient architects. It only took a century of rebuilding to get things set up."

The doors opened to a room of cubicles bustling with men and women in business casual.

A woman met Linus as he entered. "We received word you were on your way, Professor Atticus."

"The system is running." Linus handed the woman the disk. "I'll be in my office. Keep me updated."

Imagination is more important than knowledge

Albert Einstein

Theoretical physicist

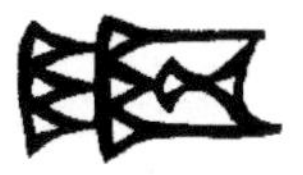

Chapter Twenty Three

Fred sat engrossed in his screens, vigorously typing code as it scrambled across the field entitled Cloud Master TEST SYSTEM: C2C Search Engine.

He shifted the cursor to the navigation menu: Akashic Record Query, On-realm Connection, Off-realm Connection, Help - knowledge store, Consultation. He rubbed his eyes. A yawn escaped his lips.

A new chat window popped up, jarring him from his work. His boss's face appeared in the rectangle on the center screen.

"Fred, we've got a problem." The man's balding head had a sheen of sweat. "Grab Evan and meet us in the boardroom, ASAP."

The chat box closed before Fred could offer a response. He considered the pages of open code laid out in front of him.

"They couldn't know. Could they?" He struggled to lock down the numerous files without losing information.

He stretched and turned to leave the cubicle. He wasn't even sure if Evan was in the office. He shook free the clouds of code that fogged his mind and checked the time. They had both been taking additional precautions, for differing reasons.

When was the last time he ate, slept? He pushed away from the desk. His legs wobbled under him. His back cracked and popped as he straightened.

Fred grumbled as he hobbled from his cubicle.

He turned the corner of the cubicle to rap on the frame of Evan's cube. "You home?"

He poked his head in, half expecting to see an empty chair.

To the contrary, Evan pivoted in his chair and stared wide eyed at Fred. "Hey. You're unplugged. Something must be up."

"Board Room." Fred nodded. "We've been summoned."

"Crap." Evan pushed his fingers through his hair.

He, too, locked down his work stations. Fred took note the process was much slower as the connection to the actual ITower network slugged along.

Fred wandered down the narrow hallway to the great frosted glass doors of the board room. Evan followed quietly. Fred waited at the door for the younger man. He swallowed his concerns about the work he had been doing. Meeting with the Board wasn't something he'd planned to do so soon. How long had it been? A week? Had Evan been working on anything substantial in that time? He felt as uncertain as Evan looked. The two exchanged a glance as they assessed their combined ill-preparedness.

The energy in the room felt stiff yet agitated as Fred and Evan entered. Men and women in standard hues of greys and blues sat around the oblong table. Docked tablets lay dark—instead, folders occupied the space in front of each board member. Evan slid into a seat closest to the door. He eyed the folder in front of him. Taking it in his hands he tipped it causing the papers to scatter free. Fred assisted in gathering the stray papers as he claimed the seat beside Evan.

"It's a folder, kid." Fred allowed a smirk to peek from his lips.

"Right." Evan frowned.

"Gentlemen." The head of ITower offices sighed as the pair settled in. "It appears our situation has become more dire than first thought."

Evan and Fred exchanged sidelong glances. A silent curse passed between them.

"If you could, please, start the presentation." He waved to the presenter at the front of the room.

The man cleared his throat and began with a stutter and a cough. "You'll notice in the following sequence, some people have been able to connect to unauthorized Cloud data." The man adjusted the sleeves of his suit as he changed the image on the screen. "This woman, for example, queried family photos and accessed what appeared to be video clips of her ancestors from the 1800's."

"Nonsense." A man in an equally stuffy suit sniffed. "Video didn't even exist then."

With little more than a nod and a glance directed at Evan and Fred, the presenter continued. "Precisely." He clicked the next slide. "This man queried economic projections for the coming year and what appeared to be historical economic data for the next fifty years."

The head of ITower piped in. "Historical?"

The presenter again cleared his throat and adjusted his shirt sleeves. "Yes. It appears to be a corruption of data. Is it possible you know something more about this Fred? Evan?"

Evan shrugged, as confused as the Board members. Yet, Fred squirmed.

Before Fred could offer a response, another suit inquired. "Fred, you know our data. The madness in this is clear. Find out what's going on. Fix it."

"Of course. It has to be some sort of glitch resulting from the shut downs." Fred waved it off as nonsense.

With a trusting nod, the man turned to Evan. "Evan, you're our security man on this. Find out who's getting in, how they are doing it. Lock 'em out. Lock everybody out for as long as you have to."

"Including businesses and emergency?" Evan frowned. "We're already straining to keep things as normal as possible."

"Everyone. If you have to." The man's hand came down heavy on the table. "We have to get this cleaned up before the Feds climb down our throats because some gamer kid accessed a real war game."

Military protocol slipped into Evan's posture as he offered a curt nod.

The man at the other end of the table straightened his tie as his posture relaxed. "ITower's command of all things InfoStrada is tenuous enough. We don't need to prove the activists right about monopolies and global control. It's not as if we are locking everyone out for our own elite use."

As if on cue, Fred's mobile device chimed a text message alert.

"Is that your phone?" Evan frowned and leaned in to whisper while other board members checked their own devices in confusion.

Fred snatched his mobile device and swiped his hand across the screen to decline the incoming message from Hannah. "The mobile network system has been down since the start of this mess. How are you getting messages?" Evan hissed. "And from whom?"

Silencing the ringer, Fred returned the device to his pocket.

"What was that?" The boss frowned in Fred's direction before scanning the rest of the room in search of the disturbance.

Another board member leaned over the table and focused again on Fred. "Was that a mobile message?"

Fred coughed and waved off the idea as if it were insane. "Uh, no, of course not. It was a reminder. For me to take my meds. I use the old text notification chime for nostalgia's sake."

The board member's eyes narrowed before he shook off the interruption. "Of course. Take your medication. Get back to your desk."

"Of course." Fred was out of his chair without a second thought. "Give us a couple days to shake this out. We'll keep you in the know."

"Fred." The boss's voice called from the front of the room. "You go right ahead and use my protocols to get what you need. Get it done."

"Of course." Fred offered a curt nod. "As you say."

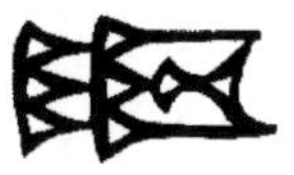

Chapter Twenty Four

Fred's pace took him to the end of the hall before Evan could catch up.

"Fred. Uncle." Evan breathed out the words. "Geez, old man, slow up."

Fred came to a halt at last.

"That wasn't a med reminder, was it?" Evan rested a hand on Fred's shoulder.

Fred remained silent. The idea of telling Evan still troubled him.

"You're connected, aren't you?" Evan's eyes were wide.

Fred shrugged as he pulled his shoulder from Evan's grasp.

Evan smirked. "That's all I need to know. What's going on with the corruption? I know you. I saw that look. You have intel on what's going on."

Against the accusations, Fred again shrugged and carried on to his cubicle.

"Oh no." Evan scuttled behind his uncle. "You are not getting away with a shrug and a nod."

"Okay." Fred leveled his gaze on the younger man. "Come on then. I'll show you. But not a word."

Fred and Evan rounded into the cubicle as another notification sounded from Fred's mobile device.

He pulled the device from his pocket and tossed it onto the desk. "Hannah. Hannah. Hannah."

Evan glanced at the blank screen. "Who? Wait. The chick from the crazy shop you've been visiting?"

Fred smiled at the question as he logged into the desktop computer and settled into the chair. "Yes, and I do hope you will get a chance to meet her."

Evan wheeled the chair from his own cubicle in beside Fred's.

As the windows popped up on the screen Hannah's face immediately appeared in a chat window.

"There you are. Why aren't you answering my messages? I found something for you," Hannah bubbled.

A wistful smile spread across Fred's face. "So that *was* you."

Evan nudged Fred with a smirk. "She's a bit young for you old boy."

Fred scowled as he shushed his nephew. "I was in a meeting, and my mobile kept going off." He returned his attention to the young woman in the chat. "That's not supposed to happen."

"Oh, sorry, didn't mean to interrupt your meeting. You could've snuck a quick message."

"Yeah, except mobile devices don't work. Everything's offline, remember?" Fred tapped at his temple as he reminded the young psychic of the deeper dilemma of text messaging during the shutdown.

Evan watched the exchange in confused silence.

"My mobile is fine. As I've explained before." Hannah waved her device in front of the laptop camera. "My friends and I message all the time."

Fred's smile curved into a curious frown as he recognized once again the curtains behind Hannah. "And you're in your store again."

Hannah shifted to peer around the store. "Well, yeah. It's midday."

At this Evan snapped from his silence. "Wait. What?" He nudged Fred away from the screen to glare at the chat. "Wait. She's not in a message center? Is this a secure line? What is going on?"

Fred pulled Evan's arm. "Calm yourself, Evan. Hannah's a friend. We're working on the whats and hows as much as we are able."

"Working on it?" Evan stammered. "GlobeNet's been down for months and you two are messaging from phones!"

Fred rose from his chair to be certain no one on the floor had heard the outburst. "Evan, please."

Evan again pushed into view of the screen. "Where are you? What service are you on and who do you work for?"

From the chat window Hannah offered an inviting smile. "Oh, Fred this must be your nephew." She waved a hand in view of the camera. "Hi Evan. I'm Hannah." She paused a moment to assess Evan's demeanor.

"Ooh. You should drop by next time Fred visits and try an aura cleansing. On the house."

"Wait." Evan's gaze flipped from computer to his uncle. "Fred, you told this woman about me? I thought we were incognito. What else have you told her? Who else have you told? What if she has connections to Wave7 or some other organization? Or the media?"

Hannah interrupted before Fred could offer an explanation. "He has a hard time centering, like you, Fred. Same chaotic energy. Same karmic frequency."

Hannah shook her head and continued to smile. "You're like twin souls in separate bodies."

Fred's smirk was met with disdain from his nephew.

"Ahem." Fred refocused the conversation. "Right, well, Hannah, we'll stop by the store in a little bit to introduce you in person."

Evan frowned. "Store?"

Fred shushed him once again. "I have to show Evan something here in the office first." He squeezed Evan's shoulder. "Oh, and Hannah."

"Yes?" Hannah offered an impish smirk.

"No more texting until I can see about these messages." Fred offered a thumbs up.

"Right." Hannah returned the gesture.

Fred disconnected the chat with a click of the mouse. In the sudden void of conversation, confusion and concern settled on Evan's face as he leaned against the wall of the cubicle.

"What the hell was that about?" Evan cursed.

"Evan, my boy, I need you to relax and stay with me for this." Fred rose from his chair, beckoning Evan to follow. "We should pop out for lunch. Somewhere comfortably busy."

Evan frowned, but followed.

Fred managed to remain silent on the topic of supernatural, big data, ITower, and Hannah until after the pair settled in at the bustling bar and grill.

"The presentation was not showing a data corruption." Fred ran a hand through his hair. "I can't even believe what I'm about to say."

Evan sat across from his uncle, arms crossed, beer untouched.

"How can I even put this into words?" Fred released a nervous laugh. He, too, had yet to touch the drink in front of him.

"Out with it already." Evan leaned his arms on the table. "Are you going to have me guess? If it's not a corruption or hackers, what then?"

Fred closed his eyes and took a deep breath. "The best I can say is it's access bleed over." He shook his head. "A cross-over, if you will, from something I was working on. Something I'm still working on," he corrected at the last.

"Okay. Bleed over from what?" The frown on Evan's face gave Fred pause as he fought to form the words for a proper explanation.

"How can I even begin. Your technological understanding is at least on par with mine."

Evan raised a brow at the comparisons of skills. "At least."

"My apologies. On par with mine. But, there's another realm of understanding. Or rather more the understanding of the other realm, you have no grasp of." Fred ran his hands over his hair again. "Hells, I've only started studying this myself, because of what happened on the train."

"On the train?" Evan interjected. "Shit, Fred, is this about that jackass who got you all fired up?"

Fred waved off the assumption. "Oh, no, no. Where I went after."

"The hospital?" Evan's contorted features displayed his struggle to understand.

"No. My dear boy." Fred leaned across the table. "Before that."

Evan's face contorted in confusion. "What. Are. You. Talking. About?"

Fred patted Evan's shoulder as he sought the right words to explain his near-death experience.

"Evan, I was there." He glanced conspiratorially around the bustling bar. "I saw the other side."

Evan leaned into the seat. " Are you having another stroke?"

Fred released a burst of laughter. "I suppose it could sound like that. But no. Evan, I saw the great data stream in the sky, for lack of better description."

"What the hell are you on?"

"I was dead. And for a moment, I saw all of life." He paused. "I saw the code, Evan. The code of the Universe."

"Shit. You are having a stroke." Evan brushed Fred's hand from his shoulder.

"What? Ha! No." Fred slapped a hand on the table. Jostling the as-yet untouched drinks. "Evan. I'm serious. Hannah helped me understand."

"Shit. This is worse than a stroke. You're caught up in some crazy shit with that woman in the chat. You're in a cult." Evan waved his hands.

"It's not crazy. It's metaphysics." Fred shrugged.

"Damn it, Fred." Evan pushed the hair from his brow with both hands.

Fred smirked at the familiar act of frustration. "I thought it was zany too. I did. But it all made so much sense."

"It's no wonder you're slipping. You're chatting to civilians out there." Evan waved his hands in frustration. "Somewhere! On a network that's not worked for months. Gods, are there even any controls or safeguards on these chat links?"

Fred turned away from Evan's ranting. The two pushed their hair from their foreheads in the same smooth sweep of wide-spread fingers.

"Maybe I should have offered a more technical explanation," Fred murmured. "Oh and not to worry, you only see what you're allowed to access."

"Shit." Evan finally took up his glass and dumped half the beer down his throat. He slammed the stein back to the table.

"So, what, is this some new thing you and that woman are working on? A totally secured, wireless, networkless connection? Is she a hacker? Where did you find her?"

Fred let a short laugh escape his lips. "Who, Hannah? No, she doesn't work in tech. Like I said, she's got her own thing." He tried to picture the young women doing more than chatting and checking her email. "Hannah connects in other ways. And she's been helping me since the NDE."

Evan sighed. "N-D-E?"

"Near death experience." Fred elaborated.

"I need another drink. Or a better dose of meds." Evan flagged down a waiter.

"Evan, please. Have an open mind." Fred plead with his younger self. "I've managed to connect to something bigger than our own physical world's Big Data cloud."

"No, Uncle. You had a massive stroke. You were in a coma. You're a bit drugged up, and had some funky ass dreams." Evan twirled his finger beside his ear. "And you might have left a few marbles in that hospital room."

Ignoring Evan's sarcasm, Fred drew his phone from his pocket. With a few slides of his fingers across the screen, he pulled up the bare-bones application he had been toying with. A screen opened to read: Cloud Master C2C Search.

"Say what you will. I can prove I'm not crazy."

Turning the screen for Evan to see, Fred queried a video: Battle of Gettysburg. After a moment, a streaming image buffered into view.

Evan waved at the screen. "Okay, so you can stream the History Channel."

Fred pointed to the live stream notation at the corner of the window.

Evan raised a brow. "Re-enactments?"

"Fine." Fred's fingers thrummed the screen in aggravation. He queried again for video: Space Exploration 2119.

Images of colonies on distant planets appeared in the search listings. Maps of galaxies and travel guides, including time and distance approximations, filled the GPS read out.

"Sci-fi Channel, NASA mockup videos." Evan crossed his arms and scoffed at the display. "These could all be archived files in the lesser data servers. This is good stuff, a solid connection, but not new."

Fred's frustration peaked. "Boy, you are raising my blood pressure." Finally Fred's eyes lit up with an idea Evan might respond to.

"Fine. Who's your favorite team nowadays?"

Evan rolled his eyes. "I don't know. Cardinals. Football."

Fred typed the query for the Cardinals football team season record.

"You're off by about thirty years on that date, old man." Evan laughed.

Evan's sarcasm caught in his throat as the search revealed streams of statistics, injuries, retirements, videos, and week-to-week summaries of the football season. His jaw dropped as he rose to stare at the screen.

"Is this for real?"

"One hundred percent." Fred smirked and allowed Evan to take the device from his hands. Satisfaction filled his chest.

"Fred. If this is real, we could make a mint." Evan's eyes glittered as he turned the device in his hands. "Let me try this."

Evan's fingers flew as he entered a search query for the next year's Super Bowl.

Fred reached over to strike delete before Evan could hit enter. "Don't get any ideas, boy. Profit is not the point of this."

Evan waved the comment off as he deflected Fred's hand. He tapped send on the query. The device blinked. The only words remaining on the black screen; Data Inaccessible. Evan reworded the query multiple times. Same result—nothing.

Fred scowled at the darkened screen. "What did you do, break my connection?"

Gripping the edges of the table, he leaned toward Evan's side of the table. Fred's fingers flew as he tapped the same series of queries prompting a search protocol. Without issue, information for the next several Super Bowl events-- advertisements, videos, links to potential scores--populated the screen.

Fred took in the sudden access before turning his attention to Evan. Evan shrugged as the pair exchanged glances from screen to one another. Confusion filled Evan's eyes, as well as a sense of deeper concern.

"There. All fixed. Now hand it over, old man." Evan nudged in jest.

"Fine. But no betting." Fred tossed up his hands as he slid the device back across the table.

Even as Evan slid his fingers over the screen the streaming stopped.

"What?" Evan tapped at the screen hoping to jostle the data back to life.

"Fascinating." Fred leaned over Evan's shoulder.

As Fred neared the proximity device it again began to flicker and shift. Data streams of future Superbowl information buffered to life once again.

"What the hell is going on here?" Evan groaned.

A wry smile coursed Fred's lips. "I can't say for certain, but I think we might want to visit Hannah sooner rather than later. This could be more in her field than ours."

Evan scowled at his uncle's ambiguity. He swallowed back the remainder of his drink.

Your vision will become clear only when you can look into your own heart. Who looks outside, dreams; who looks inside, awakes.

Carl Jung

Swiss founder of analytic psychology

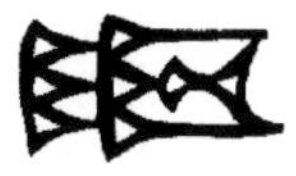

Chapter Twenty Five

From the table behind Fred and Evan, Linus listened in on the conversation. As the men left, Linus leaned around the wall of the booth.

He glanced at the screen of his mobile device. It had gone dark. He tucked the device into his pocket, tossed a handful of crumpled bills onto the table, and slid out of the seat to follow Fred and Evan.

His thoughts raced as he strived to maintain the distance between himself and the two men.

"Which one is the architect though." He grumbled as he slipped between the crowd of pedestrians.

The leaders would want to know which of the men to track. It had been nearly a century since the last potential architect had incarnated. Linus scowled to himself as he thought of how that attempt at rebuilding the grid had gone.

The discovery of the Arc battery source, and the Grail memory core, had been amazing. Oligarchal collapse set the project back when items and research were seized because of shifts in simple minded governments.

Linus lingered to allow more space between himself and his quarry. As he paused at a street crossing he caught a glimpse of a printed news article stating the world governments' considerations on breaking the ITower monopoly.

"If they do I'll fade out of history like the men before me." He grumbled.

A rush of panic waved over Linus as he momentarily lost sight of Fred and Evan. He hurried through the intersection, ignorant of the signal.

The bustle of the commercial district seemed to fall away when he crossed the street. He hung back as Fred and Evan approached the gated garden to one of the homes down the street.

In nature we never see anything isolated, but everything in connection with something else which is before it, beside it, under it and over it.

Johann Wolfgang von Goethe

German writer and statesman, 1800's

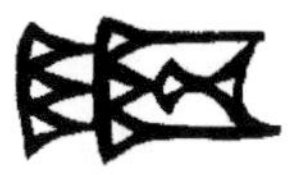

Chapter Twenty Six

Fred lead the way as he and Evan traversed the sidewalk.

"I still don't understand that glitch, or why you think this Hannah chick can help," Evan complained as he increased pace to keep step with his uncle. "Geez, old man, you're getting better after all."

Fred quirked a brow at the younger man. "We gotta get you back to boot camp or something, boy."

"As for the glitch..." Fred fell into step with Evan. "I think it may have to do with a network a bit more powerful than the one we are working on for GlobeNet. And I think Hannah may be the one to help with the answers. We'll find out in a moment."

Fred came to a sudden halt in front of the patio adorned with a quirky collection of chimes and pinwheels. The front window glittered with displays of crystals, perched on shelves and sills or dangling from delicate chains. Various diminutive statues of deities and angelic beings intermingled with potted greenery. Fairy lights in pastels illuminated the menagerie.

Evan's gaze wandered the display before pausing on the purple and white sign above the door.

"Conscious Connections?" Evan read. "You can't be serious."

"Dead serious." Fred winked.

He led the way to the top of the stairs and opened the door.

Fred waved an invitation for his nephew to enter. "After you."

"This must be a front for something," Evan grumbled as he passed into the sage and patchouli cloud.

"Fred!" The cheery young woman from the chat session turned her attention toward the door as bells tingled at the frame.

"Greetings, Hannah dear." Fred beamed at the sight of the woman.

Evan nudged his uncle. "I've never seen that look on your face, old man.

Hannah moved from behind the counter across the showroom of the store. Arms open, she met Fred with an embrace. The two connected as if they'd known one another for a lifetime.

As Fred broke from the greeting, his hands remained on Hannah's shoulders.

"Hannah, my dear, I would like to introduce you to someone I feel will be important to the task at hand." Fred turned Hannah to face his nephew. "This is Evan."

The light in the young woman's vibrant green eyes shifted. The softness and joy she greeted Fred with muddled with something deeper. Emotions and connections struggled to host recognition.

"Evan, this is Hannah." Fred caught the look between the two, as well as a subtle note of distrust behind his nephew's level gaze. "She's going to help us. You'll see."

Though Hannah moved to offer a similar embrace as she'd extended to Fred, her advance was more cautious. Cutting off the awkward greeting, Evan offered his hand.

"Of course. Evan." Hannah welcomed the retreat from her jovial greeting in exchange for the disimpassioned hand shake. "It's a pleasure to finally put an energy to the name."

As their palms connected, Hannah's expression shifted once again. Fred had come to recognize this shift. A premonition. Hannah blinked, as though trying to re-center after being lost in thought.

"Oh. My." Hannah caught her breath and retrieved her hand in an attempt to disguise the wave of energy with a vacant smile.

Evan smirked at the waver in the woman's demeanor. "Yeah. That's how most girls react."

"Evan." Fred nudged his nephew's rib.

Hannah waved off the retort. "I'm sure at one point that was true, but things are changing. It's okay Fred, he's still learning. And he has been taking prescriptions inhibiting his consciousness."

Hannah closed her eyes for another breath and exhaled. When her eyes focused once again on Evan, the intensity of her energy sent visible goosebumps up his arms.

"Whoa." Evan stepped back, clearly annoyed at being put off his game.

"Relax." Hannah winked. "I'm checking that wild energy of yours at the door."

"Right." Evan coughed. "Let's hear more on this project you and my uncle are working on."

Fred smiled. It wasn't often witnessed his nephew rattled in such a way. Evan crossed his arms as he shifted the conversation to something in his realm of understanding. "First, what's your security clearance with ITower?"

Hannah turned her attention to Fred.

"Hannah's not with ITower," Fred explained. "Or any network company."

As Hannah caught Evan's concern, she offered a knowing nod to Fred. "Well, none in this realm, anyway."

A short laugh escaped Fred in response to the quip. "Of course."

"What are you two on about? What does any of this have to do with a magic tricks and trinket shop?" Evan glanced around the store.

"Evan, have a little faith." Fred clapped a hand on Evan's shoulder before returning his attention to Hannah. "Let's see the setup you've been working from."

"Of course." Hannah grinned. "I think you'll be somewhat disappointed."

She slipped past the two men to lock the front door as she flipped a sign that read 'Out to Lunch'.

She led Fred and Evan through a short labyrinthine hallway of classrooms and meditation nooks. Evan's eyes widened. Fred suppressed a chuckle. He, too, had been surprised by the size of the space which appeared deceptively small from the street.

Evan peered into the various spaces with mild curiosity.

"It's always a bit of a shock to first timers." Hannah glanced back at Evan, as if understanding his thoughts.

The trio ascended the narrow flight of stairs to an apartment quite in contrast to the store below. A cozy workspace at the top of the stairs served as Hannah's office. Beyond that, a kitchen and sitting room filled the living space. Three doors led off the main living space to a pair of bedrooms and a closet-sized bathroom.

"Welcome to my humble abode." Hannah waved over the space as Fred and Evan entered.

An old-world energy filled the home. The muted hues and soft natural furnishings were a far cry from the bustling commercial district beyond the walls, and equally so the glitter and whimsy of the space below.

"Hannah, you are an individual with many facets." Fred smirked at the mid-century kitchen as he settled into a well-worn office chair.

"Not so much. Customers get the flash and the fantasy, my soul pod gets to see the real Hannah." She turned her attention to the rolltop desk. "Well, here it is."

She gave her best showroom smile as she rolled back the top of the desk to reveal a wireless tablet propped against a wire stand.

Fred gaped at the basic device lifting the standard tablet in his hands. "No wires."

"That's all there is, gentlemen." Hannah crossed her arms as she leaned against the wall of shelves. "Same old gal I've been using for five years. Have fun. I'll be back in a minute with some tea." Hannah made her way to the kitchen, leaving Fred still turning the tablet in his hands.

"There must be more to it." Fred leaned into the office chair.

Evan moved in beside his uncle. "What's the deal here?"

Fred shook his head. "This is how she was talking to us this afternoon."

"Nah. This chick is pulling your chain." Evan shifted the desk from the wall to peer down the back in search of wires.

"Where's the service?" Fred mumbled.

Hannah called from the kitchen. "Oh! I should have shown you guys while we were downstairs. The modem is by the counter out front. I still don't trust it too far from the shop tablet."

"It's not even on the same floor?" Fred tapped the surface of the device to wake up the screen, disbelief coursed through him..

Opening the cloud browser, the screen populated with code and messages. "Impossible."

"What are you looking at?" Evan frowned at the blank screen.

"It's working. But I have no idea how she's accessing anything. I mean. This code is hard to read, even for me." Fred tapped the edge of the device to zoom in on a section of code.

"What are you talking about?" Frustration painted Evan's tone. "There's nothing *on* the screen."

Fred raised his attention to Evan. "What do you mean?"

Hannah returned with a tray containing three mugs of hot water and a basket of tea bags.

"Oh good! Fred, I've been meaning to show you that video."

Fred and Evan turned to the woman in matched confusion.

"Video?" Fred struggled to follow the streaming data flitting across the screen.

"I don't see anything!" Evan threw his hands out in exasperation.

Setting the tea tray on the desk, Hannah dusted off her hands. She peered over Fred's shoulder at the tablet. "Yeah. That's the one, alright."

"What video?" Fred shook the tablet in his hands. "Hannah, can you actually read this code?"

Hannah released a curt laugh. "Code? Of course not. Why? Wait. What do you see?"

"It's all data. Streaming data. Code flashing on the screen." Fred tapped the edge of the device again in an attempt to adjust the activity on the screen.

"Code. Video." Evan ran his hands through his hair. "Come on. What's the gag, Fred?"

"You don't see anything." Hannah's cast a smile of wistful amusement. "I was right. You guys aren't connected."

She plucked a tea bag from the basket and dropped it into one of the cups. "Well, I suppose, Fred, you are at least partially connected. You can see data, but you're not seeing what is coming in."

She handed a teacup to Evan and followed the same routine to offer a cup to Fred in exchange for the tablet.

The two accepted the tea, though Evan scowled, his eyes darting between screen and Hannah. "What the hell are you talking about?"

Hannah shifted the tablet in her hands. She tapped at the edges and slid her fingers over the screen.

"We're all energy," she explained as she toyed with the device. "People, places, plants, data, technology, everything." She looked from Fred to Evan to ensure both followed her explanation.

"You know. Computers only work when they have a connection to the network, to a source of energy, to the Cloud." Hannah's words caused both Fred and Evan to tilt their heads. "People are the same. We are merely lumps of flesh without connection to global consciousness. With connection to consciousness, we get to the Akashic, other souls, other realms, our data, our memories. You know, the big Cloud in the sky." She offered a wink to Fred. "In this current case, we can use devices to interface with the big data in the sky."

Fred leapt from his seat, upsetting the tea in his cup. "Of course!"

He settled back into the chair as Hannah offered a linen napkin to mop up the splatter of tea.

Hannah took a sip from her tea as she perched on a bench beside the desk.

"That's why my C2C search works for me, but not Evan." Fred waved the napkin at his nephew. "But. That still doesn't explain how other people are getting to a higher connection, or any connection, for that matter."

Hannah frowned. "C2C? What have you been doing?"

"I'd like to know the answer to that one, too." Evan set his tea cup aside.

Fred's enthusiasm abated moderately, as a sheepish grin spread across his face. "Well, I've kind of connected to the other cloud Hannah was talking about. The Akashic. My new connection engine, it can span both clouds. Like Hannah is able to."

Evan crossed his arms as he eyed both Hannah and his uncle.

"I know how it sounds." Fred scowled. "But beyond that, we have a problem. Evidently, other people are connecting too. Since before my program."

"Wait." Hannah interjected. "So you *are* able to connect to the Akashic with your computer! That means you're progressing. That's amazing!" She wrung her hands as she stared at Fred. "It's also dangerous."

"No one at ITower knows it's me. We're completely safe," Fred assured both Hannah and his nephew. "Right now, ITower sees my program as another corruption in the data."

Fred took up his cup of tea once again.

"Geez, Uncle." Evan released an exasperated sigh.

"Oh!" Fred's excitement was returning as he set his cup on the desk to continue. "Remember the guy I met in that metaphysical chat room?" He shook a finger at Hannah.

"Well. Yes." Hannah sipped her tea. All the while her eyes flitted from Fred to Evan, watching, calculating. Fred wondered what she was doing--she'd mentioned something about reading the shifting expressions and noting waves in energy. That must be it.

"Yes. Well," Fred continued. "He fired off all these data dumps on my machine. Tons of data."

"Tons of random data." Evan pressed his lips together. "From some dude in a chat. Yep. Great."

Fred offered a vigorous nod. “Indeed! I sifted through the data and reverse-engineered it in order to build the C2C interface. That’s how I can connect.”

Evan scowled at this flood of information. “I repeat. Some guy on a chat room? Fred! You've got somebody else in on this? Damn it, there are all kinds of security issues, here. You can't be doing this. You know the protocols! ITower is going to string you up.”

“Oh, that's who he was? The Coach.” Hannah’s eyes grew wide as she ignored Evan’s concerns.

“Yeah.” Fred nodded. “Coach. That's his username.”

“What do you know about him?” Evan pressed.

“I was meditating the other day.” Hannah closed her eyes. “This entity who called himself The Coach popped in. He started spewing technical jargon and lost me, though.” She opened her eyes and took another sip of her tea.

“Slow down.” Evan pressed his palm to his forehead. “Let me see if I have this straight. You,” He pointed at Fred, “connected with this Coach dude in a chat room online. And you," he turned to Hannah, "had a little chat with him while meditating?”

“It seems so.” Fred rubbed his chin.

“I need something stronger than tea.” Evan set down the teacup to put both hands on his head.

“Yes! Something stronger.” Fred slapped the desk, rattling the tea cup. “Only seeing code on Hannah's screen is driving me crazy. If we want to see the images we need a stronger connection.”

Hannah clapped her hands together. “Now you’ve got it!”

“ITower allowed me to set up a direct line to our Cloud at the house. Maybe it will help if we use that. It’s one less variable.”

“Maybe you don’t got it.” Hannah mumbled.

“Hannah, could you come with us?” Fred rose from his chair in his excitement, ignoring his nephew shaking his head in protest.

“I feel I probably should.” Hannah smiled. “To keep an eye on the two of you. Besides, this is the most action I've had all day. Give me a minute, I'll get one of my Reiki Masters to watch the shop for the rest of the day.”

As Hannah disappeared to the front of the shop Evan leaned toward Fred. “Are you certain it is wise to continue to involve this chick? We hardly know her.”

A knowing smile filled Fred's cheeks. "You only think you hardly know her."

As the trio exited the store a figure watched from the coffee shop patio next door.

Hannah scanned the street as the feeling of being watched washed over her. Her gaze fell upon Linus for only a moment. Her breath caught as the word "Pythia" formed on her lips.

"Did you say something?" Fred paused for Hannah to catch up to him.

"No." Hannah shook off the feeling and smiled at Fred. "It's nothing."

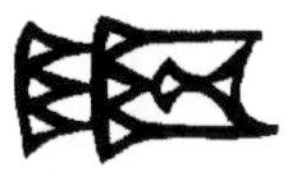

Chapter Twenty Seven

Hannah meandered the house as Fred and Evan settled in with consoles and devices.

"Your home has wonderful energy." She ran her fingers gently along the window frame. "A bit chaotic, but full of positivity."

The two men ignored her as she continued to glide through to join them in the wire cluttered office space.

"I'm on ITower's cloud. In the admin console. But I don't see anything yet." Fred grumbled as he leaned in toward the monitor. "My search engine is still not working. Evan, what do you think I should I be looking for? I'm not getting a full connection."

Frustration edged his voice, yet Hannah could feel the sense of excitement permeating the man's aura.

"You know, this is kind of exciting." Fred's eyes glued to the screen. "It's a little like war."

Evan scowled at the code streaming across his screens. "Hell if I know. You're the one who says you connect to this other cloud. Maybe it will look like some kind of login screen. Or an encrypted link."

Fred and Evan attacked their respective keyboards, leaving Hannah to lounge on the couch. She passed the time flipping tarot cards in an absent-minded game of solitaire.

A frown furrowed her brow. "Linc?"

"Yeah. Like a hyperlink, or maybe a mapped gateway." Evan continued to type. "Do you suppose there is some kind of a validation code? Like a password?"

"Communications is the key to war. Dude?" Hannah spouted as she continued to stare at the cards laid out on the coffee table.

Fred offered a glance and a confused smirk to Hannah's statement before returning to the business at hand.

To Evan he shot a wry reply, "I don't know, man, it works for me."

"Evan, check your frequency." Hannah's eyes were suddenly focused on the man. "You've gotta get on frequency?"

At this Evan paused his flurry of typing at last. "What?" Something resembling anger drew down his brows.

Unperturbed, Hannah raised a card into Evan's view. The Knight of Wands was scrawled beneath a ruddy haired rider on a rampant steed, a staff in his hand.

"Linc says you have to get on frequency."

Hearing the name, Fred, too, halted his assault on the code to lock eyes with the young woman.

"Hannah, don't go there. He's not ready." Fred shook his head.

"What are you doing?" Evan turned a stern gaze on his uncle. What did you tell this chick about Linc? Is this so she can play games with me with her crazy cards?"

"This is not a game. And I am not going to be your medium to Linc with all of this technical mumbo jumbo he keeps streaming into my head." Hannah shot from the couch and marched to Evan's side. "Talk to him yourself. Calm down. Type this in."

She paused as if listening for directions. "Five dogs eat three snakes for breakfast today."

Evan turned to his keyboard. Reluctance and frustration slowed his fingers.

He looked to Fred as if for a sign to reveal this sick joke clearly being played out on him. Hannah suppressed a smile. Nothing betrayed the sincerity in Fred's eyes.

"Fine." Evan pounded the keys. "Five. Dogs. Eat-" He stopped again. "Wait. That's. That's our old team validation code." His eyes burned as he shot a brief glare between Fred and Hannah. "How did you get that information? That was Top Secret."

Hannah held up the card and once more waved it at Evan. A wry smile drew up her lips.

His scowl deepening, Evan typed the code he had nearly forgotten.

5DE3 S4BT. He struck the enter key and shoved away from the desk.

A pop up window suddenly opened. All code halted on the screen.

Link Established filled the small white text box.

A chat window appeared.

LINC: Hey, Dude, long time no see.

The words filled the box in a flash, leaving Evan shaking his head as he shifted his attention once more to Hannah. At this, though, his gaze was more dumbfounded than angry.

"How are you doing this? We don't have time for parlor tricks." Anger reemerged on Evan's features.

Fred rose from his chair and sidled to view Evan's screen. "Hannah's not doing anything." He set a hand on his nephew's shoulder. "Answer him."

Sweat beaded Evan's brow, he blinked back the moisture rising in his eyes. Still, he typed.

EVAN: How do I know it is you?

Fred and Hannah shared a knowing glance.

LINC: Only you and I know the authentication code. What more do you want? The phone number for the hot chick I banged on our last R&R in Singapore?

Evan allowed a smile to crack his features.

Linc's video image flickered into view within the pop-up window. "Trust me, Chief, I know a lot more about her now than I care to. You don't want to go there."

Evan chuckled as shock merged with awe. "How?" Was all he managed to say.

"Magic!" Linc wagged his fingers in front of his face. "And if you would quit taking those damned pills, we could chat so much more often."

Evan frowned.

"Yeah." Linc tapped at the side of his temple. "You're not crazy, man. You're on frequency. Those pills shut you down."

"The voices?" Evan sighed.

Fred put a hand on his nephew's shoulder. "How long have you been hearing voices?"

"Since the zap wagon." Linc nodded.

When both Evan and Fred returned near disgusted faces to face the screen, Linc shrugged.

"What?" Linc shook his head. "Too soon?"

"I thought I had gone nuts." Evan's features danced between a wry smile and concerned frown.

Hannah leaned into view of the screen in an attempt to make out the images displayed there.

"Nice." Linc smiled.

As the trio focused on Evan's computer and Linc, a secondary window popped up on Fred's display. The speakers on Fred's system crackled to life as Coach appeared within the video chat window.

"Hey, Fred! Dear Hannah!" The image of a bald and bearded man waved. "Good to finally see you in person." Laughter echoed from the speakers.

Hannah's tarot cards fluttered to the floor. "Did you all hear that?"

Fred side-stepped back to his chair and flopped into the seat. Linc shifted his attention to the left as if glancing across the room to Coach.

"Are you Coach?" Fred stared at the face looking back at him through the screen.

"Oh good! You can see me." Coach clapped his hands together. "Congratulations on leveling up." The bald man offered a thumbs up to the still-confused Fred.

"You are real." Hannah could almost see the wheels turning in Fred's head as he recognized Coach from his NDE on the train. "You were there when I died."

"Indeed! Great memory!" Coach snapped his fingers. "But it's going to take more than a death experience and some techno stuff to get to the level of Little Miss over there."

"Of course." Fred turned to Hannah. "I understood how we connected the two clouds. But Hannah connects devices in her store to either cloud with no code knowledge."

"She's been connecting a lot longer than this most recent crash. She's using the grid." Coach winked at Hannah. "You have to use the grid to connect. Right, my dear?"

Hannah's retort dripped with amicable sarcasm, "Don't patronize me, old man."

Coach laughed aloud. "You are much older than me. But, you are incarnated this round, so play your role, dear one." He belly laughed at his own joke.

Evan paused his chat with Linc to peer over at the strange conversation taking place on Fred's screen.

"Grid?" Fred interrupted the side chat and surveyed Hannah, his eyes probing for information. "What grid?"

Hannah shook her head. Her shoulders rolled in confusion as she considered the words of the man on the screen. At once it dawned on her.

"Aha!" Hannah snapped her fingers. Her eyes glittered in understanding. "My store! It's on a ley line! I picked that spot for spiritual reasons…" She paused to make eye contact with each of the faces looking back at her. "I never thought. Even for a moment I was using it for my devices though."

"This is so far beyond all of us, it seems." Fred smirked.

"Who are you talking to?" Evan peered across the space to Fred's computer.

"Here." Linc's image flickered out of the window on Evan's screen. "Let me help."

As the two screens flickered, Linc appeared beside Coach. All three clustered around Fred's screen.

"Is this the chat room guy?" Evan's eyes narrowed. "How is Linc with him? Is he dead, too?"

"I've been off the mortal coil for a long time now." Coach offered a sage nod. "Though not nearly as long as I had been on it."

Hannah leaned away from the desk to perch on the arm of the couch.

"He's a guide." She proclaimed. "He's on the other plane."

The image of Coach nodded once again. "You have all been here as well, dear lady. And *you* have been to many of the other planes, as well."

Evan and Fred turned their attention to Hannah.

She raised her shoulders. "I have only guessed at some of my past incarnations."

"You have done more than guess, dear Hannah." Coach smiled. "You have known. For a long time."

"This is all well and good, but what about now?" Linc interjected.

"Of course." Coach brought his hands together. "I concur. Our whole concern is the grid."

Fred and Evan shook their heads side to side as they shrugged at their levels of lack of understanding.

"You need to get the grid back on-line." Coach pressed, as if the answer was obvious.

"And you have a lot of work to do." Linc rubbed his hands together. "Time moves no matter what plane we're on, and while you may not be able to see the countdown, we can."

"Great. Sure." Evan waved in frustration. "But what the hell is this grid thing?"

"Are we still talking about ley lines?" Hannah raised her hand from the couch.

"Our prize pupil, indeed!" Coach jutted a finger in Hannah's direction. "Ley lines, vortices, ancient sites. Stonehenge, pyramids, temples." He rattled off a list, both spiritually and technologically important. "These are all used by civilizations like Atlantis, well at least as long as that one lasted."

"And others before them," Linc piped in.

Coach nodded. "They built the grid. They used it for creating, storing data, and moving energy."

Fred sighed as understanding weighed on his shoulders. "That's how they communicated, too. On a different level."

Evan scoffed. "I suppose this includes crop circles and crystal skulls?"

Linc nudged Coach. "See! I told you he would get it!"

Evan threw out his hands and turned from the screen that was now flickering with interference.

"Maybe we can try this connection again at my place?" Hannah hopped from the couch. "Since it's located on the grid line already."

Linc winked at Evan. "Hey Dude, I like this gal. She's quick."

Evan frowned, but both Fred and Linc caught the fleeting glance at the young woman and a faint reddening at his collar.

"You and Hannah go ahead." Evan tilted his chin at Fred. "I'll hang back here. To catch up with Linc."

"Of course." Fred patted Evan's shoulder.

Hannah moved to protest but a subtle look from Coach was enough to silence her. Instead she gathered her tarot cards from the floor.

Her breath caught as a pair of cards revealed face up beneath the scattered pile. The card with a Hierophant priest beside a tower and with two subjects kneeling in front seemed to stare back at her. She nods.

Fred's shadow cast over her as she swept the cards into the deck. "Are you ready?"

"Yes." Hannah shook the concern from her expression. "What can I carry?"

Hannah and Fred packed wires and devices into bags and boxes as Evan continued to shake his head at the image staring back at him.

"You're here." He whispered to Linc.

The two hardly noticed Hannah and Fred slip out of the house.

No sensible decision can be made any longer without taking into account not only the world as it is, but the world as it will be.

Isaac Asimov

American writer and professor

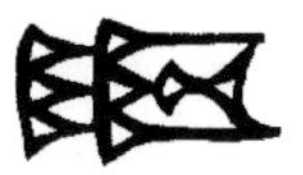

Chapter Twenty Eight

The van rolled to a stop outside Fred's house, blocking the driveway.

"This it?" Linus's companion put the van in park.

Linus removed his camouflage jacket at tugged at the sleeves of his black shirt.

He tossed his jacket into the rear corner of the van and stepped into the cargo space. From the mounted cabinets along the vehicle walls he pulled a small black box.

"Do you need me to set that for you, Mr. Atticus?" His companion peered from the driver's seat.

"No thank you." Linus offered a taunt smile to the younger man. "I think I can recall how to use a device I aided in building."

The young man swallowed and returned a sheepish nod. "Right. I forget sometimes."

"It happens." Linus turned his full attention to the black box device.

He sighed as he reminisced of his first encounter with the much larger black boxes. His mind flashed to the Serapeum of the Library of Alexandria, adorned in sashes bearing crosses. He imagined the heat of the flames that licked the scrolls and manuscripts.

His thoughts receded as he and his companion emerged from the sliding door of the van and snuck to the rear of the house.

His cohort kept watch as Linus planted a small digital device among the shrubbery. He set the timer and slipped back along the walkway beside the house.

Linus glanced through the side window to see a somber Evan staring at a seemingly blank screen. "If this one is the architect this will solve Wave7's problems for another generation."

"Mr. Atticus. Please, sir. Come on." Linus's companion hissed from the driver's seat of the van.

Linus hopped into the passenger seat and slammed the door as they pulled away.

"I mean no disrespect, Mr. Atticus, but do you think it will be this easy to deal with the architect?" The young man watched the house shrink in the rear view mirror.

Linus shrugged his coat onto his shoulders. "I can only do as much as those above my station will allow, and hope it is enough."

Linc's countenance shifted mid-sentence.

"What?" Evan smirked at Linc's sudden look of concern.

"Hey. Buddy." Linc scanned the space surrounding Evan. "We've been chatting a while. You still live in a biosuit. Take a break. Go get some fresh air. I'll be here," Linc assured him.

"Don't worry about it." Evan leaned back in his chair. "Fred's place is nowhere near as stuffy as our old commo-van. I'm fine. And check it out. No squeaking chairs."

Evan laughed. He felt a lightness only familiar in distant memory.

"No." Linc's tone had turned stern. "You need a break. Now."

"Shit. If you're going to order me around." Evan shoved his chair back. "I'll hit the head and be right back."

"No." The frame surrounding Linc's image began to emit a dark aura. "Outside. Take a walk. Up the street. Get some air. Or a beer at that bar a couple blocks away."

The chat window abruptly closed. A moment more and the screen flickered out and blinked to black.

Aggravation pulled Evan to his feet. "Damn cables."

He struck the side of the screen. Dropping to his knees, he wiggled the array of wires stemming from the tower and monitors.

"Go." Linc's voice filled Evan's ears.

"Well. Hell. I guess I'll take that break, now." Evan pushed up from the floor.

At the front door Evan stopped. Air filled his lungs as he stretched. "Okay. Maybe I did need a stretch."

"Keep going." The persistent din of Linc's voice permeated Evan's every thought.

"Damn it. If this is how you're going to be, I'm going to pop a couple pills to shut you down."

As Evan's feet touched the curb of the street in front of the neighboring house, a faint glow filled his peripheral vision.

From the side of Fred's house, ripples of electricity rattled a row of flower pots.

Lights in neighboring houses flickered. A dull rumble reached out to Evan as he turned to face the light.

"Down!" The order assaulted on his ears.

Evan was blown into the street by a rush of air and energy. A rain of glass sprayed from the windows of Fred's house peppering Evan with the shrapnel. Electric popping filled Evan's ears as he rose from the cracked edges of the sidewalk.

Disorientation and vertigo wobbled Evan's legs as he brushed debris from his arms and hair. Ringing continued to block out the din of car alarms, barking dogs, and neighborhood doors opening.

Through it all, Linc's voice emerged like a bell. "Keep moving."

Evan shook the buzzing from his ears and cupped his head in his hands as his mind flashed to the battlefield years before.

"Son of a bitch. Again."

He turned his gaze to the skies.

"You could have warned me it was incoming mortars." He cursed the empty sky.

"Much worse than mortars." Linc's voice cut through the growing din. "Much worse. Move."

The most momentous thing in human life is winning the soul to good or evil.

Pythagoras

Ancient Ionian Greek philosopher

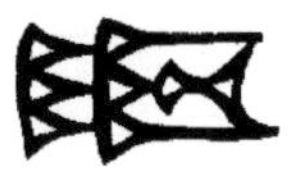

Chapter Twenty Nine

Fred sat across from Hannah in the rear office of the store. He squinted at the screen of the wired tablet as he struggled with the connection. Coach's smiling face filled a video chat window.

"If you want to get everyone re-connected, you'll have to get the grid on-line."

Mid-message, Coach averted his gaze to one side. In the same moment, Hannah's chin tipped to the ceiling. Eyes wild, she gripped the arms of the chair, her breath momentarily caught.

Coach scowled as he returned his attention to Fred.

Confused and concerned, Fred set a hand on Hannah's shoulder. "You okay?"

"Well, that was a close call." Coach sighed.

His smile returned.

"Not good." Hannah fought to slow her breath. "What was that? Evan?"

"It's not something for you to worry about this time," Coach's voice soothed the woman.

"What about Evan?" Fred interjected.

"It's okay." Coach turned his calming tone on Fred. "You'll find out shortly."

Something in the demeanor of the ethereal being settled the concerns of both Hannah and Fred.

Changing the subject to the project at hand, Coach cleared his throat.

"Hannah, my dear."

With a sigh Hannah nodded. "Yes."

"Are you aware, dear one, your store is on a third-tier ley line?"

"Well, I knew it was a line." She shrugged, her face coloring slightly as she could not offer more information.

"This is helpful. And more so, the two of you are connecting fairly well." Coach gave the pair an approving smile.

Fred and Hannah exchanged approving smiles.

"Of course, If you can get the full grid running again, it's possible everyone on our little planet will gain connectivity again." Coach knit his fingers together at the idea.

"Amazing." Awe sighed from Fred's lips. "Imagine it. Every person accessing the Akashic with a mobile device."

Fred released a brief chuckle at the thought of it.

"Not exactly." Coach wagged a finger. "If someone wants to use the grid, they'll also need to raise their biological frequency."

"Enlightenment." Hannah rested her head in her palm.

"Indeed." Coach nodded. "Then they can use a device with a physical frequency generator," he explained.

"Like a crystal." Hannah offered.

"If we start in on crystal skulls, we may have to repeat this for Evan. He won't believe it." Chuckling, Fred slapped his knee.

Coach paused. "Well, yes. Most electronics have crystal components much like the skulls. Ultimately, all of this is a placebo."

"A placebo?" Fred's face curled in confusion.

Coach took yet another breath to focus. "It's silicon and quartz. But if it helps the physical being to focus, they can be helpful." Coach shifted his gaze to Hannah again. "It's no different than tarot cards, pendulums, divining rods, runes, crystal balls... it's all a crutch."

"Hey." Hannah sneered in mock offense.

Fred snickered. "So, what you're saying is we don't need a device to connect."

Coach held out his hands. "It's all up to you. And the grid."

Hannah nodded. "Alright then. Back to this grid. Why can't you get it running?" She waved at Coach. "Why not snap fingers and done?"

"I'm not doing your job." Coach laughed. "I'm not incarnated right now. There's far less I can do." Coach tilted his head toward Fred. "That's why we sent him back. To help."

"Wait. You sent me back?" Fred frowned.

"You needed a little nudge." Coach shrugged.

"I'm here to fix this giant grid." Fred slumped back into his chair. "How? Where do I start?"

Coach's laughter echoed from the speakers. "Like I said, I'm not doing your job for you. It's not my challenge." Reassurance colored the being's voice. "Before we sent you back, you reviewed your soul contract. You agreed to it. Remember?"

Hannah turned to gauge Fred's reaction to this new information.

Fred mustered a stammer. "I don't know. I guess. Well, maybe." Visions of his NDE struggled to surface in his memories. "Even if I do remember, I don't know what it all meant."

The store's door chimed, shaking Fred and Hannah from the depths of the conversation.

"Hello!" A woman's voice called from the front of the store. "Hannah?"

"Oh!" Hannah rose from her chair. "I forgot! There's a group tonight."

She returned her attention to Coach. "Will you still be here?"

Fred caught the reassuring smile Coach offered Hannah.

An idea struck Fred as he heard the bell at the front door once again. "Maybe we can covertly run some of this past them?"

He jutted a thumb toward the front of the store.

"What about Evan?" Hannah tipped her gaze to Coach.

"He may interrupt the gathering." Coach offered a cryptic smirk.

Then, as if a joke suddenly came to his mind, Coach piped up once more. "You know. A couple of your group members are waning. You want me to shake them up?"

Hannah waved her hands. "No, please don't. I see them as a challenge. And, I think you might scare them off."

Hannah waved as she scurried to the front of the store. Her cheerful, welcoming voice traveled faintly back to Fred and Coach.

"Take good care of her." Coach's tone leaned serious as he gazed after Hannah. "She has much to offer, though she lacks the tech savvy of our boy Evan."

Fred frowned at the cryptic nature of Coach's words, though he acquiesced.

"Of course."

Coach's chat window flickered and the screen returned to a stream of code.

The river of time may fork into rivers, in which case you have a parallel reality and so then you can become a time traveler and not have to worry about causing a time paradox.

Michio Kaku

American theoretical physicist and futurist

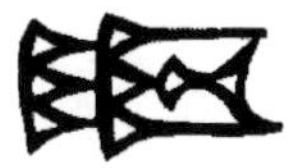

Chapter Thirty

As Hannah was busy arranging the familiar semi-circle of folding chairs, support group attendees milled within the store.

Fred straightened his collar and entered from the office, receiving a few looks from the other NDE group members. He cleared his throat and subtly joined Hannah in arrangement of the chairs.

The handful of attendees finally settled in when the bell on the door clanged to life again. This time, Evan burst into the tiny store. Disheveled, dirt and blood smudged his face. Tears marred his clothing.

Chairs squeaked on the hardwood floor as members of the support group turned intense stares at a panting Evan.

Fred moved to his nephew's side. Hannah, however, struggled to maintain a facade of calm.

"I'm glad you rushed to join us." She released a nervous giggle.

"Uncle." Evan swallowed.

He eyed the crowded room.

"Hannah, may we use your office a moment?" Fred held Evan's arm.

He lead the younger man into the main lobby of the store even before Hannah offered a response.

"Of course. It's. I mean." She pointed. "You know where it is."

Fred caught Hannah's eye as her gaze followed Evan.

As he led Evan past the circle of seated attendees, an older woman raised her palms to Evan.

"Oh my goodness! Your aura is expansive. Are you staying for the meeting?"

Evan frowned at the woman. "Lady. No offense, but I couldn't care less about your little meeting." He flashed an unapologetic glare at Hannah. "I hope I'm still alive by next week."

Fred bustled Evan through to the office at the rear of the store.

"Please. Let's ground and focus before we begin," Hannah diverted the group's attention, closed her eyes, and rested her wrists on her knees.

Fred glanced back long enough to see the others following the woman's request without question.

"I'm glad you decided to drop by after all!" Fred settled Evan beside the computer and poured a glass of water from the filtered pitcher on the counter.

"Did you run the whole way here? Looks like you rolled the way." Fred jokingly fanned Evan. "We have some insight on the grid project! How's Linc?"

"Yeah, well, we have other issues before we move on your grid madness." Evan gulped the water and slammed the glass on the table.

"Are you okay?" Fred frowned as he checked the glass for cracks.

"How do you think Hannah will feel about a pair of techie roommates for a while?" Evan jabbed his thumb in the direction of the store.

"What are you talking about?" Fred returned with the glass full of water again.

"Unless you have another place we can set up more secure than what your house used to be." Evan ran his fingers through his hair and slumped into the couch.

"Wait. What?" Concern tightened Fred's jaw as his heart raced.

"The house is compromised, Fred." Evan shook his head.

Linc's voice filled Evan's head. "Compromised. Yeah. That's sugar-coating it."

"Okay. Yes." Evan tugged at his hair. "The house is toast."

"What?"

"Somebody blew it up. Someone's got it out for you, or me. Or both of us." Evan took Fred by the shoulders.

Fred waved apologetically for his nephew's intrusion as he took a moment to peer through the doorway into the store lobby.

Hannah forced a smile and urged the support group to continue in sharing their stories.

"Maybe we should wrap up early, Hannah." One of the group members' voices wafted into the office. "It seems you have more pressing issues."

"No, it's fine," Hannah began.

"We know Fred is going through some things," another member of the group offered.

"Right." Hannah's shoulders slumped in acquiescence. "Let's postpone." She perked up a moment. "Wait, if any of you are available tomorrow..."

"A special meeting," An older woman smiled and winked.

"Yes." Hannah gripped the woman's hand. "You could call it that."

Fred looked on as Hannah bit her lip. He offered a sheepish glance at Evan as he entered from her office.

The members of the group filed out of the store and into the street as Fred returned to the office.

"If you need anything before tomorrow, let us know." One of the men offered before crossing the street to his car.

Hannah waved. "I will."

She locked the door and turned the sign to closed. Looking down the hallway to the rear of the building, Hannah froze, her eyes glazed over, as a premonition swept over her.

She spun to look across the street again.

Fred called from the end of the hallway. Concern flooded through him. "Hannah?"

"A strange vision. Unfamiliar, and dark. A cage in a large room, and electricity crackling all around. I'm sure it was nothing." Hannah turned from her reflection in the store window to march toward Fred.

She waved off the experience. "How's Evan? And the house?"

Fred frowned. "Evan will be fine. I won't even ask how you knew about the house."

"There's a room upstairs." Hannah didn't miss a beat as she swept past Evan. "You two are going to be here a while. I'll get the beds ready."

"Why would anyone attack the house?" Fred sighed.

"Linc warned me to get out before it blew." Evan watched Hannah as she gathered sheets and pillows from a closet. He continued in a whisper, "Like last time, on the battlefield."

"Should we tell ITower?" Fred sipped from the glass of water in his hand. "Should we see if anything is salvageable?"

Evan glanced at Fred's hands, and Fred took notice of the growing tremor shaking them.

"Fred. Man. You should sit."

Fred allowed his nephew to lead him to the couch.

"The house is still there, but every piece of electronics is fried. They EM-effed up half the neighborhood too." Evan shook his head. "Someone targeted us."

"We should have everything stored in our sub-Cloud." Fred contemplated. "Still. Who would do this?"

"Wave7?" Evan shrugged. "They could have backtracked us from ITower network logs and found your place."

"But why?" Hannah interrupted.

"Why wouldn't they?" Evan snapped.

"No." Fred sighed. "I don't think we should assume too easily this was Wave7."

He rose and set the glass on the table beside the tablet.

"It may be more complicated." Fred lifted the tablet from the table as he turned to Evan. "Did anyone see you come here?"

"No." Linc's voice filled Evan's mind.

"I don't think so," Evan replied, half expecting to see Linc.

Hannah crossed her arms as she leaned in the doorway. "I'm thinking it's a good idea to increase my insurance."

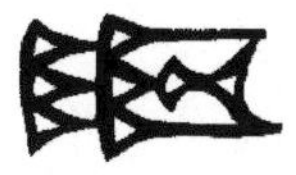

Chapter Thirty One

Evan spent the next several days smuggling wiring and components out of the ITower offices. He and Fred opted to continue to work opposing shifts, though both manned their computers nearly around the clock. With Fred still unable to do much heavy physical labor, Evan accepted day shift at the office, physically wiring functions at Hannah's place after dark.

Once the sun was down and the offices were all but empty, Fred periodically disabled facility security monitoring systems. Though unrelated, he used the pretense that aggressive network and data testing could overload security systems with false alarms.

Evan took these windows as opportunity to smuggle as much out of the ITower building as his laptop bag and a single filing box would contain. It was all he could do without alerting the one lazy night guard at the garage entrance.

Evan transported equipment to Hannah's, taking a new route every evening, stopping sometimes for dinner, evading those who might target them again. On a few occasions he brought flowers, cakes, or small tokens of appreciation to Hannah for her inconvenience.

More importantly, anyone surveilling or tracking his movements would assume Evan was up to his old habits of wooing a new conquest.

Hannah, for her part, had begun hosting more free events, talks, and classes in store. The constant stream of new cars, patrons, and instructors, worked as cover while Evan secreted shopping bags and gift boxes, filled with electronics, in among the patrons.

While the population of Conscious Connections flowed on the mortal plane, their collected energy powered the link to the ley lines and the cloud.

Within the hallways and classrooms of the small establishment, wires ran over floors, up the stairs, and across tables.

One afternoon, the older woman who had shown such concern at Evan's presence the night of the EM attack, stopped in. She picked her way over the increasing number of cords littering the storefront as she collected her items and brought them to the counter. Hannah stepped over a tangle of cords leading from her tablet to the back side of the main counter. The woman surveyed the path of the wires.

"Hannah. My dear girl. What is going on?" The woman looked from Hannah to the wiring and up to the wall of crystals.

Hannah offered a polite smile. "Please, excuse the wires." She waved off the mess. "I have a couple of temporary house guests in the spare apartment. "They work in the tech field," she offered as explanation. "Tread carefully. Don't trip on anything."

"I wasn't talking about the wires, dear one." The woman pressed her hands to her heart. "I am certain you can sense it. The energy in your space. It's," The woman paused to find the correct wording. "The frequencies are strange. It's intense."

Hannah offered a nervous giggle. "Yes. Well. As I said, it's probably all the electronics."

"It's something else." The woman pressed. She set her fingers to her temples. "I am getting all this data? All this information."

Hannah hurried to fill the woman's bag and complete the sale on the register. "Maybe you're experiencing the planetary retrograde." She plastered a professional smile on her lips. "It can cause disturbances. Have you fully cleared your aura lately? Here, we got some sage and new crystals."

Hannah thrust a handful of small stones and a grip of sage into a small bag. She held out the bag. "Free of charge."

"I don't think it will help." The woman turned from Hannah, leaving her holding out the bag of trinkets and dried leaves.

Hannah set the bag on the counter. Once the store emptied after the typical lunch break rush Hannah slipped into the back office.

As she rounded the stairwell she came face to chest with Evan. A spark of energy transferred between the pair as they stepped apart.

"Sorry." Evan leaned against the stairwell wall. "I was popping out for something to eat. "You want anything?"

Something sent unfamiliar emotions through the pair. Evan had been with dozens of women, yet his interest in Hannah felt different. There was a calm about the young woman that surpassed her age.

"No. No, I'm fine." Hannah stuttered. Her energy settled after a moment, yet Evan seemed to have had an increasingly disrupting effect on the woman since their first meeting.

"Is Fred up there?" Hannah shifted the conversation.

"Yeah." Evan tilted his head up the stairs.

Evan released a slow sigh as he watched Hannah climb the steps.

He continued his descent and slipped out the back entrance of the store.

Evan slid into the driver's seat of the Tesla and sat in silence.

***

"Fred?" Hannah tapped the door frame to the office.

Seated at a bay of towers, half a dozen monitors blinked and streamed data at Fred as he typed.

Coach and Linc peered from separate monitors.

"Fred." Hannah scanned the room, taking in the array of devices. "Wow. I guess you boys have been as busy up here as I have downstairs."

"Oh." Fred turned to face Hannah. "I apologize. I didn't hear you come up."

"Yeah." Hannah picked her way to the desk.

"Isn't this amazing!" Fred splayed his hands at the monitors.

"Amazing." Hannah's eyes wandered the cluttered space. "Yes."

"Hannah. This is the brink of something astounding. We could be on the path to the next step in human technological evolution."

Fred rose from the chair and put his hands on Hannah's shoulders.

His excitement waned as he locked eyes with the young woman.

"What?" Fred frowned.

"Well." Hannah struggled with the words.

She had no desire to put the brakes on what was clearly an amazing accomplishment for the man in front of her.

"It's just... I know you and Evan want to keep this away from the ITower offices for now. I realize they will think you are both a little bonkers if you tell them what you are up to. But, the people who visit my store, they can sense what you are doing. Is there perhaps, I don't know, some way of encasing the information you are connecting to?" Hannah took Fred's hands in hers. "Fred, you need to, I don't know, ground this or something."

Fred's brow furrowed as he turned his gaze on the image of Coach on the screen.

"The data you are accessing is spilling out all over the store," Hannah continued. "And who knows how much further. People are beginning to take notice, and ask questions I know you are not ready to answer."

Fred nodded. He returned to his chair. "I am in agreement. But, I'm in uncharted territory here." He looked to Coach for some assistance.

The guide merely shrugged.

"Hannah. I am not even sure when we are connected to the other Cloud, let alone know how to block or disconnect anyone else." Fred attempted to explain.

"Wait." Evan appeared at the doorway.

"I thought you were going to lunch?" Linc smirked from his box on the screen. "Couldn't stay away, huh?"

Excitement glinted in Evan's eyes though he tried to shrug off Linc's words. "Look. Hannah might be right. It feels, weird, out there."

Hannah crossed her arms. "It's not weird, it's spiritual energy."

"Right. Whatever." Evan stepped over the wires and strewn electronics to his chair. "Fred, maybe this is more of a security issue."

Hannah leaned on the desk beside the monitor with Coach peering out at her.

"It's about access control and encapsulating data; like encryption." Evan's eyes glinted.

In the second screen, Linc's face mirrored Evan's. "Yes! Of course!"

Evan peered over his shoulder at Fred. "You've built access control systems in the past."

"Use the same concepts," Linc piped up. "Authentication and authorization for access."

"You need a directory and network pathing to vector where people are allowed to go," Evan rapid-fired in response.

"Then apply ciphers and codes to protect the data." Fred clapped his hands in understanding.

He whirled his chair to face the monitors again.

Hannah's head spun as she applied her own comprehension to the various words filling her ears. "Vectors? Ciphers? I don't know your words, but I think you guys are speaking my language. Veils, shrouds, mental blocks, not grounded or clear, not on the right frequency."

"In this case they are, my friend." Coach winked.

Fred, Evan, and Linc exchanged perplexed looks.

Hannah's expression shifted as Coach's words sunk in. She jumped from her perch. In a matter of skips she disappeared down the short flight of stairs.

Hannah marched to the rear of the store. She ran her fingers along the titles of the texts shelved against the wall. Heaping a pile of books into her arms, she hurried upstairs.

She dropped the books onto one of the few cleared spaces on the desk beside Fred. The man lifted the topmost book off the stack.

"What could you know about security systems and access." Evan quipped as he pushed clear of the pile of books she placed inches from his arm.

"Magical Systems and Mysticism," Fred read aloud as he took up one of the books.

"Yes!" Hannah snagged the tome from Fred's grasp.

She flipped the pages excitedly.

"Here." She settled on a page and flopped the book open for Fred, Linc, and Coach to see.

Sighing, Evan leaned in to peer at the display.

The page revealed an array of ciphers and vectored symbols.

"What is this?" Evan swiped at the book, flipping the pages at random.

"It's high magic." Fred smirked. "Arcane Witchcraft."

"Crowley level." Hannah snickered. "Now this is exciting. I haven't studied much high magic since college. Then I was experimenting with casting circles and calling corners." Evan's eyes rolled to the ceiling.

Hannah snatched the book out of Evan's grasp and began fanning through the chapters.

Evan snapped his fingers. "Jinkies. And here I left my Ouija Board at home."

He shoved free of his chair and rolled his eyes. "I'm going for tacos. Here I thought something interesting was about to go down."

He shook his head as he passed his uncle. "You guys are too much. I'm going for food, then I'm going to get some real work done with Linc. Maybe we can get something accomplished at the office on the project we are supposed to be focused on."

Hannah's shoulders slumped as Evan pushed past to descend the stairs.

Fred set his hand on the top edge of the book. "Forget him for now. He needs more time."

Hannah returned a definitive nod. "Right."

She lowered her gaze to the open pages in her hands.

"The purpose of high magic is to secure your space from negative energy. And to prevent other souls from accessing your environment." She waved her hand around the room. "It's to protect your world. Your manifestations. Your stuff."

Fred, Coach, even Linc, were watching, listening.

"Okay." Fred crossed his arms and leaned into his chair. "How do you do it?"

The question gave Hannah pause. "Well. I suppose..." Her eyes flicked around the room searching for solutions.

She fanned the pages yet again. Stopping, she reached over the desk and snatched a Sharpie marker. From the other edge of the desk she nabbed a short stack of Post-it notes.

"What are you doing?" Fred leaned forward in his chair as Hannah hopped over wires to a far end of the room.

"Building a circle." Coach grinned from the monitor.

Hannah scrawled a symbol on a Post-it and slapped it on the wall.

"Precisely! I'm building us a sacred space." She pivoted to face Fred and marched to the opposite wall. "Securing it."

"A firewall". Fred rose to analyze the square of bright pink paper. "What are you writing?"

"Ancient symbols," Hannah called out as she slapped another Post-it to the wall. "Seals. Bind runes. They all have different properties and purposes."

Linc put his hands atop his head. "It's like coding. Specific syntax. Network protocols."

Hannah paused to shrug. "I guess. I am not too keen on tech stuff."

Fred laughed as he crossed the room to view another of Hannah's sticky note symbols. "If so, King Solomon must have been quite a geek. He had forty-four seals on his temple alone."

For a moment, all movement in the room stopped.

Only Coach continued to smile. The others stared at one another, letting this new information sink in.

"Solomon's temple." Fred ran a hand through his hair. "A grid point?"

The revelation held them.

"How many are there?" Fred sighed in awe.

Coach's voice broke the silence. "Fred. Tune in. Lift your frequency. Or should I write an access rule to the data." He chuckled at his own jest.

Hannah stepped back from her Post-it circle.

She settled on the couch to review the words associated with each of the symbols she chose.

"I'm not sure what to do next." She confessed.

"What would you do if this were a typical sacred space?" Fred peered over her shoulder at the book.

"Call the corners, I guess." Hannah turned the pages.

She balanced the book in one hand as she raised her other to the symbol on the first wall.

"Lords of the Watchtowers of the North, Lords of Earth. I thank you for attending this rite. We thank you for joining us from your fair and lovely realms. I bid thee Hail and Farewell."

She took a deep breath and glanced at the others before continuing.

Pivoting to the adjacent wall she intoned. "Lords of the Watchtowers of the West, Lords of Water. I thank you for attending this rite. We thank you for joining us from your fair and lovely realms. I bid thee Hail and Farewell."

Coach grinned at Hannah and the woman smiled back. "Lords of the Watchtowers of the South, Lords of Fire. I thank you for attending this rite. We thank you for joining us from your fair and lovely realms. I bid thee Hail and Farewell."

"Lords of the Watchtowers of the East, Lords of Air. I thank you for attending this rite. We thank you for joining us from your fair and lovely realms. I bid thee Hail and Farewell."

Hannah lowered the book to gaze around the room.

"Are you certain you did that right?" Fred reached out to touch the nearest symbol on the wall.

In a sudden flash, Hannah watched as the room is netted in an iridescent, nearly holographic web. The symbols seemed to glow.

Fred drew his hand back. "It feels warm."

Hannah allowed her expression to reveal her accomplishment.

Fred tapped the tips of his fingers together feeling the warmth ebb as he pulled his hand from the symbol.

"What are you looking at?" He rested his gaze on Hannah and her almost smug smile.

"I have never seen it do that before."

Fred scanned the room. "I... don't see anything." He turned to Coach. "Should I see something?"

Hannah moved through the web, her hands caressing the strands of indigo light.

"That is a highly elevated aura," Coach applauded.

"It's not a white light, though." Hannah's voice almost seemed disappointed.

"Give yourself time. It will improve." Coach's approval gave Hannah a small sense of pride.

Fred shook his head. He flipped his attention from Coach, to the room, and around to Hannah.

Linc watched Fred's confusion. "Old man, get on frequency. This shit is amazing!"

Fred frowned. A sigh escaped his lips.

"Right." He closed his eyes and allowed his breathing to even out. "On frequency."

Hannah smiled as she watched Fred's shoulders relax. As the man stood at the center of the room an aura of warmth and light shimmered the space around him.

As his eyes opened amazement drew a smile to his face as the web brightened into view.

Visions of the Akashic library surrounded Fred and Hannah. Symbols, data, and information seemed to alight on every surface in the room.

"Is this always like this?" Awe overwhelmed Fred.

"And so much more." Coach's voice cut through the visions like a ripple. "Go back and ground."

"What?"

Fred was suddenly staring straight into Hannah's eyes as she slapped a Post-it note to his chest.

Fred glanced at the symbol.

Fred shuddered as his senses snapped into focus on Hannah's symbols swirling within the circle.

"Ground, Fred." Hannah ordered. "Ground. Anchor yourself."

"Yeah, yeah." Fred mumbled. "I got it, I got it."

Fred's gaze followed the strands of the circle to where the symbols had started to shift.

Fred dove for his keyboard. His hands touched the monitor. Symbols appeared beneath his fingers. Movement shifted behind the surface of the screen. It pulled at Fred's fingertips. Drawing and redrawing, he created new symbols, re-positioning them as they appeared.

Fred's face contorted with a new level of consciousness and understanding. As he studied the images an impish grin bloomed across his lips.

He closed his eyes. "Watch this." He whispered into the swirl of light and dark.

Science is always discovering odd scraps of magical wisdom and making a tremendous fuss about its cleverness.

Aleister Crowley

English occultist, poet, painter, novelist

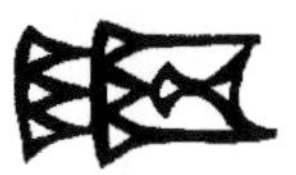

Chapter Thirty Two

As Evan returned from his dinner mission, Linc's voice filled his mind once again.

"I hope you saved your work in the Cloud."

"What?" Though Evan recognized by now he was talking to himself.

Linc's tone urged him to quicken his pace as he neared Hannah's storefront.

He mounted the stairs to the second-floor and called into the apartment. "Hey! I got an odd message from Linc. What have you done now?"

Evan halted in the door to the main office space.

Still clutching the bag of tacos, he scanned the strange symbols on the walls, monitors, and people in the room.

Fred looked up from his screen. "Oh! Tacos! Yes, we've worked up an appetite."

Hannah turned from the markings she had been adding to the walls "Oh! Evan! Don't move!"

The young woman skipped across the room. She halted toe-to-toe with Evan and slapped a Post-it to his chest.

"What the-" Evan balked at the woman.

Hannah lingered a moment more with her hand on Evan's chest, closed her eyes a moment before inviting Evan into the sacred space with a sweeping gesture. "Okay. Safe. You may enter."

"It worked. We locked him out." Fred clapped his hands.

"I, I mean we..." Fred offered a wink and a nod to Hannah, "...we built a security system."

Hannah lifted the bag from Evan's grasp. "I'll go get some plates. You guys have some catching up to do."

Evan's confusion allowed him to release the bag from his grip as he turned his attention on his uncle.

"What is all this?" Evan wandered toward the note-covered walls.

"Don't touch," Fred called out as Evan's hand raised to the nearest square of paper.

"It should keep others from tripping across data in the Cloud." Fred continued. "A sort of firewall. Well, I guess, an Earth, Air, Water, Firewall." Fred snickered at his own joke.

"What has this chick got you on?" Evan scowled at his uncle.

"We're on a whole new level." Fred beckoned for Evan to be seated. "We have to be open to new levels of understanding. And, you need to do your part, now."

Evan slumped into the chair. "Yeah? What part is that? Seek out crop circles and henges?"

Fred's mouth opened, then closed again as he considered his nephew's words.

Linc's face appeared in a window on the monitor. "The task at hand first, Fred."

"Of course." Fred leveled his gaze with Evan. "Find the jerks that nuked my house. Find out everything about them. Past, present…"

"And future," Linc interjected with a smile.

Fred agreed. "That too. We could use some help from you guys." Linc shrugged.

Evan narrowed his gaze as he looked from his friend to his uncle.

"But you need to get on frequency," Linc admonished his friend. "You have a lot of catching up to do. You shouldn't be this far behind. Those meds messed you up."

Hannah reappeared with plates, a small bottle of wine, and a trio of stemmed glasses on a tray.

"It's not champagne, but I thought we deserved something to celebrate this latest discovery. It's been some time since I've had cause to use the good glassware." She checked the glasses for remaining dust.

She set the glasses on the table and removed the screw cap from the bottle of wine.

"I'm thinking a reiki session might help clear Evan's chakras so he can expand his capabilities." Hannah continued as she filled the glasses and passed them to Evan and Fred.

She glanced into the monitor at Coach and Linc. "I would offer a glass to you guys, but, well." She shrugged. "Maybe an offering table?"

The sentiment garnered a smile from all but Evan who continued to hold the glass at arm's length. "This is insane."

Evan dumped the glass back in one gulp.

"Cheers." Hannah shrugged.

Of what use is a philosopher who doesn't hurt anybody's feelings?

Diogenes

Ancient Greek philosopher

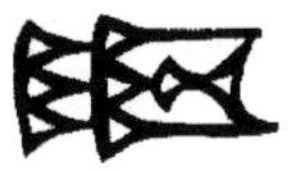

Chapter Thirty Three

The man on screen was little more than a background silhouette.

"What do you mean your team is locked out of the grid?" Linus could sense the fury in his tone and guess the scowl that must have accompanied it.

"I've recruited a new technician. He is digging into it. He's good." Linus assured the silhouette. "I can only assume it's something to do with both the architect and the woman in the metaphysical shop.

"And what of the potential architect?" The silhouette inquired.

Again the darkness in the man's tone sent an anxious tension through Linus. He swallowed and steadied his breathing before responding.

"It seems he stepped outside the building before the pulse struck." He shook his head. "But, we know his equipment was destroyed. It will set his research back again. Gain us more time."

"None of the architects who came before have ever been able to get this close to controlling the core of the grid. We have not been able to control it ourselves." The silhouette paused. "Professor Atticus, you were put in the lead of this case because you are the best in your field and the most connected in your sector. If this is too much for you, we can make more substantial arrangements to put an end to this."

Linus considered the man's words carefully. Though he had set the pulse bomb on the house, resorting to the more obvious means of wholesale violence suggested by his superior did not thrill him. He preferred the appearance of accidents, vandalism or faulty equipment.

"I would rather not involve any other teams until I can be certain that architect's energy will not be compromised. I am certain he is the source now. He cannot be terminated, yet. We have to learn more from him." Linus confided.

"I agree our options for confrontation are limited with the incarnation of a potential Delphi conduit and an architect in such close proximity to one another; both in time and space." There was almost a hint of amusement in the silhouette's tone at this. "However, this could be a good sign that we are incredibly close to bringing up the grid."

"I agree." Linus relaxed his shoulders as the tone of the conversation seemed to be leaning more to the amicable.

"We will continue to allow you to maintain lead in your sector. Keep a close watch on the progression of their work. And Professor Atticus, check your locker in the university archive this afternoon."

At this the screen flickered and went dark.

Linus glanced at his wristwatch. Only past noon. If he hurried he would arrive at the university before evening classes started. He wouldn't need an excuse to linger in the archives too late.

Linus gathered his coat from the back of the chair and slipped from his office into the main floor of cubicles.

One of the assistants met him in the corridor.

Leaning in close, Linus informed the young man, "I'm heading back to the university for the evening. Unless something dire comes up, continue with the tracking and uploads."

"Of course." The man gave a curt nod, then paused. "Oh. Professor, did you want us to continue to trace and confirm the whereabouts and identity of the Pythia?"

Linus shrugged his jacket onto his shoulders as he eyed the young man. "Potential Pythia." He hesitated. "Yes, I think so. But, keep that information in our sector only. Until we can be certain of course. We wouldn't want the whole organization excited if it turns out to be nothing."

"Right." The young man smiled. "There've been enough wild goose chases over the decades."

Linus offered a short laugh. He took his leave of the man and made for the elevators.

Wave7 had indeed seen many potential oracles come and go over the years. Linus sighed as he walked, recalling the research by the United States military. Some files were nearly a century old, more recently buried in nonsense about alien technology, and CIA MK-Ultra research. But he was fully aware Wave7 operatives had been testing psychics, primarily twins, as potential Delphi entities.

The woman in the occult shop didn't have a twin though. As far as Linus could tell Hannah was an only child. It would make little sense if the woman was this century's Pythia, but her energy had stood Linus's hair on end the first time he so much as glimpsed the storefront.

Linus continued to wander in his thoughts as he rode the train to the university.

He fumbled with the ring of keys tucked in his pocket as the stop closest to the university was announced over a crackling speaker system. Linus wondered how the transit system had managed to bypass the automated broadcast system within the trains and allow the engineer to make announcements over the train car speakers. As he stepped onto the platform his wonder at the communications systems merged with concern over where the city had found enough human drivers to man the trains. Certainly technicians used manual overrides for repairs, but how many had been available for a sudden full time work day?

Concern etched Linus's face as the strain of the shutdown weighed his thoughts.

"It's a necessary evil." He mumbled as the train pulled away.

Keeping the grid safe from widespread knowledge had been the purpose of Wave7 since the first discoveries. Linus shook his head as he entered the campus and descended into the basement level library entrance. The archives behind the main library housed files from as far back as the nineteenth century. Then, of course, everything had been hard copy documents due to lack of technology. Now, it was a required form of secrecy. Privacy and technology had been enemies since the mid twentieth century.

Linus often wondered if this was a manifestation of Padua's adventures of Lovelace and Babbage, bringing their Analytical Engine to life. Or perhaps it became clear only after the confirmation from the discoveries in Egypt less than a decade later.

As he strode down the dim corridor past a series of darkened vacant rooms Linus glanced back down the hallway to be certain no one had followed. The campus was enormous and the lower level spaces were seldom used since the turn of the century. But it was still wise to remain cautious. At the farthest end of the passage Linus coughed as he opened the door to the Wave7 archives. Secrecy and steady custodial maintenance rarely went hand in hand. Linus was almost certain his hands were the last to have disturbed the thin film of dust gathered on the door frame.

"Though perhaps not." He mumbled as he flipped the switch on the wall beside the door.

A manilla envelope sat on the center of the counter at the far end of the room.

Linus closed the door to the archive, which from the inside was clear to be made of much sterner stuff than institutional building materials. He passed the shatterproof glass cases lined with neat shelves of books and archive boxes and tossed the keys on the research counter.

As he drew open one of the metal drawers, he pulled a pair of gloves from the box and tugged them onto his hands.

The manilla envelope bulged from the contents within. Linus unwound the red string and opened the flap of the envelope. He slipped the contents gingerly onto the table.

At first glance, Linus was uncertain what he was looking at. The dull pages had no cover though a series of grey green threads bound one edge. The title page was missing as well, leaving Linus to stare at the jumble of images and figures scrawled on the first page.

"The drawings look Voynich." He pondered aloud as he leafed through the opening chapter. "But these figures almost read like programming code. COBOL or assembler code-like, maybe?"

Linus flicked an overhead lamp on as he continued to study the volume. In frustration he shook the envelope. A single slip of paper floated free.

Linus read the single line of hand written text, "Latest download from Paquimé. Enjoy."

He stood silently pondering the prehistoric archaeological site in the northern Mexican state of Chihuahua.

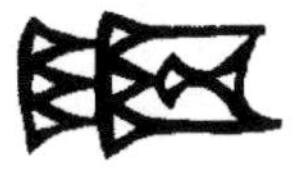

Chapter Thirty Four

Following the creation of the Earth, Wind, and Firewall, as Fred had taken to calling it, the pair worked to create a similar barrier within the confines of their ITower cubicles.

Evan focused intensely on his work, as he fought to avoid staring at calendars, Post-its, and various otherwise benign cubicle decor doubling as symbolic boundaries. This included the plethora of other meaningless wall hangings intended to obscure the strangeness of their cubicle adornment.

"Next thing you know we'll be setting up crop circles in the lobby." He grumbled.

A familiar voice pierced the earphones of his headset causing his head to jerk back. "We need to get you up to speed with your uncle and this Hannah chick." Linc's face appeared at the corner of the monitor.

"Man. You gotta give me some sort of warning before you do that." Evan leaned away from the keyboard.

"What motivates you these days?" Linc avoided Evan's concerns.

"Motivation." Evan snickered. "The usual, I suppose. Sex, money, food." Evan counted the vices on his fingers.

"You haven't changed at all, man." Linc sighed.

"At least I'm honest about my vices." Evan shrugged. "Hanging in that crazy shop with all those lights and brights makes me nauseous. No one can be that pure."

"They're at least trying." Linc quirked a half smile. "Better than your failing to hook up with a tech witch."

"What?" Evan shook his head and averted his attention to another monitor. "Yeah. Whatever. Also, I'm not sure she would be too keen on that nickname."

As Evan tapped at the keys, Linc surveyed his friend.

"Seriously. What do you think will happen if this works?"

"Works? I think we should be plotting to tear the whole deal down instead of open-source it." Evan scowled.

Evan continued to work through the project Fred laid on his shoulders.

"I mean, look at this." Evan tilted the monitor to face Linc, though he knew the man could see it regardless of the angle.

"Fred has me poking around on the Wave7 creeps, but meanwhile I can peer into more than the big data trail they left."

"And this is from my side of the Cloud." Linc confirmed.

"Yeah." Evan stared at the files open on the screen. "Past, present, and.... Wait a minute."

Evan straightened. His fingers flew across the keys. A renewed interest sparked his search.

"Future." Linc nodded. "Yep!"

"Yeah. But not theirs. Not yet," Evan whispered.

Linc watched with concern and curiosity as Evan typed into the search fields.

"I know he showed me game stats, Fred did. The other day. They were for the entire year." Evan's heart raced. "Think we can peek at next week's stocks?"

Linc was caught up in the excitement in Evan's voice. "Pish. Next week. How about until it completely crashes in…" Linc laughed, then paused. "No. I mean. Don't do anything too obvious."

"I knew it." Evan raised his hand to catch a virtual high five from his partner. He immediately dropped it back to the keyboard. "Right. Okay. So how do I do this?"

Worry crossed Linc's face.

"Well, Coach did say to light a fire under you though." He mumbled.

"Okay." Evan scowled at the screen, leaning in to study the data. "Now. How did the old man manage access."

"It's about your belief, dude." Linc shrugged. "If you believe it, you can see it."

Beyond the cubicle wall Fred focused his search on history concerning the grid. Eons of data and information poured across the screen.

His CloudMaster commands pulled information from the directory beyond the mortal realm, as his mind reeled from the knowledge at his fingertips.

At last, designs for the grid unfolded before him. Most of the languages were foreign to Fred as he focused on a spread of blueprints based on the great pyramids and pyramid-like structures.

It took Fred off guard as a roster of names on the blueprints seemed familiar.

"Are these all names of architects who built the grid?" Fred murmured to himself as he input one of the names that caught his attention into his Cloud search engine.

A moment passed before the results populated. Typical historical sites and information filled the page yet as Fred clicked, the connected lives spread like a family tree.

"Reincarnation. A string of past lives for this soul." Fred released a short laugh. "Right there in black and white."

As Fred read the flood of names one stood out.

"That's me." Fred clicked to stop the data from continuing to populate his screen. He sat expressionless, eyes wide, mouth agape. As he recovered, beginning to breathe normally again. He tilted his head and focused his gaze. "Wait. Who else?"

Curiosity drove Fred to type his nephew's name. He clicked search.

The lineage of Evan's soul stemmed out across the eons. Fred did a command-F search compared the list of architects who touched the grid in some fashion.

He was less shocked at the discovery at one of Evan's lives matching this list, though his excitement grew.

In his enthusiasm, Fred typed Linc's name.

"We were all there." Fred whispered as a command search found a match on Linc's list of lives as well.

As the magnitude of the situation settled, Fred considered the other players currently in this strange game.

Fred wracked his brain to recall Hannah's full name and typed it into the search box. To his surprise, the autofill assisted in rewriting her name.

"Pythia?" Fred's eyes grew in confusion.

As if on cue, Hannah's face blocked the site window.

"Fred!" The woman bubbled. Then seeing the man's expression she frowned. "What are you up to?"

"Your ears must be ringing. How did you know I was thinking about you?" Fred joked.

Hannah offered a sly smile and tapped at her temple. "I got the craziest sensation I needed to know what you were doing."

Her smile returned.

"Right. Of course." Fred leaned back in his chair. "Listen. I think I found something!"

"Enlighten me, oh geek of boundless knowledge." Hannah struck a yogi pose.

Fred relaxed and released a laugh.

"We have been on this grid project before." He explained. "All of us. You, me, Evan, even Linc. I was in the Akashic Records. I have seen the history of our past lives. Every alias our souls have used while incarnated." Fred breathed in the reality of his search.

"I might like some warning next time you go poking around my soul files," Hannah joked. "But, at least that explains why my head is spinning."

"I apologize. I had no idea." Fred's excitement ebbed as the realization of how powerful his connection had become. "Am I actually connecting with the souls I search?"

"It's possible." Hannah waved it off. "I'll be fine, but you might want to slow down. Others might not appreciate unsolicited hits to their akashic profile page."

Fred's face fell at the thought of causing a disturbance to the souls of real people.

"Hey," Hannah snapped her fingers. "You meant no harm. And, this is a good thing."

Fred perked up. "How so?"

"If we've done this before." Hannah clapped. "I'm sure we can tap some of that knowledge for this round."

"Yeah." Fred eyed the information laid out on his screen. "Evan was a big player. The translations seem to come up with, architect, or something similar. It's hard to be sure."

"Great. Don't tell him that." Hannah smirked at Evan's expense. "We don't need to boost that ego of his any higher."

Fred laughed at the truth of the statement. "The poor boy. Give him a bit of slack. Maybe I'll temper the information with news of less than extraordinary lives."

"Wait. You can see everything? About all of us? More than grid related experiences?" Hannah's brow furrowed. "Don't go probing into any unladylike histories of my past lives."

"What about the more manly ones?" Fred winked.

Hannah rolled her eyes. "If we release this to the world, I'll need a new career path."

"That may well be true." Fred nodded.

With a laugh and a promise to behave, Fred signed off.

As he considered how aware Hannah had been to his queries Fred opted to stick to his own past and that of his nephew.

My whole belief system is that our paths are drawn for us. I believe in reincarnation. I believe we're here to learn and grow. We choose how we come into this life based on what it is we have to learn. Some people have harder lessons than others.

Gillian Anderson

American actress; The X-Files

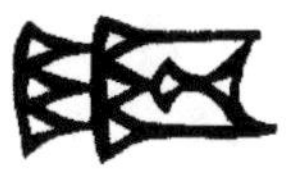

Chapter Thirty Five

Hannah's anxiety was not quelled by the conversation with Fred. To the contrary, her energy continued to feel chaotic as she sat on the edge of her bed and stared into the blank screen of her tablet.

"So." Coach suddenly appeared on screen, shaking Hannah from her struggle to find a moment of peace. "Have you tried a search into your past lives?"

"Well. I mean..." Hannah stammered. "Not exactly. I've had some inklings, and there have been a couple friends who offered readings. I've been busy. I live in the now." She settled on the explanation.

"What if the now depends on the then?" Coach persisted.

Hannah eyed the screen. Unprompted, Fred's CloudMaster search engine activated. As the cursor moved across the screen, the letters D-E-L-P-H-I appeared in the search bar.

Hannah's hand hovered the *enter* key.

"What are you waiting for?" Coach's voice beckoned.

"For the computer to catch up with me." She clicked the icon.

As the data filled the screen Hannah felt an energy pulling her soul toward the screen. She had experienced trance states before, but this was much stronger. The technology in front of her was only a tool, a connection between her and another time and place.

We don't know a millionth of one percent about anything.

Thomas A. Edison

American inventor

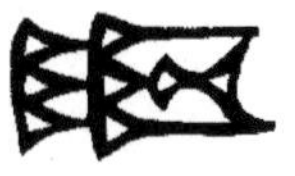

Chapter Thirty Six

Before her, the vision of a parade of young women formed in silhouette. She sensed they were more than women of noble rank--these were venerated goddesses in human flesh. Some part of her soul beckoned her to avert her eyes as they moved past in a procession of glamour and silks. Their faces shrouded. Bodies wrapped in fabrics that whispered as they walked.

The Oracles of Delphi. Hannah allowed the thought to form in her mind.

As a child, she had imagined the world of Oracles. She wondered what exotic lives they led in temples high above an ancient city. Ivory pillars, shrouded in clouds, as their Oracles were veiled in robes. She had wondered, until the dreams began.

"Tell no one." A young woman's voice filled Hannah's mind. "It is not what they say it is."

Hannah watched the girl's grey eyes shiver with tears. It had been a mistake. Hannah remembered the name Penelope from her last summer in the small town.

A father-like figure appeared and pulled Hannah from the grey-eyed Penelope.

A grim smile shifted through the man's dark beard. "You can write letters."

A mother's broad smile took the place of the grim man. "Your sister was chosen for a wonderful experience, an amazing life. We are all happy for her."

Even with the centuries and lifetimes between them, Hannah felt she understood a darker truth behind her former mother's smile. Families of Oracles were well cared for. Her family in this lifetime would want for nothing.

Hannah's mind flickered with visions.

She saw her sister, her Penelope, in dreams. She recalled shared experiences once attributed to her gifts and an overactive imagination.

Her visions of Penelope, ethereal rendezvous, begged her never to speak of her strange visions to anyone, including her mother and father.

She shared her experiences with Penelope, the only person she could trust. The two had been alike in so many ways, like twins. Gifted, blessed or cursed—with the sight of Oracles.

Through Penelope's eyes Hannah saw lives differently. This vision wanted to protect young Hannah from a dark fate. From being torn from family, friends, a normal life.

Then Penelope changed again. She was one of them, gossamer and silk, quiet smiles, and twisted messages. In that lifetime they changed her, but not the part who dreamed with Hannah; who was part of Hannah.

Hannah's previous incarnation had lost contact with her sister Penelope. They grew apart, as they both grew older.

Years passed in Hannah's vision. Delphi, the Oracles, and Hannah's understanding changed.

"If the Oracles can see into the future," Hannah's breath moved the mist surrounding her, "why didn't they know what would happen to them?"

The silhouette of Penelope shivered through pale purplish clouds as she responded. "If I knew that, do you think I would be here?"

Hannah reached out to part the curtain of clouds between them. "Maybe."

She was greeted with a frown as the veil lifted.

"That was unkind of me." Hannah bowed in apology. "But you don't know the waking like I do."

"I know." Penelope reached for Hannah's hand. "The wall that separates two parts of me is the answer."

Hannah sighed as she looked into the young woman's grey eyes. She embraced the phantom of her soul and walked through the dream space to the cottage that always appeared for her meditations. Flowers in the front yard shifted with the mist, their colors blurred like powder as she passed to the narrow wood door. Hannah was certain she could walk through the door, but it felt more appropriate to push open the portal and enter the room.

"Ten years and not a cobweb or a speck of dust." Penelope's smile was contagious.

"I wish I could do the same." Hannah set a small square table with a plate of grapes and cheese beside a pitcher of water.

Penelope poured a cup for each of them and unfolded the cloth from the basket of flat bread.

"Are you well?" Hannah tore a piece of bread.

"As can be expected." Penelope rested her hands in her lap.

"I need to talk to you." Hannah straightened in her chair.

Penelope nodded, her eyes losing some of their light. They were both familiar with how these visits had changed over the years.

"There's a thief in the walls of the forum. An elder." The mist shifted in response to Penelope's words. "He has come on hard times. He will resign. Let him plead his case."

Penelope's pale lips turned slightly. "The Oracles will convince those in power to offer a careful sum to keep the man silent and alleviate his need."

"I had a vision of war." Hannah gripped her hands around her cup of water.

"I need to hear you say it," Penelope's cool hand touched Hannah's fingers, "though I sense our visions have been a match this time."

"The destruction." Hannah closed her eyes to a lingering vision.

Penelope squeezed her fingers. "It's farther off than it seems, do not trouble your heart with this. We need to focus on the more pressing issues." Penelope's tone was firm.

"Yes." Hannah looked across the table. "If we can change things now, we might avert disaster."

"Nothing is set in stone." Penelope opened her hands.

The mists shifted away. Hannah felt a waking tingle at the back of her my head. She looked across the table at Penelope's fading form. The cottage faded, the mist rolled in.

Hannah shook her head, leaned over on her side on the bed and rolled onto her back. She sighed away the vision of Penelope as she began to snap out of her trance.

"Good morning, beautiful." Soft lips were warm against Hannah's cheek. "No nightmares this time?"

She rolled over, startled, not knowing if she was still in the vision or back in her apartment.

"And how is good Penelope?" The man leaned away and began to fade from Hannah's view.

Hannah lolled her head against a pillow of mist. The scent of a kitchen fire and olive oil filled the air as she made her way down a hall to a hearth. A young girl with curls skipped to a table with a plate of grapes as dark as her hair.

Hannah slid onto a wicker couch along the table. She leaned her head around to look out onto a patio. The man from the earlier vision was hunched by a small fire pit.

Breakfast carried on while the man spoke of the Agora and topics slated for discussion that day. Hannah's mind wandered to her conversation with Penelope.

"What's the matter?" The man's question drew her attention.

Chapter Thirty Seven

As Fred and Evan worked feverishly on their personal projects, neither considered the impact if they did manage to recreate the grid. For the first time in weeks both were so deeply immersed they failed to notice the time.

Late in the afternoon, a coworker knocked on the wall separating the pair of cubicles. "Hey there!"

Fred and Evan frantically closed the series of windows unrelated to jobs they were supposed to be working on.

"You missed lunch." the man smirked. "And, you're both requested in the boardroom."

The duo attempted to appear to be calmly working the GlobeNet crash concerns instead of the side searches which had stolen the better part of their day.

The man paused to send a dark glare in Evan's direction. "I hope you have something accomplished on the data side."

"Of course!" Fred waved the comment off as he pulled his jacket onto his shoulders.

"What was that all about?" Evan straightened his tie as he met his uncle in the walkway.

Fred fell into step beside his nephew. "Have you figured out what to tell them about security?"

Evan sighed. "What security? They nuked us."

"Yeah." Fred put a hand on Evan's shoulder. "They know that. But, how do we cover it in professional lingo?"

Both Evan and Fred were sweating in the stark brightness of the boardroom. The pair eyed the suits seated around the large glossy table, which itself was once a massive shared touch screen. The war-room like table was now just another relic of past days when the world was connected.

Eyes stared back at them without the distraction of technology.

Fred's chair shrieked as he drew it out from the table.

"Might wanna get that fixed." He pointed at the offending wheel.

Silence swallowed the humor in the old man's words.

Evan claimed the moment to slide into his seat and appear as controlled as possible.

"Gentlemen." Evan recognized the chief of information security. "Please. We require an update. What can you tell us?"

The man's tone was far more subservient than either of the men had expected. Desperation, rather than power lingered in the eyes that awaited a response.

Evan took the opening to cut through the 'typical bullshit' of the meeting. "You mean besides having our house and equipment blasted? And it taking your security boys how long now to reach out to us?"

Fred's face was the only shocked expression in the room as Evan's eyes narrowed on the sea of stoic faces.

A gentle hand rested on Evan's arm, startling him from his moment of righteous ire.

"Yes." Fred breathed before adding. "That was sort of a setback." He paused to feel the energy of the room. "We found another place, but it's been a bit hectic."

With a nudge, Evan halted his uncle. "It was a major setback. Having an offsite location is critical for certain activities. We cannot trust who might acquire access inside ITower facilities. Our current setup is temporary. We do need to find a new location. We are putting in eighteen to twenty hour days and an off-site location with accommodations is absolutely necessary. Maybe the company can help out with that."

"ITower offers condolences concerning the damage to your personal property, Fred." The regional lead acknowledged with a bow of his head.

"But these things happen." A new voice cut through the empathy. "And, it appears the insurance company considers the event an accident. Something due to faulty wiring."

The man at the far end of the table leveled his gaze with Evan.

Fred and Evan adjusted their posture as they turned their attention to the man seated at the far end of the table. "We appreciate your continued diligence and confidentiality," the dour man continued. "Longer hours of access to the office would perhaps help."

The tone of the man's voice did not denote a question.

"We are spending more hours here than there already, but if ITower finds that to be a viable solution, then so be it." Evan recognized a military man, and this one had rank.

"As noted," Fred leveled with the man at the end of the table. "We have a new location and are efficiently utilizing it in our off-site work. There may be prying eyes inside the facility, so it's important to have a secluded alternative."

Evan's expression betrayed his uncertainty at revealing the location Fred spoke of. The quirked brow of the man with the dark eyes and darker aura only served to raise Evan's paranoia.

Evan diverted attention from their quarters to the technical issues. "We've made progress on blocking both Wave7 and the public from selected portions of the Cloud." Evan added.

"We're still not sure how anyone was able to modify the data in the Cloud." Fred took the hint from their reaction and ran with it. "As long as we can block it, maybe it's enough for now… until we regain full control"

The regional lead seemed pleased with this information. "Is there a way to set this security system in place here in the offices to give our people access while still protecting the data?" He pressed. "We need to protect our data wherever possible."

It was Fred's turn to command the conversation. "Well, it's still in testing stages. I'm not sure if staff will be comfortable working within the new security measures."

Evan allowed his face to betray the inside jest. "Yes, I agree. They might be a bit put off by the methods to get access. We need to work on it more."

The regional lead flashed a brief glance at the man at the end of the table. "Of course. As long as it's working." He cleared his throat. "We'll deal with the comfort of the others."

The man at the end spoke again. "My apologies gentlemen, but exactly how is it you are connecting into networks at all if you are not in a major controlled complex?"

Evan watched as the man folded his hands and leaned into the table.

"We're dealing with systems and organizations not necessarily compatible with the business world. We both have concerns about the nature and security of our location, as well as our personal safety. We're not convinced the explosion at Fred's house was an electrical short." Evan shifted his posture to match the man who had become his verbal opponent. "However, it is better for all if this information remains need-to-know."

Fred offered a vigorous nod at his nephew's command of the situation. "Yes. Plausible deniability. We'll fill you in when the time is right."

Taking the opening offered by Fred, Evan continued. "Please be assured the data and connections are safe where and with whom we are working. Though any aid in locating a more permanent and secure housing situation would be welcome."

The room was silent.

Evan smiled down the table at the man. "Keeping our work separate from the bulk of the staff and ITower buildings is best for everyone for the time being."

The man at the head of the table had begun to redden. "We would not want the Feds or anyone getting curious and poking around the office. ITower's contractual control of the Infostrada could be at stake."

"Exactly! Better to keep us remote as needed." Fred agreed.

"Fine." The adversary at the end of the table frowned. "How long are we going to wait? The clock is ticking, gentlemen. What do you have to show us?" He seized command again.

Evan allowed only the most minor of stammers escape his composure. "We're still dealing with loss from the destruction of our work, but I assure you, I'm closing in on the perpetrators. But I have to maintain distance so as not to set off alarms. We can't afford another incident." He dared a bold maneuver. "Though, maybe it would be wise to leverage the Feds. Fred and I could use the additional protection. I can assure you it was not faulty wiring."

Fred followed Evan's lead. "We would have something to show much sooner if had the additional man power of government security teams."

It was exactly as the pair hoped.

The regional lead was sweating. His eyes darted from the duo to the man at the end who responded, "No. No. Let's not be hasty. You take all the time you need to make this right. We don't want to let the cat out of the bag and have federal agencies breathing down our necks."

Evan let a smile slip as he shot a glance at the man.

Everyone in the boardroom was well aware of how long it had taken ITower to be off the government leash. None of them would be eager to have the shackles of regulations strapped on again.

"Very well." Fred claimed the moment of stillness in the room to rise from his seat.

The wheel shrieked again. This time Fred smiled. He gestured for Evan to follow him from the room.

"If there is nothing more. Gentlemen, ladies. We will take our leave. Lots of work to do."

The pair backed for the exit with a wave and smile.

Fred allowed the door to latch behind them before raising his eyes to Evan. They hurried further down the hallway before breathing a sigh of relief.

"That wasn't so bad," Fred quipped.

Daggers shot from his nephew's eyes. "Old man."

"Well. Your little tip about government involvement bought us some time at any rate." Fred wagged his brows at the younger man.

"Except the Feds were sitting in the room." Evan stabbed the air back toward the boardroom.

Fred's eyes grew wide. "No."

"Yeah." Evan swung into his cubicle.

"The suit with the crewcut?" Fred considered.

"He gave off some serious G-man vibes." Evan nodded. "Unless he's connected to something worse."

He dropped into his chair and keyed his login passwords while Fred hovered at his back. He took a moment to grin at the escalating stocks on the screen before he realized Fred still eyed the screen over his shoulder.

He spun his chair to obscure the monitor. "What have you been working on, anyway?"

Fred scratched the back of his neck. "Uh, yeah, it's as I told the board. I've been working on locking down the Cloud. I mean, making Hannah's magic a little less magic looking. More Gartner Quadrant, less Gardner Quarters."

Evan rolled his eyes at the play on words.

Fred shifted to peer around his nephew. "And what about you?"

Evan knit his fingers behind his head. "Protecting our futures, Uncle." He winked.

Fred shrugged as he thought back on the information he discovered earlier about Evan. "Yeah, kid, don't get too much of a hero complex."

"Aye aye, sir." Evan offered a mock salute.

Fred scoffed and pivoted from the cubicle.

Evan turned his attention to the computer screen, a smirk spread across his face.

Before his eyes the stock market ebbed and flowed over a series of months. Evan considered what might be visible to the watchdogs on the ITower server. He was clearly on Fred's Cloud connection, but how much leaked between the two was still a mystery.

He rose from his desk and peered into his uncle's cubicle. "Hey. Fred. I think I'm going to go over to Hannah's to work for a little while. That meeting sort of rattled me. I need some space from the suits."

Evan was met with a wry smile from his uncle. "Sure. Rattled by the suits. That's why you want to spend more time at Hannah's."

"Don't get any ideas, old man." Evan scowled.

"Me. Ideas? Never." Fred waved Evan off with a wink before he continued his work on the Cloud-to-Cloud program.

Chapter Thirty Eight

The bells clattered against the door as Evan breezed through the front of the Connections store. He continued up to the office on the second floor. He offered no more than a curt wave to Hannah as she stared at the screen in her office.

He slid into the wheeled chair, a cocky grin across his face as he waited for the machine to boot.

He was less than shocked when Linc appeared on screen. "Glad to see we've found the key to your motivation."

"Absolutely." Evan dragged the chat window to the corner of the screen. "This is going to be amazing."

"Come on." Linc expanded the chat box to fill the screen, blocking Evan's view. "Isn't there anything else that gets you going?"

Evan grumbled as he flipped on the second monitor and shifted his stock views from behind Linc's window to the new screen.

"Come on." Linc's face filled the second screen.

Evan sighed. He shifted to gaze to the room behind him. "Maybe, there's one other thing."

"Always the hound," Linc taunted.

"Are you going to let me see these stocks or are we going to delve into how you're still jealous I always got the girl?" Evan pushed away from the desk.

"How about we see if you can still get the girl." Linc winked as the screen flickered off.

"Fine. Challenge accepted. Maybe I can convince her to put some tech version of a salt circle around my workstation to keep you out." Evan sneered bemused at the blank screen.

He scooted his chair across the floor and peered into the room where Hannah had been seated when he first came home.

The little office was dark and empty, though her tablet still glowed from the desk. With a shrug Evan rose from his chair and descended to the main floor of the shop.

Glancing around the beaded curtain separating storage area from shop front Evan scanned the display area for some sign of Hannah.

He spotted the young woman bent behind the counter. Her black yoga pants hugged her hips as she troubled herself with a tray of gems within the glass case. She seemed to be checking each one as she held it a moment before setting it back into the tray and moved to another next to it.

Evan eyed her as she worked. He had little interest in the brick-a-brack and stones as he watched the loose sweater slip from Hannah's shoulder.

"Target acquired," he murmured.

A sly smirk spread across his face.

Evan straightened suddenly as Hannah pivoted to face him.

"Did you say something?" Her eyes were at once wild and filled with exhaustion.

A sudden heat rose to Evan's cheeks. He was taken aback by the sudden frenetic energy of the typically demure young woman.

"Yeah," he stammered. "Wow. Are you feeling okay?"

Hannah caught sight of her reflection in the glass case. She combed her fingers through her hair and straightened her sweater on her arms in an attempt to tame her disheveled appearance.

"I'm. Fine." She flashed a crooked smile at Evan. "It's been a busy morning."

Evan glanced around the empty store. "Right…."

"Restocking." Hannah waved at the stones. "Heavy boxes. Lots of counting."

Evan shook his head as Hannah continued to flounder through excuses for her stranger than normal behavior. "Anyway. You wanna grab something to eat?"

A grin brought dimples to Hannah's cheeks. "Sure." She slid the case closed. "You buying?"

As Hannah closed the space between them, Evan felt a surge unlike he had experienced when approaching a conquest.

"Of course!" He squelched a stammer. "I can behave like a proper gentleman."

Hannah let her brow to raise at the statement. She closed the space between herself and Evan. Her gaze locked with his. "I think your definition of that term has a different meaning."

Evan searched the woman's eyes for signs she knew more than he was comfortable with. "I."

"Think your future is looking pretty good?" Hannah hooked her arm through Evan's to guide them both toward the front door.

Unperturbed, Evan pushed the door open for them to pass through. "Let's work on the next hour. What does the future say about dinner?"

Hannah rolled her eyes at Evan's mocking tone, but played along. She set her fingers to her temples. "I'm seeing something round--a donut, no, pizza. Yes, it is all clear to me. Pizza with meatball and pineapple."

"I am thinking maybe not so much on the pineapple." Evan squirmed.

"Well, the future is never a certainty." Hannah laughed.

The pair ambled the block down the street to the nearest pizza place.

Evan ordered as Hannah claimed a table near the windows.

She took a moment to gaze around the space. It was off hour, yet a few tables hosted guests. The low tones of music could be heard. CDs, or possibly radio, Hannah assumed as she tried to pick out the song.

Evan lowered himself into the seat across from Hannah.

"Not much different at this level." Evan mused as he followed Hannah's gaze around the dining area.

"Raise your own energy a smidge and you might feel differently." Hannah sighed.

Her focus fell on a group of four young people in a far corner table.

Two were chatting, one held a book, the other fidgeted restlessly, his eyes ever scanning the walls of the room.

"You see." She tipped her head in the direction of the young man.

Evan shifted in his seat to look. "Bunch of kids."

Hannah continued to watch the fidgeting boy.

"He's a bit on edge." Evan shrugged.

"He senses the need for the new connection." Hannah observed.

"He is probably feening for a social media fix or a video game." Evan snickered.

Hannah turned a glare on Evan.

"What!" Evan threw his hands up. "You want every moment in life to be some sort of magical experience. It's not." Evan jabbed a thumb at the kids at the table. "These kids have never been without a connection. Hell, for that matter, neither have we."

Hannah conceded to listen to Evan's perspective.

"Come on." Evan leaned on his arms. "I mean, how old are you? Twenty-two, twenty-five?"

"Thirty, as of last Thursday." Hannah crossed her arms. "What of it?"

"Wow." Evan paused his narrative to take in the full appearance of the woman across from him. "Well, an older woman then."

Evan smirked. Hannah's impending retort was interrupted by the arrival of their pizza.

"Seriously though," Evan offered the first slice to Hannah, before taking one for himself, "When did you first log into a screen?"

Hannah's expression fell for a breath of a moment.

"I don't remember. I was three. Maybe?" She took a bite of her pizza.

"And I'm sure you were introduced to technology pretty much in the crib. "We all were. Even my crazy mother was a techie in her way."

"I've never heard you mention your mother." Hannah smiled. "Was she that bad?"

"Is." Evan corrected. "But, nah. She's a good mom. She's just-" Evan cut himself off as he realized how he was about to describe his mother.

"She's like me isn't she." Hannah guessed. "Is that what you meant by crazy?"

"Shit." Evan tried to back out of the pit he had begun to dig. "I guess crazy's not quite the word for it. But, yeah. She would dig your store."

Hannah stifled a laugh behind a napkin.

"In fact, Fred was always the grounded one." Evan explained. "After that episode on the train though…."

Evan trailed off.

"People often come back changed after an NDE." Hannah's hand covered Evan's.

As their eyes met Hannah drew her hand back. She swallowed and averted her attention to the kids at the far table again. With a sigh Evan followed her gaze.

"Every generation since the dark ages has sought connection," Hannah shifted the conversation as she slid another slice of pizza onto her plate.

She twirled the strands of cheese still connected to the pie until they broke free.

Evan mumbled a muffled, "What?" around a bite of pizza.

Hannah passed him a napkin as she set down her slice.

"Real connection." She clarified. "To that bigger data Cloud." She directed her eyes to the ceiling before taking another bite.

"And what do you think people would do if they had a *real* connection?" Evan added air quotes as he questioned the woman.

"For some, little would change. They would go on as if all was normal, but with a greater sense of understanding and purpose." She leveled her gaze. "Others. Well, they would do what you have been up to."

"What is that supposed to mean?" Evan's brows creased.

"And that." Hannah circled Evan's face in the air. "Confirmed it. I don't need metaphysical tools to see you're acting like one. I know what you've been up to. It is not all about making money and shaking down the system." Hannah finished her slice of pizza and moved for a third.

"You cut right to the chase. What happened to peace, love, and kindness?" Evan snagged another slice and flopped it onto his plate.

"Being a lightworker is not about being a nice guy. Though, some of the Sedona types are pretty fluffy. It's about honesty, and seeing past false faces walking around." She tore a bite from her pizza.

"How did you know my mom lived in Sedona?" Evan's shoulders dropped.

Ignoring his question, Hannah sighed. "I don't know what would happen if everyone had access. I've never known otherwise."

She seemed at once lost and sullen. Evan struggled to keep up with the roller coaster of emotions and energy emanating from the woman.

"Why not check one of your broken phones or crazy cards for the answer," Evan mused.

Hannah set her pizza onto the plate. "Is this all a game to you?"

"No." Evan's face showed he was treading volatile ground. "I mean..." He fought with his thoughts, as he gazed across the table. "It's all a lot to take in. Humor is my coping mechanism. And, I'm still not completely sure I believe the same way you and Fred do."

"What about Linc?" Hannah frowned. "Does your connection to him mean nothing as evidence of how powerful this work is?"

Evan frowned. He'd been enjoying the conversations with his old friend. They looked like any other chat session to Evan. Yet, the reality of it was staring him in the face through a pair of beautiful eyes.

"Just remember, this is not a game, Evan." Hannah dropped a few dollars on the table as she rose to leave. "I have to get back to the shop."

Evan stared after the woman, dumbfounded by her sudden exit, yet he remained in his seat. He beckoned the waiter to the table to pay for the pizza and order a beer.

The entire date, if it could be called that, had gone entirely opposite from what Evan anticipated. Over his beer he reviewed the conversation. He eyed the group of kids as they too exited to the street.

They seemed like typical kids. As they crossed in front of the window, the one Hannah pointed out suddenly stopped. He turned his gaze directly on Evan.

The interaction lasted the span of a breath, yet it left Evan feeling exposed.

He finished off the beer, pulled his card from his wallet, then replaced it as the state of things settled on him anew. He didn't want to wait the time it took to process a manual credit card charge. He drew out a crumpled wad of cash and dropped it on the table.

The walk back to the store was a fog. He opted to enter through the rear of the building.

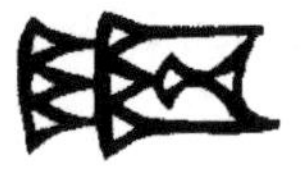

Chapter Thirty Nine

The moment Evan dropped into his office chair, Linc appeared on screen.

"Well. It didn't go so well, did it?"

"I think I need a new angle," Evan grumbled.

Linc laughed. "Man, you have never been good with real women. It's not about money. It's not about cars. It's more than that. It's about the connection. Trust me. Don't blow this one."

"Connection." Evan collapsed into his chair. "That damned word is turning into a curse."

An alert on Evan's screen interrupted before Linc could continue.

Evan snapped out of his funk to check the stock screens. "Romance or not, connection is certainly offering a lot in the money department."

He smiled as the summary page of his stock portfolio displayed large green positive numbers down the net return column. Since his new-found ability to query the future, he had made a lot of money in the stock market on simple one day buy and dumps. Using ITower's access to the temporary emergency global network for financial services was a fortunate enabler for Evan's profiteering.

Yet as Evan flipped through the stock links and investment pages his screens flickered again with an emergency weather alert.

"What is this nonsense now?" Evan read the screen.

> ***Warning: China Coast Hit by Massive Tsunami from Undersea Earthquake.***

He continued to read the article from the *next* week where he found the connection to his stock alerts.

> ***Company Stocks Plummeting.***

Evan popped tabs open as fast as his fingers could fly. "Damn, I can make millions, tens of millions on this catastrophe. I just have to short as many of these stocks as I can."

As simple as the broker's temporary website was during the tech crisis, Evan began to setup stock shorting orders on the tumbling companies listed in the news bulletin. Flipping rapidly between screens, he suddenly stopped.

His eyes narrowed on the screen as he quietly said to himself, "When exactly did this tsunami happen.. uh.. when *will* this happen?"

He clicked furiously on the news bulletins.

9:18AM Taizhou, China on the East China Sea.

"It is happening today. Where the hell is Taizhou? And what time is that here?" More rapid clicking on the keyboard. "OK, on the coastline South of Shanghai; North of Taiwan." Clicking continues. "1:18AM GMT… ok, ok, what time ... 5:18pm here. Damn, that's less than three hours from now.

"What is it?" Linc queried, though his tone hosted more knowing than just curiosity.

Ignoring him, "Some company page," Evan's eyes narrowed. "It's a memorial. Casualty count. Shit. That's a big number for just one company. Damn, here's another article from next week. Oh, man, that's a lot of people getting crushed, drowned or washed out to sea. More than 384 thousand people."

"In disasters like this, it's not just money that's lost." Linc exhaled. "Money can always be made again, later."

Evan continued to scroll the death tolls. He clicked to another page. More articles and photos of devastation assaulted his eyes. Evans face contorted.

"Where is the epicenter of the undersea earthquake? How many miles offshore? How fast does a tsunami move? Dammit, I need more time. People have to get off the coast"

"Oh. You do have a heart in there somewhere," Linc responded with a smirk.

Evan continued to ignore Linc's comments. "It hasn't happened yet. The earthquake is… 174 minutes from now." More rapid clicking. "The epicenter is 105 miles offshore... tsunami traveling almost 500 miles per hour. These people are lucky if they get ten minutes notice, even if they knew exactly when the earthquake happened. There won't be time for people to get inland. That's why the casualties are so high."

He looked puzzled as he scanned the room. His face turned from scorn to gritty determination as his eyes flicked in search of a plan.

"This global network doesn't work for shit, dammit. There has to be a way to warn people."

Turning back to his keyboard he searched for contact methods and emergency addresses and sites to Chinese national, regional and also international emergency service agencies. He pulled up lists of hundreds of large companies located in the impacted coastal areas. After collecting lists of contact points, methods and emergency network electronic addresses, Evan glanced at the time. He lost over fifteen precious minutes just gathering basic information. There was hardly two and a half hours until impact.

He rocked back and forth in his chair as if posturing. "All of these corporate security offices and news agencies subscribe to just a handful of international weather and crisis organizations. If I can get these orgs to send out alerts on what is about to happen, people will get evacuated from the coastal areas." He sat back. "That will never happen. They will think I am nuts and demand proof."

Evan pulled his chair back up and began hacking the global emergency broadcasting systems after mumbling, "Thankfully their defenses are down. They're lucky to have any connection at all to this flimsy temporary governmental infrastructure."

Adrenaline and military cyber hacking experience kicked-in. His fingers flailed across the keys intermixed with mad swipes at the touchscreen. He hacked into the China Earthquake Administration warning system admin account.

"Dammit. It's all in Chinese. I can't do a thing, here." He looked down his list and proceeded to hack into the International Tsunami Warning Commission of the United Nations. After gaining full control of the emergency notification admin account he typed out a global message recalling the information he pulled from his search of next week's news articles.

> ***2324 GMT: EARTHQUAKE-TSUNAMI EMERGENCY; East China Sea - At 2318 GMT an 8.7 magnitude undersea earthquake occurred 105 nautical miles off the coast of Taizhou China. A series of extremely dangerous tsunamis are enroute to the central China coast. All personnel in coastal***

areas of the East China Sea are urged to evacuate coastal areas immediately for at least four hours following this notice.

Evan leaned back as he proof-read the alert bulletin. "That should give them two hours notice and two hours after the tsunami hits." He pressed the enter key. "Now for the other sites."

He sequentially hacked into both the International Geological Survey Bureau and the International Oceanographic Service. After sending the same notice through both of their international alert systems, he sat back in his chair, let out a huge sigh and smiled.

"I can't stop a tsunami, but I can move people."

Linc grinned and clapped his hands in a slow mocking congratulatory gesture. Evan glanced at his ghostly friend. "No cheers, yet, Casper. The proof is in the pudding."

Now that the alert messages had been sent, he pulled up Fred's cloud search engine and entered the same searches for future headlines. The responses popped back on his screen.

> ***Massive earthquake and tsunami hits central coast of China. Billions of dollars of damage occurred while miraculously only 137 lives were lost. A mysterious hacker known only has NetNostradams is attributed for saving potentially hundreds of thousands of lives. According to sources, this modern day Batman sent a fake, yet totally accurate emergency notification to major world agencies two hours before the actual catastrophe. This action enabled local authorities to evacuate the coastal areas. International authorities are investigating.***

Shock and relief washed over him as data changed almost before his eyes. His heart rate lowered as did the number of lives lost.

"What have I done?" Evan stared at the screen.

"Saved lives," Linc replied. "It's something you have a lot of practice at."

"Man, I changed the future." Evan whispered as the essence of power washed over him.

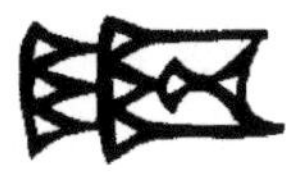

Chapter Forty

Linus paused at a storefront to watch the latest news on an array of televisions displayed in a sidewalk storefront window.

The reporter rambled in practiced tones: "Breaking news. More updates on the mysterious NetNostradamus. In the past few hours the unknown hacker broke into several international weather and crisis organizations in order to send several emergency alert notifications concerning a potential earthquake and tsunami predicted to hit coastlines in the East China Sea. Notifications were sent to tens of thousands of local organizations who immediately activated emergency evacuations. Hours after the initial organizations still struggled to discover the source of the intrusion, an earthquake and tsunami struck exactly as the initial alert stated. Authoritative sources are stating the hacker, dubbed NetNostradamus, was precisely correct on location and magnitude of the earthquake hours before it occurred.

Linus's face contorted as he considered the report. "NetNostradamus?"

He turned from the televisions and rushed along the street, eyes narrowed in contemplation.

Linus entered the GlobeNet command center. The facility had been vacant since the crash of GlobeNet. For ITower, it was too far from the centers of commerce to bother reconnecting to the core network.

He faced the elevator with eyes wide as he approached. The biometrics scanners emitted a pleasant ding as the green light flashed. The door opened. Despite global network instability his organization managed to use the technology at their disposal.

Gazing lazily around the carriage, he rode the several floors above the city.

The doors opened to the bustling command center. A handful of workers, some in jackets similar to Linus's, were seated at clusters of computers arrayed in front of a wall of screens. He glanced at one large screen on the left depicting yet another similarly arranged command centerspace with more, uniformed attendants.

Linus closed on the nearest worker. "You. Pull up the news station. All Channels." He waved his hand at the remaining screens on the front wall.

"Yessir." The worker keyed in names for local, national, and international news stations.

After a moment, the screens in front flickered and cascaded to the requested news sites.

"What do we know about this NetNostradamus?" Linus barked. "Anyone?"

His eyes narrowed as he scanned the silent room. Confused faces were on him, yet none offered an answer.

"I want information. Start the searches." Linus paced the room. "Is he one of us? Where did he log in from? How did he access global crisis center systems and push alerts out?" Linus pivoted on his heel to stare down the seated workers. "I thought we pulled in the best. You guys built GlobeNet. Now get control of it."

Linus turned his attention once more to the giant screen. "Someone is on *our* network. Find him. There shouldn't be any deviations from our directive."

Linus stormed through the side door into the adjoining conference room. He slammed the door, leaving the workers to their task.

He opened another screen on the wall of the room. At the center of the image, the shadowed figure appeared.

"Do you have an update from your sector?" The shadowed figure's voice was as obscured as his face.

"Our former GlobeNet techs have regained much of the previous access to the network again. No news on the damage that might remain from the lock out. They could have planted traps, honeypots, tracers. We just do not know yet."

"Are we keeping the other networks subdued?" The figure pressed.

"All other firewall blocking rules are functional. We are substantively in control," Linus assured the figure.

After a moment, he cleared his throat. "Though..." Linus struggled for the words. "There is a new concern. An individual the media is calling NetNostradamus."

"We are aware." The figure's tone darkened. "Is he one of your sector's agents or technicians?"

"I cannot confirm, but he must be someone on the inside." Linus swallowed. "I have no reason to suspect anyone in this sector. He may be a GlobeNet employee, or some ITower code monkey."

"Or the architect." The figure growled.

"I am aware of the possibility," Linus conceded. "At least we know its not the work of a civilian. Our firewalls would have kept them out. Though, if it is the architect, he seems to have a bit of a hero complex."

The shadowed figure remained silent.

Linus took this as permission to continue. "He accessed the networks capable of traversing time. We've seen this phenomena, too, and are trying to stabilize it. This hero used the information to pre-warn of this tsunami disaster and save lives. He could have easily used this information for personal gains."

"Is this your way of speaking on behalf of this hacker and against the directives of our organization?"

"Not at all," Linus assured the shadow. Though to some degree he struggled to assure himself. "I have always been loyal to our research and the goals of our predecessors."

"Considering how much Wave7 has funded your research and how much knowledge we have conveyed to you, your loyalty should be unwavering." the shadow intoned.

"Of course." Linus nodded.

A secondary window popped open in the corner of the screen. One of the former GlobeNet techs seated in the other room appeared onscreen.

"Sir. My apologies for the interruption," the young woman stammered. "You need to see this. It's about the NetNostradamus."

The window closed as she concluded her transmission, leaving the silhouette to command the screen once again.

"Go, go." the silhouette dismissed Linus. "We want updates as soon as you have anything of substance."

Linus nodded and remained in the office a moment more as the silhouette signed off. He rushed to the main floor of the command center once the anxiety from the encounter ebbed. He was met by the young tech, tablet in hand.

"We traced the IP address, sir," she informed him. "It's a location here in the city."

Linus snatched the tablet from her hand. "How close?" He scowled as he zoomed in on the pinpoint on the map.

"She is close. The address led us here."

The name "Conscious Connections" appeared on the blue flag beside the pinpoint.

He shoved the device back into the woman's hands. "She? Search the Cloud. Find out everything you can."

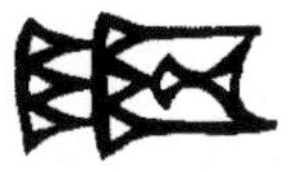

Chapter Forty One

Hannah busied with breakfast. She was growing accustomed to roommates, though for the most part they met in passing. She arranged a bottle of milk, container of juice, and plate of hard boiled eggs on the table and set a short stack of bowls on the counter beside a box of cereal. Before taking her seat, she snagged a bowl of fruit and flipped the coffee maker on.

Evan swept into the room, tablet in hand. "Did you see what happened?"

Hannah accepted the tablet and peered at the screen. Allowing for the lag as the device passed between their energies.

She read the headline. "Tsunami Strike Lands with Few Casualties."

Evan pointed at the next line in the article.

Hannah continued. "NetNostradamus? Rogue Wave7 tech terrorist." She quirked an eyebrow at Evan. "He must be well connected to arrange something like this."

"Seriously connected." Evan winked. "So, how many lives did your psychic powers save last night?" He snickered.

Hannah frowned as her shoulders slumped.

Fred interrupted the exchange as he entered the kitchen. "Good morning, team!"

He made a beeline for the coffee pot. Filling his mug he glanced over his shoulder at the pair stoically seated at the table.

"Well. Okay then." He grunted.

Hannah leaned away from the table. "Do you want me to fall at your feet? Do you have any idea what you're doing? What about the butterfly effect? You're messing with the future."

"You're jealous." Evan's smug smile peeked over the edge of his coffee cup.

Fred glanced between the two to the tablet on the table.

"You've never used your powers to get results like this," Evan continued as he waved at the article. "Besides, you're the one who told me I should use my gifts to help others and shouldn't take advantage of the future."

"You think I'm jealous?" Hannah shoved away from the table. "You don't know how much damage you could have done. Have done. You don't know what you have affected. This is not some corporate challenge for top results and earnings."

Fred pulled the tablet towards him. He scanned the article as the pair continued to berate one another.

"Oh, I know what it affected. It affected my bank account. Do you know how much I lost by doing this?" He waved at the tablet. "Instead of letting those waves crash on people and the markets crash on investors."

"You didn't lose squat. That profit didn't even exist yet," Hannah pointed out.

Hannah sighed as she caught Fred's attention bounce between her and Evan as he struggled to keep track of the dialogue. At last he lifted the tablet and shifted his attention to Evan.

"Are you Nostradamus?"

Evan began to smile in affirmation.

"No, no need to answer. I know you are." Fred scowled.

The weight of the situation began to settle on the room. They sat sipping their coffee in silence.

"Did you use the Cloud search engine? Did you hack the crisis centers from here?" Fred set his coffee heavily on the table. "You realize the Feds, and ITower, can probably track it back here, even through the unstable networks and arcane log files. And what about Wave7? Do you think they're going to be pleased this is connected to them?"

"I saved people!" Evan cried out. "Shit. Does nothing make you two happy?"

In a soft, slow tone Hannah responded, "Those hundreds of thousands of people may have had their soul contracts and their life plans disrupted. They'll all have to be recalibrated."

Evan gaped. "What? Are you people crazy?" He stopped,, then swiped an egg and his cup of coffee from the table before storming from the room.

Fred and Hannah were left to stare after him.

"He'll catch up." Hannah sighed.

"He has to." Fred glanced at the tablet. "We can't do this without him."

"We never could, but he has to know this is serious." Hannah sipped her coffee. "He can't mess with our timeline to such a drastic degree."

We have it in our power to begin the world over again.

Thomas Paine

American philosopher, theorist and revolutionary

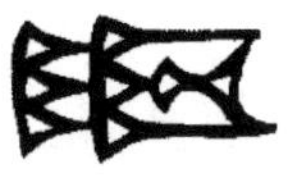

Chapter Forty Two

Later, Fred and Evan's continued discussion concerning the NetNostradamus drew Hannah from the front of the store. She lingered at the foot of the stairs.

"*Your* Cloud?" Evan scoffed. "I thought the entire point of this was to get the whole happy world connected. To share the great Cloud in the sky with the unenlightened."

Evan waved his arms as he rocked in his office chair.

"Yes." Fred sighed. "But it's not for personal gain, or stroking your ego, or to impress some girl." Fred waved a hand at the stairwell.

"Some girl?" Evan laughed.

"None of this impresses her!" Fred jabbed at the rising and falling stock data Evan left open on his computer. "She could connect to the global grid without any of this silicon garbage." Fred snatched up a tablet and let it slap onto the desk.

"Oh please!" Evan reeled in his chair. "Her magic cards, and woo-woo boards are not a guaranteed connection to anything besides her own psychosis. We both know that."

"Evan, be real. We never would have gotten this far without her, or her magic cards." Fred slapped the desk. "This connection is so much more ancient than you seem to understand in this lifetime!"

"The firewall idea." Evan acquiesced. "I will give Hannah points for that one."

"That's all?" Fred scowled. "Is this a bruised ego talking? Linc mentioned a lunch date that didn't pan out all that well."

"What? No!" Evan whirled his chair to face the keyboard.

Coach blinked onto the screen. "Evan. You know all about the grid. Even as closed off as you are in this life. If what you have seen doesn't convince you, what about the fact that Wave7 took enough interest in your work to wage an attack."

Hannah forced herself to walk up the stairs and into the static of the combined energy. "Maybe this is not the right lifetime for him to understand." she interjected.

Fred and Evan both whirled their chairs in Hannah's direction.

"What happened to your soul over the last few millennia may have damaged you in some way. Slowed your progress." Her voice was soft compared to the exchange between the men.

"Damaged soul. What are you talking about?" Evan tugged at his hair. "Look. I'm the only one who doesn't sound damaged. Talking about extra lives. Millenia of experiences." He turned on Fred. "You were always the sane one, Uncle. Now you sound like your sister."

"I confess, I haven't admitted how right your mother was about all of this. I had to die to find out." Fred released a short laugh.

Evan shook his head.

"Past lives, my boy." Fred continued. "Yes, you had many. We all did. And, more than one connects us to the grid. We are soulmates."

Evan gaped at his uncle. "Crazy is contagious. What are you talking about now?"

The tablet screen came to life on the table. Linc appeared, rounding out the team.

"I prefer the term soul pod. Mates sounds a bit too romance and candy hearts." Linc smiled.

"Oh, come on." Evan lifted the tablet.

"Try to remember." Linc pled with his friend.

Coach popped into the screen beside Linc. "If you will allow me, I think I can help you understand, Evan."

"What is this? An intervention?" Evan tossed the tablet at Fred.

Fred turned the tablet to face Evan.

"Here it comes." Coach prompted.

Evan waved off the warning as he pushed past Hannah toward the kitchen.

A wave of vertigo tipped Evan against the doorframe as he struggled to steady himself.

Fred rose from his chair, "Just relax a moment."

Concern marked Hannah's features, yet she hung back. The air buzzed with a familiar vibration, though one she had not felt with such strength in a long time.

"Okay." Evan put a hand to his head. "What was that?" He took a few uncertain steps. "I think. I need to get out of here."

He stumbled from the room in the direction of his sleeping space.

Fred moved to follow, but Hannah's hand stilled him.

"Wait until the download is finished," Hannah murmured. "It takes a lot out of a person, you know." Her gentle eyes shined on Fred.

"Yeah." Fred turned his attention to the tablet and Coach.

The entity offered a slow nod.

"I'm going back to the store." Hannah disappeared down the stairs.

Fred picked up his things. "I guess I'll head to the office. It should be about time for more updates, anyway."

Before Linc and Coach disappeared from the screen, Coach turned to Linc. "Updates and uploads. It will be an interesting few hours."

Evan collapsed onto the bed. The room seemed to tilt and float as he stared at the ceiling. His vision flashed to a screen deep within his mind.

A flurry of past-life images assaulted his senses, visually and physically. His body tumbled back through time.

My doctor told me to stop having intimate dinners for four. Unless there are three other people.

Orson Welles

American actor, director, writer and producer

Chapter Forty Three

Evan slammed onto the stool. The papers before him fluttered to the floor.

"να προσέχεις" <Na prosécheis>. The man beside Evan took up the scrolls and arranged them once more on the expansive marble table. Evan understood though he didn't know Greek.

Evan laid his palms on the table as he fought off the last of the vertigo. His head swam as he took in the rest of the room. Bright rays of sunlight illuminated the scrolls as the man arranged them neatly.

"Who are you?" The question fell from his lips as the realization struck him.

He scowled. "You were on the train!"

As the words struck the air Evan heard them change. He recognized what he had tried to say, but instead the sentence sounded foreign.

"What language is that?" He blurted.

"Which one, sir?" The man from the train narrowed his eyes.

Evan realized he looked nothing like when they first met. "These are our translations in Coptic. These are still in the demotic script."

Evan shifted his gaze to the scrolls. After a moment the meaning in the shapes and squiggles became clear to him. "I can read this?"

"Sir." The man from the train, who wasn't the man from the train, looked at Evan in concern. "Are you feeling well? Maybe we should stop for the afternoon."

"No." Evan smoothed the scroll closest to him. "No. I'm fine. Where were we?"

The man waited a moment more before responding to the question.

"Here." He pointed. "The glyphs here seem to be a measurement, but the number is nowhere near the dimensions of any pyramid-like structures on maps."

Evan analyzed the inscriptions indicated by the man who assumed to be his assistant.

"Unless there's an enormous stone structure hiding out there that we have yet to find?" The man shrugged at his own quip.

Evan failed to acknowledge the jest as he frowned at the numbers and symbols. "It's not size. It's the output." He murmured.

"Excuse me?" The assistant peered at Evan.

"These are ohms." Evan tapped at the scroll. "Or, I suppose, the ancient Egyptian derivative."

It was the assistant's turn to frown in confusion. "I'm sorry. Ohms? Output?"

Evan locked eyes with the man. "Energy. This is how much energy the power plant can produce. Where did you say you found these?"

The assistant stared another long moment at Evan. "The scrolls are from the temple priests. They are from the collection of Pharaoh Djoser. You took over the translations yourself."

"The pyramids were power plants?" Evan blurted the words without considering their bizarre nature.

When Evan at last glanced up from the scrolls the assistant was gone. Concern etched Evan's face. He realized he had been here before. He slid the scrolls aside and jostled a lamp with a reflective plate mounted to one side. His face peered back at him, though at first he didn't recognize it as his. The features were so different.

Evan staggered back from the table. He looked down at his hands, his legs. "What?"

The words caught in his throat. "Am I dreaming?"

"If that will help you understand what is happening, yes."

Evan recognized the voice, but it did not quell the shock as he turned to see Coach standing in an archway into the room.

"You're not in a screen?" Evan balked at the bearded man.

"And I'm not serving you a drink this time." Coach smiled.

He approached the table and shuffled absently through the scrolls. "It's amazing work you're doing this time around."

Evan continued to offer a blank stare in response.

"This is a vision, Evan. But, it's also quite real." Coach poked Evan in the shoulder to prove his point.

"The desert?" Evan's brow knit. "That was how long ago?"

Incomplete thoughts tumbled from Evan's mind.

"The city in the desert is later, though I suppose for the purposes of this conversation, it was before." Coach raised his shoulders. "Time is not as relevant as we make it out to be."

Evan put a hand to his head. "Yeah. I'm getting that."

"For the moment, we are here in this now so you can use the lessons you forgot." Coach waved to the table.

"Are you here? Like here, here?" Evan stared down at the scrolls.

"We experienced this time and place in a corporeal form, yes." Coach nodded. "You knew me as a teacher, then as a colleague."

"We worked on the Cloud project." Evan studied the papers.

"You called it by a different name then, but yes." Coach rested a hand on Evan's shoulder. "Study. All of your other questions will be answered once you finish the project."

At this, Coach patted Evan's shoulder and dismissed himself from the room.

Evan settled onto the stool beside the table. His mind whirled as he scanned the scrolls. The notes, his notes, slowly began to make sense.

"How long have I been here?" Evan searched the walls for a clock.

As he did so he caught a glimpse of his assistant before the young man disappeared around the frame of the door. Recognition flashed again. His thoughts wandered to the train and the man in the military coat.

Focus. It was Linc's voice this time that burrowed into his thoughts. *If you lose focus here you will snap back, and the ride will not be pleasant. Study. Remember what these plans look like.*

Electric communication will never be a substitute for the face of someone who with their soul encourages another person to be brave and true.

Charles Dickens

English writer and social critic

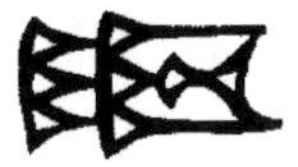

Chapter Forty Four

Linc and Coach stood before a misty screen as projected images played out on the surface. Coach turned his attention to a scene of Fred bustling down the street to catch the bus.

Coach quipped, "This is about to get interesting."

"He needs to take a car." Linc frowned as he appeared beside Coach.

"How is our boy doing?" Coach ignored the comment about Fred's use of public transit.

"Evan is getting a whole new perspective on the term *network*," Linc smirked.

Coach gave Linc a sidelong smile. "You didn't think it was fun the last time you learned that lesson."

Linc shrugged and returned his attention to Fred on the cross-town train.

"What is he doing there?" A look of concern flooded Linc's face.

"Uploads and downloads," Coach offered. "An interesting few hours indeed."

In the projection Fred settled into an open seat on the train. Force of habit had him draw his phone from his pocket. The screen was black once again.

"Nothing outside the circles." Fred murmured. "Nada. No connection."

He felt a sudden shift in the seat as another passenger settled beside him.

"Mine either," the man in the military jacket pointed at Fred's phone.

Recognition fell upon Fred's face.

"You." He tilted away from the man.

"Whoa. Easy." The man set his hand against the side of his face. "I'm still wary from the black eye our last encounter gifted me." The man peered around the nearly vacant train car. "I hold nothing against you and I hope the same is for you. It looks like your health much better. No sign of that nephew of yours?"

The man smirked. Fred squinted and positioned to flee to another part of the train.

Sensing Fred's dismay, the man offered his hand. "Let me start over. Linus Atticus."

Fred raised his hand in conciliation. "Fred."

"Come on, then. I am open to admitting the wrong foot was mine in our first meeting." Linus bared his teeth in a wide grin.

Nothing about Linus put Fred at ease. Even as their hands parted a sensation of connection remained.

"I'm a professor, as well as other things. Here, at the campus." Linus gestured at the passing university.

"I work in tech." Fred settled into his seat.

"Must be slow work at the moment." Linus laughed.

It was a cold, sharp sound that put Fred once more on edge.

"Yeah," was all he offered to the query.

"I'm more focused on the past than the future in my work," Linus carried on. "This outage has actually done wonders for my projects."

This new dimension to the conversation served to lower Fred's guard. "The past you say. History?"

"Yes and no." Linus offered. "I'm part of a group researching fringe understandings of historical monuments."

"Fringe?" Fred allowed the man to enlighten him.

It had thus far been a strange day, no reason to fight for normalcy now.

"I'm only the latest in many generations of work, but I think we are at last coming to a new connection within the studies." Linus relaxed in the seat. "I had attempted to go into greater detail upon our first meeting. But I guess that conversation took a wrong turn."

Fred struggled to recall what had been said on the train. It seemed like another lifetime ago, and in some respects, it was.

"My organization has been following your work for sometime and my sector estimated that our meeting should take place on that train ride." Linus pressed his lips together. "Our people are not as precise as we would like. But, you understand the issue with time and space not always matching up." He shrugged.

Fred raised a brow. "I'm afraid I'm not following."

"The Cloud." Linus cut right to the meat of the conversation causing Fred's brows to raise all the more. "More accurately the connection to it."

Fred intended to continue to deny understanding what Linus was talking about, but his face betrayed him.

"Wave7." Fred hissed. "That symbol etched on your uniform. It's a lambda."

Linus put a finger to his lips. "Not so loud my friend. Not everyone understands the work you and I are doing."

"You and I are working on completely different wavelengths." Fred had not caught his own play on words until Linus snickered.

"Your organization is a bunch of hackers who crashed the infostrada and may cause a breakdown of society soon if I don't clean up your mess." Fred fumed.

"Did we? Crash the connection, as you say?" A knowing look passed over Linus's face.

For the first time since the crash Fred doubted the information his employer and the media had claimed.

"Wave7 is about research and rebuilding. What is ITower about?" Linus pressed.

Fred could not argue in favor of his company based on the actions he had been an accomplice to.

"Where did the crash originate?" Linus continued. "Who called in the order to shut down GlobeNet?"

"They thought the glitches were a danger to the public." Fred admitted. "They still may be."

Until this character had sat beside him, Fred had not questioned the potential long term hazards of connecting the Clouds for public consumption.

"How could they not be?" Linus set a hand on Fred's shoulder.

The connection sent a wave through both men. Their eyes locked in dark recognition as silence enveloped them. Linus withdrew his hand to his side.

"Hannah seems to think it's safe." Fred absently dropped the woman's name.

Linus's eyes glinted at the mention of Hannah, yet he refocused on the matter at hand. There would be time to talk with her soon enough.

"Safe for whom?" Linus continued. "For two centuries Wave7 has curated an elite team of scientists, historians, and enlightened individuals to protect the information surrounding the Grid. What would happen if everyone had access to the information we are talking about?"

Fred considered his nephew's stock market profiteering and interference in a natural disaster. Evan was likely the best example of how most of humanity would react if given connection to the etheric Cloud. However, something in Linus's smile set Fred on edge.

"Who controls the access?" Fred leveled his gaze with the strange man.

Linus laughed at the question. "The most enlightened of course."

"And who decides what qualifies as enlightened?"

The train slowed at a stop. Fred was suddenly aware how far he and Linus had traveled together. He was far beyond his usual stops.

"Before Wave7 there were priests and scholars." Linus began. "And before that shamans, medicine men, oracles, and wizards. Access has always been sanctioned to an elite few for the sake of society. It would be foolish to think this generation of mankind has come far enough to take the gates off the temples."

Fred moved to rise from his seat. "Maybe. Or maybe it's time to see what happens next."

"Fred." Linus's hand shot out and clutched at Fred's arm. "This does not end with you, or with me."

"Why do I feel like you've said that before." Fred shook his arm free and strode toward the doors of the train as it slid to a halt at the platform.

He swept off the train and looked back only when he had both feet on the concrete. When he did, Linus was gone. Fred scanned the platform, but there was no sign of the Wave7 operative.

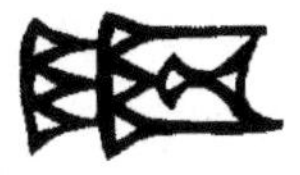

Chapter Forty Five

As Hannah busied herself at the front of the store, the bells chimed.

"Good afternoon!" she called from behind a shelf of crystals.

Two men entered. They browsed the books and charms collected around the store, making a broad circuit before closing in toward Hannah.

Something about their attire plucked at Hannah's memories. The uniform jackets and hashed-out military devices on the sleeves set her senses on edge.

She hefted one of the larger salt crystals in her hand as if to move it from one case to another, "Can I help you gentlemen with anything? Past lives, or understanding current issues?"

She crossed the room, crystal still in hand, and wandered to the counter between the main storefront and the stairs to the second floor.

"We're more interested in the future," the first gentleman explained as he rotated to study a miniature statue of Anubis, ancient god of death and afterlife.

"The future is never set in stone, my friend. It can be difficult to interpret." Hannah offered her typical response.

"Don't be so humble." The second man offered a dry smile. "We've seen the amazing skill you have."

The man continued to close the space between Hannah and himself. "NetNostradamus."

"Excuse me?" Hannah tightened her grip on the crystal in her hand.

She tossed a subtle glance to the stairs.

"Who else are you working with?" The first man swept up to Hannah as his compatriot locked the shop door and flipped the sign to closed.

Hannah focused her attention carefully on the two men. They were after Evan, yet they seemed to think she was NetNostradamus. Evan was likely still comatose from the information Coach was feeding him. She sighed in acceptance of the premonition of what was about to happen.

Her fingers loosened from around the crystal. A calm smile flowed across her lips.

"No one. I'm not working with anyone. It's all me." Hannah's shoulders relaxed as she rested her hand on the counter. "I suspect you want my help."

"In a manner of speaking." The first man moved toward the stairs either to pass Hannah or block her.

Hannah made a sudden shift, causing both men to close on her once again.

She held out her hands. "I was just going to gather my things."

The pair passed a look between one another, confusion danced in their eyes.

"You're not going to run." It was less a question than a command.

"You look a lot faster than me." Hannah nodded. "And, I don't need to be psychic to sense it wouldn't be pleasant when you caught me."

Hannah picked up her bag from behind the counter.

The man closest to Hannah reached for her arm. "Smart choice." The other one stepped off the stairs.

"Are you hiding any devices?" Her captor reached for the bag.

Hannah glanced into the woven satchel. "If so, what would it matter?"

"No devices allowed." The second man closed on Hannah.

His hand gripped her shoulder.

"You won't need them." The first man stilled the other with a look.

"And you won't need those." Hannah gestured to the handcuffs hanging from the hip of the first man.

The two turned to lead Hannah out the front of the shop.

"We should take the back exit," Hannah offered. "It will save you gentlemen from having to explain anything to approaching customers as to why you're hauling me away.

The men's eyes narrowed on the ease with which this encounter was progressing.

The pair followed Hannah through to the rear door of the building.

"A lot of wires for a store with no connection service." One of the men commented as they picked through the lines threaded along the hallway.

"I was experimenting." Hannah continued toward the rear door. "It's all fried though." She added. "Tracking that tsunami did it in."

The explanation seemed to suffice, though Hannah didn't slow her pace, forcing the men to follow her out the back.

As the three entered the alleyway the men flanked Hannah.

"Hold her here." The taller of the two commanded.

The other offered a curt nod and tightened his grip on Hannah's arm.

"How did you find me?" Hannah shrugged her bag onto her shoulder.

The man didn't answer.

"It was the protocol address wasn't it? Or maybe the volume of data when I connected, that set off your alarms?." Hannah sniffed. "Or maybe you were monitoring the scale of the magnetic etheric fields?" She shook her head.

The man remained silent.

"Or the signals to the satellites?" Hannah struggled to remember convincing jargon tossed around by Fred and Evan.

The man tightened his grip once more. Hannah fell silent.

After a moment a dark van pulled up along the alleyway.

The pair hustled Hannah into the vehicle. As the door closed, Hannah sent a focused glance to the second floor window.

I hope you've been working up there all this time. I hope you are connected right now. Otherwise this is not going to go well. Hannah sent the thoughts and an image of the two men and the van through the deep consciousness of her mind.

"What are you looking at?" The man seated beside Hannah glared out the window.

"Nothing. Hoping I get to see my store again."

Deep into that darkness peering, long I stood there, wondering, fearing, doubting, dreaming dreams no mortal ever dared to dream before.

Edgar Allan Poe

American writer, editor, and literary critic

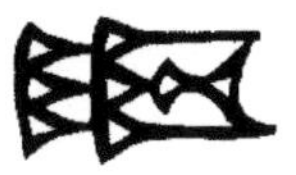

Chapter Forty Six

Evan awoke in the dim warmth of his room. The weight of visions, dreams, and memory heavy on his mind.

He rubbed his eyes and temples before turning to the clock beside the bed. Hours had passed. The sky was darkening.

A silence fogged the apartment level of the building.

"Hello?" He called as he moved through the rooms in search of Hannah or his uncle.

He rubbed at his head and made a path to the kitchen for a glass of water.

An energy buzzed around him. It crawled over his skin and in the air as he walked. An uneasiness groped at him as he peered into the empty rooms. Time felt slower, heavier, encumbered.

"Where the hell is everyone?" He listened for the familiar din from the store below.

Nothing.

He flopped into one of the chairs beside the table. Images of the marble table from the past, or future, rippled through his mind. Through the fog of visions, Evan picked the tablet from the kitchen table. As if commanded, the device came to life.

In a breath, Fred's image formed on the screen.

His uncle's face flickered and shifted. He appeared to Evan as the multitude of people in past lives where they had known each other. It made Evan nauseous as he struggled to bring the images into focus. He clapped his eyes shut.

"Finally up from your nap?" Even Fred's voice took on a layered tone.

"Stop." Evan snapped.

He opened his eyes and at last Fred, as Evan knew him now, stared back.

"Still grumpy I see." Fred smirked.

"Sorry." Evan relaxed as the vertigo faded at last.

"It's a rough ride. Be grateful you didn't have to go on a full NDE roller coaster. It's harder to grasp and retain data when your body dies." Fred consoled his nephew.

Evan remained silent. He didn't quite trust his senses yet.

"Oh! But the reason for my call! I've been trying to contact you for at least an hour!" Fred clapped his hands. "The office has gone mad."

"What do you mean?" Evan stifled a yawn as he absently tapped at the tablet to find the applications fully functional.

He leaned forward in his chair. "Is the network up? Did you fix it?"

"What? No." Fred shook his head in confusion, then his eyes filled with understanding. "My boy, that's you. You are fixed."

Evan's smile faded. "I wasn't broken?"

"Right." Fred winked.

Evan's view of the cubicle suddenly shifted as if the camera had been titled hard in another direction.

"I can explain more when you get here." Fred's voice was suddenly low. "And you need to get here," he urged. "They're poking around the cubicles. Including mine. And yours. You need to get down here!"

"Wait, who?" Evan rose from the chair.

"The FBI. They're here. In ITower." Fred peered into the camera. "Gotta go. Get here fast."

The screen winked and Fred disappeared. The tablet clattered to the table. Evan grabbed his bag. He paused a breath as he hit the foot of the stairs. He scanned the empty store. Concern weighed on him, yet there was little time to worry about Hannah or the rush of images and visions that flashed through his mind earlier.

Evan's eye caught sight of a large crystal resting on the counter. It seemed to glow as if illuminated from within.

"Look for her later. I'll keep an eye on her." Linc's voice cut through the silence of the store.

Evan scanned the room for the source of Linc's voice. His eyes fell upon the crystal once again.

"Hannah's fine," Linc insisted in a familiar military tone. "Get moving, Lieutenant."

"Where are you?" Evan called.

"Same place I've always been," Linc replied. "Now go. Fred needs you."

Evan frowned at the crystal. He wanted to deny what was happening, even as the glowing continued, at least in his mind. He rubbed at his face and turned for the door.

As he crossed the street to his car he caught sight of a pair of ITower repair vehicles slowing to park in front of Hannah's store.

The communication of the dead is tongued with fire beyond the language of the living.

T. S. Eliot

Poet, essayist, publisher

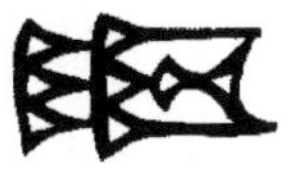

Chapter Forty Seven

Evan rushed through the disheveled chaos of ITower into the boardroom. His entry drew attention from Fred and dark looks from the administrators seated around the table.

To Evan's shock, the large monitor at the far end of the room was functioning. Moreover, Hannah's image filled the screen.

Fred's look was enough to give Evan the hint he should wipe the recognition and concern from his face. Fred waved him to an empty seat.

"It's nice of you to join us Evan." The ITower sector security officer cleared his throat.

Evan offered a nod and a wave as he settled in the seat beside his uncle.

Once Evan was seated the security officer returned to his debrief and passed a stack of folders to one of the many assistants milling around the room.

"Evan, I think we have a problem." Fred murmured he leaned in toward Evan's ear. "Where's Hannah?"

"She was out of the store when I came to. I didn't see anything weird though. Did you tell these suits something about her?" Evan scowled. "What's going on?"

"Gentlemen." The head of the security cleared his throat. "We have a serious issue."

All eyes turned to Evan and Fred. The pair straightened in their seats.

"The FBI is crawling all over this place. They have warrants and subpoenas specifying searches for terrorist investigations," the security lead continued. "It appears we have been compromised. The FBI wants full access to everything the two of you have been working on."

Fred and Evan exchanged anxious glances.

"How soon do we need to prepare the files?" Fred leveled his tone.

Evan was impressed at how calm his uncle appeared to be.

"In their words, yesterday." The security officer frowned.

"Right." Evan breathed. "Of course."

"The files and Feds are not our biggest problem."

Of course it wasn't. Evan's eyes floated to the screen.

"Do either of you know this woman?" The security lead flung his hand in the direction of Hannah's image.

The picture of Hannah seemed to stare directly on Fred and Evan. The duo shared a look yet neither were prepared to respond.

"The FBI confirmed that this woman is collaborating with cyber terror group, Wave7. They are further investigating concerns that she is the NetNostradamus talked about on the media."

Fred and Evan remained silent. Uncertain where to go from here. Wondering how much more the FBI knew. They didn't have to wait as the next bit of news dropped like a bomb.

"They also tell us you are living in this woman's house." The security lead's eyes hardened, daring Evan or Fred to deny the allegation.

Fred shoved himself out of his chair. "Yes," he blurted. "Yes, we are living with her."

Evan's eyes volleyed from his uncle to the suits in the boardroom.

"You know what happened to my house." An accusatory tone colored Fred's words. "We reached out for help from ITower. We kept this out of government hands, at your request."

The admission of keeping company secrets drew dark looks from the agents in the room. The security officer reddened as he shook his head.

Fred spoke assertively. He was on a roll, as if in control of the present situation. "As for Hannah, I can guarantee she's not a terrorist. She wouldn't work with these Wave7 nuts."

Fred's knuckles whitened as he pressed his palms into the table. Evan could sense his uncle was holding his breath, yet could not will himself calm as he scanned the room.

"Does this woman have access to the projects you have been working on?" The security lead was stoic.

"Yes." Evan answered with a sigh.

Fred vaulted a glare onto his nephew. Evan refused to make eye contact.

"She has no understanding of networking, tech communications, or data management." Evan leveled his gaze with the lead.

"Can you be certain?" The lead pressed.

"She still thinks a piece of tape over a mic will keep hackers from listening through her device." Evan scoffed in supplement to Fred's assertion.

"What is her connection then?" The lead crossed his arms.

"Her connection." Evan rubbed at the bridge of his nose. "Shit." He murmured. "She's a psychic," he added flatly.

Evan caught Fred's expression from the corner of his eye but could not discern the emotion behind it.

"I see." The lead's frown seemed to deepen. "So exactly what *have* you been working on?"

"We've explained everything we are able to. It's all stored on the GlobeNet working and archive files. The board has full access." Evan dead-eyed the men and women in the room.

"As well as new information on our side project." Fred's voice cracked.

Evan's eyes went wide as he shot his full attention to his uncle.

A sheen of sweat glistened on Fred's brow.

"My NDE, near-death experience, allowed me to see things I never expected; I never believed in."

Fred ignored the raised brow from the security lead as well as odd looks rising from the board members and assistants in the room. Yet Evan noticed; even the Board member who leaned back and rolled her eyes.

"There is a Cloud out there," Fred continued as he stood. "It's so much bigger than ITower's Cloud. You have no idea." Fred smiled down at Evan. "Everything is in that Cloud. Everything and everybody who ever existed, who ever will be."

A voice shot across the room. "Nonsense. If the technology you are speaking of existed, ITower would have accessed it by now."

The man at the head of the table who leaned forward.

Evan swallowed. This was the same military-esque man he saw in the board meeting after the crash; when this whole mess started.

"Fred." Evan tried to silence his uncle.

Fred held up a hand to his nephew. "No. This is bigger than ITower." He wiped his brow. "Evan and I managed to build the tools for a Cloud-to-Cloud interface. We can search that Cloud with the same ease as the one in this realm, the physical realm."

Fred stabilized against the table. The room seemed to close in around him as the information settled on them. Members of the board exchanged glances and whispers. The absurdity of Fred's explanation weighed on them.

"There is no Cloud bigger than ITower's." A flat response from the man at the end of the room sliced through the murmurs.

"Wait. What are you trying to say?" The security lead cleared his throat and refused to make eye contact with anyone besides Fred despite the side chatter.

Evan shifted his gaze to his uncle. He waited as the others in the room for the next information dump.

Fred's eyes however were set across the table, boring into the gaze of the man with the military haircut.

"What I'm saying is, none of you know what the hell you are talking about. You have no idea. This is so much bigger than us, than ITower, than this country." Fred clenched his left hand. "We can talk to the dead. We can see tomorrow. We have access to all the knowledge of the universe."

Fred's gaze shifted from the man across the table to the screen displaying Hannah's image. In her place Coach's face appeared.

"Fred, that's enough."

Fred's brow knit as he sensed no one else heard the voice.

"They're not ready for this." Coach sighed. "It's time to step into your new role."

Fred caught his nephew's gaze. He turned his attention to the screen in time to see the image flicker back to Hannah's picture.

As Fred caught Evan's gaze, sweat beaded on his brow. His breath caught. He struggled to continue his tirade about how little the ITower executives understood real connections they had made.

Color sapped from his cheeks. Evan was at his side as the floor slipped from under Fred's feet.

In a sudden shift, Fred felt the world spin away. His vision narrowed. Then, as if every light in the room illuminated, he was blinded by a bright white light.

He watched as Evan caught his pale form while he collapsed to the floor of the board room.

Before he could react further, a voice cried out like a far off echo to call an ambulance.

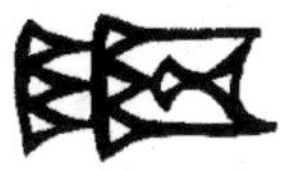

Chapter Forty Eight

EMTs finally called off their attempts and covered Fred's face. His body, now vacant of energy, lay on the gurney. As they wheeled his body from the room, the military man from the far end of the table put a consoling hand on Evan's shoulder.

"We feel your loss. He was like family to us, too." The man smiled sympathetically.

Evan continued to watch as the EMT's and suits filed out of the boardroom.

Once the last of the administrators had cleared the door Evan was left alone with the man with the greying crew cut. "We are not doubting Fred's work. But he did seem to be struggling for some time, and this latest heart attack, though sudden, wasn't all that surprising. I apologize if I come off harsh, but, was there any truth in what Fred said? Or was the rant a symptom of a stroke?"

Evan scowled at the man. "I don't know what to tell you."

He pulled away from the man's grasp to follow the EMTs along the corridor. He glanced through the glass wall at the lingering image of Hannah on the screen.

As the gurney disappeared down the hall, Evan was drawn back to his cubicle. He made his way to Fred's cluttered workspace.

"What are you doing here?" Evan set a hand on the back of Fred's occupied chair.

"How much did you actually complete?" Staring at the flickering screen sat the man with the military haircut.

Stacks of papers, Post-it notes, and multitude of opened tabs were spread across the workstation.

Evan knew it meant nothing to the man in the chair, to some degree it still meant nothing to Evan. Whatever Fred had been accessing, it was beyond what he shared at Hannah's.

The man reached for the keyboard.

"What the fuck are you doing?" Evan all but tore the keyboard off the desktop.

People in surrounding cubicles peered over their walls.

The man continued to stare at the screen. "How much did Fred complete? How deep did he get?"

"I don't know." Evan lied. "I've been focused on the network security issues."

Hannah's name suddenly flashed across the screen.

The man quirked a brow at Evan. "It appears you may have been securing the wrong data."

Evan swallowed. He licked his lips.

"Would you like your old office back?" The man rose from Fred's chair to stand toe to toe with Evan.

"Excuse me?" Evan was taken aback by the unexpected offer.

"Your former office. Would you prefer to work there?" The man repeated the words with such stoicism Evan was left speechless.

"You mentioned a need for a new living arrangement as well." He pushed the chair neatly in alignment with the desk before side stepping Evan.

"Yes." It was the only word Evan could purge from his mind.

"Good." The man stood and stepped into the walkway outside the cubicle. "I think it's best if ITower keeps a close eye on you Mr. Gabriel. We wouldn't want anything to happen to you."

The man's words burrowed into Evan.

"You may, of course, take some time to mourn and get your uncle's affairs in order." The words should have felt sympathetic, but the man's tone was so hollow Evan sensed them more as a command, or perhaps even a threat.

"What if it was just nonsense?" Evan knew how poor the lie sounded even as it left his lips.

"It's not." Finality weighed the words.

In the next breath the man had straightened his jacket and stepped out of Evan's view.

"Fuck." Evan gripped the back of his head.

He paced the tiny cubicle and stared at Hannah's name burned into the monitor.

"Damn it."

In a burst of frustration he shoved the stacks of papers to the floor. Most of Fred's equipment remained at the store. Evan threw a stack of papers into a box and stormed out of the office.

Eyes watched Evan storm from the office. He could feel them, all of them, including the man with the military haircut.

Humankind cannot bear very much reality.

T. S. Eliot

Poet, essayist, publisher

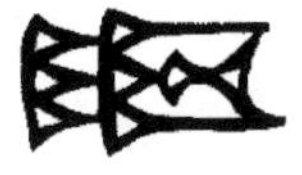

Chapter Forty Nine

As Evan disappeared from the cubicle, the computer screen flickered once again. All other tabs disappeared to reveal Fred's concerned face.

Within the halls of the Akashic Library, Fred turned away from his view of his vacant cubicle. Beside him, Coach looked on. The library was abuzz with guides, streaming data, and flitting entities of various shapes and intensities.

"What will happen now?" Fred turned to Coach, seeing him more clearly than the first time he visited the other side. "Evan? Hannah? How can I help them if he won't see me?"

"He will," Coach assured. "No need to ask about Hannah. We have someone working on that as we speak. All will be as it should be. Data is moving."

Fred nodded in acquiescence as Coach led them to another section of the library.

"I am certain you have questions." Coach lead the way between what appeared to Fred as towering shelves of books, bristling with energy and light. "All will be answered. For now, we have much work to do."

Fred glanced back to where he had peered through to see his former cubicle. It seemed much further away than they had walked.

"Right." He sighed as he realized how permanent this new position was about to be.

He clasped his hands together and turned his attention to Coach. "Show me what to do."

Coach offered a reassuring nod. "We have a coding project I think you may enjoy."

As they rounded yet another hallway within the great data library, Coach waved his hands as if opening a cabinet. A screen of numbers expanded before him and Fred. The numbers were quickly followed by a wall of words. Hundreds of languages, symbols, and images expanded across the air space.

Fred stepped forward, astounded. "It's so fast. And so vast." His eyes raced over the images in a struggle to make sense of it all.

"It should be." Coach fell in beside Fred. "It's the fabric of reality."

"We're going to have to change a few settings to help Evan along." Coach allowed the information to sink in.

"Change?" Fred turned from the plethora of flowing data to quirk a brow at Coach.

"Reality." Coach swept his hands across the field of data.

Suddenly the symbols and numbers surrounded Fred and Coach as they, too, were enveloped as part of the Cloud.

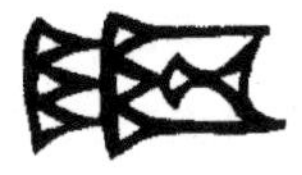

Chapter Fifty

Evan threw open the door to Hannah's store. The space was dark. He dropped the file box of papers at his feet and searched the wall for a light.

As his eyes adjusted he stepped into the room, crystals crunched beneath his feet. He toed at cards and trinkets strewn across the floor. Abandoning the file box, Evan rushed to the second floor. The light from the stairwell was enough to see the tangle of wires and shattered equipment.

"They didn't leave us half a chance." He fell against the doorframe.

He made his way to Fred's room and shoved aside a stack of books blocking the entryway. A stash of vintage CDs tumbled into his path, shattering the aging plastic cases.

"Seriously." He stooped to restack and pick up the cracked plastic boxes.

The cover of the top case fell off in his hand. Inside the shattered case he spotted something loose. He tipped the case and a mini-SD Magna chip tumbled into his palm.

"Sometimes your old fashioned ways are wonderful, old man." Evan turned the tiny chip between his fingers. "You didn't trust the Cloud, after all."

The chimes of a phone rang in the store below. Startled and curious, Evan wrapped the tiny SD chip in a tissue and slipped it in his front shirt pocket. Side stepping into the kitchen, he grabbed a knife from the scatter of utensils on the floor.

Picking his way through the front of the store, Evan sought the source of the ringing. He worked his way toward the front windows.

Outside, a shadow moved across the empty street, catching Evan's eye.

"Linc? Is that you?" Evan called quietly. He shook his head questioning why his friend would physically manifest. Looking again, he could swear the figure shifted to stare across the street into the store window.

"Damn thief. This day cannot get any more messed up." Evan ran outside and bolted across the street.

The figure was gone.

Stricken and certain he had lost his mind, Evan turned back to the store.

"Only a few seconds left, Dude." Linc's voice filled his ears.

Evan caught his breath as sparks rippled over the edges of the building.

"You know the drill. Hit the dirt." Linc's voice barked into Evan's mind, all but shouting.

Out of conditioning, Evan leapt over the curb away from the store and dove behind a transit bus bench for cover.

The front of the store glowed a deep, electric blue. The force of the EM Pulse tore through the glass in the front window. The blast cleared the store's front porch of the bells and dangling suncatchers, firing them over the street toward Evan.

Chapter Fifty One

Hannah sat with eyes closed, a high-backed chair supporting her as she reclined. A series of wires adorned her fingertips, temples, while bands surrounded her arms. Leading from the connections were an array of physical adapters, monitors, keyboards, and radios.

"Things are going to move much faster with your assistance, Hannah dear." Linus Atticus approached the screens.

He keyed in a series of codes. Hannah's eyes snapped open, yet she stared vacantly into the room and over the heads of the dozen others within the space.

A circle of monks sat in meditation, maintaining an energy field prison preventing Hannah from extending her aura beyond the reach of Wave7's control.

"Well, good morning. I hope you're finding the accommodations comfortable." Linus sneered.

Hannah continued to stare unseeing at the man, yet visions flickered behind her vacant eyes.

"There is little chance of ITower catching up now, even if the architect continues. No one can punch keys as fast as your mind works, dear Pythia." He chuckled. "Perhaps this is a little reminiscent of your time in the Temple of Apollo."

The earth grid slithered within Hannah's mind. Layers of code flitted across the screen as Linus watched. Ley lines flicked on and off with each passing thought, yet the world around Hannah blurred into a thick fog.

"What does this look like from inside your mind, I wonder?" Linus stepped closer to the wire frame.

Hannah awoke to the tone of temple bells. She covered her head to drown out the din. The sound shook all memory of her dreams--she wondered if that was the idea.

Keep the Oracle from dreaming. Keep visions focused on the Grid.

Lack of proper sleep served to maintain fatigue and decrease her risk of over thinking.

The chill of the morning awakened her skin with the same harshness the bells had rattled her mind.

The sky was bright and clear, though her vision was not. Hannah made her way to a narrow window. As puffy as they were, her eyes narrowed in contemplation if she was really looking out a window, or if she was back in the temple, or in the oracles' cave or perhaps in some hidden hostage room. Where were the monks that surrounded her before? Or were they here but just not visible to in this state.

Below she could hear bickering. The words were not clear.

"Can none of you think for yourselves?" The male voice was weary and strained.

A pair of women in plain beige dresses arrived without so much as a knock on the door. They roughly requested the clothes Hannah wore and offered a uniform of silk scrubs.

A vision flashed in Hannah's mind as her arm brushed one of the women. A pale blonde haired woman expressed something otherworldly. Her death will be sudden, electric, Hannah thought.

"They're waiting for you." The woman's voice shook away the vision.

Hannah reached out for the woman. "Are you real?"

It had been the same script every morning, at least in the state where there was a small window. They took the same walk to the lower chambers of the temple. Though sometimes Hannah thought it looked more like a warehouse. The varied visions made it confusing to decipher.

Each time, three people, typically women, guided Hannah's steps. Her time alone ended at waking and would not return until sleep took her.

At the foot of stairs a handful of monks stood around the large cage. Food was laid out on a large oak table. It always smelled fresh and looked bright. Hannah's stomach gurgled.

The women assisted Hannah to the head of the table. She waited as they gathered a plate for her. The monks always remained standing until Hannah took the first bite.

The behavior at first confused Hannah. She was clearly a captive, though they performed this pantomime of servitude.

Once all were seated, the true course of the meeting commenced.

"Pythia." The monk closest to Hannah addressed her.

She did not raise her eyes this time.

"We are prepared to commence the great work of the Grid." It was almost an invocation.

Once the meal was complete each monk cupped Hannah's hand in theirs and pressed his lips to her palm. The women always waited for the last monk to be seated on a circle of cushions surrounding the large metal cage.

Hannah opened her eyes as a gentle hand rested on her arm. The sweet young woman's smile was full of the utmost desire to be of service.

"Come, Pythia." The woman gripped under Hannah's arm and led her to the cage. "We must hasten to the temple to prepare you for assemblage today."

Hannah nodded. She learned to look forward to the strange calm about to envelop her. The walk to the seat of their temple brought a chill to her arms and a fresh pit of discomfort to her stomach.

The sweet smell of electrically driven ozone rippled off the wires as the air in proximity was ionized. It was real magic, the women had explained on one of the occasions. It may have been the first time they led Hannah to the device they called the temple.

Copper tendrils swirled in grey-green curls encompassing the metal orb. The cage loomed in an arching canopy to a domed roof. It trapped a perceptible haze of static. It was only as they ascended further that the throne could be distinguished from the mass of metal and wires. The seat almost beckoned Hannah. It was little more than a darkened leather bowl suspended at three points to the curves of the cage.

A crevice penetrating imperceptibly deep into the ground below was only about the span of a grown man's foot. Still, Hannah paused before crossing the slitted mouth in the earth that seemed to gape at her.

The women donned cotton masks over their mouths. Only the Pythia was allowed to breathe what the monks had called the Breath of the Goddess. Hannah had tried to identify the smell, a mild sweet odor. It was more than the sweet ozone; it was something else. The women took Hannah's hands and carefully lowered her into the seat.

Bowing as they stepped back the women scurried down the ramp and out of the room.

Hannah instinctively gripped a set of leather knobs in each hand. They allowed her some stability as the mist overcame her. Her head lolled against a pillowed rest mounted to the back of the seat. Her breath drew smoky tendrils past her lips and through her nostrils. It was now a sour burning, though only for a moment.

"Shh." the vision's voice hushed Hannah as she watched a fountain pool ripple and blur into view.

Hannah clutched at the mosaicked walls of a fountain. Her legs buckled. Her knees crunched into coarse gravel surrounding a public fountain. Soft hands encircle her shoulders before the fog surrounded her once more.

"Penelope!" Hannah shouted against the mist. "You can't call me to this place!" Hannah's eyes fought the dark and the fog. She batted at the encompassing swirls.

"Hannah?" The echo masked any emotion, but Penelope seemed equally confused by Hannah's struggle.

"Penelope." Hannah's own voice echoed again in the gloom.

A hand was on her before the familiar face of her visions came into view. "Hannah! How are you here?"

Penelope drew Hannah to her and crushed her in a bold embrace. Hannah's arms folded around her waist.

"Penelope. I'm not supposed to be here. You told me yourself. Remember?"

Hannah held the vision of Penelope at arm's length. She looked different than in the cottage. This vision was gaunt, hard, and stricken with anxiety.

"We spoke for the last time at the cottage." Hannah pressed the spectre.

The vacant stare reminded Hannah that there were different versions of this guide. This was not the one in the cottage.

"You must have been dreaming." Penelope whispered. "I wish I could dream."

A green mist wafted in and choked Hannah's lungs. She coughed and looked away.

"It takes some growing used to." Penelope's smile was somber. "But this is a place of peace."

Penelope took Hannah's hand and lead them through the fog to a reflective wall. "This is how we will see through the Grid."

Hannah watched the rippling world. She struggled to understand if she was seeing through her eyes or those of this fractured fragment of her soul.

"Atticus? I know him." The words tumbled from Hannah's mouth, but they were not her's.

A cluster of men and monks beyond the rippling window murmured om's and grimaced in varied forms of concentration, wonderment and anticipation.

"Can they hear me?" Hannah turned to Penelope.

Penelope's smile was blissful at Hannah's ignorance. "Of course. You spoke as Pythia."

"Penelope, you can help me." Hannah focused her mind inward struggling to keep the words between herself and the guide.

"Hannah," the sweet placating voice fell sour on Hannah's ears, "I did not bring you here. I cannot help you."

Hannah's shoulders fell. She returned her blurred vision to the image beyond the ripples. The caroling alarms rang in her ears as she fought to maintain a measure of control over her own consciousness. She did not want to be herded back to the grid just yet.

Hannah scanned the room from her perspective adjacent to the door in the ring of monks outside the cage. The monks appeared to be deep in meditation even as the two men Hannah recalled from the store tried to calm the man she recognized as Professor Linus Atticus. After a moment, another man entered. He scowled and pointed past the monks, where Hannah could only assume her physical form was seated.

This man she did not know, though something about his greying crew cut was familiar. She was certain a curse passed his thin lips as he scowled at Linus. Then he turned and left the room.

Linus leaned a leering face toward the rippling window to Hannah's world.

Hannah drew away.

Penelope's arms caught her. "They cannot see us. Be calm."

Another wave struck Hannah and words once more tumbled from her lips. "Code is shifting. The wave patterns will crash."

Penelope's pale eyes stared at Hannah. "What?"

The moment passed. Linus's frown deepened. Worry glistened in his eyes and on his forehead.

This was the image Hannah was left with as the world faded around her. The green mist stole Penelope as Hannah snapped back into the body. She coughed again at the acrid stench of metal, hot wiring and ozone.

"Shh," a voice soothed her.

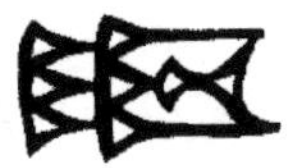

Chapter Fifty Two

Evan settled into his former office within the ITower high security building. He found himself wishing he had taken the two week bereavement leave before unpacking equipment and kickstarting the process of implementing Fred's system. He considered how much time that would have opened up to visit with his mother. Training ITower geeks on a system based on something that bordered on magic seemed far less tedious.

He fired up the array of computer screens and lowered into the ergonomic seat. Eyeing the smooth glass of the large workstation, Evan felt for a moment all was as before the crash.

A quick look out the window at the late afternoon light and typical summer grey-green of the sky was enough to bring Evan back to reality. There was still not tech magic to shutter out the world.

The now too familiar face of ITower security appeared on one of the screens.

"Evan. We need an update on the issues with the last Tesla site collapse." The man's words were cold.

Evan let a sigh release as he fought his distaste at the mention of the sites. They had nothing to do with a long-dead scientist or recently defunct solar electricity manufacturing entity. To Evan, they were Fred-sites.

ITower expanded on the data and maps decoded from Fred's SD card, as well as information Evan rescued from his things salvaged from Hannah's store. This included his own notes and progress on the project he and Fred had been working on with connectivity. ITower could have at least named one of the new generation sites after Fred.

ITower and the FBI still considered Hannah a suspected terrorist, still Evan was not totally convinced. In the first few days Evan held hope that Hannah would turn up, safe, claiming some vision, an impromptu ayahuasca trip to the Amazon or perhaps to visit a friend. It had been nearly a month though and he was losing hope of a good ending. Evan now hoped she would simply turn up at all, even if the Feds caught her, ending with a peaceful arrest. He wanted her to be alive, hacker terrorist or not.

Evan continued to stare at the flowing streams of code filling the screens in front of him. His fingers flew over the keyboard as he actively ignored the man on the screen.

"What do you need to know?" He paused. "Sir."

"Well, for one, when will that Tesla site be back online?"

"Tomorrow." Evan continued his frantic typing. "Unless I'm interrupted again."

With barely a nod to the man on the screen Evan flicked his hand over a secondary keypad. The chat window flickered out.

The sun, the real sun, continued its path across the Arizona sky as Evan plugged away at the code. The building echoed in emptiness as Evan finally closed the screens and left the office. Deep in the parking garage he clicked the fob on his key ring. The headlights of his car blinked to life.

The city felt so nearly pre-crash as he drove home, Evan allowed himself a momentary pause to shift his gaze to the empty video billboards.

As he pulled into the front drive of his luxury apartment complex, a valet approached to offer a professional smile to Evan and an appreciative nod at the vintage vehicle.

Evan ignored the man. A glass of whiskey and a moment of peace awaited several stories up.

The concierge in the front lobby waved Evan to the desk.

She handed him a letter. Evan barely returned a nod of thanks.

Evan turned the paper in his hands. Another invitation to join the nightlife of irritating tech CEOs patting themselves and Evan on the back for the discovery of a new, more powerful data system.

ITower executives resumed offering gifts, dinners, dates with stunning young women. It was a return to the life Evan had pre-crash, and so much more. The true cost of this quid pro quo was more than the ITower masters understood.

Fred had left everything Evan needed on the SD card and his computer files. There were moments as Evan first opened the files he thought Fred planned it all. With the strange series of events Evan experienced leading up to the final meeting in the boardroom it wouldn't have surprised him if Fred had known he was about to die.

Armed with the work that Fred left behind, ITower wasted no time restructuring their sites to support the new access systems. ITower expedited building new locations based on a list of GPS coordinates in Fred's architectural plans. Evan wished he'd had the wherewithal to review the underlying construction designs. It meant nothing initially, yet his higher ups seemed unwilling to release the locations of the newer towers, especially the ones flagged as Teslas. Everyday Evan promised himself he would dig into the databases once the offices cleared out. With his focus on securing the new network superstructure, every night he was too mentally and physically drained to even think about it.

Evan's mind wandered as he made his way down the hall of the apartment building. He could swear the presence of those he lost lingered around him as he made his way home.

He felt Fred's eyes on him in the curve of a metallic sconce. He could swear he saw Linc in the glint of a beveled glass window. It could have been Coach's smirk in the chrome frame of an art deco revival painting.

Evan let the ice fall into the glass as he shook off the ethereal sense of being haunted. However, the unfortunate reality was how few of these haunting experiences he'd had since his uncle's death. As much as Evan wanted to believe the fleeting visions, his contact with Linc and Coach had come to a halt the day of Fred's final meeting at ITower.

Evan hoped that once he activated the cloud to cloud interconnection that the old man would appear on some screen as Linc had done. To the contrary, not only had Evan not heard from the ghost-soul of Fred, he had also lost contact with Linc, and even Coach.

If they were around, none of them were talking to him.

"Maybe giving the files to ITower was a mistake. Shit." Evan cursed as he filled his glass from one of the bottles of whiskey that graced his kitchen counter.

He couldn't take it back now. At least not without the consequence of being fired, or possibly handed over to the FBI as an accomplice to Wave7. The thought brought Hannah to mind again.

Only the dreamer shall understand realities, though in truth his dreaming must be not out of proportion to his waking.

Margaret Fuller

American journalist, editor, critic

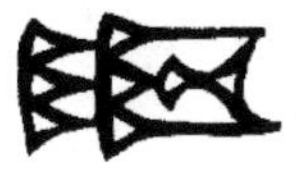

Chapter Fifty Three

Linc turned a somber frown to Coach as the trio looked on at Evan through life-sized screens within the Akashic library.

"He's a mess," Fred interpreted Evan's melancholy expression as the younger man flopped on the couch. "Even when he's laughing and drinking with the ITower execs, he's not himself."

Coach swirled the mist and Evan's image dissipated. "If we want to help him. We have to work on this side. Not too much help."

Before they returned to the Akashic code, Fred lingered at the misty dome, "Will he learn?"

"There is a path for Evan to follow this time around. As far as he may stray, we must trust he will find it." Coach set a hand on Fred's shoulder.

"He's alone." Fred sighed.

"Only because he refuses to see he's not," Coach offered.

Linc turned his attention to the pair as they approached another screen he claimed as his own for the moment.

"We're still unable to make a connection with Hannah." Linc's voice strained in concern. "It's as if she's fallen off of the universe."

Coach and Fred fell into step behind Linc. They, too, squinted at pinprick lights arrayed across an ever-turning globe before them.

"Is it possible she's dead?" Linc crossed his arms.

Ever the voice of reason, Coach leaned closer to the globe. "If Hannah had left her body, she would be with us here." He rotated the globe with a wave of his fingers. "No. She is alive, somewhere. She has been shrouded somehow. We can only hope Evan can do what needs to be done to find her."

"If he even has the desire to do so." Fred peered over Linc's shoulder at the screen depicting his nephew at yet another lively event. The trio exchanged nervous glances.

"Does he still believe she's helping Wave7?" Fred asked, peering into another moment in Evan's day-to-day life.

This time, Evan was in his office. Alone.

"Linc?" Fred returned his attention to find Linc no longer among them.

Coach raised his shoulder. "We all have our jobs to do."

It was all he offered before he, too, faded to another part of the great library. Fred was left to watch as another day turned to night in his nephew's busy, shallow world.

"We were so close." He whispered to the image of Evan, head-down on his desk, recovering from a hangover, and an all nighter at the keyboard.

"So close." Evan grumbled the words in his restlessness.

"I should have shown you the designs and maps." Fred lamented. "It would mean so much more if you could see the plans."

Fred moved to the globe and flicked his fingers. Blue pins alighted on the surface. He spread his fingers and the image soared to a trio of pyramids surrounded by sparse vegetation.

As Fred looked on the area around the structures came to life with the bustling of workmen and machinery.

"I do hope Coach was right about who's using who." Fred faded from the library to join the others.

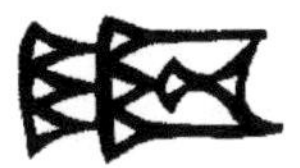

Chapter Fifty Four

A sudden wave of electricity, shot through the computer screens before they blinked out. The lack of light and hum of electricity caused Evan to stir.

He raised his head to the flickering of hundreds of windows opening and closing. Code screamed across the screens.

"What the-. Damn it." Evan fought with the keyboard and clicked at the mouse.

He struck the walls of the external hard drive and cursed the sudden vibrations of the cell phone as it ran a violent course through the full spectrum of ring tones.

With sudden recognition, Evan stared at the dance of images, tones, words, song lyrics, and data. "Talk. To. Her."

Evan shifted his attention from screen to phone in an attempt to follow the ripple of electricity chasing around the room.

"Hannah. Help. Her."

Punching at the keys he fought to halt the machines haywire activity.

"Hannah. Needs. You."

His attention focused at the sight of Hannah's name in a flash of bold-type letters filling all three primary screens.

A glimpse of Linc alighted on a nearby tablet. "She. Needs. You. We. Need. You. You. Are. The. Key."

"How do I get you to come in clear?" Evan poured his frustration into focusing on the tablet.

"Even after. All. This. You still. Have to. Tune-in. Come. On. Man. Get. On. Frequency."

As if the words had taken Evan back to the van on the battlefield, when he and Linc were synced in their actions, the tablet image suddenly became clear. Evan's mind wandered to when the duo were able to tap code and relay communications as if they were of one mind.

"Man, this has been such a long time in the making." Linc's image took on a stretched, almost three dimensional, appearance as it expanded from the confines of the tablet. "Lifetimes. Millennia. Now is the time. You and Hannah were meant to meet now." Evan tilted his head as he strained to understand the choppy connection. "Don't you understand yet? Coach. My escape from the meat suit. Fred."

Evan tried to turn the volume up as he struggled to hear Linc more clearly. He frantically rummaged through one of the boxes he had salvaged from Fred's house. He smiled.

"There you are." Evan pulled the headset he had used in the communications van with Linc many years before. "I hope my ounce of nostalgia will come in handy."

Evan docked the headset with the tablet. He breathed in the lingering familiar odor trapped in the cushioned earpieces.

"Now that's a stroke of brilliance!" For the first time since their days together, Evan felt as though Linc and he shared the same space.

"I still have a few tricks." Evan closed his eyes, then reopened them to a room completely transformed.

The office had closed in around him leaving only the workstation in front of him. The pitted metal panel housed a monitor array, keyboard, and toggles, similar to their old Army van.

"That's new." Evan's fingertips brushed the cool metallic surface. He smiled. "It's real."

"Real's a funny thing." Linc released a short laugh as he tilted back in the seat beside Evan.

Evan reached out and hesitantly jabbed his partner's shoulder.

"Everything is data," Linc grinned and nudged Evan in return. "Fred tried to tell you. We live on in the streams of data that create everything. Think quantum, Dude. Waves or particles, waves or particles. Without waves of consciousness, we do not exist in the physical."

"So you're not dead." Evan didn't try to conceal the catch in his voice. "And Fred?"

"No one actually dies, Evan. We leave the meat suit, that's all." Linc's smile was soft, yet a hint of sarcasm toned his words. "It's like saving your documents to the Cloud. It doesn't matter what device you use to access it, the data is always there."

"Then how do I access Fred and his files?" Evan rubbed at the bridge of his nose.

"Fred's been busy." Linc adjusted the sleeves on his uniform. "He'll connect with you again soon though."

"You've seen him then?" Relief coursed through Evan. For the first time since the boardroom meeting, he relaxed.

"Of course. What? Did you think he would abandon the project?" Linc crossed his arms as he gauged Evan's next reaction. "You still don't get it."

"What's to get." Evan sighed. "As long as I can contact you and Fred, what else am I supposed to do?" Evan waved his hand over the tablet. "As far as the public at large knows the Cloud is up and running again, same as before."

"But they don't know what's behind it. And you don't believe in what's behind it." Linc pressed.

"So what?" Evan scoffed. "I'm doing my job, man. It doesn't matter to me how the sites work as long as I can keep the data flowing between the clouds. Hardware versus software."

Linc shook his head. "Tsch. And what about Hannah?" Linc flicked his fingers and Hannah's image appeared on the monitors.

"I've been looking." Evan gazed at the image.

"Look harder. She needs you." Linc paused. "And you need her, even if you don't get it yet."

A curt knock interrupted Evan before he could respond. The door to Evan's office opened. Startled, Evan threw the headset from his ears. In the doorway stood the head of network security.

The setting of the office snapped back to reality. The image of Linc disappeared as if a plug was pulled.

"Evan." The man took a moment to scan the room before continuing. "There are reports of a power surge and a lag in data coming from this section of the building. Have you noticed anything?"

"No." Evan stammered. "I mean, I haven't noticed any problems."

"Right." The man frowned. Uncertainty holding him in the room a moment more. "Well, keep working on it. Let's get some progress by the end of the day."

Sighing into his chair, Evan scowled at the headphones in his hand. He turned his attention to the computers on the desk. All screens displayed normal data streams and coding sets.

Linc was gone.

"I think the lag issue fixed itself." Evan murmured.

Evan set the headphones on the desk.

An overwhelming urgency to find Hannah swept over him as a rush of air passed over his shoulder. He opened a supplemental program to run an automated scan.

"Shit. This could take hours." Evan snatched the tablet, rose from his chair and headed for the door.

He paused and returned to his desk. Snatching up the headphones he took one more look around the room.

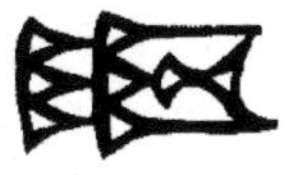

Chapter Fifty Five

Linc found himself surrounded once more by the streams of data.

"You spoke to him?" Coach sidled up beside Linc.

"I did." Linc gauged the facial response of the guide. "He's on frequency."

Coach offered a somber nod, yet Linc could tell the guide was still pleased.

"I tried to tell him about Hannah." Linc eyed the latest lines of data. "We were interrupted."

"We've done all we're meant to do for now." Coach rested a hand on Linc's shoulder. "It's up to Evan from here."

As Coach turned aside, Linc noticed Fred in the distance.

The man's hands danced before him in waves and patterns, manipulating data.

"What is he doing?" Linc closed the space between them.

"Changing the framework of reality." Coach smiled.

"So, when do I get to do that?" Linc's lip curled into a half smile.

Coach chuckled. "You already have." He continued to watch Fred. "Remember."

Linc felt a tug as his being was flung into a new space. "What the-."

"You haven't been at this quite as long as Fred and Evan, but your work has been equally valuable."

Linc scanned the dimly lit, yet expansive room for Coach. But he was alone.

"I don't think I want to visit this one." Linc's voice cut through the silence of the barren room.

He approached an archway directly across from him. A dark hallway on the other side expanded away from the room. Linc set his hand on his chest.

He felt his heart pounding and smiled. "Haven't felt that in a while."

Linc followed the tunnel toward a distant light. As he moved forward the angle of his ascent decreased. As he neared the opening the sound of water filled Linc's ears.

"It's leaking again." He frowned as the knowledge of his purpose filled him.

Emerging from the tunnel Linc stared out across the vast expanse of mountains. A sheer drop marked the end of the walkway, forcing him to turn and follow a narrow path along the face of the mountain.

Far above, silk ribbons and flags fluttered lines of cables connecting the mountain to another. Linc could almost make out the dragon heads peering from the tiered roofs on the adjacent buildings.

He followed the path to another opening in the face of the mountain. Here a stream of clear water trickled from the tunnel.

"It's not as bad, but it will change the pressure." Linc grumbled as he ducked into the tunnel.

"Hardware versus software." Linc muttered as he neared the source of the leak.

Linc leaned to pick up a wrench-like tool from a basket at the entrance to this new room. Light glinted off the smooth dome of the enormous copper bowl whose edges nearly brushed the walls of the cavern.

"Why are you always the trouble maker?" Linc's hand caressed the cool surface. "Can't you be like your six soul sisters?"

Linc traversed the bowl, careful to lift his sandal-shod feet over the maze of pipes coursing the floor. Water dripped steadily from a joint in the pipes. It was less about repair as it was maintenance, though no less concerning. It was more than the acolytes and priests who relied on the power and connection offered by the monstrous device atop the mountain. The villages in the surrounding valleys would fall into a dark age if the grid collapsed.

Linc watched his own wrinkled hands as they tightened the connection on the pipe. The leak slowed to a halt.

Linc called out, "If we do get it running again, who will maintain it?" His question drifted into the silence.

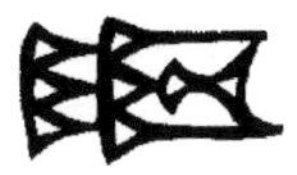

Chapter Fifty Six

Evan closed and locked the door to his apartment. In his usual routine he pulled a glass from the cabinet and a bottle from the shelf. He paused. His eyes traveled to the tablet resting on the counter.

"This probably won't help." He left the bottle on the counter and filled the glass from the tap in the kitchen.

He struggled to recall any of the insane magical nonsense Hannah and Fred had discussed months before. Centering, circles, chakras. None of it meant anything to Evan. His mind had learned to block out information concerning auras, mysticism, or anything that sounded like it would come from his mother and her Sedona friends.

Evan settled on the couch, tablet at arm's length. He focused his mind with a mantra he could understand. "It's all data."

A heavy knock on the door shook Evan from his attempted meditation.

He rose and peered through the peephole. He sensed he recognized the man on the other side of the door, yet he couldn't place from where. The uniform meant little to him. It wasn't standard issue. He slid a nine millimeter pistol from the drawer beside the entryway.

"Can I help you?" Evan called though the small speaker.

"Evan, my dear boy." The man on the other side of the door smiled. "It's been too long."

"Have we met?" Evan's query lay flat in the space between the two men.

"In this life, only briefly." The man's smile faded. "My condolences about Fred."

At the mention of his uncle, Evan opened the door against the security chain.

A wave of anxiety sent shivers up Evan's spine as he removed the barrier between himself and the uniformed man.

The sensation ebbed as quickly as it had arisen, yet it left Evan with a sharp memory.

"The train." He scowled and shifted to close the door in the man's face.

Linus set his foot in the jamb of the entryway. "Please."

Evan eyed the man a moment more. "I'll be out in a moment. Meet me in the bar outside the lobby."

A sweep of Evan's foot and a shift of body weight against the door left Linus in the hallway.

Evan rested against the door. "Okay. Linc. Where are you now?"

The words fell on an empty room. Evan was on his own. He checked the magazine on the pistol and tucked it into his jacket pocket.

He glanced into the hallway through the peephole. Clear. Part of him hoped he had scared the man off and he wouldn't appear downstairs. Evan entered the hallway and locked the apartment door. He recalled Fred's notes had mentioned a conversation with a professor Atticus on a train. Evan couldn't shake the anxiety that struck him at the sight of the man.

Evan scanned the bar. It was early enough on a weekday, the crowd was reasonable. His gaze fell upon the uniformed man seated in a booth near the rear of the dining area. A pair of drinks garnished the table.

"I didn't want a drink." Evan slid into the seat opposite the man.

"Yes you did." Linus raised his glass. "It's single malt. A good vintage."

Evan peered into the glass set before him.

"It's not drugged," Linus assured him.

Evan raised the glass and sipped. The flavor was flawless.

"It would be a waste to taint this flavor with poison." Linus leaned over the rim of his glass and inhaled, closing his eyes to savor the aroma. He then enjoyed his own drink once again before setting the glass aside.

"How do we know one another? How did you know Fred?" Evan eyed the man.

"In this life, I am certain you remember it clearly." Linus traced circles with the moisture drops left by his glass, connecting them like constellations.

"The train." Evan frowned.

Linus released a sharp laugh. "Yes. That shiner you gave me stuck around for some time."

"What do you want?" Evan leaned into the chair. "Compensation?"

Linus smiled and waved the idea off. "Of course not. Not for the eye, in any case."

Evan felt anxiety rising in his spine.

Linus's eyes flashed. "I'll cut to the chase. Shut down the sites. Stop working for ITower."

It was Evan's turn to laugh. "Right. I'll get right on that."

Linus's frown deepened. "Hannah would prefer it."

At the mention of Hannah, Evan's heart felt suddenly choked off.

Linus noted the white-knuckled fists balled on the table's edge. "As I said. Shut. Them. Down."

"Where's Hannah?" Evan leaned across the table.

"Working." Linus let the word fall between them. "For the greater good. We've worked too long and too hard to allow the uninitiated access to the world as we understand it. Governments will spoil the nature of the Grid. It will destroy the minds of anyone lacking understanding of how great this power is. You know this."

"It's a data cloud." Evan remained calm.

Linus's brow dropped into a hard line above his eyes.

Evan glared at the man across the table. "Is that what your cult, Wave7, or whoever is blowing shit up and kidnaping people think this is? You think you're creating some sort of temple?"

Both men felt the continuing rise in Evan's anxiety.

Linus leaned back in a defusing manner and calming responded, "That's what they used to think." As Linus relaxed so too did Evan's anxiety ebb. "Two centuries ago when the industrial age peaked, it seems everyone initially fought the mysticism of archeological discoveries. They were so naive." Linus caught Evan in an amused stare. "You've heard of Babbage I assume."

"The inventor of the first computer?" Evan humored the question.

"Far from the first, though it would be the first in the era we consider modern." Linus smiled. "Do you know why it was created though? No." Linus took a slow, calculated sip of his whiskey. "No. You know what you were told. The Difference Machine. A device for computations."

Linus lowered his voice to a conspiratorial whisper. "It was the beginning of the Grid rebuild project. You could call it the first modern access point to the Cloud."

"What are you talking about?" Evan coughed out a nervous laugh.

"I thought by now you would've seen everything you needed to be convinced." Linus sighed.

"I've seen some shit in the past few months." Evan nodded. "Some of it tracking back to you. Enough that I should be calling the cops about now."

"But you won't." Linus was firm in his certainty.

"No."

"Because you want to know what you're working on." Linus let a satisfied laugh escape his lips. "Your uncle, Fred, he started this. My organization, or cult if you prefer, sent me to meet him on that train. It was meant to divert his skills into our service and out of the hands of ITower."

"The crash happened after Fred's coma." Evan frowned.

"Time is a funny thing." Linus again raised his glass to his lips.

The words hung in the air. Evan had heard the same sentiment from Linc, Coach, Fred, and even Hannah. His discomfort grew again.

"The interconnection and grid rebuild has to be put into the hands of people who know what they are dealing with." Linus insisted.

"What makes you the authority?"

"Wave7 is a selective organization." Linus explained. "Every member is chosen because of a connection to the Grid. Over lifetimes. Some souls, if you will, are more difficult to track in the physical realm."

"Like mine." Evan dropped the tease and awaited Linus's response.

The man offered a calm nod that set Evan's anxiety through the roof.

"How do you track them?" Evan breathed.

"Babbage's machine. Oracles. The Cloud." Linus's smile was almost vicious. "Sometimes our prayers are simply answered." Linus shrugged at his jest.

"And your guy at ITower?" Evan fired the accusation to see if Linus would bite.

He was surprised when Linus's expression shifted to one of confusion and concern.

"You don't have a guy on the inside." It was Evan's turn to command the exchange.

"No." Linus's tone was uncertain.

"I'm not turning off the sites." Evan finished his drink. "And I'm going to find Hannah."

Linus lunged for Evan's arm as he rose to leave. "Even if they connect the Grid, you can't power it."

Something about the deeply personal way Linus said the word 'you' gave Evan pause.

"If I see you again, I'm calling the FBI." Evan drew his arm from the man's grip. "I don't know how good your people are are at covering your tracks, but at least the investigation will keep you out of my hair for a while."

With that Evan left Linus in the booth. Evan's heart continued to race even as he closed the door to his apartment. The conversation with the man he had assaulted on the train left him with far more questions. Although he had an inkling where to start on at least one of them.

Back in his apartment, Evan swept the tablet into his grasp and pulled up the list of ITower employees. Linus might have thought it required magic to dig up information on people, but Evan had more than a few tricks of his own. Intuition told him where to start his search, but evidence confirmed his suspicions.

"Found you." As the records for the man with the military crew cut opened on the tablet Evan was less than shocked that most of the profile had been blocked from access. "Okay Mr. Jeremiah Price. It's about time our employer knew about some of your references."

Death is no more than passing from one room into another. But there's a difference for me, you know. Because in that other room I shall be able to see.

Helen Keller

American deaf-blind author, political activist and lecturer

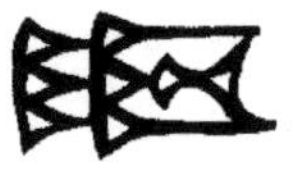

Chapter Fifty Seven

The exchange with Evan had unexpectedly put Linus off. He finished his drink and ordered a second before leaving the bar. As he passed the towering apartment building he glared toward Evan's floor.

His superior had never mentioned a contact within ITower. "At least not other than Evan or Fred." He growled.

It made sense, of course, that more than a few of the ITower employees who had defected to work with Linus were still employed by the company. Linus had taken for granted that his superior would have told him.

Linus knew he had to return to monitor the Pythia, but his feet took him instead to the train and his offices within the city.

He ignored the questions and glances from the men and women on the command center floor and in the cubicles. He made a beeline for the meeting room. The screen was on when Linus entered. It shouldn't have surprised him.

"You spoke to Mr. Gabriel." The silhouetted figure asked.

"Who is our contact within the ITower security building?" Linus demanded.

"I am." The response was so abrupt Linus nearly asked the silhouette to repeat himself.

Instead Linus nodded. "Of course."

"Your meeting. With Evan. Will he be assisting our cause or will I have to take other measures?" The darkness in the voice hung over Linus.

For the first time he questioned the responsibility he held within the organization.

"Evan Gabriel remains under the impression that our work is unimportant. He thinks the Grid is an ITower construct and a just another data service." Linus licked his lips.

"That is a shame." The silhouette sighed. "I will take care of him from this end. Unfortunately, I'm uncertain if the Grid can be secured or if we will be forced to discontinue construction altogether."

"But, we have the Pythia." Linus frowned. "The organization has never been this close."

"There is still some hope, professor. Stick to your orders and allow me to perform mine." The monitor was dark before Linus could formulate a response.

His conviction to the Grid wavered as his thoughts thundered over the sound of the helicopter engine.

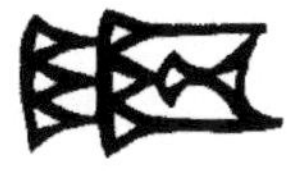

Chapter Fifty Eight

Evan rushed through the hallways of the ITower building. His meeting with Linus had given him the information needed.

"And, why hadn't you told me anything, Linc, my friend?" Evan grumbled as he slipped into his office.

Evan laid the tablet on the desk. Data pinged on his monitor.

"That's quite a power surge." The words slipped into the silence of the office.

Evan rummaged through the drawer of the desk in search of some analog means to note the information on the screen.

"That's south of here." Evan searched the GPS coordinates offered by the search.

"You need to leave." Linc's face filled the monitor.

Evan lurched away from the screen.

"I'm not supposed to help this much, but shit, man." Linc's eyes were wide. "You have to get it together and get out of Dodge."

"Why?" Evan frowned.

"You gotta go." Linc insisted. "Look. I'm about to give you way more intel than I'm supposed to, but time is-"

"A funny thing." Evan finished.

"Not so funny in this case." Linc shook his head.

Linc's image gave way to footage from the ITower CCTV cameras. The man with the military haircut strode through the lobby towards the elevators. As the doors closed, Evan could see the man reveal a small black box from the folds of his jacket.

"What the fuck." Evan cursed. "What good will zapping the office do?"

"It will make your death look like an accident and probably mark you as a terrorist in one stroke." Linc exclaimed.

"I'm going. I just need to find some files first." Evan upended a file box leaving the contents strewn across the floor of the office. "I need some hardcopy info on the sites and the core."

A sudden smile spread across Linc's face. "Why didn't I think of that?"

"Hardware versus software." Evan quipped gripping the file box and making for the stairwell.

As he turned the corner, Evan slid into the alcove leading to the emergency exit as he caught sight of the man with the crewcut approaching his office.

Evan took the stairs two at a time as he descended to the lower floors of the office building. He emerged in a windowless hallway.

He scanned the ceiling before turning his attention to the door he had come through.

"I must be too far under to get a connection."

He wandered down the hallway. Doors lined the passage, though few were marked.

"I should've written down the damn door number or something." Evan grumbled.

He glanced again at his watch. He hoped Jeremiah would hold off on frying the office until he was certain Evan was in the building.

Evan scanned the ceiling again. If not, he might still be safe so far under the building. He wandered deeper into the basement of the structure.

The sticky note with the GPS coordinates suddenly fluttered from the bottom of the file box. Evan caught it as it floated toward the floor.

Hannah first.

The voice rang in Evan's ears. For a breath he wondered how long it had been since he had taken his meds.

"Great. Sure." His voice echoed in the vacant hallway. "But how?"

Evan waited for the voice to come again. Instead he felt as though a wall had brought him to an abrupt halt in the hallway. He frowned and attempted to continue to the next door but found his feet all but frozen in place.

His eyes ran the length of the hall. On the opposite wall he caught sight of an aging poster advertising one of ITower's ancient handheld devices. The screen of the device was half the size of a modern phone to allow for an analog keypad to occupy the lower half.

Suddenly struck by Hannah's words of the past, Evan's eyes grew wide. "Just a tool to connect. Like a tarot card... or a phone. Just a means to focus and connect."

Evan removed the poster frame from the wall. With another glance down the hallway, he dropped the corner against the solid metal of the doorframe shattering the glass that protected the image.

Evan shook the poster free from the broken glass. He tore the image of the phone free from the advertisement.

"So now what?" He turned the paper in his hand. "Dial? Call."

As Evan stared at the paper phone, his mind shifted the screen. The numbers seemed to take on a three-dimensional feel.

"Yes." Evan subdued his excitement. "Call. Um, call Hannah."

He burned his gaze into the coordinates on the sticky note.

***

Linc waved his hands at the image of Evan in the hallway.

"He's trying to call her?" Linc paused. "With a paper phone?"

"Of course he is!" Fred crossed his arms and allowed a broad grin to spread across his face.

"He may not be strong enough to get through directly," Coach noted.

A small body of determined spirits fired by an unquenchable faith in their mission can alter the course of history.

Mahatma Gandhi

Indian lawyer, anti-colonial nationalist and political ethicist

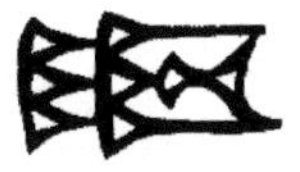

Chapter Fifty Nine

Within the Wave7 base, Hannah blinked into awareness of her surroundings.

Though she sensed the cage, the ring of psychics surrounding the Faraday prison disrupted her ability to experience anything beyond the physical and logical confines of the room. A static blur of information fought through her mind as she focused on the message being sent to her.

She saw a bald man seated beyond the cage. Her mind reached out to him. His energy felt more calm than the Yogis who visited her shop as his consciousness floated in deep meditation. She sensed others in the room equally enlightened.

"Him." Hannah directed a mental image into the static buzzing against the cage. "Call him."

As if via satellite, Hannah's voice crackled through the paper phone to Evan's ears.

"It worked." Evan's joy echoed in his voice. "Hannah it worked! I can hear you! Where are you?"

Hannah's eyes wandered the coils surrounding her. "In a cage."

"Damn it." Evan's voice sliced through her mind. "Are you okay?"

"I'm in a cage, Evan." Hannah took a breath.

"Right." The man's voice was sheepish. "I'm sorry."

A long pause lingered between them as Hannah swiveled her head in search of the exit she knew to be there.

The monk seated in front of her shifted and mumbled.

The static surrounding the cage crackled and snapped. Hannah released a frightened yet quiet yelp as she avoided a spark arching toward her.

"Hannah." Concern filled Evan's voice.

"I'll get you out." Hannah slid her arms from the seat and reached her toes down to touch the narrow stand on which she was perched.

She gagged as a wave of mist found its way to her nostrils. "There's a constant cloud of smoke in here." She whispered.

The monk stirred again. This time another beside him shifted as well.

"Evan. They can hear us." Hannah sent the words through her mind.

"Who?"

"The monks." She murmured.

She could sense Evan's confusion before his words confirmed it. "Are you in a church?"

"No." Her shoulders slumped. "They're surrounding the cage. They're somehow powering this cage I'm locked in. It's been an odd couple of weeks."

As Hannah's feet stabilized on the narrow platform she dipped to evade another circuit of sparks. She closed her eyes to calm her thoughts.

It's okay. I'm with you.

"Evan?" Hannah whispered.

"I'm still here." He assured her.

"I think someone else is too." A soft smile settled on her lips.

"Friend or foe." The tension grew in Evan's voice.

"Friend. I think. She's in my head. It's okay." Hannah stepped toward the opening in the cage.

"What?" Hannah could hear his confusion through the connection.

"It blows my mind that you still have to question reality."

Traversing the short platform was far more difficult without the aid of the women who typically guided Hannah's steps.

"The door is closed." Hannah sighed. "And I'm pretty sure I'll get a healthy zap if I touch it."

Reach for the door. Penelope's voice blocked all other sounds surrounding Hannah.

Hannah did as she was bid. Her palms stretched toward the sizzling coils. As they neared the walls of the cage small tongues of lightning snapped at Hannah's fingertips.

Instinctively she drew away.

Trust me. Penelope urged. *We can do this together.*

"Hannah." Evan called to her.

"Give me a minute." Hannah wasn't certain who she had intended the words to mollify.

With a deep breath she held her palms out once again. This time she felt the energy arching away instead of toward her. The smoke which had surrounded her legs seemed to roll away and return to the vent in the floor.

The gauzy fabric of her garments rippled against her skin. Her head hummed as the energy around her warmed her palms. Evan's voice hissed through the crackle of static obscuring his requests. Hannah's eyes grew wide as she witnessed a pair of faintly blue fingers emerge from her own. Veins formed from the electricity emanating from her body, creating hands, then arms stemming away from Hannah's palms.

"Holy…." Hannah's words trailed off.

She clamped her eyes closed and felt the energy of her lost twin slip from her body to connect with the door to the cage.

Her breath caught as the air within the cage filled with the smell of ozone and hot metal.

The hinges of the door groaned for only a moment before the metal screamed. Hannah's eyes shot open in time to see the door tear from it's frame and hurled across the room.

"Well." Hannah took a wobbling step through the opening ducking clear of the bare sparking tendrils jutting from the cage.

"Hannah?" Fear traced Evan's words.

Hannah listened for the voice of Penelope, but was met with a hollow silence.

"Yeah." Hannah swallowed. "I'm okay, Evan."

The monks surrounding the cage had broken from their trance at the din created by metal striking the concrete walls of the room.

"I think I need a step two to this plan." Hannah's eyes darted around the room at the dark and confused gazes of the monks.

A few of the men were on their feet. It was only as Hannah watched a pair of the monks approach the door that Hannah considered her position.

"Stop!" She called out in a clear command.

She held out her palm in the direction of the nearest monk. "Don't come any closer!"

To her surprise and relief the men held their position.

"Okay. Now what?" Hannah murmured.

In response the cage behind her began to crackle and spark again. This time the arcing electricity shook the cage with a violent shudder. The monks backed from the platform and edged for the exit.

A series of long tendrils of blue lightning ripped toward the corners of the room.

Lightly folding her arms across her chest and taking small steps, Hannah emerged from the cage. She eyed the stairs leading to the floor with a wariness borne both from the electricity and the monks.

Neither seemed to be advancing on her as she descended.

"Where do I go from here?" Hannah held her ground as she stared at the monks.

"I'm trying to get a lock on your location again but there's a ton of interference," Evan grumbled through the paper phone in his hand.

"Pythia." One of the men dared to approach Hannah.

He was met with a warning jolt that scorched the floor near his feet.

The man stepped back. Another of the monks ran to a lever mounted on the wall. His hands were on the kill switch before another jolt of electricity could reach him.

His arms drew the switch down throwing the room into darkness and sudden silence.

In the dim aura offered from seeping daylight Hannah bolted for the nearest exit.

Hannah panted as she navigated the labyrinth of the building. "Evan, can you tell me which way to go? I'm trying to get to a window or something."

Hannah peered down yet another hallway.

"Are you being followed?"

"No." Hannah paused to glance around her. "No. Not yet."

She considered the monks and the cage. Had they been the only ones in the building?

"I think I'm alone." she turned yet another corner. "I found a window!"

Hannah made a break across the lobby to a bank of low windows. As she peered through the glass her heart jumped.

"Evan." Hannah's hands trembled against the large pane of glass. "I know this place."

As Hannah gazed out over the desert and the fallen walls of the distant ancient ruins, the reality of her situation weighed on her. "Evan. I'm in Mexico."

Checking once again to be certain none of her captors had followed, Hannah exited the building. It was more a stack of freight containers, mobile labs, and military trailers than a building. She vaguely recognized the set-up as one she had seen years ago on a visit to the sacred sites while touring ley lines and ancient cities. Students, archaeologists, and locals had bustled across the site. It was a ghost town for the moment. Caution tape in both English and Spanish enclosed the site. A few vans stood parked near the cluster of buildings. The town wasn't far if she recalled correctly.

As Hannah made a beeline for the row of vehicles a hand caught her arm.

"Shit." She breathed.

Evan's voice met her ears as if through a tunnel. "Are you okay?"

"I could use another ball of lightning." Hannah pivoted to face her captor.

Hannah recognized the man she had seen as a priest of Delphi. His energy burned the memories of her soul. Nausea and anxiety rose through her as her gaze drilled into the man.

"Linus Atticus." Her words sliced through the air surrounding them, though her lips never shifted.

"He's there?" Evan hissed.

"That was an impressive display in there." Linus continued to grip Hannah's arm. "I am so thrilled we finally found someone with the energy to power the Grid. And not even a twin."

The weight of Linus's words shook Hannah. Penelope, the spirit who lovingly haunted Hannah's childhood wasn't a guide. Hannah was a twin flame in a single body. A twin flame who had seen the worst this entity of Linus Atticus had to offer.

"This is your fault." The words fell from Hannah's lips but they were more Penelope's than her's.

Linus scowled at the woman.

"You burned the Library of Alexandria. You killed the Pythia." The words continued to flow from Hannah. "You destroyed the Grid."

"What are you talking about?" His head reeled back, he winced as his hands flew to his temples.

A ripple of crushing energy tore through Linus's mind.

Hannah took advantage of the man's pain to pull away from his grasp and run for the vans again.

"Agh. What are you doing?" Linus managed a groan from behind Hannah.

Her feet stopped suddenly. Hannah pivoted to face the man as he crumpled to his knees. "Avenging my sister, and myself, and all the incarnations of our souls."

A darkness overtook Hannah's energy. It was a feeling she knew only too well. Her childhood marked with therapy and medications to settle episodes her parents and doctors named as severe anxiety and depressive bouts. Only Hannah's grandmother understood. Karmic bindings curled themselves around Hannah's soul. At last, with Linus so close she tapped the residual energy of the monks and the cage.

"Hannah what are you doing?" Evan's voice crackled in her mind.

Hannah ignored his voice and focused to release her higher self from lifetimes of karmic attachments.

The exchange would not be kind to Linus.

"Spirit Guides, help me heal, release, and sever etheric cords no longer in service to my higher purpose. All cords not aligned with love, light, and positive attention release." Hannah's words merged with the part of her who had remained a disembodied soul. She raised her arms to accept the energy emanating off the surrounding ruins rekindled by the work she had been forced to complete within the cage.

Linus had forced his actions on others over hundreds of lifetimes, it was all about to snap back like a psychic rubber band.

Hannah felt her connection to the surrounding psychic monks elevate. She could not have known that they, too, had at one lifetime or another fallen victim to Linus, though as she felt the release of her own karmic bondage she could sense the others as well. She summoned the rites and watchtowers as she had when creating the psychic firewall surrounding Linus with the luminous barriers and symbols.

Linus buckled under the sudden weight of persecutions, inquisitions, manipulations, and excommunications, dealt over millennia of lifetimes.

"Karma's a bitch." Hannah murmured as a surge of static and energy pulsed the dry gravel around her.

In a final rush of energy Linus crumpled, gripping the sides of his head. The final blow of Hannah's assault ripped an agonized scream from his failing lungs.

Hannah didn't wait. She pivoted on her heel and darted for the nearest van. She slid into the driver's seat and pressed the ignition button on the vehicle's dash. She popped the van in gear, leaving a cloud of red dirt in her wake. As she glanced in the rear view mirror she caught sight of two monks leaning over the vacant corpse of Linus Atticus.

The artist alone sees spirits. But after he has told of their appearing to him, everybody sees them.

Johann Wolfgang von Goethe

German writer and statesman, 1700's

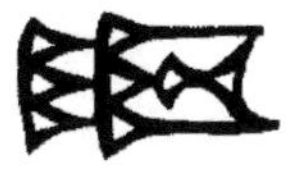

Chapter Sixty

"Hannah?" Evan watched the paper phone turn to ash in his hands. "Shit."

She's fine. You're not. Move.

Evan shook off his concern for Hannah and continued down the hallway.

Library.

The word came to him like a command as Evan stepped in front of a non-descript heavy door.

"More binders? How much did ITower commit to hard copy?" Surprise and confusion filled Evan's voice. "It's the Library."

He entered the room and let the door close behind him. He automatically reached and pulled a particular binder from the shelf. He let it fall flat on a nearby table. "What *is* this?"

Scanning the documents within the folders Evan noted the similarity to the scrolls of the Alexandria Library in his vision. In this life however, Greek was not a language he was able to pull from his understanding. The images and numbers caught his attention though.

"Pyramids?" He turned the pages. "This looks like Stonehenge. Is that Angkor Wat?"

Evan gathered the binders that caught his attention into a file box and made his way to the exit. Glancing down the hall to be certain he had not been followed, he continued to the maintenance elevator.

A voice sounded in his head he couldn't identify as his, Linc's, or anyone else he could recall. The voice suggested to him it would be wiser to take the stairs. He complied.

He cut through the levels of the parking lot avoiding eye contact with the few passing employees. At his car, he dropped the file box in the passenger seat. He cleared more than five blocks before pulling over to breathe.

"Hannah's not a traitor." Evan sighed. "Crew cut is more trouble than the Feds." He dropped his head against the headrest. "Fred is 'working'." He laughed. "ITower is building pyramids and temples. What the fuck am I supposed to do now?"

In response to his question, the navigation screen on the dashboard blinked to life.

Evan frowned at the device that hadn't worked in months. A list of directions scrolled up the screen as the voice of the navigation assistant announced the first turn.

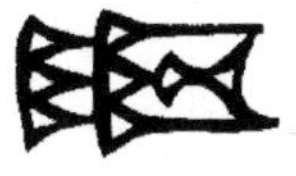

Chapter Sixty One

Hannah sighed as she opened her eyes to assess her surroundings. The van contained a surprising array of equipment, though little of it meant anything to her, but the box of supplies were a blessing. She leaned back a moment in one of the high backed swivel chairs mounted to the floor of the van. Insatiable with thirst, Hannah opened a bottle of water and poured it down her parched throat. She hoped the final power surge created while inside meant her signal to Evan had actually gotten through.

"I feel like having only half the skills makes this a bit more difficult." Hannah opened another small water bottle.

She hadn't heard from Penelope, Evan, or anyone else since leaving the depth of the ruins. Glancing out the window she hoped whoever was left at the site didn't know how to find her. Taking in the expanse of desert that surrounded her, Hannah realized she could barely find herself in the vast empty space.

She toggled a few of the switches and dials on the van. "Nothing."

As she pushed back into the seat, a box tumbled from a shelf on the side of the van. Hannah leaned to rummage through the contents and discovered an ancient portable AM/FM radio.

A wry smile spread across her lips. "I haven't seen one of these in a long time."

She turned the device in her hands and fumbled with the telescoping antenna. She rotated the knob on the face of the radio until she heard a click followed by static.

Her mind wandered to stories her grandmother had told about ghost boxes and spirit phones. Hannah settled into the chair and rested the radio on the narrow table.

Locating the tuning dial she scanned through the channels. Slowly at first, then more steadily she sifted through the static.

"Hannah." Her name burst from the speaker.

"Wait." She scanned back through the channels again.

"Hannah. Stop." Clipped messages popped between the waves of static.

She stopped rotating the dial to wait for another response. Nothing. She moved to scan again.

"Wait." A single word in a familiar voice.

"Fred?" Hannah's eyes glittered. "Fred! Thank goodness! Is Evan with you?"

"I certainly hope not." The response crackled through the speakers.

Hannah frowned. "What?" Realization fell upon her shoulders. "Fred. How are you accessing this station?"

"I'm getting better at reaching out from this side of the connection." Fred's laugh echoed in the cabin of the van.

"Fred. Oh, Fred." Tears welled in Hannah's eyes. "What happened?"

"The work I needed to do was a bit more than the flesh suit could handle." Fred was matter of fact as his voice pushed through the speakers. "I can do so much more from this side of the pond."

Hannah wiped the tears from her cheeks. "Of course you can." She sniffed. "Does Evan know?"

"He knows. He took it a bit rough, but I think Linc helped him understand." Fred offered.

"What's it like?" Hannah asked.

"You know, and you'll see it again." Fred laughed again. "But, not too soon. Still a lot for you to do over there."

"Of course." Hannah sighed. "But, I'm in a bit of a fix at the moment."

"Help is on the way." Fred reassured her. "Just trust them."

"Them?" As the question fell from Hannah's lips a knock rattled the van. "Shit." She hissed and slid down to the floor of the vehicle.

"Trust them, Hannah." Fred's voice emitted from the radio on the table.

Her breath caught as another knock struck the side of the van. She slid from under the table and moved for the handle on the rear door.

"Trust." Fred urged.

She gripped the lever and pushed the hatch open.

There, standing in an arch behind the van stood a trio of the monks from the ruins.

"Damn it!" Hannah moved to swing the door closed.

"Wait!" The monk nearest the van caught the door. "Please. Don't zap us."

Hannah released the door but did not move from within the van.

"We meant no harm to come to you." The monk spoke again.

"You locked me in a cage." Hannah crossed her arms.

"To focus your abilities, not to imprison you." He continued.

"So, then you used me as what?" Hannah eyed the other two men.

"The Conduit." The monk replied. "But, it is clear you are not the one they have been waiting for."

Hannah raised a brow at the men.

"We are trying to power the Grid." He explained as the others moved closer to the opening.

Hannah stepped back.

"Please. We want the same as you do." He held his hand out to Hannah.

"Kidnapping is sort of a deal breaker." Hannah continued to back away.

"Wave7 kidnapped you." The monk looked to the others. "And us too in a way."

Hannah stopped to look at the radio. "Well?"

"I told you." Fred responded. "Trust them."

The monks' eyes were wide.

"And explain as much as you can on the way." Fred's voice carried to the front of the van. "You will need them."

The dash navigation panel illuminated behind Hannah. She focused her attention on the waiting monks.

"Fine. But, I'm driving." Hannah claimed the driver's seat and started the vehicle.

She glanced in the rearview mirror to see the monks helping one another into the van. They closed the doors. Hannah saw two exchange a high five.

Hannah grabbed the AM/FM transistor radio as she pulled away. "Evan. Evan. Tune in."

Personally, I would be delighted if there were a life after death, especially if it permitted me to continue to learn about this world and others, if it gave me a chance to discover how history turns out.

Carl Sagan

American astronomer, cosmologist, astrophysicist, astrobiologist

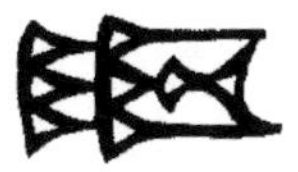

Chapter Sixty Two

Evan waited in the rear of the small library of Bisbee, Arizona. It was more active than he had anticipated, recalling the last time he visited the tiny mining town-turned-artist retreat. Though, that had been before the crashes, when far fewer people bothered with actually entering a library.

Before she even came into view, Evan sensed Hannah climbing the stairs. He turned to see the woman in a broad sun hat, large glasses, and a cotton scarf wrapped high on her neck and chin.

"Movie star chic, or terrorist camouflage?" He whispered as the woman lowered herself into the chair back to back with his.

"I'm so glad you have a sense of humor about all of this," Hannah grumbled.

"You can relax now. I promise." Evan hoped his words carried as much weight as he wanted them to.

"We're parked out back." Hannah whispered. "Shall we continue to travel separately and meet at my shop?"

Evan twitched at the mention of the little store.

"What?" Hannah sensed his shift.

"Change of plans." Evan turned to glance over his shoulder at the woman. "They know all about your store. Plus, there is no place to meet."

"What did you do to my store?" Hannah hissed over her shoulder.

Their faces were so close, Evan could not help but feel something else stir within him.

"Ask your friends at Wave7," Evan shot back. "They seem quite skilled with EMP bombs."

Hannah slumped in her chair. "Damn. Is it really all gone? And I am not their friend."

"I'm sorry about your place. Truly." Seeing her grief, Evan reached for Hannah's arm behind him.

Hannah slid her arm away. "So what's the new plan?"

"My mom's house." Evan grumbled. "And what do you mean we're parked out back?"

"I acquired a few assistants." Hannah murmured.

Anxiety flooded Evan's senses. "Wait. Are you actually working with the terrorists?" He hissed.

"Keep your voice down." Hannah insisted. "No. I mean, they're working with us now. I guess."

Evan pushed his fingers through his hair. "Linc told me to trust you."

"And Fred told me to trust them." Hannah countered motioning toward the back lot. She added somewhat facetiously, "Thanks for telling me Fred crossed over by the way."

Evan closed his eyes. "Right. I didn't think about it. Things were a bit chaotic when we connected. And, I didn't think it would be a great way to open our little conference call with 'Hey, Fred's dead'."

"It's fine." Hannah sighed. "He told me himself, and maybe that was better for all of us."

"How did you call Fred, anyway?" Evan pressed.

"You haven't talked to him since he crossed over?" Realization filled Hannah's voice. "Come on. Meet me in the van out back. I'll show you."

The pair left the library separately. In an incredibly archaic choice, Evan passed a handwritten note to Hannah indicating the directions and address where they would meet and when.

***

Hannah took in the site as she left the library. The top of the crumbling staircase was an icon in the tiny town. She wondered how many people had walked those stones. What would remain of them in another thousand years? Would the graffiti mean anything, if it remained at all? What strange rites would the future attribute to this staircase to nowhere? She wondered this as she wondered at the crumbling notions of the past that fell around her. With each new discovery on this adventure, new questions flattened old answers.

She slid into the driver's seat of the van and unfolded the handwritten directions to the spot Evan had chosen. It was off the path and off the grid. That was all that mattered for the moment.

She glanced back at the trio of monks toying with the radio and some of the other equipment in the vehicle. "Buckle in gentlemen."

"So you're sending me to your mom's house while you try to save the world?" Hannah grumbled as she picked up the sandwich Evan offered her.

The pair sat in the rear of the parked van with their impromptu picnic. Just outside the vehicle the monks wandered the open field. Evan maintained his mistrust enough to want them out of earshot.

"When you put it like that…" Evan frowned.

"Not at all my dear!" Fred's voice emitted from the static of the radio.

Laughter burbled from an old AM/FM walkman with the headphone jack connected to a portable speaker.

"Linc, you are *not* helping, man." Evan turned the volume down on the speaker.

Shaking her head, Hannah leaned across Evan and turned the volume back up.

"We will need more than Hannah if this is going to work." Coach's voice echoed through yet another small radio.

"I can gather more backup. If you need more psychics and their energy. But, I need to know everything. What exactly are you gentlemen planning?" Hannah leaned against the wall of the van.

"Evan is going into the core of the ITower grid," Fred said.

"We will use the new technology to reconnect the gaps in the original grid," Linc added. "It's been done multiple times over the centuries."

"You make this sound like a poorly rewired hack job." Evan sighed.

He set his sandwich aside and opened one of the binders obtained from the ITower archives.

"But, you're not wrong in this case." he flipped through the pages. "The new sites and servers are based on plans I can confirm are Egyptian."

"You can confirm?" Hannah frowned at the heavy binder.

As she flipped through the pages, the images and structures depicted within the varied script were of Greek, Egyptian, Latin, and what looked to be Chinese.

"Stop." Evan put his hand between the pages as they fell.

He drew the binder closer to him, though not out of Hannah's reach. "I wrote that one." He wondered at the Greek script on the page.

Hannah stared at him.

"Well, whoever I was then wrote that one," he corrected.

"What are we actually planning to do here?" Hannah continued to stare at the pages.

"Turn on the grid." Linc's voice echoed against the walls of the van.

"Why?" Hannah looked toward the monks wandering outside.

"She always asks that." Coach chuckled from the radio.

"Well?" Hannah pressed. "I don't know why I'm the voice of reason in past lifetimes, but this time I was kidnapped by people who seemed to want what you are attempting to accomplish. The same people who don't seem to take issue with property damage and possibly murder."

"Linus Atticus was trying to shut down the sites. At least, that's what he claimed." Evan folded the rest of his sandwich into the paper bag and returned to the driver's seat. "Whose side is he on?"

"Yeah." Hannah lowered her gaze. "He's not really a concern either way."

"We may yet have to contend with him on this side." Coach added.

"It's time to move." Linc's voice cut through the conversation.

"Better get your friends." Evan thumbed in the direction of the monks.

"Yeah." Hannah gathered the radios and tucked them into a backpack from the shelves.

She called out to the monks who closed in on the vehicles. As they approached she felt her connection to each of them. Though they were far from the ruins, the residual energy fed her intuition as if quantumly entangled with the monks.

Turning to the monks she asked, "What happened to Linus?" Her question was flat, without concern.

One of the monks responded, "He has crossed over." His voice was equally free of emotion. "It looks like an aneurism … perhaps."

"Right." Hannah nodded.

"We took him inside before we followed you." It was the closest any offered as a gesture of sympathy. "His contract for this life was complete. You understand."

Hannah didn't say either way. Her gaze drifted to Evan as he waited for her beside the Tesla.

"You guys are taking the van." Hannah shifted the subject abruptly. "Don't lose track of us."

Even as she said it Hannah sensed it was an unnecessary command; perhaps too abrupt. But considering they kept her physically, emotionally, and metaphysically trapped inside a literal cage for weeks, she did not have a lot of empathy.

She strode toward the Tesla and opened the passenger side door. Evan slid into the driver's seat.

"Everything okay?" Evan asked as Hannah set the radios on the dash.

Hannah settled into the passenger seat and set the binder in her lap.

"Where are we going?" Hannah fastened the belt across her shoulders.

Evan sighed. "Sedona."

***

Later that day, Evan pulled the car into the driveway at the foot of a cobbled path leading to a single-story brick ranch. He shifted the vehicle in park as the van with their three new partners parked behind them.

"Let's keep things about Fred and the grid stuff on the downlow," Evan instructed.

Hannah acknowledged but asked, "So then, what is our reason for visiting your mother?" She glanced in the rearview and the approaching monks. "And with these guests, no less?

A snicker crackled from the radio.

"Business." Evan flicked the radio off and stepped out of the van.

"Evan!" His mother appeared from behind the copse of oleander bushes. "Oh! I thought that was you on the screen."

Hannah stepped from the vehicle as Evan's mother approached. The elder woman paused, a broad smile spreading across her lips.

"And who is this lovely young lady?" His mother put her hands out to greet the young woman.

"This is Hannah. A coworker." Evan's words ripped the smile from his mother's face.

She quickly replaced her apparent disappointment with a professional grin.

"So you are here on a business venture?" she raised a brow.

Evan sensed his mother's letdown. "We have some network connection issues to work on here in town, so I thought we would pop in to say hello."

Gesturing to the trio clustered behind Hannah she asked, "And they are with you?"

"They're on a tour of the ITower facilities." Evan explained, then looked over the attire of the monks.

Hannah saw her confused look and interjected, "They're from Asia, on an exchange program for technicians. I hope you don't mind if we come in for a moment."

Evan's mother hesitated only long enough to give a sidelong glance to her son.

"No at all. Come on in for some iced tea. I picked some fresh lemons from the back." Evan's mother led the way under the pergola into the little house.

Hannah snagged the radios off the dash and passed the binder to Evan.

She smiled as they entered and took in the eclectic decor of the little brick home. The smell of leather, wood, and the scent of creosote filled the rooms.

Evan flopped onto one of the overstuffed leather chairs and rested his arms on the thick wooden frame.

"Keep your shoes off my driftwood table." His mother's voice paused Evan's foot mid fall above the oblong wood and turquoise table.

He set his feet back on the woven area rug.

Hannah stifled a giggle as she settled on the large cowhide ottoman.

The monks lingered graciously at the door until Hannah beckoned them to enter. They proceeded to peruse the knick knacks and artwork adorning the room.

Evan's mother emerged from an arched entrance that lead to the kitchen. She set out several glasses filled with iced tea, a small bowl of wedged lemons, and a spice container marked 'cinnamon'.

"Oh." She paused as she reached for the cinnamon. "I apologize. I'm so used to Fred being with you when you visit."

A wave of grief passed over Evan, a feeling he saw reflected in his mother's eyes. Hannah put a hand on the woman's arm.

"He is always close by." Hannah glanced at the little radio careful not to linger. "He talked about you often."

Evan's mother let a sad smile spread across her lips. "Oh. I know, dear. It's still hard not to have the crazy old fool in the room, is all."

Evan took a deep drink from his tea.

"What did you say you did for ITower?" Evan's mother narrowed her gaze.

"Cloud services and connections." Hannah replied without missing a beat.

Hannah raised her glass and sipped at the tea.

The monks blundered through small talk and attempts to make insightful commentary about ITower.

Evan was mid explanation of how Asia's connections appear to have held up better than those in the United States, though not as well as those in Europe, when the tiny radio crackled to life from Hannah's bag.

"Evan." Fred's voice shattered the awkwardness of the moment.

Evan's hopes that his mother had not heard the voice were shattered as she leaned around to stare at the bag beside Hannah.

"Fred?"

"Samantha." Fred's voice crackled from the radio once again.

"You can hear that?" Hannah smiled.

"Well, of course I can." Samantha rose from her chair.

Hannah fished the radio from her bag and set it on the table.

"Hannah. What are you doing?" Evan protested.

Hannah waved him off. "She can hear him, Evan. She's connected."

"Of course she is." Fred's voice beckoned from the radio. "Sam's always been into the weird, freaky stuff. Much more than I ever was."

"Oh! Oh my goodness! Fred, that is you?" She plucked the radio into her trembling hands.

Evan's mother shot a momentary dark glance in her son's direction. "This isn't one of your sick tech gags, is it?"

"What!" Evan held his hands out to her. "Of course not, Mom! I would never!"

Tears shivered in the woman's eyes. "Oh, my dear, stupid Fred."

"Don't start that now, Sam." Fred's voice soothed his sister. "We have work to do."

Realizing the nature of the conversation, the monks' eyes were wide. Their complete attention focused on Hannah and the radio.

"What?" Evan stood. "I thought we agreed to keep this on the down low?"

"I think Fred feels his sister should know what we are up to," Hannah said.

Evan flopped back into his chair. He looked from the glass by his hand to the women awaiting his response. "I'm going to need something stronger."

Evan's mother settled onto the couch between Hannah and Evan, while the monks rested on the floor. Evan drew the remaining devices from the bag and set the radios up at either end of the coffee table.

Coach's voice whipped up in a chuckle from one of the other radios, "I love it when a plan comes together." Laughing again at his obvious reference to an old TV show.

Hannah shifted to adjust the volume on the radios. "You can hear both of them?"

"I can hear Fred." Evan's mother smiled as she offered a gentle pat to the top of one of the small radios. "I don't seem to hear anything from the other radios."

"That'll work!" Fred's voice crackled from the speaker.

"And you three?" Hannah shifted her attention to the monks.

The trio appeared to enjoy the experience unfolding before them. "We have seen many amazing things in our temples, but this is astounding."

Hannah confirmed, "So you can hear them?"

All three nodded.

"Of course they can." Coach added. "They are well connected." The monks snickered.

"Okay, well, for Samantha, I'll repeat anything Coach and Linc have to say," Hannah offered.

"Linc?" Evan's mother put her hand to her chest and looked directly at Evan. "Your dear friend from the Army?" Her eyes instantly misted as they had at the sound of Fred's voice.

"Yeah." Evan cleared his throat.

Evan cut off any flood of impending questions and set the binders on the table with a bit more force than necessary.

"This is a bit more than your Sedona meet and greets, Mom." Evan shook his head.

"It's more technical." Fred added.

Evan's mother gave a curt nod. "I can keep up." She crossed her arms.

Evan laid the binder across the coffee table. "It's a grid,"

Hannah, Samantha, and the monks, leaned in to peer at the scrawlings and diagrams on the open pages.

"How do you know what any of this means?" Evan's mother laid a hand on the center of a pyramid-shaped diagram.

"That part I'm having trouble explaining even to myself. I know it. I don't know how, but I just do." Evan ran a hand through his hair, eyes wide with confusion.

"Past life memories. Soul memories," A monk stated.

"What?" Now, both Evan and his mother shared matched confused stares.

The monk took a deep breath. He turned to the radio for a moment. "May I?"

"Take it away." Fred's voice emitted from the device.

"Evan, you know you have done this before." The monk began. "Built the grid, I mean."

Hannah interrupted at the sight of Evan's befuddlement. "When you experienced the download of information back at my store, you most likely saw the, well, data from all of your past experiences."

"Your soul's past experiences. Before you were Evan," Fred's voice interrupted.

Evan's mother continued to stare at the images in the binder, turning each page with a delicate sweep of her hand.

"Are you okay with all of this? Do you understand?" Evan put a hand on her shoulder.

For the first time since opening the binder, Evan's mother turned to him. "Oh, my dear, this is all so exciting!"

It was not the reaction Evan expected. Disbelief, concern, possibly anger, but excitement, not so much.

"You knew about this." The monk smiled at the woman.

She turned to the monk. "I wouldn't go so far as to say *knew*. But I always had inklings about these things. Fred was the hard-sell on stuff like this so I couldn't talk to him. My little group of Sedona confidants had no idea what I was seeing."

They all looked to the small radio as the speaker crackled.

"Well. Things are different now," Fred defended himself. "Come on. Move on. Move on. We need to plan our next move."

The stillness in the room lingered for more than a few seconds.

Evan broke the silence and announced, "I'm going to turn on the grid."

"How?" Hannah asked as all eyes suddenly focused on Evan.

Evan dangled a pair of USB access cords and a case containing Fred's SD card from a chain. "The drives were with the binders and a map to the server warehouse." He paused and jangled the drives in his hands. "ITower has been working on this a long time. Way before your involvement, Fred."

"Since Wave7 hired them." The monk was stoic as all eyes now settled on him.

"Jeremiah." Evan all but growled. "That damned crewcut G-man."

"Only if G stands for Grid." Linc piped up.

"Linus may have inadvertently alluded to having contacts within ITower." Evan smiled.

"Did he know everything about the grid?" Hannah frowned.

"Not as much as he wanted to." Evan laughed.

The monk interjected, "I am sorry to say, but you are going to need protection from Wave7 and their people." We have worked for them a long time. We should have left long ago. You will need protection from them.

"And ITower." Fred added.

"And you're going to need a lot more power if you are going to fire up this grid." Coach's voice crackled from the radio.

"What sort of power?" Hannah ignored Evan's confused expression.

"I think he means psychic, or spiritual energy," Samantha offered.

"I think I can help with that." Hannah eyed the three monks. "You can help, too."

Linc's voice crackled through the speaker, "Hey Man. Trust her. Trust them. Trust the plan."

Evan took a deep breath and exhaled in resignment. "Okay. We have work to do. Let's get on it."

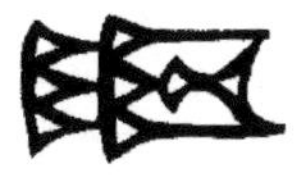

Chapter Sixty Three

Hannah silently stood with Evan, arms crossed, at the edge of the bricked path to the house.

Evan broke the silence. "We have our plan." Even though his hands itched to reach out to Hannah, he struggled to keep them in his pockets.

"Yeah." Hannah's response was little more than a mumble.

"I trust you." He rested a hand on Hannah's shoulder. "Almost as much as I trust Linc." He smiled, "And I think Linc has more faith in you than he ever did in me."

Hannah's eyes shimmered as she stared at Evan. "It's a good plan." She offered the words as a vow more than mere statement.

Evan peered around Hannah to the pair of monks who lingered in the doorway of his mother's small home.

"I suppose I trust them, too. Crazy as this all feels." Evan offered a nod to the men.

The duo returned curt bows before turning to re-enter the house.

With a sigh, Evan turned toward the van. A second thought struck him as he reached the door to the cab.

"Here." He fished a set of keys from his pocket.

He tossed them to Hannah. She caught the jumble of plastic between her palms.

"If things go completely sideways." Evan shrugged. "The Tesla still has a decent charge and there's a couple battery cans in Mom's shed. Fred used to stow them here for long trips. Otherwise, maybe you can Delphi magic something."

Hannah fumbled the keys in her fingers. "Right."

"That's plan Z." Evan smirked. "I always have an A through Y before that."

He tapped at his temple and climbed into the driver's seat of the van.

He again fought the urge to leap from the vehicle and claim Hannah in a farewell embrace. He slowly shook his head. It was a foolish thought. Worst-case scenario, he would have a ton of explaining to do at ITower come Monday morning.

"Right?" He started the van.

When he looked again, Hannah was no longer in the driveway.

"She's certainly not worried," Evan thought as he backed into the street.

As he drove, first the house, then the familiar neighborhood rolled into the distance behind. Evan tried to focus on the task at hand. Absently, he flicked on the radio.

"It's you and me, cowboy." Linc's familiar voice soothed Evan's thoughts.

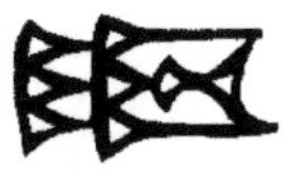

Chapter Sixty Four

Hannah stood in the entry of the small house, her eyes transfixed on the taillights of the van. Her soul crying out for her to follow Evan.

Her eyes fell to the keys in her hand. "Plan Z."

A gentle hand found Hannah's arm, drawing her mind to the present moment.

"Pythia. We should begin." The monk's eyes were solemn yet strong.

"Yes." Hannah pocketed the keys.

The sitting room of Evan's mother's home had been cleared of all furnishings where other psychics; monks, seers, and NDE experiencers had gathered.

As they sat in a circle, the scene was all too familiar to Hannah. She recalled not only the Faraday cage, and faintly the priests of the Oracle millenia ago as well as other temples, caves, and incarnations.

"Okay, Penelope, have we done this before?" Hannah murmured. "Don't make me do this alone this time."

"Do you need anything?" Evan's mother whispered as Hannah stepped past her.

Hannah took the woman's hands. "Maybe some water."

Samantha nodded and made for the kitchen leaving Hannah to face the expectant gazes in the circle.

She approached the large pillow at the center of the circle. Settling in she opted to sit in the direction of a friendly face. The woman had been a regular at the NDE meetings since Hannah first opened the store.

She reached out to grasp Hannah's hands and offer a reassuring smile. One of the monks broke the moment with a hand on Hannah's shoulder.

"Pythia." He leaned close. "You must face the eastern quarter."

"Oh." Hannah nodded. "Of course." She shifted her position on the large pillow.

Samantha returned with water in a lidded bottle. "It's glass. No metal or plastics. I hope that's okay."

Hannah smiled at the woman's concern. "I think it'll be perfect."

She thanked Samantha as she accepted the water and turned to the monk.

"How do we know this will work?" Hannah asked. "We aren't on a site or ruins."

"The home is brick; brick is earth. We disconnected the electricity and grounded the wires." The monk explained. "It should allow the energy of the ley lines to flow freely."

Hannah's brow furrowed. "There's a line here?"

"Oh!" Evan's mother quietly clapped her hands together. "Yes! It's why I bought this land in the first place. I was told it was centered on a large vortex."

The monk patted Samantha's hands and offered a smile that Hannah tried not to sense as condescending. "Large enough for our purposes anyway."

"Right." Hannah shifted the conversation. "The plan."

"Yes." The monk settled in beside the others in the room. "We are two fold in our purpose."

Hannah began, "First, we act as a jump between the closest sites," She paused. "Second, we focus our energy on anyone or anything who may mean to stop or harm Evan while he enables the grid."

"Think of yourselves as a magnetic shield and an electrical breaker." Coach added from the radio on a nearby shelf.

"And what happens if the breaker fails?" Samantha's question silenced the room.

"Plan Z." Hannah rested the keys in her lap. "I drive to the nearest power station and turn everything up to eleven. The surge with blow the server core forcing a meltdown."

"If the surge doesn't wipe the servers the potential ire will render them useless." Fred added.

"What will happen to Evan?" Samantha pressed her palms into her lap.

"ITower has a waterless suppression system." Fred continued.

"A vacuum." Hannah sighed.

The room was silent again.

"Then we better not mess this up." Linc's voice crackled from the radio on the coffee table."

A nod from one of the monks sent a collective sigh through the circle.

The collective closed their eyes as they leaned into chairs or positioned themselves on pillows surrounding Hannah. Finally Hannah also closed her eyes and steadied her breathing. The sounds of the house faded from her mind as her consciousness left her body to connect with the energy deep within the earth.

She sensed her spirit stretch like roots deeper and deeper while the light of her third eye beamed toward the Cloud. A warmth closed around her from the others in the circle. Reiki waves flowed between them. The rush of light claimed Hannah's senses as her consciousness tumbled away from her body.

As the visions in her mind stabilized figures emerged before her.

"Fred?" Her voice wafted through the air like a rippling wave.

"Hey." His face emerged from the blur of the mist. "Relax. You're doing great."

At Fred's shoulder another figure appeared. Coach smiled. "We have one more job to do while you're here."

Hannah took in the pale surroundings. The pillars, nearly too bright to rest her eyes on, waves of energy creating a semi-solid floor to stand on. In the distance loomed a dark orb.

"What is that?" Hannah whispered into the mist.

"You have known him as many faces, though most recently, Linus Atticus." Coach took Hannah's hand in his and lead her forward.

"Your release of his karmic connection to you, and the others at the ruins sent his physical body into a shock that ended his time on earth," Coach explained. "But, it sent his soul into a place of darkness as his past finally caught up with him."

The dark orb pulsed in front of Hannah and the others. She struggled to see anything beyond the deep swirling darkness.

"This is our chance to remove one of the souls that has blocked the Grid for so long." Coach brought Hannah's hand to the edge of the dark mass.

Penelope's familiar voice drew Hannah's attention. "The combined positive energy of these souls gathered on the ley line, as well as ours being in such close proximity may release him permanently from this darkness."

A pale golden glow that seemed to mimic Hannah's silhouette hovered beside her. As she reached out to touch the light it enveloped her, completing her own aura.

"Next round I get to hang back here." Hannah laughed. "You can run a store and balance the accounts."

A warmth of amusement surrounded her. The experience lasted only a moment more before her consciousness shifted once again to the dark mass of energy.

"Release him." Coach urged. "Reassign the darkness to less harmful nodes and distribute the power to the Grid."

Hannah raised her palms to the swirling mass. Her vision clouded once more. She allowed her eyes to close again, blocking out the growing darkness.

The release was less violent than that of his physical form yet Hannah felt the waves nonetheless. The resulting ripple sent Hannah's consciousness tumbling back into her body.

Hannah fell back in the center of the circle. "I cleared it. But it's not right. Something is not as it seems. I saw, I felt, but I do not understand."

"Hannah?" Samantha's voice drew Hannah into the room.

She found herself again surrounded by the circle with Evan's mother at her side. A jacket now draped her shoulders.

"You took quite a trip." The monk rested a hand on Hannah's head. "And you've been busy clearing the way. But we must continue soon."

"Yes." Hannah sought the bottle of water and sipped. "Have we heard from Evan?"

"We're in the building, now." Linc's voice emitted from the radio. "I'll keep you updated." The sound cut in and out as he spoke.

"Not once you are in the core, Linc." Fred noted. "The energy will be too powerful there. You'll be on your own."

Worry traced Hannah's features. She had seen something in the darkness when she had released the being last known as Linus Atticus. The information had emerged almost as an apology.

She caught sight of the keys in her lap. "This was a distraction. Like a trap." She mumbled. Her gaze fell on the monks. She scowled.

"No. It was a means to an end. A small piece of a bigger picture." The monk bowed his head a moment before leveling his gaze with Hannah. "The Grid has been waiting so long for the right alignment."

"No." Hannah was on her feet before the others could protest. "You must continue. You have to focus, channel the energy. Send it to me and Evan, both. You are the only way." She sprinted for the door.

"Hannah!" Samantha called after her.

She turned to connect her gaze with the woman and scanned the others as well. The monk was right. As much as Hannah wanted to deny it, she could see the life contracts of every soul in the room. They all understood as well. It was no different than a tsunami or an earthquake. Inevitable. Natural in the superlative.

Her eyes fell on the keys clamped in her hand. She had to try. She bolted for the door.

Men die in despair, while spirits die in ecstasy.

Honore de Balzac

French novelist and playwright, 1700's

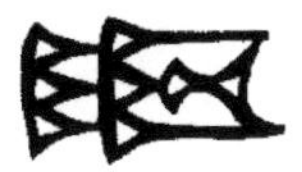

Chapter Sixty Five

Evan stopped short as the man with the crew cut met him in the lobby of the ITower server farm core complex. "I've been expecting you."

He turned and motioned for the guards to open the large steel doors leading into the inner sanctums. He continued as Evan followed him inside.

"All of the greatest empires had access." The man chose a drawer from the wall of identical openings. He removed some object and slipped it into his pocket. "You see, it was the means by which they connected to one another, the means by which their greatness was possible."

Evan kept his distance. "If that's a gun from that box, I have a backup on the way."

The man smirked. "Of course you do."

He made his way to the elevators leading to the lower center levels of the server core. He looked back to be certain Evan was following before he continued. "The mechanics and methods by which connection is made varies extensively, of course."

Evan entered the elevator with the man, keeping his back to the wall.

"The Maya, used planetary and cosmic energies, harnessed by rituals, what we would call programs, powered by magnetic fluctuation, determined by astrological alignment." The man waved a hand at the hieroglyphic-like symbols decorating the walls of the elevator carriage.

"Explains the calendar." Evan grumbled.

"Precision. Precisely. However, without the ability to access required output levels of electricity, the Mayan method of accessing the data waves required unwavering attention to detail, mathematical prowess, and patience." The man nodded in approval of Evan's apparent understanding.

Evan completed the point. "So, because they couldn't flip a switch to get the lights to go on they had to wait for good ol' nature to do it for them." Evan glanced at the doors as they opened.

"Correct again, in a manner. After you." The man gestured for Evan to exit.

"Nah. You first." Evan leaned against the wall.

The man acquiesced and continued his speech as Evan followed. "But, power is not the only obstacle. Much as you or I see it as commonplace to sit before a screen connected to a powerful machine, so too did the Maya."

"Ancient computers with internet access." Evan maintained the space between himself and the man with the crewcut. "Imagine the size of that machine."

"For that, it is best to use Egypt as an example." The man emitted a curt laugh.

"Pharaoh's had desktops?" Evan mused.

"Oh, no," This time the laugh was darker. "Well yes, of a sort. And you are correct in your thinking, they were quite large."

"You've seen an ancient Egyptian computer, with Cloud access." Evan held back as he recalled the images in the binders.

"Egyptian scientists discovered the power generated by the decomposition of the human body, the soul, and methods by which to use and even improve the outputs of each organ through purification and chemical manipulation." The man stopped short at the entry to the glass doors leading to the primary server core.

Evan frowned at the image the man's words projected into his mind. *Mummy powered.*

"The pyramids of the great Pharaohs were not burial mounds. They were simply a method of harnessing the greatest power from the greatest power source, the decaying souls of earth bound gods. Each pyramid was an enormous computer tower, with the ability to link into the mysteries of the collective consciousness." The man pointed a finger at Evan's chest. "But you know all of this from your uncle's research."

Evan separated the clasp at the nape of his neck. The SD chips clicked against one another as his hand closed around them.

"You have it." The man's smile was calm, yet dark. "Access to every truth in the universe, from its conception. A keystroke away."

"The world could have it." Evan stared at the man.

"We cannot know what that would bring." The man sighed. "In these incarnations, we experience greed, power, control, hate, spite and jealousy.

Much more. Couple that with what we could reveal or provide to these people and the results on this planet would be disastrous".

Evan caught Linc's reflection in the glass behind the man.

The man reached into his suit pocket to remove the same small black box Evan had seen before; outside Fred's house.

"I have a contract to fulfill, just as you do." He rested his finger over the switch.

"You know the pulse will blow every server in here." Evan nervously licked his lips. "And probably kill us both."

"Oh I know." The man smiled. "Linus was supposed to be the one to go this time, but your friend Hannah saved him from making that choice. Likely for the best. He was wavering anyway."

The electronic locks to the server room screamed and flashed as Linc's grinning reflection shifted in the glass doors. The man scowled at the sudden disturbance behind him, offering Evan open access to the core.

Evan lunged for the box in the man's hand as the doors flung open. He claimed the black device as he threw his shoulder into the man's chest, sending him crashing to the floor. Taking the opening offered by Linc, Evan dove through the doors into the server core.

The doors slid back into place barring the man with the crew cut from entering.

He pounded the thick glass with his fists and growled profanities at Evan.

"Sorry. Bullet proof glass is a bit dense. Can't hear you." Evan mocked the man.

Linc's image reappeared on the glass door. He motioned for Evan to disable the door lock. Puzzled, Evan shrugged in response. "Use the Force, Luke." Linc burst out laughing. Evan now looked more confused than ever. Linc motioned for him to put his hands on the door's control panel.

As Evan moved to the panel and raised his hands to the front, a bluish glow permeated throughout the room. As he touched the front panel, some form of electrical or magnetic discharge flailed around his hands. Evan heard crackling and arching sounds coming from inside of the door's control box.

Back in Sedona, the circle of meditators remained deep in trance, the same bluish energy swirled around the circle and spiraled outward through the wall in multiple bursts. The senior most monk smiled with his eyes still closed, raised his arms in the air in exhilaration.

"You all doing so well. We must focus and continue. Send your energy. He is calling for it."

***

Evan pivoted from the doors and made his way to the control station. He set the EM device on the control desk as he nestled into the cool chrome and leather chair.

"Thanks partner." Evan murmured into the now empty space of the room.

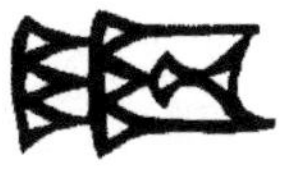

Chapter Sixty Six

In the misty room of the ethereal, Fred asked Coach, "Where is she going? I can't connect to her. I can't even see her."

"Plan Z." Coach smiled as he peered through the mist into the room of now deeply meditating psychics, still settling after the burst of energy.

"She won't make it ... Plan Z" Fred frowned.

His eyes were on the swarms of data cascading through the air surrounding them in the mist.

"I know." Coach faced the data, studying the flows and contexts.

"I'm locked out here, too." Fred groaned as he attempted to rearrange the data as he had before.

His fingertips sparked as he reached into the stream.

"You locked it." Coach put a hand on Fred's shoulder. "Because you knew that even you would try to change it when the time came."

Coach added, "Evan is incredibly preoccupied. He obviously sent for an energy boost. He got it. I hope it helped."

Fred ran a hand through his hair. It was an act he had done so many times in life. An act he had seen his nephew mimic. An act he always considered a family quirk. He looked at his hand as he pulled it away from his scalp. It twinkled with crystal-like flecks of energy. It was his and not his, similar yet familiar.

"But how?" Fred turned to Coach.

"The concept of time and space are meaningless to the soul not incarnated. We simply have our contracts to fulfill when we are there."

Fred stepped away from the mist. Deep in focused concentration, his recently released soul still readjusting to reality. As his veil of incarnation continued to lift after sixty years of living in a carbon suit, his thoughts reassembled what he already had stored in the cloud, in his book in the library.

There is always static. No matter what your mechanism of communication, from human conception, there is an echo, a feedback. CB Radio had disembodied voices, claimed to belong to truckers cursed to remain behind the wheel even in death. The television, audio and visual representation of streams of data waves fed to tubes, silicon chips and pinpricks of light; this device too, was surrounded by rumors of ghostly images. Computers, did we think they would be any different? Once connected to the internet, that ever expanding cloud of collected consciousness, via cell phone, laptop, desktop, any number of digital means, then we discovered the extent of this ether.

It is always there. It was there before us, this data, information. We, the people of the most modern age, merely re-discovered it; we found methods by which to access it; without an ounce of sense of what to do with it. All of human history, an echo on the waves of collective consciousness, the truth, all laid out and file shared from reality's primary, desktop mainframe.

Fred tuned back into the frequency of the misty images in front of him and Coach.

"Does Hannah know?" Fred's voice warped between several tones.

"She will." Coach consoled as he rested his arm across Fred's shoulders.

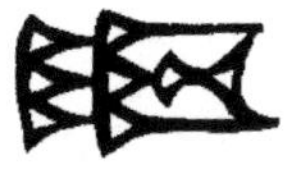

Chapter Sixty Seven

The old electric car hurtled down the highway as Hannah pressed the pedal hard to the floor. Her senses battled between maintaining focus on the road in front of her and the shifting Earth Grid whirling around her.

Deep within the server core of ITower's desert site outside Phoenix, she sensed Evan's busy mind.

Newly erected power lines lined the roadside, their posts alive with electrical current, buzzing with energy only confused and blocked her signals. The earth itself shimmered blue energy along the edges of the gravel.

From behind the Tesla, blue lines raced forward into the horizon. Bursts of metaphysical energy fired past her.

The engine of the car bogged down as it sapped the remainder of the charge. She wouldn't make it in time. Her soul knew it even before Linc's voice hissed through the radio.

"Pull over!"

Hannah hesitantly did as the voice commanded. Stone and dirt spat against the undercarriage of the vehicle. She stared in silence into the distance at high fences surrounding the ITower server complex.

"I should have been stronger." A tear rolled over her cheek.

She stepped from the car and stumbled to the side of the road in front of the car. A chill pushed her hands into the pockets of the jacket Samantha had given her. Her knuckles brushed the contents.

She held a small mobile device and a pack of tarot cards in her grip.

"Evan!" She cried out.

A bemused smile flitted over her lips allowing a short laugh to escape amid a cascade of tears.

Hannah raised her eyes to the horizon. She let the items fall from her grasp into a roadside puddle.

The learning and knowledge that we have, is, at the most, but little compared with that of which we are ignorant.

Socrates

Ancient Athenian philosopher

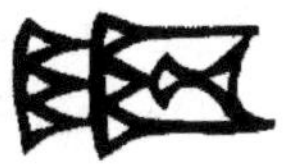

Chapter Sixty Eight

Evan seated himself at the console at the fore of the server room, lowering into the office chair in front of a glass desk. The slim screen and keyboard seem to be formed from the surface of the desk itself.

Searching the framework of the console configuration, Evan pulled the SD card from his pocket.

He turned the tiny device back and forth in his fingers. Contemplating. If Fred truly was onto something, Evan quite literally held the world in his hands.

Finding the single port to the backup system, Evan inserted the SD boot-up chip into the narrow slot.

Those few seconds seemed to be an eternity before the screen booted to the BIOS.

In relief, a wisp of breath curled from his lips. Evan shivered from the chill of the server room. He drew from his pocket a USB cord. He would need to connect in similar fashion as Hannah had connected to the cage within the Wave7 base. He considered the implications of his next actions.

The USB end of the cord slipped snuggly into the port on the screen. He rotated the clip at the other end of the cord between his fingers. He then slid the clip onto the tip of his finger and reclined into the chair.

"At least this is more comfortable than the communication van," Evan mused at himself. "Time to get on frequency, Lieutenant."

As he leaned back, Evan eyed the flickering lights filling his vision like stars.

"Something's not right." Evan frowned.

He scanned the server room. "I'm too exposed. I need sensory deprivation. I need to cut off all stimulation." Evan looked around the room for some solution to his problem. Nothing inside his self-made prison seemed suitable.

His gaze fell upon a server tower being prepared for installation in the back of the room. Next to the tower sat the packing box on its side, the size of a refrigerator. Inspired, Evan pulled the clip from his finger and rushed to the box on the floor. It was completely full of foam packing peanuts.

He sifted a handful through his fingers. The images from his visions in the temples rose to his mind. The incense, medicinal herbs, comfortable robes and the chanting oms, all deprived of them, him, of bodily sensors.

"Fit for a Pharaoh." He elevated his voice.

Hurriedly, he dragged the box toward the control station. He kicked the rolling chair clear of the desk. The horizontal box fit snug against the side of the desk allowing Evan to swing his leg over the side. As he sank into the sea of foam packing pieces he slid the keyboard onto his lap and reclined into the box.

"Okay. Maybe not exactly Pharaonic."

To Evan's surprise, Linc's voice echoed across the room. "More like MacGyver."

Evan chuckled at his friend's quip. He adjusted into the center of the packing peanuts and rested the keyboard at arm's length.

"Much, much better. I feel it now. Connecting."

He clipped the cord to his fingertip once again and closed his eyes. The first tendrils of the surge stole the light from the room pitching Evan into darkness.

He understood. He wondered if he would be recorded on ethereal history as the man who connected the clouds and restarted the grid; the man who gave mankind truth. The familiarity of the action, once so commonplace, flooded his emotions. Nothing at first, then, as his heart began to sink, as his emotions subsided, the window appeared.

Finally, as his senses fell away his fingers trembled over the keys.

Var func = outer():// *EXECUTE CLOUD MERGE*

{ END }

J.J.M. Czep Bio

J.J.M. Czep lives with her husband and cats in a home full of magic near Phoenix, Arizona. As an author, performer, tarot reader, and adventurer, Czep explores a range of studies. She was voted Phoenix Magazine's Reader's Choice for Best Local Author in 2015, and currently spends part time shelving books in her local library as she continues to work on multiple projects for print, audio, and stage. She has written, produced, directed, and/or performed in production shorts including shows at Comic-Con conventions.

Bob Frank Bio

Raised on an Iowa farm, he spent summer afternoons in corn fields dreaming of adventures in faraway lands. At 17, while war raged in Southeast Asia, he joined the Army and graduated from West Point as an airborne paratrooper with years of duty staring down Russian machine guns. For the next twenty years he was a cyber security road warrior for the largest oil company in the world chasing hackers across Europe and Asia. He traveled to every God forsaken corner of the world: Nigerian savannas, Saudi Arabian deserts, Sumatran jungles of Indonesia - even Bakersfield, California.

Always known for fantastic storytelling, he ended his travels and delivered the *Third Eye Trilogy*. In researching deep ethereal topics for the Trilogy, he became embedded in metaphysical world, ultimately spending two years as president of the International Institute for Near Death Studies. This connection to metaphysical circles led him to connect with co-author Czep to deliver a wildly adventurous, rough and tumble Cloud to Cloud novel.

Other works by J.J.M. Czep

Other works by Bob Frank

Before dying, Steve Jobs looked at his sister Patty, then for a long time at his children, then at his life partner, Laurene, and then over their shoulders past them. His final words:

"Oh wow --- oh wow --- oh wow!"

Steve Jobs

American business magnate, co-founder of Apple, Inc

Made in the USA
San Bernardino, CA
02 March 2020